Some more praise from Dan

"*Borgel* . . . is the first one I read, and is my favorite.
I named my lizard after it."—Molly Jordan

"If it weren't for the *Snarkout Boys* books, I wouldn't have had a tough punk girl
named Rat as my childhood idol . . . and I most certainly would not have
been so excited about being a weird kid."—Kirthi Reddy

"It's like (Pinkwater's) books have this wild fantasy element . . . yet the kids in
the books are very real and easy to relate to."—Camilla Aikin

"How weird . . . to be . . . reading *Yobgorgle* . . . and realize that possibly the
world was even stranger than you could imagine. And this is not even to mention
The Worms of Kukumlima . . . sheer genius at work."—Jesse Rossa

"If I had not read the Pinkwater books I never would have understood the true
meaning of the word 'Nettlehorst.'"—Michael Sideman

"My five favorite books used to be *Deadeye Dick* by Kurt Vonnegut,
The Outsiders by S. E. Hinton, *To Kill a Mockingbird, Catcher in the Rye,*
and *The Great Gatsby*. Then I discovered you."—Colin Cable

"Your books have always inspired me."—Erika H.

"*Borgel* is simply delightful. Who would've thought the physics of time could be
explained with a map of New Jersey?"—E. S. Weiss

"*Borgel* . . . changed my life."—Christel Gause

"What a thrill to find it back in print."—Emily Lloyd

"I have read and reread *Borgel* so many times that my copy at last vanished
entirely, no doubt reduced to subatomic particles during a long car trip."
—Shaenon K. Garrity

4 FANTASTIC NOVELS

DANIEL PINKWATER

4
Fantastic Novels

Foreword by Scott Simon

Aladdin Paperbacks

New York   London   Toronto   Sydney   Singapore

First Aladdin Paperbacks edition July 2000

Copyright © 2000 by Daniel M. Pinkwater
Foreword copyright © 2000 by Scott Simon

Aladdin Paperbacks
An imprint of Simon & Schuster Children's Publishing Division
1230 Avenue of the Americas
New York, NY 10020

The text of this book was set in Elektra

Printed and bound in the United States of America.

10   9   8   7   6   5   4   3   2   1

Library of Congress Cataloging-in-Publication Information:

Borgel was originally published by Macmillan in 1992. *Yobgorgle* was originally published by Houghton Mifflin/Clarion in 1979. *The Worms of Kukumlima* was originally published by E.P. Dutton in 1981. *The Snarkout Boys & the Baconburg Horror* was originally published by Lothrop, Lee, & Shepard in 1985.

ISBN 0-689-83488-8

Contents

4 FANTASTIC NOVELS

Foreword

Daniel Pinkwater is goofy. I offer this considered evaluation after hearing the testimony of my friends Emily and Eliza Green of Tallahassee, Florida, ages 8 and 3 respectively. The Green Girls, who are widely read, volunteer that Daniel is their favorite author. "Because," they say, with persuasive conviction, "he's just so *goofy!*"

They recall with particular affection Daniel's creation of Larry.[1] Larry is a polar bear who eats muffins. What were you expecting a polar bear to crave—raw, oily, smelly sub-arctic fish? Cranberry or crustacean muffin—you choose. Anyway, Larry migrates to warmer climes in search of the snack that sustains him. But on this trek, he encounters a series of uncomprehending people who are scared by his predilection for pastry; it seems to turn their view of the world upside down. What might be next—brown bears who crave pesto sauce?

At last, however, Larry meets a hotel owner with a round crescent head, a warm, nonplussed smile, and a silhouette that betrays a craving for muffins, too (the man also seems to betray a superficial resemblance to Larry's creator). The hotelier does not flee from Larry's reach, or lecture him as to why polar bears cannot hunger for muffins. Instead, he makes a place for Larry to lounge and snack in the pool of his resort. The polar bear is transformed from outcast to celebrity. His tastes are enlarged by a sampling of other confections. As the book closes and the last scene fades, man and bear, belly to belly, are abiding partners.

[1] (*At the Hotel Larry*, Marshall Cavendish, 1993.)

The message, at least to me, is that those with the courage to be creatively, independently goofy will find themselves rewarded. They will win new friends, new experiences, a new view of the same old world. Goofy is *good*. Goofy is *healthy*. Goofy can make the world feel as if it's spinning round in a different direction—and what a view!

Emily and Eliza can grow up with Daniel Pinkwater, as two generations of readers have done already. Practically unique among authors in the field, Daniel has acquired an enviable following ranging from young children to aging adults. The four novels in this collection have been read with relish (not to mention mustard, onions, and hot peppers), by persons of every age.

In addition to Larry and his friends, the adventurous Green sisters can move on to encounter the sprightly Snarkout Boys (one of whom is a girl), the one-hundred-and-eleven-year-old Uncle Borgel, Sir Charles Pelicanstein, the African explorer, and an unexpected reprise of Die Fliegende Hollander in Lake Ontario. The books are genuine literature evolved in a straight line from the world which contains that affable polar bear.

Daniel Pinkwater taught me that there ought to be no clear line between writing for young people and writing for adults. Each should require care, craft, and consideration for the reader. If Daniel has devoted much of his writing life to young readers, it may be because they are more willing and eager to inhabit a piece of literature than older readers. Adults often look for escape clauses in a story. They wait like highway patrol cops lurking behind billboards to catch speeders. They look for chances to depart, hang back, and disbelieve in a

xii   SCOTT SIMON

story. But young readers tend to open the pages and leap in, swimming along with the author's current of imagination.

Daniel and I work together, talk together, and like each other. But at this writing, we have never actually met. I don't know that limited contact is the key to a steadfast friendship. But my regard for Daniel is so staunch, I am loathe to trifle with the winning formula. Instead, we get together electronically every few weeks to share our love of words and nonsense by reading and talking on the radio about a book that Daniel has discovered. In these conversations, I am continually impressed by the fact that Daniel is a maestro of children's literature who does not sound paternal, avuncular, or juvenile when talking about the books. Instead, Daniel is a fan. He has fun. He reads the stories for merriment and enjoyment, not homework or medicine.

I regret that after several years of latching onto Daniel's insights to locate some of the most promising and pleasurable to children's books, the ethics of journalism at National Public Radio prohibit us from having Daniel on to speak in behalf of his own books. I suppose that the ethics are sound. But I regret Daniel's generosity awards valuable, marketable attention to the books of other authors, but not to those of Daniel himself. I am therefore glad to have the chance in another forum to invite readers to inhabit Daniel's expansive imagination and vast heart. The man makes goofy sound grand.

Scott Simon
Washington, D.C.
November 1999

BORGEL

1

This is how Borgel turned up. I don't remember any of this myself. It's the story the family tells. Nobody quite knew who Borgel was. There was some vague idea of him, but neither my parents nor anybody else could remember having seen him. There was an old aunt in Cleveland, Ohio, who knew all about the family, and who was related to whom, but she had died years ago. There was nobody left who remembered much—for example, no one remembered for sure where we originally came from. I assume it was someplace in Europe, but no one knew exactly where.

The family name didn't provide much of a clue—Spellbound. Spellbound is an English word. English Borgel certainly was not. Where he came from I never found out. He had an accent. He came from the Old Country. That's what he called it. He never said which old country.

Borgel turned up one day with thirty-two large, lumpy, black valises. He brought them in a taxicab. My mother was home alone at the time.

"Missus Spellbound?" he asked when my mother came to the door.

My mother said yes, she was Mrs. Spellbound.

"Congratulations!" Borgel said. "You are going to be allowed to take care of an old man. God will like you for this."

Then he carried his thirty-two valises up the stairs, two at a time. He refused to accept any help. After he had brought all the valises up to the apartment, he asked if he could have a cup of hot water. My mother was in a state of something like shock. She didn't know who this old man was, and she couldn't understand why she had allowed him to carry thirty-two large leather valises up the stairs and to send the taxi away. She had even offered to help him carry the valises.

"No thank you," Borgel said with an accent. "When I have to have a woman help me carry thirty-two valises up three flights of stairs, I will lie down and die—which I am not ready to do yet, thanks God."

My mother led Uncle Borgel to the kitchen and put the kettle on. "Hot water, you said?"

"Yes, beautiful Missus," Borgel said. My mother liked that. When my mother poured the hot water into a cup and placed it in front of Borgel, he took an old-fashioned purse out of his coat pocket. My mother thought he was going to offer to pay for the hot water, and was about to tell him that it was not necessary, but what he took out of the purse was a tea bag, which he swished in his cup a time or two, squeezed out, and then returned to the purse.

"I won't be any trouble," he said.

At this point my mother screamed. She said it surprised her that she screamed suddenly like that. She said she had felt a scream coming on for a while, and it just suddenly got out. It didn't have anything to do with the tea.

What she screamed was, "Who are you anyway?"

"You didn't get my letter?"

DANIEL PINKWATER

"What letter?"

"The letter I sent you."

"I didn't get any letter!" My mother was still screaming. It didn't seem to bother Borgel.

"So you didn't get the letter. What does it matter as long as I'm here, right?"

"I don't know who you are!" my mother shouted. "Who are you?"

"That's easy," Borgel said. "I'm Borgel. I'm your relative."

"Borgel?"

"Borgel."

"You're my relative?"

"Yours or your husband's—I'm not clear about which."

My mother had stopped screaming. Now she was repeating everything Borgel said. "Mine or my husband's and you're not sure which."

"That's right," Borgel said. "Do you remember the old aunt, the one in Cleveland, the one who died?"

"Yes."

"Well, she probably knew. I never paid attention to things like that. The important thing is that I'm here, right?"

My mother felt numb all over. "Right," she said.

"A hundred and eleven," Borgel said.

"A hundred and eleven?" my mother asked.

"How old I am," Borgel said. "A hundred and eleven years old. I could go anytime. It's nice of you to take me in."

"I have to call my husband," my mother said.

"Sure," Borgel said. "How is he anyway, health okay?"

"He's fine," my mother said.

"Good. I'm glad to hear that. Which is my room? I may as well put the valises away."

That was how Borgel came to live with us. There was some more discussion, of course. My father came home from work early, and he and my mother talked with Borgel.

Borgel had a little to add to what he'd said already, but not much. It appeared that his old apartment—he referred to it as "the old apartment" in "the old building" in "the old neighborhood"—was slated for demolition. Somehow he knew that we were his only living relatives, so he came to live with us.

He wasn't specific about how he was related to us.

"What's the difference how I am your relative?" he asked. "I am your relative, and I am a hundred and eleven years old, and you have to take care of me—what could be simpler than that?"

Borgel had already moved the thirty-two valises into the little spare bedroom at the back of the apartment. There wasn't much more to say.

All this happened when I was quite small. I don't remember any of it. At that time, my world wasn't as big as the whole apartment. I don't remember when I began to notice that Borgel was around. He continued to live in the little room, and he continued to give his age as a hundred and eleven, year after year.

I have an older brother and sister, Milo and Martha. They were and are more or less perfect. Honor students. Extra good manners. Religious. Boring. I only bring up their names in the interest of accuracy, because I feel I should mention everyone living in the apartment.

DANIEL PINKWATER

Obviously, Uncle Borgel wasn't a standard uncle. He was more along the lines of a great-great uncle, or a second cousin of my father's grandfather, or something like that. We called him "uncle" because that was the best we could think of. It seemed to satisfy him.

Occasionally my parents would have conversations about him. "Of course I feel sorry for him," my mother might say. "It's too bad they tore down the building he lived in to make room for the new sewage treatment plant—but is this the right place for him? I mean, wouldn't he be happier in one of those communities they have for older people?"

This conversation would be taking place in the living room. From nearly a hundred feet away, back next to the kitchen, behind a closed door, over the sound of the television, over the sound of Milo practicing the French horn in his room, would come a shout that everyone in the apartment could hear clearly.

"Phooey!"

"That was a coincidence, of course," my father would say.

"Of course," my mother would say.

And they would drop the subject for another few months.

Frequently, Uncle Borgel would not come out of his room for two or three weeks at a time. The second bathroom was in the hall right outside his door, and he could dart in and out without being seen—at least he never was. My mother said that sometimes she could hear a blender working in Borgel's room, and sometimes she could smell cooking. Evidently, he had a hot plate in there.

In the beginning she would worry about Borgel, and

knock on the door and ask if everything was all right. Borgel would answer that everything was fine, and please not to bother about him. He never opened the door.

The only member of the household to see the inside of Uncle Borgel's room for the first few years was Fafner the dog. From the day Borgel arrived, Fafner spent almost all his time there. Uncle Borgel would open the door a little and let Fafner out when it was time for a walk—that is, when Borgel didn't take him himself. When Fafner came back, he would sit outside Borgel's door and whine until he was allowed in.

On a couple of occasions, I remember hearing growling and scuffling and happy barking coming from the room. They were wrestling.

My mother reported to us that while everyone was away at school and work, Borgel would come out of his room. He would have his hat and coat on. He and Fafner would go out for two or three hours. When they came back, Fafner would appear to be tired. My mother thought they were going for long walks.

One night, Borgel appeared in the living room where we were all watching TV. He pulled a straight chair into the middle of the room, and sat with his back to the set.

My mother said hello to him. He bowed from his chair. She asked him if he would like a cup of hot water, tea, or perhaps a cookie.

"No thank you—I just had an eggplant," he said.

One Saturday afternoon—maybe I was ten or eleven—I ran into Uncle Borgel. I was just hanging around, not doing much of anything, when Uncle Borgel suddenly appeared.

　　　　　　　　　　　　　　DANIEL PINKWATER

He had a way of doing that. One second he would not be in the room—and then he was.

"Okay, sonnyboy," he said, "answer me this—what is an *eft?*"

"It's a lizard, isn't it?" I said. "Like a salamander."

"HO-kay," Borgel said. "Now, what is a *wok?*"

"That's a Chinese frying pan."

"Prew-ty good," Borgel said. "Now tell me, please, Mr. Smartypants, what is a *roc?*"

"It's a big bird," I said. "Sinbad the Sailor met one in the story."

"Bingo!" Borgel shouted, and handed me a dime. Then he went to his room.

The next day, I received a letter. It was an invitation.

> *To Mr. Melvin Spellbound:*
> *You are invited to visit me in my room after*
> *supper tonight.*
>
> > *Borgel*
>
> *Wear a tie.*

I later got to know that one could only visit Uncle Borgel's room by invitation. Walking up and knocking on the door was no good. The invitation might come hours, minutes, or weeks in advance. It would read

> *You are invited to visit me in my room*
> *at seven o'clock on the first of June.*
> *And wear a tie.*

The invitations always ended with "wear a tie." When I visited Uncle Borgel, with my tie on, for the first time, I found him sitting in a room crowded with valises and suitcases—the ones he had arrived with. They were all made of dull, scuffed-up black leather with bumps on it. They were stacked almost to the ceiling, and I could see more of them through the partially open closet door. In addition to the suitcases and Borgel, there was a bed, two chairs, an empty bookcase, and a framed photograph of a man with a bushy beard wearing a big cowboy hat. There was nothing else visible in the room.

Apparently, Uncle Borgel kept all his possessions in those suitcases, and took things out as he needed them, putting them away afterwards.

"Hello, Melvin," Uncle Borgel said. "Would you like a cup of Norwegian vole-moss tea?"

"I've never had any," I said.

"So you'd like to try it," Uncle Borgel said. He opened a valise, and took an electric hot plate, a couple of cups, and a kettle which turned out to be already full of water. He put the hot plate on top of the bookcase and plugged it into a wall socket.

"It will be ready in a few minutes," he said. "Sit there." He pointed to a chair. I sat.

"Good! Now—a surprise quiz!" he said.

"Huh?" I said.

"Wait for the question," Uncle Borgel said. "No guessing—besides, 'huh?' is not an answer. First question: What is an *asp*?"

DANIEL PINKWATER

"It's a little snake—a poisonous one," I said.

"Hooray! Ten points for that one!" Uncle Borgel said. "Now the second question—what is a *boa*?"

"A boa is a big snake—a boa constrictor."

"Right again! You didn't make an asp of yourself that time. Here comes a tricky one. What is a *fry*? Take your time."

I took my time. "A fry is a . . . baby fish?"

"Whoopee! You got them all, Mr. Genius. A perfect score!" Borgel dug out a dime and handed it to me.

"Excuse me," I said. "Why do you do that?"

"Do what?"

"Only ask questions about three-letter words?"

"I don't know—I just happen to like three-letter words today. There are a lot of big topics with only three letters— God, for example, and Art, and bugs."

"*Bugs* has four letters."

"Bug then—look, the water is boiling already. I'll get the teapot."

Uncle Borgel took a teapot from the suitcase, shook some horrible-looking gray leaves into it, and poured in boiling water.

"There are more kinds of bugs than anything, you know," he said, "except stars in the three-letter *sky*."

I couldn't decide whether the Norwegian vole-moss tea tasted more like moss or vole—never having tasted either to my knowledge. It wasn't exactly bad, but it was very strange.

"The Laplanders drink this like Grepis-Cola," Uncle Borgel said. "It's good for the brain and other muscles."

"What's Grepis-Cola?" I asked.

"It's the seventy-fifth most popular soft drink in the world," Uncle Borgel said.

That interested me. I like topics like that. I already knew the twenty most popular soft drinks in the world. I thought I would make a point of asking Borgel sometime what the other fifty-four were.

"Okay!" Uncle Borgel said. "Now it is time for the musical entertainment. I hope you like music."

"Sure, I like music," I said.

"You like Beethoven?"

"I'm not sure," I said. Classical music was a topic I didn't know very much about. Nobody in the family cared much about music, classical or otherwise—unless you counted Milo, but he only played French horn in the high-school band because things like that are supposed to look good on your college application. He already wanted to become a dentist and drive a German sports car. I don't think he was any good as a French hornist.

"Beethoven is a first-class genius," Uncle Borgel said. "He's maybe as good as the human race can produce. If you listen to the music he wrote, you'll find out things about yourself. If you listen to music by Beethoven a lot, you will never become stupid—unless you already are, in which case there's still no harm in it."

Uncle Borgel got a radio out of a suitcase. It was made of wood. He unplugged the hot plate, and plugged in the radio. There was a friendly light in the dial, like a Christmas tree light.

"This will take a minute to warm up," he said. "I watch the newspaper to see what is going to be on. Tonight they are playing Symphony number five. It's just right for a boy who doesn't know Beethoven. It's exciting. You'll probably like it."

He was right. It was exciting, and I did like it. The music made me feel the way I did when I watched certain adventure movies—better in a way, because the feeling was inside me instead of being connected with a story on the screen.

While listening to Beethoven's Symphony number five, I also got to like Norwegian vole-moss tea.

When it was over, I asked Uncle Borgel, "Would you invite me the next time something by Beethoven is going to be on?"

"Of kee-ourse!" he said.

I got to be invited to Borgel's room more often than anyone else in the family.

My parents were practically never invited. Milo and Martha visited him occasionally, but they appeared to regard it as charity—being kind to an old man, part of their perfection program. I doubt that Borgel had much fun with them, but he'd invite them from time to time so they could feel virtuous.

I visited Borgel at least once a week. We listened to the radio, drank cups of Norwegian vole-moss tea, and had discussions about all sorts of things. I would also go for walks with Borgel and Fafner. He liked to walk at a fast pace for fifteen or twenty blocks. It was hard to keep up with him. It was difficult to believe he was over a hundred years old.

Of course, Borgel saw the rest of the family, even though

they didn't visit him in his room very often. He would pass through the apartment on his way out with Fafner—and at long intervals he would join the family in the living room, always sitting with his back to the television. It turned out that he disliked television because the people in the pictures appeared so small. He said it gave him the willies.

I wasn't able to find out from Borgel where the Old Country was. He would never say. I had developed a theory that it was one of those countries that don't exist anymore, like Bosnia or Herzegovina. Borgel only referred to it as the "Old Country." It didn't seem likely that he had forgotten. He didn't appear to ever forget anything.

He'd say things like: "See this button? It's a bone button. I remember when all buttons were made of bone, or shell, sometimes wood. There weren't any plastic buttons until Matthias Klopmeister invented a celluloid button-making machine in 1883."

Someone who remembers who made the first celluloid button-making machine, and when, isn't likely to forget where he was born, but Borgel never mentioned the place by name.

"Melvin," Uncle Borgel said to me, "some details are important, and some details are unimportant. I pay attention to the important ones."

I asked him if the history of button making was important.

"Of course buttons are important. Next to zippers, buttons are among the most important inventions of mankind. Imagine how much trouble getting dressed and undressed would be if you had to deal with strings and pins and knots and such."

I asked Borgel what some of the other important inventions of mankind were. He said they were underarm deodorant, window screens, long-playing records, and Chef Chow's Hot and Spicy Oil.

I liked it very much when Uncle Borgel would let me come with him on visits to the Old Neighborhood. The Old Neighborhood was where Uncle Borgel lived before he came to live with us. He lived in the Old Apartment in the Old Building.

2

The Old Building wasn't there anymore. In fact, the Old Neighborhood was hardly there anymore. It was mostly a bunch of vacant lots. The apartment houses had been torn down to make way for a new sewage treatment plant that was never built. They tore down the Old Building (with the Old Apartment in it), filled in the basement with bricks and rubble, and left it that way.

Uncle Borgel didn't leave many traces. Assuming he was born in some defunct country like Herzegovina, it was interesting that he should have most recently lived in an apartment that wasn't there anymore, in a building that wasn't there anymore, in a neighborhood that wasn't there anymore. It isn't exactly accurate to say that the Old Neighborhood had ceased to exist entirely. There were still a few buildings standing, and the main business street, Nemo Boulevard, was not quite dead. That was where Uncle Borgel and I would go when we visited the Old Neighborhood.

Uncle Borgel said the Old Neighborhood was the only place in town where you could get a bottle of Chef Chow's Hot and Spicy Oil. It's one of the essential ingredients in most of the cooking Borgel did. He bought a bottle of Chef Chow's Hot and Spicy Oil at least once a month. I asked him why he didn't buy it by the case and save trips. He told me he liked to go back and visit the Old Neighborhood—and besides, it would be dangerous to keep many bottles of Chef Chow's Hot and Spicy Oil together in one place.

"Safety first," he said.

Another thing Uncle Borgel liked to do when we visited Nemo Boulevard was to go to the Star Spangled Banner All-American Cafeteria. The Star Spangled Banner All-American Cafeteria was Uncle Borgel's favorite place to hang out. It was a place where not a word of English was ever heard.

Whenever we went there, he would have two or three glasses of coffee. They served it in thick, barrel-shaped glasses. Uncle Borgel would put a lot of milk in his coffee and stir it with a spoon. He would also eat a rhinoceros roll. A rhinoceros roll is an ordinary hard roll. In some places they call them kaiser rolls, or kimmelwicks, or stale-o's. At the Star Spangled Banner All-American Cafeteria they called them rhinoceros rolls.

When we went to the Star Spangled Banner All-American Cafeteria we would usually meet Uncle Borgel's friend Mr. Raspelnootzpiki.

Mr. Raspelnootzpiki was also very old. He claimed to be even older than Uncle Borgel, but Borgel said he was probably not even a hundred yet. When they met at the cafeteria they would speak in some strange language. It was unlike anything I had ever heard. It sounded as though they were clearing their throats, but they were communicating.

I asked Uncle Borgel a trick question, hoping to get a clue about where he had come from: "Is the language you speak with Mr. Raspelnootzpiki the language you spoke in the Old Country?"

"No. Mr. Raspelnootzpiki doesn't come from my Old Country."

"Is his Old Country anywhere near yours?" I was still hoping to get some information I could use. I could look up Mr. Raspelnootzpiki's Old Country in an atlas and see what countries were nearby.

"His country was next door to mine."

I was really getting somewhere.

"What is the name of Mr. Raspelnootzpiki's Old Country?" I asked.

Uncle Borgel made a sound. At first I thought he was preparing to spit, something he did better than anybody, but I realized he was saying the name of Mr. Raspelnootzpiki's Old Country.

"How do you spell it?"

"In English?"

"Yes. How do you spell it in English?"

"You can't spell it in English."

Mr. Raspelnootzpiki wore a thick black overcoat, winter and summer, and he smoked horrible, cheap cigars. He also wore thick eyeglasses and a funny slouch hat. He and Uncle Borgel would alternately talk and listen.

I would sit, sipping my coffee and nibbling my rhinoceros roll, and wonder what they were talking about.

Another reason I liked to go to the Old Neighborhood with Uncle Borgel—in addition to sitting around in the Star Spangled Banner All-American Cafeteria with him—was that I liked the stories he told on the bus. Sometimes he'd tell true stories from his own life, about climbing a mountain in Asia, or being a cowboy in Brazil, or sailing in the South Pacific. Other times he would tell a story about some criminal, and how the police caught him. Halfway through many of these stories, I would realize it was the plot of a television program the family had watched the night before while Borgel sat with his back to the set.

Very often he'd tell stories from the Old Country. They were nursery stories or folktales. They were all about animals. At the end of each story, he would pause—then he'd say "moral," and then he'd tell the moral.

Here are some of his stories:

The Story of the Rabbit and the Eggplant

Once upon a time there was a race between a rabbit and an eggplant. Now, the eggplant, as you know, is a member of the vegetable kingdom, and the rabbit is a very fast animal.

Everybody bet lots of money on the eggplant, thinking that if a vegetable challenges a live animal with four legs to a race, then it must be that the vegetable knows something.

People expected the eggplant to win the race by some clever trick of philosophy. The race was started, and there was a lot of cheering. The rabbit streaked out of sight.

The eggplant just sat there at the starting line. Everybody knew that in some surprising way the eggplant would wind up winning the race.

Nothing of the sort happened. Eventually, the rabbit crossed the finish line, and the eggplant hadn't moved an inch.

The spectators ate the eggplant.

Moral: Never bet on an eggplant.

The Story of the Mole that Thought It Was a Fox

There was a mole that was unusually large and beautiful—for a mole. It was stronger and faster than all the other moles. It decided that it must not be a mole at all.

"A terrible mistake has been made," said the mole. "I have been raised as a mole, when all the time I have been a fox."

The mole told all the other moles, and all the other animals, that it was really a fox.

"Is that a fact?" said all the other animals, none of which had ever seen a fox.

One day, a real fox passed through the part of the forest where the mole that thought it was a fox lived.

"I am a fox," said the mole to the fox.

"Well, you sure are an ugly one," said the fox, and continued on his way.

Moral: Who cares?

The Story of the Fish that Thought It Was Drowning

A fish in a forest pool called out to the animals that passed by, "Help! Help! Help me out of here! I'm drowning!"

An elk spoke to the fish, "You're not drowning. You are a

fish. You live in the water. If you were to come onto dry land, you would die."

"Oh," said the fish.

Moral: Don't listen to anything a fish says.

The Moose and the Squirrel

In olden times, everybody knew that the moose was a great trickster. The moose always played jokes on the other animals, and cheated them, and got them into trouble. So, when the moose came upon the squirrel, who had collected a great number of nuts for the winter, the squirrel resolved to have nothing to do with him.

"Oh, squirrel," said the moose, "why don't you let me put all those nuts of yours in my pocket? I'll take them wherever you like, and you won't have to run back and forth with one nut at a time."

"Oh no," said the squirrel, "you'll play some sort of trick on me."

"No I won't," said the moose, "I'll just put your nuts in my pocket, and take them wherever you say."

"Oh no, you'll cheat me," said the squirrel.

"No I won't," said the moose.

"Oh no," said the squirrel, "you'll get me into trouble."

"No, honestly," said the moose. "I just want to help you."

"Really?" asked the squirrel.

"Sincerely," said the moose.

"All right, I'm going to trust you," said the squirrel. "You may put my nuts in your pocket."

"I just realized," said the moose, "I don't have a pocket. Let's forget the whole thing."

Moral: Animals are stupid.

Of course, stories like that would have appealed to me much more when I was a lot younger, but I still liked to hear Uncle Borgel tell them. He was a good storyteller. He'd imitate the animals, and sometimes—if he was telling about a squirrel, for example—he'd get up and hop around the bus, imitating a squirrel. He really got into the spirit of whatever he was telling. Sometimes everybody on the bus got involved.

DANIEL PINKWATER

3

One night, Uncle Borgel tiptoed into the room I shared with my brother, Milo. We were both asleep. Uncle Borgel pressed a flashlight and a scrap of paper into my hand and then tiptoed out. I switched on the flashlight, and read what was written on the sheet of paper:

> *Come to my room in one hour. Get dressed, and carry your shoes in you hand. Also bring some extra clothing—a spare shirt, underwear, socks.*
>
> *Don't make any noise.*
>
> *Borgel*
>
> *Tie not necessary.*

I waited until the luminous hands of the alarm clock indicated that three-quarters of an hour had passed. Then I got up, dressed in the dark, rummaged around for some spare clothes, and carrying my shoes in my hand, made my way through the dark apartment to Uncle Borgel's room.

"Come in."

I went in. Uncle Borgel had on his hat and coat. He was sitting on his bed with one of his lumpy leather valises on his lap.

"Thanks for coming," he said. "I just wanted to say good-bye."

"Where are you going?" I asked.

"I thought I'd take Fafner with me. It would be too cruel to leave him here. He wouldn't understand."

"You . . . you're . . . you're going?"

"Yes. Going."

I didn't know what else to say, so I said, "Why did you ask me to bring these extra clothes?"

"It's cold in the apartment. I thought you might want to put them on. Do you want to put them on?"

"No. I don't want to put them on."

"If you're tired of holding them you can put them in this valise." He opened the valise. "Here, put them in the valise."

I put my clothes in the valise.

"Well," Uncle Borgel said, "I will be going now. Come, Fafner."

"Wait," I said. "You're just going to wander off in the middle of the night? I mean . . . just leave?"

The truth was, I was a little worried that maybe Uncle Borgel had gone crazy. I couldn't just let him wander off like that.

"If you're going, I'm going with you," I said.

"That's okay by me," Uncle Borgel said. "I'll wait while you put your shoes on."

I laced my shoes, grabbed my coat from the coat tree in the hall as we passed it, and followed Uncle Borgel in his long black coat and broad-brimmed hat, carrying his black

DANIEL PINKWATER

lumpy leather valise and followed by Fafner, down the stairs, out of the building, and into the street.

This was my situation: I was out in the street, in the middle of the night, with the family dog and my sort-of-great-uncle who was at least a hundred and eleven years old. What it amounted to was that we were running away from home.

It was very strange. I had overheard conversations between my parents about the possibility that Borgel might go soft in the head sometime. This didn't seem to be very likely in Borgel's case. He always did the crossword puzzle with his leaky fountain pen in under two minutes. Once I got him as a present a book of the world's hardest crossword puzzles. He did them all in about half an hour.

Borgel could also figure in his head faster than I could work my father's adding machine. And he could juggle five balls.

Still, it seemed very odd, this taking off in the middle of the night. Probably the right thing to do would have been to wake up my parents and tell them Uncle Borgel had gone crazy and was running away. I couldn't do that. He was my favorite relative. If Borgel was going to run away, the only thing to do was to run away with him and see that nothing bad happened to him.

I myself had no particular reason to run away from home. I wasn't mistreated or anything of that kind. On the other hand, it occurred to me that there was no strong reason not to run away. I was fairly bored by my family, except Borgel. There wasn't anything better to do. But it seemed to me that I was entertaining foolish thoughts—after all, how far could we get? It would probably all come to nothing within a couple of hours.

Borgel was making his way along, peering at the parked cars. He was sort of mumbling to himself. I considered offering to carry his valise for him, but he never allowed that sort of thing. We went a block, turned the corner, went another block, turned another corner. We were going around the block! Borgel was obviously confused. Maybe he had gone soft in the head after all.

He continued to peer at parked cars. I couldn't imagine what he was up to. Then he put down the valise, opened it, and took out a length of stiff wire—a straightened-out coat hanger. He worked the wire into the window frame of a beaten-up old sedan, fished around, and caught the door-lock knob with the hooked end of the wire.

It only took a few seconds. "Get in," he said. Fafner jumped in. I followed him.

Uncle Borgel had broken into a parked car! Now he was fiddling around under the dashboard with another piece of wire—this time it was insulated electrical wire. He was hot-wiring it! Uncle Borgel was a car thief!

"Uncle Borgel, are you sure this is a good idea?"

"Sure. It's the only way."

"Suppose the police caught you and threw you in jail?"

"Ah-ha! Hypothetical questions! So what? What could they do to me—give me life in prison? Besides, I'm a cute old man. No court in the world would convict a cute old man. Anyway, I haven't done anything to get arrested for."

"Haven't done anything? What do you call . . . ?"

"Shhh! I have to concentrate."

Uncle Borgel felt around under the dashboard, poking with his piece of wire. Suddenly the engine turned over. Borgel smiled.

"That's got it," he said. The engine was coughing and sputtering. Borgel stamped on the gas pedal. The car vibrated and lurched forward. We were moving. We were criminals. I was an accessory to grand larceny. I knew this because I had watched a lot of police shows on TV. Grand theft auto was what I was an accessory to—a felony. I thought you could get about seven years for that.

Not being a cute old man, I figured they'd throw the book at me. I wasn't feeling very happy. Uncle Borgel obviously was. He was singing as he drove.

Uncle Borgel had often cautioned me not to be a wimp. He was of the opinion that the rest of the family had wimpish tendencies, and had warned me against falling into those ways. I bring this up because I do not want to give the impression that I was unaware of the thrills and excitement available to persons who have committed Grand Theft Auto. I appreciated that we were taking a lot of risks, and I could see that it was a sort of adventure—but my thoughts kept returning to the prospect of getting caught and thrown into prison.

The old sedan chugged onto the interstate, and in fifteen minutes or so had worked up to cruising speed. I was thinking that if one commits Grand Theft Auto and then crosses a state line, it becomes a federal crime, and one stands a good chance of being machine-gunned by the FBI. I considered working this into the conversation, but I couldn't be sure whether it would have the effect of discouraging Borgel or just making him happy.

Fortunately, there wasn't much traffic on the interstate at that time of night—just the occasional convoy of trucks, which would shoot past us and be out of sight in two minutes. I began to cling to the hope that we would get so far away from the scene of our crime that nobody would be looking for us. When we got to a city, I'd persuade Borgel to dump the car, and we'd go home on the bus.

Oh no! The state line was coming up fast! We'd be across it soon! That was it—the big time—professional crime. It was going to be death in a hail of bullets for me.

"Melvin, look in the glove compartment and see if there are some whole wheat fig bars in there." I had to hand it to Uncle Borgel—he was a cool one thinking of fig bars at a time like this. I opened the glove compartment and rummaged around.

"A Super-Yeast candy bar, raisins—anything you find in there," Borgel said. "I'm feeling hungry, and I don't want to stop until we've burned up this tank of gas."

I found a cellophane bag of whole wheat fig bars and passed it to Borgel.

"Care for one?" he asked.

"Maybe later," I said. I was examining something else I'd found in the glove compartment. It was a plastic folder containing a card. It had Uncle Borgel's picture on it. I could read the card by the light of the tiny bulb in the glove compartment. It said that the car was a 1937 Dorbzeldge sedan, that it had four cylinders and weighed 5,307 pounds, and that it was owned by Borgel MacTavish. MacTavish was

Borgel's last name—not that he was a Scotsman; MacTavish was as close to any English-speaking person could come to pronouncing his last name, which sounded nothing like MacTavish, but even less like anything else.

"This is your car," I said.

Borgel sprayed whole wheat and fig crumbs all over the dashboard. "Naturally it's my car. What did you think, that I stole it?"

"Why did you break in with a coat hanger, and start it without a key?"

"Because I lost my key after I had the car about a year, and then the country where she was made went out of business, so I couldn't get a new one. How about this car? Forty-five years I've had her and never changed the oil once. She's a honey!"

Honey was making about forty miles per hour and clouds of white smoke. I took a bite of a whole wheat fig bar and settled back against the seat cushions.

"This is the life!" Uncle Borgel said. "The open road, a good machine, and a whole wheat fig bar! By the way, see if the dog will eat one of those."

I offered Fafner a fig bar, which he accepted without enthusiasm. He didn't like food that got stuck in his teeth.

"This is the life all right," I said. "By the way, are we going any place in particular?"

"Yes, we are!"

"Do you feel like telling me where?"

"I feel like telling you a story from my life."

"Will we be gone long?"

"That depends on what you call long. We'll see."

"I was just thinking about my parents."

"I left them a note."

"Oh, that's good. What did the note say?"

"The note said, *Melvin and I have gone away. We took the dog. Don't anybody go in my room. Love Borgel.*"

"That should do it," I said.

"Sure," Borgel said.

It sank in. We really had run away, Borgel, my hundred-and-eleven-year-old super-great-uncle, or whatever he was, and I.

"There are some bottles of natural honey-sweetened ginger beer in the back," Borgel said. "See if you can reach a couple."

I hung over the seat back and felt around. Under Fafner, I found a brown paper bag that clinked. I reached in and fished out two bottles of ginger beer.

"What do I do with these?" I asked.

"Give them here," Uncle Borgel said. "Pardon my teeth."

With his teeth he pried the cap off one of the bottles, and handed it to me. He did the same with the other bottle, and spat both caps out the window. I was impressed.

The natural honey-sweetened ginger beer tasted good and sort of burned my lips. I liked the sensation of hurtling along in the old Dorbzeldge, driving through the night with Borgel and snacking on good things.

"How come you never mentioned having this car?" I asked him.

"There are lots of things I've never mentioned. I don't use the car for little errands—just for big road trips. That's why she's lasted so long."

"When was the last time you took a road trip?"

"Nineteen hundred and forty-six," Borgel said. "I ended up in Yellowstone."

"Are we going to Yellowstone?"

"I wasn't planning on it—but you never know. We'll see some interesting things, that's for sure."

"Going to drive all night?"

"Until I get tired. You can go to sleep if you want to."

"I'm not sleepy."

"So I'll tell you a story from my life."

Uncle Borgel didn't say anything.

"Okay," I said.

"Okay, what?"

"Okay, tell me a story from your life."

"I'm picking one out."

More silence.

"Do you mind if I play the radio?" I asked.

"Go ahead, I'm still picking."

I turned the knob. A green light behind the dial came on.

"Give it time to warm up," Borgel said.

In a minute or so I could hear static. I twisted the tuning knob. I found a station. A man was talking. He sounded like someone. He sounded like Borgel's friend Mr. Raspelnootzpiki. He was speaking that same language. "Hey!" I said.

"Shortwave," Uncle Borgel said. "This car's got everything."

"He's talking in that same language you speak with your friend!"

"No, he's not. That's French."

"That's not French."

"You can speak French?"

"No, but . . ."

"So how do you know it isn't French?"

"Because it doesn't sound like French."

"The announcer has a cold and a Canadian accent. He's talking French. You can believe me. I know a lot."

It didn't sound like French. It sounded exactly like Mr. Raspelnootzpiki. Borgel's mind was made up. There was no point in arguing with him.

On the other hand, he could have been right. I was getting pretty sleepy. At one point I thought I heard the announcer say something about the Star Spangled Banner All-American Cafeteria, but by that time I was already drifting into sleep as the Dorbzeldge thundered along the highway.

"Okay."

"Okay, what?"

"Okay, I've picked a story from my life, the one I want to tell you."

I shook myself awake. "Okay, tell it."

"Okay, so here goes. Long ago in the future, in the galaxy of Witzbilb, near Terraxstein—"

"Long ago in the future?"

"Who's telling this story? Be quiet and pay attention."

"Sorry."

"Long ago in the future, in the galaxy of Witzbilb, near Terraxstein, a planet with five moons, on a little planetoid no bigger than a gob of spit in this vast and expanding universe, there was a moment."

DANIEL PINKWATER

"A moment?"

"That's right."

"This story is about a moment?"

"Absotivlutely."

"A moment, like a moment in time, right?"

"Right. Now to continue, this was a happy little moment that had never done anybody the least harm. This moment, whose name was Dennis, played with the other little moments, romping and gamboling with never a care in the world. Little Dennis never suspected that he would become a moment in history—of course he already had, because this is a story of the future in the tense of the past."

"Would you mind if I went to sleep now?"

"This isn't holding your interest, is it?"

"I'm nodding."

"Okay, how about if I told you the true story about how I became a time tourist?"

"A time tourist? What's that?"

"It really should be time-space-and-the-other—that's the element in which I am a tourist—but time tourist sounds better. It could be a story on TV. 'Borgel the Time Tourist.' 'Borgel the Time Tourist and His Amazing Adventures.' 'The Amazing Adventures of Borgel the Time Tourist.' Welcome to another thrilling episode of 'Borgel, Tourist in Time.' A watch company could sponsor it.

"The makers of Psycho watches brings you another episode of 'Borgel the Time Tourist.' Hello, I am wearing the Psycho 640-kilobyte digital watch, just like the one Borgel the Time Tourist uses. It runs in all directions, and underwater, and at temperatures up to 16,000 degrees centigrade—and you can spit on it, you can stomp on it—nothing's gonna hurt this baby. Bullets you can shoot at it—acid, magnets, vibrations!"

"So what's a time tourist?"

"I'm one. I'm a time tourist. Me."

"Yes?"

"Yes. As I said, it would be better to say space-time-and-the-other tourist, because it isn't only time, you know."

"What's the other?"

"Ha! That's easy, sonnyboy—it is that which exists in neither time nor space. It's the best part of being a time tourist."

I had read some stuff along these lines, and I had seen plenty of science fiction on television, so this sort of thing was not new to me. Neither was it new for Uncle Borgel to incorporate plots of television shows into the stories he told me. The way to enjoy this was to play along.

"So what do you do when you're a time tourist?" I asked.

"Well, the first thing you need is a vehicle. This Dorbzeldge is a first-rate time-space-and-the-other machine. The next thing, if you really know what you're doing, is to have some good traveling companions. You and Fafner have the makings of the very best fellow tourists."

"So I'm a time tourist, too."

"You are now."

"What else do we need?"

"Just the willingness for it to happen, that's all."

"The willingness for what to happen?"

"The willingness to leave one time-space-and-the-other

continuum and enter into another. Are you willing for that to happen?"

"Sure."

"You've got to be really willing. You can't just say so to be polite. Are you really willing? You really want to take the trip?"

"Yes, I really want to."

"HO-kay! We've got everything we need, and we're started! Whoopee!"

The night sky was clear and full of stars. I looked at Uncle Borgel. He was happy. There was a big smile on his face, and it was possible to see a few of the stars through his head.

That's neat, I thought, Uncle Borgel is sort of translucent. I held my hand up in front of the windshield and looked at some stars through it. They were dimly but plainly visible.

"Hot cha!" Uncle Borgel shouted. "Time-space-and-the-other, here we come!"

I came all the way awake. "Wait a minute! I can see through my hand! What's happening?"

"You have a problem, Mr. Adventurer?" Uncle Borgel asked.

"I can see through my hand! I'm transparent! What's going on?"

"Relax. It's normal."

"It's not normal! I can see stars through my hand!"

"Sort of neat, wouldn't you say?" Borgel asked.

"Except that it's terrifying. What is this?"

"Now, don't be a weenie," Borgel said. "What kind of

time tourist do you call yourself if you get all excited just because you see a few stars?"

"I'm seeing these stars through what I hope is solid flesh, and I want to know why."

"Why? I don't know exactly why. It's something that happens when you travel very fast through time-space-and-the-other."

It was sinking in. Borgel wasn't just telling me a story from television. We really were traveling through time and space—or something of the kind. I was squinting through the palm of my hand at stars, and it was like looking at them through a pair of sunglasses.

"What else happens? Tell me everything."

"All sorts. Sometimes we become completely immaterial—sometimes we turn into heat, sound, light. All sorts. It's fun."

"This is dangerous, isn't it?"

"This is no more dangerous than eating ice cream—"
I felt a little better.

"—in a hot air balloon in a high wind."
I felt a little worse.

"Don't worry," Uncle Borgel said. "I've been doing this sort of thing for maybe eight or nine hundred years. It's a snap. You'll get used to it."

"What do you mean, eight or nine hundred years?"

"It's just a guess. I lost track of myself a long time ago."

"You're telling me that you're eight or nine hundred years old?"

"Older—you can't become a time tourist where I come from until you're all grown up. You're lucky you don't come from there."

"From where?"

"From the Old Country. Where you have to be all grown up before you can become a time tourist. There aren't many boys your age have an opportunity like this."

"I feel sort of sick."

"The fig bars didn't agree with you? Have another swig of the ginger beer."

"Uncle Borgel, I'm not following this very well. Maybe you'd better start from the beginning."

"Sure. We've got plenty of time. A story from my life. You're comfortable?"

"No, I am not comfortable. I am confused and scared, and I can see through my hand, not to mention through your head. Up until a few minutes ago I was under the impression that we were riding along an ordinary road in an ordinary stolen car. Now you tell me that we're traveling through time-space-and-the-other, and that you're more than nine hundred years old. None of this makes me comfortable."

"Well, you seem to have all the facts straight. Maybe I can help you feel a little better about this if I tell you some history."

"Uncle Borgel, anything you can do to help will be greatly appreciated."

"Fine. Now settle back, look at the nice stars through your hand, and I'll tell you everything. The first thing you have to understand is that time is not like a string."

"Time is not like a string?"

"Some people think it is. It isn't. It also isn't like a series of frankfurters, a loop, a figure eight, a fast train, a fast train with a mosquito in it, a melting ice cube, a floppy pocket watch, a French cookie, rotten apples, Silly Putty, or Swiss cheese."

"No?"

"No."

"So?"

"So, *time* is like a map of the state of New Jersey—not like the state of New Jersey or even the state of New Jersey seen from the air, or from a satellite—it is like a *map* of the state of New Jersey. Got that?"

"Sure."

"Okay, next is *space*. Space is sort of like a bagel, but an elliptical one, with poppy seeds. You got that?"

"Got it. Time is like a map of New Jersey. Space is like a bagel."

"Good. Next is *the other*. This is the hardest to explain. The best I can do is that the other is like a mixed salad in which there is only one ingredient you like. Now, one more time."

"Time is like a map of New Jersey, space is like a bagel with poppy seeds, and the other is like a salad with only one thing you like in it," I repeated.

"Excellent. Have a fig bar. Now I can get on with the history."

"Am I allowed to ask questions?"

"Soitainly."

"Why is time like a map of New Jersey?"

"A good question. This is why time is like a map of New Jersey: Let's say you are in Newark, New Jersey, and you want to go to, oh, let's say Perth Amboy, New Jersey. You don't know exactly where Perth Amboy is. What do you do?"

"I look at a map?"

"Preezacktly! You look at a map. And the map shows you what roads to take to get to Perth Amboy, or Hoboken, or Elizabeth, or anywhere in the state. Now, here comes the big question. If you were in Newark and were thinking about Perth Amboy, would Perth Amboy exist?"

"Sure."

"Right. Now, let's imagine you're still in Newark, and you are *not* thinking about Perth Amboy. Would it still exist?"

"Yes."

"And if you had never even heard of Perth Amboy, and weren't thinking about it—would it exist then?"

"Yes."

"How about Jersey City?"

"Same thing."

"Keereckt! It is exactly the same thing. So, Mr. Professor of Philosophy, all the towns and cities and places in New Jersey exist, whether you know about them or are thinking about them or not, right?"

"Right."

"Trenton?"

"Yes."

"Hasbrouck Heights?"

"Yes."

"Weehawken?"

"Yes."

"Cape May Courthouse?"

"Is there such a place?"

"There is."

"Then yes."

"So there you are in Newark, and all the other places exist even though you are not in them, see?"

"I do."

"The same thing with time. All the moments in time exist, even though you're only in one of them."

"I get it!"

"You do?"

"Sure. It's easy." I was getting sort of excited. "The points in time extend in all directions, and even though we can only know about them one by one, the others are all there."

"Perfect! Now if you left Newark and went to Moonachie, would Newark cease to exist?"

"No."

"And if you wanted to go back to Newark, would it still be there?"

"Probably."

"You're an intelligent kid."

"So if you have the means to do it," I said, "you can go back and forth from any point in time to any other point in time, because they're all always there, and it works out to be like a map of New Jersey or some other state."

"Wrong. Not some other state. Just New Jersey."

"Why not one of the other states?"

"They're the wrong shape."

While Borgel was telling me this, I was noticing that the road beneath us was starting to glow.

"The road is starting to glow," I said.

"That's normal," Borgel said. "Only a couple of things

you need to understand before I can tell my story. You know about space?"

"You mean outer space, planets, and all that?" I asked.

"Space—inner, outer, near, far, solid, and immaterial; the distance between stars and the distance between an ant's ears and his hind foot—space, you know about it?"

"I know it exists."

"Good enough. You're a smart boy, Melvin. I'm glad I brought you with me. You know what is it light years?"

"That's the distance it takes light to travel in a year."

"So if we wanted to go to some galaxy that's 50 million light years away, and could travel at half the speed of light it would take us how long to get there?"

"I don't know. How long?"

"Too long, that's how long. That's space. But if you can move through time *and* space, both at once, and you sort of hit it diagonally, you can, in effect, get from Newark to Hoboken in about three seconds. That's how we travel in time and space."

"Sort of like a warp?" I asked.

"Oh-ho! We know who's been watching television," Uncle Borgel said. "Yes, that's the idea. So you should also remember from 'Star Trek' that if we change the angle a couple of degrees, we can leave Newark in the twentieth century, and hit Hoboken in the eighteenth. You still with me?"

"Still with you," I said. By this time there was no physical sensation of moving forward. Road vibrations, engine and tire noises had ceased, and the Dorbzeldge was completely silent. The road was now glowing a milky white, and to the sides of it was blackness. The only thing that told me were moving was an occasional amorphous blob of light sliding past us. It didn't look anything like space travel on TV or a video game. What really surprised me was that the windows were still open.

"Are we traveling in time and space right now?" I asked Borgel.

"Full speed ahead," Borgel said.

"You know the windows are open."

"So? You're cold?"

"I mean, is it all right for them to be open?"

"Stick your hand out and see what happens." I stuck my hand out. It vanished—that is, it ceased to exist as I put it outside the car. I drew it back, and it reappeared.

"That's spooky," I said.

"Isn't it?" Borgel said. "Now are you ready to hear the story of how I became a time tourist?"

"One more question first," I said. "How does this Dorbzeldge work? Has it got phaser drive? Has it got warp drive? Has it got improbability drive?"

"It's got Hydramatic," Borgel said. "It says so right in the middle of the steering wheel."

4

"Back in the Old Country, when I was a boy, we used to sit around eating potatoes and telling stories about how mean our parents were. Sometimes we didn't have a bottle of Chef Chow's Hot and Spicy Oil to pour on the potatoes, and sometimes we did.

"That's how it was in my childhood. Not like today. Not like some places. My family was so poor and my parents were so mean that when I wanted to have a pet they gave me a peach pit. You getting this, Melvin? I wanted a little doggy, or a kitty, and they gave me a peach pit. And I loved that peach pit! I named it Lance. I taught it tricks and everything, but it was no use. We were too poor.

"Finally, my mother and father took Lance away and sold him to a rich family as a pet for their children. Can you imagine how horrible I would feel when I walked past the rich people's house and saw those children playing with Lance, who had once been my peach pit? Now, when I say these were rich people, I mean they had water. They had mud outside their house — we only had stones. And they only hit their children on the head instead of lunch. We got hit on the head instead of three meals a day. Nobody was doing all that well in the Old Country.

"The finest thing any boy could hope to be was a time tourist. This was because a time tourist was permitted to leave the Old Country. In fact, everybody would help the time tourist, and give him things—you see, we wanted people to leave because that meant more room for everybody who stayed. Usually only the children of the extremely wealthy—families that had luxuries like clothing—could get to be time tourists. It was too much to hope for. All a boy like me could hope for was that maybe his father would knock a couple of his teeth out. But my father was too poor even for that—so what hope was there that I could become a time tourist?

"Still I had my crazy dream that somehow I would get to be a time tourist. When I was eleven years old, my father performed the ritual of throwing me out of the house and shaking his fist at me. This meant that it was time for me to begin my life's work, which in my family meant searching the fields for skunks that had been squashed under the hooves of the rich people's cattle. It was satisfying work, and after a year I found a skunk. This meant I could get married—but I didn't do that. Instead of trading the skunk's pelt for a bottle of Chef Chow's Hot and Spicy Oil, and going out looking for a wife, I went to the Great City.

"I traded the skunk skin for some Kleenexes, and I traded those for a pickle. It was the first pickle I had ever seen. I traded the pickle, and I traded what I got for the pickle, and I traded again, and I traded again. Every trade was a good one, and before long I was a prosperous man. By the time I was nineteen I had a place to sleep indoors. When I was twenty-five I owned my own hat. Most people who had a hat had to share it with five or six other people. I had a hat strictly for my own use. I was going places, but I was still far from my goal of becoming a time tourist."

DANIEL PINKWATER

"You're making this up, right?" I asked Uncle Borgel.

"Every word. Why? You don't like it?"

"It's fine—I just wanted to ask you about that thing over there."

"What thing? You mean the big pulsating thing that looks like it's made out of light?"

"That's it. Is that anything we should worry about?"

"Only if it comes near us," Borgel said. "That's some kind of monster made out of energy. It might want to consume us."

"Consume?"

"Swallow us up. If it's one of those energy monsters, it eats everything it comes near—planets even."

The thing, the energy monster, appeared to be as big as the Sun. It was glowing a sort of peach color, tinged with green. It scared the dickens out of me.

"Uncle Borgel, I think it's coming closer. Is there any chance it doesn't see us?"

"Almost none," Borgel said. "It senses our electrical field. If we don't get away from it, we're in a lot of trouble."

"How do we get away from it?"

"Easy. We shift gears and go fast. This may feel strange. Just relax."

Borgel moved the gear selector level. A red light began flashing on the dashboard. There was a high-pitched whine, and the Dorbzeldge began to vibrate, and then shake violently.

"Now I just give it the gas," Borgel said.

I felt a sensation in every part of my body. It was like

being pricked with pins everywhere. The Dorbzeldge, and the space around it, began to glow with a white light. Fafner was whining uncomfortably in the backseat. I thought that the energy monster had caught up with us. Then, suddenly, we were enveloped in complete blackness.

"I can't see anything," I said.

"Guess how fast we're going?" Borgel asked.

"Too fast?"

"Three hundred seventy-two thousand miles per second. That's twice the speed of light, sonnyboy. I hate to go this fast—it's got to be bad for the tires. What's more, you never know where you'll end up. You carsick?"

"I feel weird. Do you think we've gotten away from that energy monster thing?"

"Probably it's centuries away by now—nawthing to worry about."

"So maybe we could slow down?"

"We're slowing down. You don't just step on the brakes after going double the speed of light."

The blackness had reduced to the sort of darkness I was used to. I still couldn't see anything, but I didn't feel as if we were inside a bottle of ink. Then, gradually, I became conscious of little points of light. The points of light became brighter, more defined, and I was able to perceive some of them as nearer than others. This looked like space as shown on TV.

"Where are we?" I asked.

"I have no idea," Borgel said. "I'm looking for a place to pull off the road."

DANIEL PINKWATER

"Road! What road? We're in outer space!" I shouted.

"What road? The Interstate, naturally. We've been on it all along."

If I squinted my eyes I could imagine that there was a sort of roadway looking like diamond dust or the Milky Way.

"Look," I said to Borgel, "I don't want to hear a story. I want you to answer my questions, one by one. Is that okay?"

"Sure thing," Borgel said, "but first let's pull off. I want a cold drink, and by this time the dog needs to stretch his legs."

"Pull off? Where?"

"Right here," Borgel said. He spun the wheel and the Dorbzeldge lurched to the right.

"A cold root beer in a frosty mug sound good to you?" he asked.

"It sounds fine," I said. I could see a large orange rectangle glowing in the blackness. There was some sort of writing on it, but the characters were like nothing I had ever seen — just a series of black and yellow squares.

5

"So get out," Borgel said.

I opened the door and started to put my foot out.

"Wait a minute! There's no ground!" I said. Beneath my sneaker there was nothing but velvety blackness, infinity.

"You can walk on that," Borgel said.

"No I can't," I said. "There's nothing there."

Borgel was chuckling. "Look, I'll get out and walk around to your side. There's nothing to be afraid of. It's as solid as concrete." Borgel walked around the car and stood by my open door. "Now, just put a foot out and feel."

I felt. There was something solid under my foot. I still hesitated. "How do I tell the difference between whatever this is and a big hole in space?" I asked.

"It's a knack," Borgel said. "After you've traveled in time-space-and-the-other for a little while, you'll just know when something is all right to stand on and when it isn't. You'll develop an instinct."

"What if I don't?"

"You will."

"Maybe I can't."

"Oom-possible. You develop instincts in order to sur-vive—that's what they're for. Come over here."

Haltingly, I took a step away from the Dorbzeldge.

"Come right over here," Borgel said. He was standing by a

long yellow object that ran along what would have been the ground, if there had been any. It appeared solid from a distance, but looked more like a beam of light when I got close to it. It resembled one of those concrete barriers in parking lots.

"Now . . . if you should step over this thing, then you'd be in trouble."

"Why?"

"Because there's nothing on the other side."

"Nothing to stand on?"

"You would just float away."

"Cripes! It looks exactly the same as this side!"

"Looks the same—but it's not the same. You have to sense which is which. Besides, they've got these markers all around."

What we were in WAS a parking lot. At the far end, under the glowing orange rectangle, was a structure made of some kind of shiny metallic stuff. A space-time root beer stand.

"Let the dog out," Borgel said. "He needs to run around."

"He'll fall over the edge."

"Dogs develop instincts faster than humans. Don't worry so much—you'll turn into an old man."

I opened the rear door. Fafner was asleep on the backseat. I called to him.

He bounded out of the car, gave a horrible shriek when he saw there was nothing but emptiness beneath him, and tried to turn in midair and scramble back inside. He hit the nonground and sprawled there. He lay still for a while, sniffing frantically. Then, gingerly, he got to his feet, and gave me a look of contempt.

"You blintz!" Fafner said. "You couldn't warn me?"

"The dog talked," I said numbly.

"Isn't this fun?" Borgel chortled. "They do that when you take them out in time and space. Some surprise, huh?"

I was feeling sick. Too much was going on. I was nauseated.

"I have to pee," the dog said. He wandered over to the barrier and lifted a leg.

"See," Borgel said, "how quick they develop instincts?"

"I love you," Fafner said to Borgel, and licked his hand. "Jerk!" he said to me. "Pee-wee! Dope! Stupid kid!"

In the midst of all this confusion I was suddenly confirmed in my lifelong suspicion that the family dog, Fafner, didn't like me.

"Now, how about some root beer?" Borgel asked.

"None for me, master—just some water—but you go ahead."

"I meant for Melvin," Borgel said.

"Oh," Fafner said.

We walked over to the root beer stand. Except where there was something—such as the stand itself, the Dorbzeldge, ourselves—there was nothing. The blackness above us was identical to the blackness below us. There appeared to be no source of light, but we and the things around us were plainly visible. This had the effect of making everything seem to glow with its own inner light.

The interior of the root beer stand was illuminated, and behind the counter was the single most disgusting thing I had ever seen or imagined. It was a formless pink mass with occasional tufts of coarse black hair, slimy patches, no eyes

DANIEL PINKWATER

that I could see, and lots of red bumps and pimples.

"The proprietor is an Anthropoid Bloboform," Borgel said. "They're very industrious and clean—don't let appearances fool you."

An ugly hole opened in the repulsive mass, and an appropriately unpleasant voice came out, bubbling and rasping.

"My name is Alfred. I will be your waiter for tonight," said the Bloboform. "What may I serve you?"

"Two root beers in frosted mugs," Borgel said, "and a cup of water for the dog."

"No ice," Fafner said.

"That will be a hundred and twenty zlotys," said Alfred.

"Zlotys?" I asked.

"Common currency throughout the universe," Borgel said. "I have some."

"Any fries with that?" Alfred asked.

"He means French-fried meteorites," Borgel explained, "a little heavy for humanoids. No thank you, Alfred. Just the drinks."

"It is my pleasure to serve you." The Bloboform pseudo-handed us our drinks, and we carried them to a wooden picnic table near the stand.

"I need this," I said. I took a swallow of my root beer. It was the best I had ever tasted. It was the first familiar thing I had encountered in the last hour or so, and it had the effect of calming me down.

"Now, look, Uncle Borgel," I said, wiping the foam off my upper lip, "don't you think it's time you explained a few things to me?"

"Sure. What's to explain?"

"Let's start with everything," I said.

"Awl-rightie!" Borgel said. "Here goes! I already explained to you about time, right?"

"Map of New Jersey," I said.

"Kee-reckt! And space also?"

"Like a bagel."

"Bingo! So now you want to know how it all works, and how we travel from time and place to time and place, and what all this is, am I right?"

"You are."

"Okeydokey! Now. You ever travel in a car, back on Earth and in your own time?"

"Of course."

"How does the car work?"

"How does the car work? It's got an engine."

"Yetz? And how does the engine work?"

"Well—you put gas in, and turn on the ignition, and I guess the gas burns up, or explodes, and the energy . . . uh, it gets to the wheels somehow and . . . uh . . ."

"Good for you! You know more about how cars work than I do. Me, I just turn the key, make sure the thing has gas, oil, and water poured into the appropriate holes, air in the tires, and I go. I don't know or care to know one thing about how the engine runs. When it breaks I take it to a mechanic. See?"

"You don't know how a car works?"

"No, I don't. Next, when you take a trip—ever been on a car trip?"

"Sure."

"And when you go on a car trip, you do what to make sure you'll get where you're going?"

"Well, you might look at a map—or you could just get on the road, and watch for signs . . . along . . . the . . . road. My God! You don't know any more about how any of this works than an ordinary . . ."

"Tourist!" shouted Uncle Borgel. "That's it, sonnyboy! Oh, from experience I know a little about the people, sights, places, and customs—but as to theories, who cares? We're out to have a good time. Aren't you having a good time?"

"I'm having a good time, master," Fafner said.

"Good dog," Borgel said, patting his head.

"Hey," said Alfred the Anthropoid Bloboform, "you left your lights on." Borgel got up and walked toward the Dorbzeldge. When he was about ten steps from the car he was enveloped in a ball of orange light. Then he was gone. It couldn't have taken a whole second.

6

"What happened? Uncle Borgel? Where are you?" I shouted.

"Oh no!" the Bloboform said. "Not again!"

"Master! Where are you?" Fafner said. He was running in circles, sniffing the blackness.

"What happened? Where did Borgel go?" I asked Alfred.

"This is getting to be too much," the Bloboform said. "Nobody will come here anymore because of those darned kids and their bilboks."

"What are you talking about? What kids? What's bilboks? What happened to my uncle?"

"A bilbok is a gleep—you know, a gag, a practical joke—something that makes you go 'gleep!' Used to be you could buy bilboks in joke shops on Old Saturn 4 in the Fifth Age. Now they're prohibited, but those damn kids make their own, and work gleeps on people. I've got nothing against having fun, but maybe fifty customers of mine have been bilboked in the past couple of months. That sort of thing gets around, it can put you out of business."

"I don't understand a thing you're saying. I want to know what happened to Uncle Borgel!"

"Look. These kids, they come from rich families. They have their own time-space vehicles. They wander around playing gleeps and getting into trouble. They see your old uncle standing there, and they put a bilbok on him.

52

"That is, they subject him to an unstable transdimensional shifter. They move him—but no one can say where. He might be five minutes in the future, and all of a sudden we'll catch up with him, and he'll just be standing where he was—or he might be shifted six thousand years, and fifty billion light years, and maybe kicked onto another existential plane to boot. It's like tying someone to a rocket and just casually shooting the thing off. Now, don't cry, kid. You want a free root beer?"

"I'm starting to realize that I'll never go crazy, no matter what," I said, "because if I haven't lost my mind by now, it's never going to happen. Are you telling me that some kids passing by in some kind of spaceship . . ."

"A time-space ship," Alfred said. "They were probably here for a long time, but in our time continuum it was so quick that we never saw them."

"Okay, a time-space ship. Some kids just came along and zapped Borgel with some kind of . . . gleep . . . and now he's . . ."

"Gone."

"But not dead."

"Depends on where he landed—but not necessarily. And, as I said, he might be nearby. The commercial bilboks they used to sell would just send you a few hours, and maybe a light hour at most. Usually. Maybe all your uncle has to do is call a taxi, spend a few zlotys, and he'll be back here in a jiffy, maybe a solar month."

"On the other hand . . ." I said.

"On the other hand, he might be gone for good. That's

why those bilboks were outlawed. After a few years the humor starts to wear off."

I looked at the Bloboform. He was talking to me in a friendly enough manner. He was the closest thing to a friend I had at the moment. This did nothing to diminish his hideousness. It was, in fact, a sort of steadying element in conversing with him. I had to concentrate so hard on not throwing up that I escaped going into a panic.

"You say others have been, uh, bilboked here?"

"Many."

"And how many of them came back?"

"Two. That's two out of roughly fifty, or four percent. Your uncle stands a very good chance, considering that the chance of survival at all in this part of time-space is only about ten percent."

It was comforting to hear Alfred talk in this matter-of-fact way—even though it was nauseating in the extreme to watch him do so. I believe he was moved by my situation, and this caused him to quiver more than was strictly necessary and exude quantities of slime.

"Look, I'll make you a root beer float—with double ice cream—and you can sleep in that old Dorbzeldge while you wait for your uncle. And I'll give you free eats—he can pay me when he comes—and you can use my private bathroom, too."

This, when it came to the fact, was even more horrible than my imaginings at the moment, which were enough to bring on shudders. I went to talk it over with Fafner.

"The Bloboform says we can stay here."

"I heard, doofus. Dogs hear sixteen times better than

humanoids. And if you spread out my olfactory membrane it would be as large as my whole skin."

"I'd like to do that," I muttered.

"I heard that, too," Fafner growled. "Now that you've gotten my master lost or killed—or whatever—are you going to take care of me or not?"

"You little crud!" I shouted. "How would you like me to kick your useless rump over that barrier and let you float around thinking over what a stupid, foul-smelling, ugly, offensive little cur you are?"

"Sorry, master," Fafner said. He gave my hand a dab with his tongue.

"Don't do that."

"Sorry. You going to feed me?"

"I'll talk to the Bloboform."

"I love you, master."

"Look, you hairy little cretin," I snarled. "I know you dislike me. Now, I'm going to make sure you have food, no matter how you speak to me. So stop with the hypocrisy."

"You mean it?" the dog asked. "You'll feed me?"

"Yes."

"No matter that I think you're a jerk?"

"That's right. I'm kind to dumb animals. Now shut up. I want to think."

"Ha."

"Of course, I may not feed you very often."

"I'll be quiet."

Alfred came out from behind the counter. I wished he hadn't done that. Looking at Alfred while he was more or less stationary was nasty enough. Watching him in motion was enough to make a dog gag—of which I had evidence.

"Here," he said, offering me a root beer float.

I wiped the slime off the mug.

"I'm kind of surprised that you speak English."

"Oh, you have to know languages in this business," Alfred said. "I get a lot of New York people coming through here."

As I sipped my root beer float, I was seized with an agonizing feeling of aloneness. I moaned into the mug, "Where can Uncle Borgel be?"

DANIEL PINKWATER

7

Borgel tumbled through blackness. He was unable to see, hear, or feel. He was not aware of having a heartbeat or breathing. He might have thought he was dead, except that the odds were against that—it never having happened before.

"What is this, a gleep?" he said.

Then there was light—a dim, unpleasant sort of light. Borgel found himself in a rocky and barren landscape. The soil was black, volcanic. It was cold. There were a few blades of grass.

Borgel had landed in an uncomfortable position. It was as though he were in the middle of a somersault, his shoulders flat, his body bent double, his feet over his head, his toes on the ground. He looked up at the gray, cloudy sky between his legs.

"Hmm," he said, figuring it out. "Hoop la!" He completed the somersault and bounced to his feet. "Not bad," he said. "Not many old guys over one hundred could do that."

Then he looked around. The dismal place was familiar. He had been there before.

"I've been here before," he said.

Borgel was pretty sure he knew where he was, but he held out hope that he had landed in Iceland, or some remote part of Greenland or Patagonia. There was always a chance he wasn't where he thought he was. But he was.

A fair-sized rock whizzed past his head. Borgel saw a gnarled and shabby figure standing on a little rise of ground. An old man—he was looking around for another rock.

Yep. I know where I am, Borgel thought.

"Giddadaheere!" the old man shouted.

"Daddy! Is that you? It's me, Borgel!" Borgel shouted.

"I know that," the old man shouted, hurling another rock.

"The Old Country," Borgel said, dodging.

8

Alfred must have been exaggerating about fifty of his customers having been bilboked in the past couple of months. Either that, or he calculated months differently, because he hardly had any customers at all.

Days—or what seemed like days—might go by with nobody stopping at the root beer stand.

"It's a lousy location," Alfred said.

Meanwhile, Fafner and I slept in Uncle Borgel's Dorbzeldge and waited.

Fafner was impossible. He complained all the time. We'd gone through the fig bars, and there was nothing Alfred sold that humans or dogs could eat except root beer floats. I was plenty sick of root beer floats, but Fafner was getting wild. It was starting to look as though he would eat me, or I would eat him.

Alfred turned out to be a nice enough guy. He spent his time puttering around the root beer stand. Sometimes, he'd let me help him—but really, there wasn't much to do.

I tried to get Alfred to tell me something about where I was, but he appeared to be almost completely ignorant. He was interested in nothing but running his root beer stand, and talked about nothing but how bad business was. He didn't even remember where he came from. All he knew about was the root beer stand. It had been easier to get information from Uncle Borgel. I really missed him.

"Can't we call the cops or something?" I asked Alfred.

"Sure. We could call them. Two or three centuries and they might even turn up. And then what? Where would they look for your uncle? We're talking about infinite distances. I don't think you have any idea of what a lousy location this is."

We did ask the few customers who showed up if they'd seen Uncle Borgel. None of them had the slightest idea what we were talking about.

Incidentally, I got to see some pretty unusual life-forms at the root beer stand. We had some bean-people from Flamingus, clown-men from Noffo, and once a bus load of Freddians. It was interesting to see the different ways the various beings drank their root beer.

After a while, I was pretty depressed. I spent a lot of time hanging around the Dorbzeldge. Fafner spent practically all his time curled up on the backseat, complaining. Even though he was obnoxious, I felt more comfortable with him than with Alfred. He was closer to human.

Sometimes, we'd fool around with the radio, hoping to get some idea of where we were, or what sort of place it was—I still hadn't figured even that much out. We had no luck with the radio. When we could get a station, it was always in some language other than human. We got sick of listening to the gurgling, squeaking, and mumbling. Except for Michael Jackson records, they didn't play anything we could understand.

One day, I was rummaging around in the glove compartment at Fafner's insistence.

"Look," I told him, "we've been through and through this. There is nothing to eat in here."

"Look anyway," Fafner said. "Maybe there are some fig bar crumbs."

"I let you lick the crumbs out of the corners twice already."

"Look anyway. If I don't get something to eat soon, I'm going to die."

"You get root beer floats," I said.

"I'm sick of root beer floats! I hate root beer floats! I'm a dog! Dogs don't drink root beer!"

"There's ice cream in them," I said.

"Are you kidding?" Fafner screamed. "Licorice-flavor ice cream? Black ice cream? You think that's a treat or something? I'm your responsibility. You have to get me some real food."

"What do you suggest?"

"We could eat the Bloboform," Fafner said, craftily.

"Get real," I said.

"Okay, how about we eat the tires?"

We had been through this a hundred times. Fafner was going to list every single thing in our environment, from the root beer stand to my shoe, and suggest we eat it.

His other topic was the trunk. It was locked, and we didn't have the key. We had tried to pry it open with Alfred's ice-cream scoop, but the Dorbzeldge was built like a vault.

"We could eat the upholstery," Fafner said.

"Shut up," I said. I had found something. Stuck to the back of a card advertising Sadie's Drive-Thru Fish Market in Columbus, Ohio, was a key! It was stuck to it with what looked like part of a melted cough drop.

"Looky!" I said, peeling the key off the card.

"Is that a cough drop? Gimme!" Fafner said.

"No, idiot. Look! It's a key!"

"We could eat this key?" Fafner said. He was still going through his endless list of uneatable things we might try to eat.

"It might be the key to the trunk," I said.

"And there might be food in the trunk!" Fafner was bouncing off the roof.

We raced around to the back of the car. It *was* the key to the trunk. I fitted it into the slot, and turned it. The lock clicked. I raised the lid.

"There's food in there! There's food in there!" Fafner screamed. He was bounding around in circles.

I peered into the trunk. Fafner was standing with his front paws on the rear bumper. The trunk was full of all sorts of junk—including a twenty-five-pound bag of Kibblebitz Dog Food.

"Is that . . . ?" Fafner said, drooling.

"It sure is," I said.

"That's dog food!" Fafner snarled. "It's mine! You can't have any. It's just for dogs. Mine!"

I slammed the trunk lid and put the key in my pocket.

Fafner's mouth snapped shut, drool dripping from the corners.

"I think I'll go over and see what Alfred is doing," I said.

"Of course, I'd be happy to share my dog food with you, master," Fafner whined.

"That's better," I said. "Get your bowl."

DANIEL PINKWATER

"Right away, master," Fafner said.

I would like to say, right here, that Kibblebitz Dog Food is tasty and nutritious. It is well-balanced, and easy to digest. I would recommend it to anyone—and it is very good with root beer.

I found something else in the trunk. It was the owner's manual for the Dorbzeldge.

9

Borgel stretched out on the flattened cardboard box, the place of honor in his father's house. "Must have been a bilbok," he said aloud to himself. "I suppose Melvin is still back at the root beer stand. Well, he's a capable boy. Besides, the dog will take care of him."

Old Blivnik, Borgel's father, spoke. "Borgel?"

"Yes, Daddy?"

"Sharrap!"

Same old Dad, Borgel thought. I have to get out of here.

10

I had a pretty good idea how to drive an ordinary car. I'd spent a lot of time behind the wheel of those miniature gas-powered racers at Riveredge Amusement Park at home. Reading the Dorbzeldge's owner's manual, I couldn't see that driving it would be much different.

My plan was to get Fafner and myself away from Alfred's time-space root beer stand, and maybe try to get home. Anything was better than waiting around there—and the truth was I didn't think Uncle Borgel was coming back. Or he might come back in fifteen or twenty years. I thought we ought to go while the bag of Kibblebitz was still pretty full.

Fuel was no problem either. I read in the manual that when the Dorbzeldge operated in time-space-and-the-other, it ran on Hydramatic drive, which was inexhaustible. The manual gave a few clues about the rules of time-space-and-the-other travel. In many ways, it was easier than operating a car at home on Earth in the twentieth century. It appeared that staying on the Interstate was something Dorbzeldge would do automatically. There wasn't any need to steer most of the time, and you couldn't get lost—that is, you couldn't get any more lost than we were already. It would stay on the road, or the path, or the beam, or whatever it was. I thought I could handle it.

I talked it over with Alfred.

"Why do you want to leave?" the Bloboform asked. "Your uncle might come back any month now. Besides, I thought you were getting to like me."

"I do like you, Alfred. I just think we should go."

"Well, I wasn't going to tell you this, but I think you have a lot of talent for the root beer business. I thought maybe you'd stay and help me. When my time comes to transmogrify, you could have all this." Alfred made a sweeping gesture with a pseudopod, indicating the lonely, deserted, forlorn root beer stand.

"I'd like nothing more," I said. "But I really think we should go."

"Well, of course . . . if you think so." Alfred was really sad. "I'm going to miss you. Let's shake hands."

"Yich. I mean, before we do that, maybe you could tell me where we should go. I'd like to get someplace where I can send a letter, or maybe make a phone call. My family probably thinks I'm dead."

"Well, the Big City is probably your best bet."

"The Big City? How far is that?"

"Must be, oh ten or fifteen metaparasangs."

"Is ten or fifteen metaparasangs a long way?"

"Compared to what?"

"Never mind. What I want to know is, what sort of a place is it? Is it dangerous or what?"

"Well, you know—it's the Big City."

"You've never been there, have you?"

"Well . . . no."

"You're sure it exists?"

"Sure. Yes. Pretty sure. Sort of. I think so. Maybe."

"And it's in that direction?" I asked, pointing.

"To the best of my knowledge."

"That's good enough for me," I said. I started for the Dorbzeldge.

"Good luck!" Alfred shouted. He grabbed my hand. For a horrible moment, I thought he was going to hug me. "If your uncle shows up, I'll tell him where you went."

I slipped behind the wheel of the Dorbzeldge. Fafner was in the backseat, as usual, mumbling that I was going to get us both killed. "You can stay here with Alfred, if you like, until the kibble runs out."

"I'm going with you," Fafner said.

I remembered I didn't have a key. I stuck my head under the dashboard. There was a hunk of wire dangling down. I touched the loose end to various things until it made a spark. I heard the engine come to life.

I bobbed up and turned to Fafner in the backseat. "I got it started!" I said.

"Look where you're going, maniac!" Fafner shouted. "We're moving!"

We were heading for one of those barriers at the edge of the parking lot—on the other side was empty space.

I spun the wheel, and the Dorbzeldge turned. "According to the manual, we would have stopped automatically before going over the edge," I told Fafner.

"Did it ever occur to you that this thing might not be working perfectly?" Fafner asked. "I'd watch the steering if I were you."

"Good thought," I said. I maneuvered the Dorbzeldge out of the parking lot and onto the Interstate. It wasn't so hard to handle. As we picked up speed, I saw the root beer stand getting smaller in the rearview mirror. Alfred was waving his arm or something. We were on our way.

DANIEL PINKWATER

11

This is luck! Borgel thought. Only home a day, and what do I find? A skunk! Nice one, too. Hasn't been squashed more than a week. Well, I did it before—I can do it again.

From a neighboring field, old Blivnik shouted, "Hey! Borgel!"

"Yes, Daddy?"

"You founnaskung?"

"That's right, Daddy!" Borgel shouted, waving the prize over his head.

"Well, gerrahdaheere awreddy, y'bum!" Blivnik bellowed.

"All right, Daddy," Borgel called, with a tear in his eye. "Good-bye, Daddy! Dear old Dad!"

"Y'bum!"

12

It was smooth sailing after a while. I had the old Dorbzeldge eating out of the palm of my hand. Even Fafner admitted that I was handling the machine okay.

"So what's your plan when we get to the Big City?" he asked me.

"Well, I haven't got a plan as such. We'll have to see when we get there."

"What if we see that the people who live there are monsters of some kind, and eat people—or even worse, dogs?"

"Oh, I don't think that will happen."

"Why not?"

"Well, because nothing dangerous has happened so far."

"Your uncle got gleeped," Fafner said. "We were stuck a million miles from noplace with a Bloboform. You nearly drove us over the edge in the parking lot. We're traveling through time-space-and-the-other—and neither of us knows what those are really. The road is a sort of ribbon of light, on both sides of which is endless blackness, and if you had a flat tire, or needed to sneeze at the wrong moment, we'd probably drift away and die. Between us we've got nothing but a bag of kibble—which actually belongs to me, by the way, and I'm just sharing it with you temporarily. We're heading for some Big City we were told about by a shapeless idiot who's never been there, and isn't even sure it exists—and you say

70

nothing dangerous has happened so far! If you ask me we're doomed. We're as good as dead right now. We *are* dead, only we don't know it."

"Now, look," I said. "I was hoping I wouldn't have to speak to you this way, but you force me. I am a human being, whereas you are only a dog—a lower animal. I have the power of reason, and I have superior judgement. If I tell you everything is all right—it's all right. I give the orders, understand?"

"You know what a schmo is?" Fafner asked.

"Yes."

"Well, you're one."

The truth is, I wasn't all that confident. I just thought it would be better not to let Fafner get depressed. He remained quiet in the backseat, not saying a word.

We'd been zooming along for a number of hours. Everything was going smoothly. I was sort of enjoying driving the Dorbzeldge, and that made me feel sad—I missed Borgel. I thought how this would be fun if he were with us. Fafner was continuing to give me the silent treatment.

The road had been a continuous and uninterrupted ribbon of light. All around us was blackness—with the occasional distant glow of a star or something. At times, it was hard to know whether I was asleep or awake. I wished Fafner would say something to break the monotony.

Finally he spoke. "Pick that guy up!"

In the distance, I could just make out a figure standing at the side of the road.

"A hitchhiker?"

"Pick him up! Pick him up!"

"Listen, Fafner. It isn't a good idea to pick up hitchhikers. Don't you know that?"

"Pick him up! Pick him up!" Fafner was shrieking.

"No kidding. It's dangerous. Especially way out here. I mean, he could be a robber or a murderer. We'd better not."

"Pick him up! Pick him up! It's Borgel, you idiot!"

I stepped on the brakes.

Uncle Borgel got into the car. "Hoo boy! That was some experience! Did you guys have fun while I was gone?"

13

"Master, never leave me alone with this idiot again," Fafner said.

"Hey! No fair! I took good care of him," I said.

"Look who's driving! You're doing a good job, Melvin. Where were you heading?"

"We were on our way to the Big City."

"Poifect! That's just where I wanted to go," Borgel said.

"I smell a skunk," Fafner said.

14

"Yep. I found a good one," Borgel said.

"Say, I have a good idea," I said. "Let's throw the skunk out."

"Are you kidding? We can make a fortune with this carcass," Uncle Borgel said, pulling the flat skunk out of a paper bag he was carrying.

"Well, what if we put the skunk in the trunk?" I asked. "Maybe we could sort of wrap it in a plastic bag."

"Yes. Let's do that before I barf," Fafner said.

"Can't find the key," Borgel said.

"As luck would have it, I found it," I said.

"So pull over, princess, if you're too delicate to ride with a squashed skunk in the front seat."

"Hey, take my bag of kibble out of there!" Fafner said. "I don't want it riding with that thing."

"Such sissies," Borgel said.

When we transferred the dead skunk to the trunk, Borgel and I swapped places, and he took over the driving. It was just as well. I was pretty tired. As soon as we were moving, and most of the skunk perfume had cleared out of the Dorbzeldge's interior, I fell fast asleep.

I woke up in broad daylight. I was stretched out on the seat with my coat over me. Uncle Borgel must have put it there. I could hear Borgel outside making a great deal of noise, singing and banging and rattling what sounded like pots and pans. It hadn't quite dawned on me that the Dorbzeldge wasn't moving, and Borgel's voice coming from the vicinity of the rear bumper didn't make a whole lot of sense.

When I sat up, I saw trees and bushes and the smoke of a half-dozen campfires. Looking around through the windows of the Dorbzeldge, I saw that we were in as strange a place as I'd ever seen. It looked like a dump. There were piles of old junk, rusted car bodies, piles of old plywood, dead buses and trucks, and other things that might have been spaceships. There were stovepipes sticking out of the piles of junk—and smoke was coming out of some of them. I saw people, and things like people, sitting around on folding chairs and on boxes. Some of the beings were doing the wash, chopping wood, talking, cooking over campfires, and engaging in all sorts of activities. It was like a town made out of garbage.

It had been a long time since I was in a place with things like ground, sky, trees, and light. Later I found out that only the Interstate was like that. Where you were someplace, it tended to be a place similar to Earth, more or less.

I climbed out of the Dorbzeldge. Borgel had the trunk open and was cooking in an improvised kitchen—a folding table with a little gas stove on it beneath a hunk of cloth attached to the open trunk lid at one end and to a mop handle poked into the ground at the other. Borgel was stirring something in a frying pan, and Fafner was sitting nearby watching and drooling.

"I hope you're hungry," he said. "I'm making something special—cornmeal mush with Mexican peppers. It's my favorite camping-out breakfast."

"What is this place? And where did you get the food?" I

asked. The cornmeal mush with Mexican peppers looked lethal—but it wasn't dog kibble.

"This is the famous Gypsy Bill's Resort and Spa and Hobo Camp and Junkyard," Uncle Borgel said. "As to the food, I made a deal with the proprietor for a part interest in our skunk. I told you it would come in handy.

"I've been here before. Of course, the place isn't what it was. In my day all sorts of really distinguished people used to stay here. Now, Gypsy Bill Junior—he's the son of the founder—appears to let just anybody in. Also, he's added a duck farm since the last time I was here. Smell that?"

I could smell it. Uncle Borgel directed me to the wash house, which was just behind a clump of bushes, and told me to hurry back. "Breakfast will be served in five minutes on the front fender," he said.

The wash house was an old shack, ready to fall down. When I got back to the Dorbzeldge, Uncle Borgel had arranged breakfast on the fender and hood. In addition to his special favorite camping-out breakfast, there was also some goat cheese from Gypsy Bill Junior's goat, reconstituted mango juice, figs, and raw peanuts. Ordinarily, I might have had some criticisms about the food, but after living on licorice root beer floats and dog food, it was heaven. I had a little of everything, and Fafner made a pig of himself.

While we were eating, Gypsy Bill Jr. himself came by. He was tall and fat with a clip-on earring on one ear, and he wore two hats, one on top of the other.

"Ah, my guests," Gypsy Bill Jr. said. "Is everything to your

DANIEL PINKWATER

satisfaction?"

"Everything is first-rate, Bill Jr.," Borgel said. "It does my heart good to see how you've kept the place up since the old days."

"Then you were the guest of my dear late father, Bill Senior?"

"Oh yes," Borgel said. "I used to spend whole summers here."

"I wish you had given me some advance notice that you were coming," Gypsy Bill Jr. said. "I could have cleared the chicken out of the Presidential Suite."

"That would have been nice," Borgel said. "Perhaps we'll come this way again."

"If you do, make sure to wire ahead. Then you won't have to sleep in your car. We can have the Presidential Suite hosed out and freshened up on a day's notice. Is that cornmeal mush with Mexican peppers you're eating?"

"My speciality," Borgel said. "Would you care for some? There's more than enough."

"Thank you," Bill Jr. said. "Running a first-class resort and duck farm gives me an appetite like an ox."

Gypsy Bill Jr. spoke the truth. He not only ate as much as an ox might have eaten, he also made the same sort of noises.

"If you like, I'll be pleased to read your fortunes in the tea leaves," Gypsy Bill Jr. said. "No charge, of course, just a free reading for my guests."

"So you are carrying on the psychic work of your esteemed father," Borgel said. "I, for one, would be very interested to have you read our fortunes—especially for free. The tea leaves are wild blueberry and mint—will that make a difference?"

"Not in the slightest, my dear sir," Gypsy Bill Jr. said. "Just pour what's left of the tea in my hat." Bill Jr. removed the uppermost of his hats and held it out, upside down. Borgel dumped the contents of his portable aluminum kettle into the hat.

"We'll just shake it up to get the wet out," Gypsy Bill Jr. said, and flipped his hat up and down. All the time, cold blueberry-and-mint tea was dripping through the crown of the hat and onto Gypsy Bill Jr.'s shoes.

"Okay. That's about right. Now to read 'em," he said.

"Watch this," Borgel whispered. "I've seen his father do this. If he's half as good, it will be a treat."

Gypsy Bill Jr. gave a shrill hoot and leaped three or four feet straight into the air. Continuing to hoot, he rolled around on the ground, thrashing and kicking his feet. All this time, he was twisting and pounding on the hat full of soggy tea leaves. Then he sat up and began bouncing around on his bottom, covering a good bit of territory. He struggled to his feet, staggered as if he were hurt, clutching the dripping hat to his stomach, and then began to hop up and down until he was exhausted. Then he collapsed on the ground, panting. He was drenched with sweat and tea. Gypsy Bill Jr. lay on the ground for some time, getting his breath back. Finally, he sat up, pulled the hat open, and looked inside.

"Hooo boy!" he shouted. "You fellows have got *some* fortune!"

DANIEL PINKWATER

15

It turned out that Gypsy Bill Jr. charged nothing to read a fortune, but if you wanted to find out what he had read, it would cost you twenty dollars. Uncle Borgel turned down the offer.

"I'm sorry," he said. "It's a matter of principle with me. I never pay to have my fortune told."

Gypsy Bill Jr. walked away dripping and mumbling. Uncle Borgel whispered, "Confidentially, I'd have paid him twenty dollars *not* to tell us our fortunes."

"Can he really do it?" Fafner asked.

"I suppose so. His father could do it every time."

"If you think he's really able to tell what's going to happen, wouldn't it be useful to know in advance?" I asked.

"It would be a great big bore to know in advance," Uncle Borgel said. "I know what I'm talking about. If you know what's going to happen in advance, there would be no surprises—hence, no fun."

"Speaking of what's going to happen," I said, "are we going to keep traveling, or have we settled down at Gypsy Bill's Resort and Spa and Junkyard and Duck Farm?"

"Good point," Uncle Borgel said. "We've had our breakfast, and we've had our fortunes read but not told. Now, let's get packed up and on the road before this beautiful day is wasted. Where'd the dog go?"

I put two fingers in my mouth and whistled the way

Borgel did. Fafner appeared from behind the Presidential Suite and bounded into the car. Borgel was busy packing up the portable kitchen, when Gypsy Bill Jr. appeared again. This time he was leading his goat.

"You wouldn't be headed out Bugleville way, would you?" Bill Jr. asked.

"Might be," Borgel said.

"You wouldn't mind taking a rider along?" Gypsy Bill asked. "I know someone who might be going in that direction."

"It isn't the goat, is it?" Borgel asked.

"No, it's a human, far as I can tell."

"In that case, sure," Uncle Borgel said. "I wouldn't mind taking the goat, but we've got a dog with us, and they might get to fighting."

"That's really nice of you," Gypsy Bill Jr. said. "How about ten dollars and I'll only tell your futures through next Thursday?"

"No deal," Borgel said.

"Well, no hard feelings," Bill Jr. said. "By the way, I never did catch your name. What is it?"

"General Venustiano Carranza," Borgel said.

"Of course," Gypsy Bill Jr. said. "I didn't recognize you without your whiskers. I'll go and get your passenger."

"Hurry it up," Borgel said. "We're leaving in five minutes."

Then he said to me as Gypsy Bill Jr. went to get our rider, "Never give your right name on the road."

16

The passenger Gypsy Bill Jr. brought us was a man even shorter than Uncle Borgel. His head was bald and he had a bushy white beard that reached past his knees, which is to say almost to the ground. He wore a sort of shirt that came all the way down to the tops of his boots, which were big yellow ones with thick soles. He had a knapsack and a sign. The sign was a piece of cardboard with the word KA-POP? painted on it.

This was the conversation that passed between Borgel and our passenger:

"Nov shmoz ka-pop?" the little man asked.

"Kopka posto Bugleville," Borgel said.

"Ka-pop?" the little man repeated.

"Popso nokka," Borgel said.

"Pop-ka shmoz nov-ka. Nov shmoz ka-pop?" said the little man.

"Popoosco nobba ka-poppock," Borgel said.

"Hee hee hee!" said the little fellow. He jumped up and down, evidently very happy.

The bearded guy clambered into the backseat of the Dorbzeldge. Fafner appeared to like him. At least, he didn't snarl.

"What were you talking about with him?" I whispered to Borgel.

"I have no idea," Borgel whispered back. "I was just trying

to be polite. I have a gift for languages, but I never know what they mean. I think he was talking French."

"That's not French," I said.

"You may be right," Borgel said. "Anyway, he seems like a nice fellow. Maybe he'll tell an amusing story on the way."

Borgel was right. At least the strange man chattered away from the moment the Dorbzeldge started rolling. He was evidently convinced that Borgel could understand what he was saying. Borgel encouraged him in this belief by answering him in his own strange language.

"Ka-poski nopsi hada-dada ka-poosh?" the stranger said as we pulled out of Gypsy Bill's Resort and Spa and Junkyard and Duck Farm, waving to Gypsy Bill Jr. and his goat.

"Poopsi nopsi ka-bash ka-bash nootzle?" Borgel said.

It must have been just the right thing, because the stranger immediately answered, "Oooh, nopsi voot ka-bash sooboo fooey!"

Borgel nodded his head and said, "Difko. Fooey na-voot!"

At this point, the stranger laughed quite a bit, shaking his head and repeating, "Voot-na, voot-na, voot-na! He ha ha ha!"

"Do you have any idea what you two are talking about?" I asked Borgel.

"I believe I'm starting to pick up the language," Borgel said. "I honestly don't know how I do it. As far as I can tell, this man used to be either the advisor of a great king, or millionaire or president—something like that—or possibly a tailor, a bookie, or a kosher butcher. In any case, he's out of a job now. Also he's interested in stopping at any zoos we may happen to pass. He's never seen a penguin and it's bothering him."

"You were able to understand all that?"

"I'm not sure, of course," Borgel said. "He may also have been telling us that he has a very contagious disease. I'll try to talk with him some more."

"Pa-poosh chazza inbud nofski?" he said to the little man.

"Kla-bash ta voot-ka hada-dada ka-pop," the little man said. Then he said, "Also, if you see one of those root beer places, please stop. I'd like to buy you all a drink."

"You speak English!" I shouted.

"So do you!" the little man shouted back.

"You never said you spoke English," I said.

"How do you know?" the bearded fellow said.

"So how did I do, speaking your language?" Borgel asked.

"Not bad," the little man said. "You said you were a politically corrupt sardine and you wanted to eat the tires off motorcycles."

"Really? I said that?"

"Like a native."

"I don't know how I do it," Borgel said.

"So how about stopping for a root beer?" the little man said.

"No!" Fafner and I shouted.

"I could use one," Borgel said. "We'll be on the lookout for one of those places with the orange signs."

"Please! Not root beer!" I begged.

"Those are the ones," the stranger said. "They serve it in a frosted mug."

"Yummy!" Borgel said.

"Oh God, no," Fafner said.

"So who are you anyway?" Borgel asked our little passenger.

17

"I am Pak Nfbnm*," the little man said.

"*?"

"Exactly."

"I'm pleased to make your acquaintance," Borgel said. "I am Doctor Wiley Sinclair. This is my great-grand nephew, Colonel Sebastian Moran—and our dog, Shep."

Fafner and I nodded formally to Pak Nfbnm*.

"I am deeply honored," Pak Nfbnm* said.

"No more so than ourselves," Borgel said. "You appear to be a person of distinction. If you have no objection, might I ask the nature of your journey?"

"Certainly," Pak Nfbnm* replied. "For the most part, I travel for pleasure, and to gain knowledge of the various times and places I encounter. I also enjoy sending postcards and souvenirs of my travels to my friends and relations at home. I am a native of Benton Harbor, Michigan, where my family has been engaged in the tapioca industry for many generations."

"Who has not heard of Nfbnm*'s Tapioca?" Borgel said. "And you say you travel for pleasure? How long have you been away from home?"

"This time, something over eighty years," Pak Nfbnm* said. "I'm a habitual traveler in time-space-and-the-other. You might say I'm sort of a professional tourist."

"The same as myself!" Borgel shouted.

"I knew it!" Pak Nfbnm* said. "I could tell at once that I had fallen in with a good crowd! Let's be friends! You may call me Freddie."

"With pleasure!" Borgel said.

"And I will call you Borgel, Melvin, and Fafner. I believe those are the names by which you address one another. We may as well abandon formality, since we're all adventurers together."

"Put 'er there, Freddie," Borgel said, reaching over the seat back and shaking hands with the little time tourist.

"Were you on your way anywhere in particular?" Freddie asked.

"We were considering heading for the Big City," Borgel said. His voice became confidential. "I am the principal stockholder in a fine squashed skunk, and I thought I might as well take it where I can get the highest price."

"Congratulations," Freddie said. "But if I might venture a word of advice, the squashed skunk market is depressed at the moment. You might do well to wait a while, and sell your skunk at the great fair and market which begins in a couple of weeks. Meanwhile, if I might make a further suggestion, could you be persuaded to consider taking a little detour?"

"I can always be persuaded to take a little detour," Borgel said. "What did you have in mind?"

"Have you any particular interest in popsicles?"

"I can't say that I have," Borgel said.

"I have," Fafner said.

"Well, I have always been strongly interested in popsicles

of all sorts," Freddie said. "I'm not referring only to the well-known trademark 'Popsicle,' manufactured by the Popsicle Company, a firm almost as old and well-respected as Nfbnm*'s Tapioca, but to the generic popsicle, meaning any sort of frozen water-based confection on a stick—an ice pop, in other words, or a quiescently frozen dessert stick, also Italian Ices, Fudgsicles, and ice cubes with toothpicks in them, made of everything from raspberry soda to chicken soup."

"Fascinating," Fafner said.

"Probably, my personal all-time favorite is the root beer popsicle," Freddie said.

"Yich. Yich," Fafner and I said.

"So you like popsicles. What about it?" Borgel asked.

"When you like popsicles as much as I do, it's natural to be interested in them," Freddie said. "It shouldn't surprise you that I've traveled millions of miles and thousands of light years in pursuit of rare and exotic popsicles."

"Doesn't surprise me a bit," Fafner said. This was almost the first time I'd ever seen Fafner take much interest in what anyone was saying.

"I don't wish to brag, but it's a certainty that I have tasted more different varieties of popsicles and their cognates than any being who is alive or ever was alive. What is more, I have the honor of being a Commander of the Ancient Order of Popsicle Lovers, and five years ago received a special gold medal for my many contributions to the field. I have it here." Freddie showed us a gold medal in the shape of a popsicle.

"I am also the author of a book, *Popsikellen, Geist und*

Wissenschaft, which I wrote in German to show that it was really serious. It runs more than nine hundred pages and is considered the last word on the subject."

"Wow," I said. I felt that I ought to say something.

"And, of course, there have been my many contributions to scholarly journals dealing with popsicles, and frozen desserts, in general, and my humble contribution to the artistic side of the field—the banana popsicle."

"You invented that?" Fafner said with real admiration.

"Someone else would have if I hadn't," Freddie said modestly. "It's always like that when an idea's time has come."

"So what you're telling us," Borgel said, "is that you are the greatest expert alive on the subject of popsicles."

"In a word, yes," Freddie said.

"And why are you telling us this?" Borgel asked.

"Well, first of all to show off," Freddie said. "But also to prepare you for what I am about to tell you. What would you say if I told you there was one ultimate popsicle, a popsicle above all others, a sort of supreme popsicle, beside which all other popsicles melt into nothingness?"

18

"I'd be thunderstruck," Borgel said.

"I'd want to know where to find one," Fafner said.

"Not one—it," Freddie said. "There is only one. It is not a type or kind of popsicle, but the ideal of all popsicles."

"I don't get it," I said. "If this popsicle is so good, why is there only one? Why don't they make a lot of them?"

"You don't get it," Freddie said. "The popsicle of which I speak was not 'made' by anyone—at least not in the sense you understand. This popsicle is probably ancient—it may have existed before humans, or any intelligent form of life as we know it. It isn't something you would buy at the corner store and slurp on your way home. It is the essence of popsicle—the beginning of all popsicles. It is the Great Popsicle."

"Amazing," Fafner said.

"This Great Popsicle has powers of which we know nothing. It may have consciousness—I don't know. It may be alive."

"A living popsicle?"

"It's possible. All anyone knows about it is gathered from old stories, forgotten by nearly everyone. I first heard of it long ago while traveling in a mountainous region on a distant world. The people there had had no contact with anyone from outside for centuries before I came. They told stories of a Great Popsicle which contained the essence of all wisdom.

I wondered if there might be any truth to the stories. Years later, I found references to a mighty popsicle in a collection of Paleo-Siberian folktales. The obscure Blechkut people, almost extinct, told of a popsicle similar to the one described by those remote mountain people. Then I really began to wonder if such a popsicle might exist."

"Wait!" Borgel shouted. "I know a story about a Great Popsicle. They used to tell it in the Old Country when somebody died."

"Can you remember it?" Freddie asked, very excited.

"Well, let me see," Borgel said. "It went something like this. In the long ago time, when everything was green, people were happy and overweight. There were plenty of skunks, and the crops were abundant. In those days, people did not know how to build houses—and they had no need of them. They would lie down in the fields and go to sleep, and in the morning they would get up and dance.

"At this time there was a king, Napnik. He had a beautiful golden beard and was able to throw a rock farther than any of his subjects. The people loved Napnik because he never bothered them. He lived as simply as his people, except that he had a little cart, drawn by six peasants, in which he would ride around, displaying his beard to everyone's delight.

"Once a year, Napnik would assemble the oldest and wisest men in the land, and they would discuss how to deal with any problems that existed. Since there never were any problems, they would just sit around for a couple of days sucking on potatoes and saying poetry. Then the wise old men would return to their fields and forests for another year.

"It went on like this, as it had in Napnik's father's time, and his father's before him, and his father's before that, and his father's before that, and his father's before that, and his father's before that, and his father's before that, and his father's before that, and his father's . . ."

"Get on with it!" Freddie shouted.

"Sorry," Borgel said. "That's just the way they'd tell the story in the Old Country."

"They had plenty of time, eh?" Freddie asked.

"Nothing but. Anyway . . . his father's before him, etcetera, etcetera. It so happened that Napnik had a daughter, Glossolalia, a great beauty. She also had a golden beard, but not as thick as Napnik's. Glossolalia was not only beautiful, but clever. She tended her father's skunks and could throw a rock as far as the strongest man.

"One year, when the old wise men had gathered to suck on potatoes, Napnik announced, 'It is time for Glossolalia, my beautiful daughter, to marry. How shall we select a suitable husband for her?'

"The old wise men debated and deliberated. More potatoes were sent for. Napnik the King listened patiently as the old wise men discussed the qualities necessary in a husband for the daughter of the king. Two weeks went by, and finally the council of the wise old men had decided. The husband of Glossolalia should be a nice fellow, have a few skunks of his own, be good at throwing rocks, and if possible should have a golden beard and plenty of muscles.

"Napnik was well pleased by the decision of the old wise men, and was about to send them on their way, laden with

DANIEL PINKWATER

gifts of skunks and extra potatoes, when something extraordinary occurred. Glossolalia herself strode into the circle of wise men.

"This was something that had never happened before. In those days, although women were feared as they are today, they never appeared in the council of the wise. Even more unthinkable, Glossolalia actually spoke.

"'Phooey!' she said. 'A nice fellow with skunks? This is the sort of husband you choose for me? I reject your suggestion. I will choose my own husband. Call together all the young men of the country, and I will speak to them myself.'

"With that, Glossolalia kicked potato skins at the old wise men and departed. Napnik and the old wise men were astounded, but the king was moved to action. First, he took back the presents he had given the old wise men, and bade them go. To hurry them on their way, he threw rocks after them.

"Then he called all the young men of the country together. There were eleven of them. Glossolalia came before them, and spoke to them. 'It is time for me to choose a husband,' she said. 'Him that I marry will be king one day, for my father has no other child than me. You are all worthy young men, with skunks and everything, so how shall I choose? This is how. Are you listening? I will marry only a man of courage and wit. Those of you who hope to gain my hand will go far from this country, beyond the great forest, and learn the secrets of the world, do various brave things, and bring me a present. I get to keep the present, whether I marry you or not. The one of you who goes to the most interesting places, and does the bravest things, and brings the best present, gets me. What do you say?'"

"While Glossolalia spoke, ten of the eleven young men left. Only one remained, Grebitz, a handsome young skunkherd. Grebitz spoke: 'Glossolalia, Princess, Beauteous One—the other young men have left. I am the only suitor you've got. I am the only one willing to go far from this country and do the other things you said. So why not just get married and save a lot of trouble?'

"'Not so fast, handsome youth,' Glossolalia said. 'How do you know those other swains didn't leave early just to get started on their travels to win my hand?'

"'Because there they are, most of them, over in the next field tending the skunks,' Grebitz said.

"Glossolalia picked up a rock. 'Get started, my beloved, before I bean you,' she said.

"Grebitz left on his great journey, the first person in history to leave the Old Country. While he was gone, Glossolalia got tired of waiting, and married someone else."

"Not only is that the most boring story I ever heard," Freddie said, "but is has nothing to do with popsicles."

"That was just to get you in the mood," Borgel said. "The popsicle part comes in the story that goes with it, 'The Travels of Young Grebitz.'"

Fafner was sleeping. I was looking out the window.

"Well, get to it before I die of old age," Freddie said.

19

"Okay, 'The Travels of Young Grebitz.' Here goes," Borgel said.

"Wait! Wait! Stop!" Freddie shouted.

"You don't want to hear it?"

Freddie was very excited. "Stop! Stop the car! Back up! I think I saw it!"

"What did you see?" Borgel asked.

"Back up! Back up slowly! It's right in here somewhere," Freddie said. He was leaning out the window.

"What did he see?" Borgel asked me.

"I don't know," I said. "I wasn't paying attention."

"Come on, back up more," Freddie said, motioning with his hand. "A little more. More. Stop! There! There it is!"

We looked where Freddie was pointing. All we saw was a narrow path, somewhat overgrown with weeds, leading back to a sort of hole in the bushes that lined the road. There was a faded sign painted on a piece of wood: GREAT POPSICLE MONUMENT AND PARK

"Is that it?" I asked.

"Well, read for yourself," Freddie said.

"What are we waiting for? Let's go in," Fafner said.

Borgel headed the Dorbzeldge onto the path, which was bumpy, and we drove into the bushes.

"It looks as though no one has come this way for some time," Borgel said.

The path took us into a dark forest. Branches brushed the sides of the Dorbzeldge.

"Did you know this park existed?" Borgel asked Freddie.

"Not exactly," Freddie said. "I had reason to believe the Great Popsicle might be found somewhere around here, but I never dreamed it would be this easy."

"The sign said Great Popsicle Monument and Park," Borgel said. "It doesn't necessarily mean the Popsicle itself is here."

"Of course it's here!" Freddie said. "What else would be in a place called Great Popsicle Monument and Park?"

"We'll see when we get there—if we ever get there," Borgel said. "This path seems to go on forever."

Of course the path didn't go on forever—just for about an hour. After a while, we all were wondering if we hadn't somehow missed the Great Popsicle Monument and Park.

"How big is this Great Popsicle?" Borgel asked.

"I'm not sure," Freddie said. "It has to be pretty big. I mean, it's a great popsicle, not some dinky little thing. I don't see how we could miss it."

"I think I see something!" Fafner said.

There was something barely showing through the trees a long way ahead of us. As we got closer, we could see it was a large wooden building in a clearing. The building was a sort of round barn, like a fat tower or a silo. It needed a coat of paint. There was nothing in the area around the building but an old car. It looked abandoned. The door of the building was open. Over the door was a sign: GREAT POPSICLE.

"This is it! This is it!" Freddie shouted. "Come on, everybody! Let's go in."

"Hold it!" a voice called from somewhere. We looked around. Then we saw a skinny, dirty-looking man emerge from the old car. The way he was stretching suggested that he'd been sleeping in it.

"You folks gonna go in and see the Popsicle?" the skinny guy asked.

"Yes. It's all right, isn't it?" Freddie asked.

"Cost you fifty zlotys a head," the skinny guy said.

"Fair enough," Freddie said, paying him. "It's my treat. You are all my guests at this historic moment."

We thanked Freddie and followed him into the building. He was hopping with excitement.

Immediately inside the door was a set of dusty wooden steps. We went up, through a hot, narrow corridor. It was just like going up to the loft of an old barn. The stairs wiggled and creaked under our feet.

When we came out of the stairway, we were standing on a sort of balcony that went all around the inside of the round building. The whole interior was one open space—just like a barn. Light came from a few windows above our heads. We could look down from the balcony to the floor, which was dirt. In the middle of the floor, standing about fifteen feet high, the top of it a little higher than our heads, the sides of it just beyond the reach of our hands, was a huge, vast, outsized Popsicle.

It was the old-fashioned double kind—two sticks. It was orange. It was dusty on the top.

"That's it?" I asked.

"The Great Popsicle," Freddie said rapturously.

Fafner's nose was twitching a mile a minute. "I don't think so," he said.

"What do you mean, you don't think so?" Freddie asked.

"I don't think it's the Great Popsicle," Fafner said.

"I thought I explained to you," Freddie said. "I am the greatest expert in the universe on the subject of popsicles. While I am not yet a hundred-percent satisfied that this is indeed the Great Popsicle, I can't see any way it could be anything else. Now I ask you, what makes you think it's not?"

"I'm a dog, bozo," Fafner said. "I can sniff circles around a humanoid like you. If my olfactory membrane were spread out it would take up more area than my whole skin. I can find out more by sniffing for a second than you could find out in a library in a year."

"And your sniffer tells you this isn't the Great Popsicle?"

"That's what my sniffer tells me."

"You know what the Great Popsicle should smell like?"

"I know it shouldn't smell like papier-mâché and epoxy and wood and chicken wire."

"That's what this thing is made of?" I asked.

"Plus, it isn't cold. If it were a popsicle, it would have to be frozen—that's basic, isn't it, Freddie?"

"Yes."

"Well, do any of you feel any cold coming from that thing? It's hotter in here than outside. I rest my case. It's a fake."

"Well, I was coming to that conclusion myself," Freddie said. "Just the emotion of the moment—the illusion of seeing it—confused me. Fafner here—intuitive, simple beast that

DANIEL PINKWATER

he is—may have gotten straight to the truth of the matter without doing any actual thinking."

Fafner made a noise I'd have thought could only be made by an animal with lips.

"Still," Borgel said, "what's the purpose of this big statue? What's it doing here, and what does it mean? We are certainly in Great Popsicle country, even if this isn't the genuine article. There's plenty to find out."

"Indeed," Freddie said. "I suggest we question the yokel who took my money on the way in."

We hurried down the stairs and found the yokel.

"You came out in a hurry," the skinny guy said. "Didn't you like what it had to say?"

"I'd like to ask you a few questions, if you please, my good man," Freddie said.

"I'm not a good man. I'm a bad man. And I don't get paid for answering questions. I get paid for selling tickets to the Popsicle," the skinny guy said.

Uncle Borgel put his hand on the skinny guy's shoulder. "Of course, my colleague would compensate you for your time."

"My time is pretty expensive," the skinny guy said.

"How about two hundred zlotys for as long as it takes to give us a little information?"

"Okay," said the skinny guy. "Let's have the money, and then ask your questions."

Freddie handed over the zlotys. "First of all, can you tell what that thing in there is supposed to be?"

"That's the Popsicle. That all you want to know?"

"It isn't a real popsicle—"

"That's a question?"

"—is it?"

"Nope. It's what you call a replica."

"All right, now we're getting somewhere, however slowly," Freddie said. "What is it a replica of?"

"Boy, this is fun," the skinny guy said. "If I had known how easy answering questions was, I would have done it before this. It is a replica of a popsicle."

"Any particular popsicle?"

"Maybe. I don't know the answer to that one. You'd have to ask the guy who made it."

"That was going to be my next question. Who made it?"

"My daddy."

"Your daddy?"

"Yep. Daddy built it."

"Is Daddy anywhere around?"

"Yep, he's right over near the house. But he won't answer any of your questions, if that's what you're thinking."

"Not even for two hundred zlotys?"

"Not for two million. Daddy's been dead for twenty years. He's buried near the house."

"Well then, who *was* your late father?"

"Evil Toad."

"I beg your pardon?"

"Evil Toad. It's a family name."

"I see."

"I am Hapless Toad. We Toads have lived here, oh, forever."

"Look, why did your father, Evil Toad, build that popsicle?"

"Why ask me?"

"Why ask you? Who else is there to ask?"

"Well, I don't mean to be rude, but why come all the way back here, and pay fifty zlotys each, for you three gentlemen and the dog, and go in to see the Popsicle and not ask any questions?"

"But I am asking questions, you rural Toad!"

"Yes, but you're asking *me*!"

Freddie was hopping up and down now. "Who else is there to ask?"

"Why, the Popsicle. Didn't you know it answers questions?"

"It answers questions?"

"And you think I'm a yokel. Yes, it does. Why would anyone drive way back here in the woods and pay fifty zlotys just to look at some statue of a popsicle? My goodness, you're ignorant."

"The *Popsicle* answers questions?"

"I just told you. I was wondering why you all came out of there so fast. When Rolzup, the Martian High Commissioner, was here the other month he stayed in there most of the day."

"Rolzup came here?"

"Lots of people come here."

"Who's Rolzup?" I whispered to Borgel.

"A very important person. Some people say he's the only person in the universe who knows what's going on," Borgel whispered back.

"So what do you do, just ask it questions?"

"That's right."

"And it answers?"

"Some. It answers some."

"Questions about anything?"

"You can ask about anything, I guess. It answers what it likes."

"So there really isn't much point asking you."

"Not much."

"When we could just go back in and ask the Popsicle."

"So it would seem."

"Well, Hapless Toad, thank you very much for explaining everything."

"You're welcome, I'm sure."

"We'll just go back inside now."

"Do what you like."

"Let's go back inside," Freddie said.

We started toward the door.

"Hold it!" Hapless Toad called. "That will cost you fifty zlotys a head."

"We already paid!"

"Then you came out. If costs fifty zlotys to go in."

"But we didn't ask any questions."

"That makes no difference. Fifty zlotys to go in."

"That's robbery!"

"Rules are rules. Pay up."

Freddie counted out two hundred zlotys. "Every place I've ever been, dogs get in free," he said.

"Not here," Hapless Toad said. "Enjoy yourselves. Stay as long as you like."

We made our way up the stairs to the balcony inside the wooden building. There was the replica of the Great Popsicle, just as boring as before.

"How do you propose we go about this?" Borgel asked Freddie.

"Well, I suppose I'll just ask it a question. Great Popsicle, can you hear me?"

From somewhere within the Popsicle, a metallic voice spoke, "Yep. I hear you. Got a question?"

"This is hokey," Fafner growled.

"Try to be scientific," Freddie said. "I'll ask it something simple. Great Popsicle, how much is four times four?"

"Just a minute," the Great Popsicle replica said. We could hear it mumbling to itself. "Let's see . . . fifteen? No, sixteen! Sixteen is the answer."

"The thing is stupid," Fafner said.

"Think it'll rain today?" Freddie asked.

"Nope. Not a cloud in the sky. Had some rain last week though."

Borgel motioned for us to gather close around. He whispered, "Does that voice sound familiar to anybody?"

"It sounds like Hapless Toad to me," I whispered back.

"Just what I was thinking," Freddie said. "Obviously there's a microphone and speaker inside the replica and the scoundrel is working a trick on us."

Fafner said, "Let me take care of this. Wait here." Without a sound, he disappeared down the stairs.

"Hey! You guys got any more questions?" the Great Popsicle replica called.

"We're thinking," Borgel said.

A minute later, we heard rapid footsteps on the stairs. Hapless Toad appeared, followed closely by Fafner.

"Hey!" Hapless Toad said. "This dog bit me!"

"Nipped you," Fafner said. "If I'd bitten you, you'd know the difference. I found him sitting in that old car, earphones on his head, talking to a microphone hidden in his hat."

"I was listening to my portable stereo!" Hapless Toad complained. "And I was singing along with the Ugly Bug Band, my favorite group. What's wrong with that?"

"What's wrong with that is, one, the Ugly Bug Band is probably the worst insect country-and-western group in the galaxy; two, you are supposed to be fixing the plumbing, not goofing in your car; and three, you have a horrible singing voice," someone said. Or something said. It wasn't any of us. It was the Great Popsicle.

We looked at each other. Evidently, it was not Hapless Toad doing the talking for it, as we had thought.

"Either that or he's a ventriloquist," Borgel said.

"A vent—what?" Hapless Toad asked.

"A ventriloquist, dummy," the Popsicle said. "Someone who can project his voice and make it seem to come from someplace else. Don't you know anything?"

"Whose voice is that?" Freddie asked Hapless Toad.

"My daddy's."

"You said your daddy was dead."

"He is. When he built this thing, he programmed it to sound like him."

"Programmed it?"

"Yes. It's a computer. What did you think it was, magic? I'm going," Hapless Toad said. "Tell your dog if he bites me again I'm going to whack him with a shovel."

Hapless Toad left.

"So you're a computer?" Borgel asked the replica.

"Yes. You want me to explain what a computer is?"

"I know what a computer is. Who built you?"

"Evil Toad, a great genius and inventor."

"Why did he build you?"

"Evil Toad built me because his son, Hapless Toad, whom you've met, is a simple-minded goon. Since his only offspring has the mental power of coleslaw, Evil Toad created me to pass on the wisdom he accumulated in his life."

"Any wisdom in particular?" Borgel asked.

"Yes. Any wisdom in particular."

"Why did Evil Toad build you to resemble a great popsicle?"

"Evil Toad built me to resemble the Great Popsicle, out of respect. He respected the Great Popsicle."

"Why did Evil Toad respect the Great Popsicle?"

"The Great Popsicle was Evil Toad's friend and teacher. It taught him all he knew."

"So the Great Popsicle exists!" Freddie shouted.

"Is that a question?"

"Doesn't it?" Freddie added.

"Beyond question," the Popsicle replica said.

"And you say it was Evil Toad's friend and teacher. Does that mean the Popsicle is a living being?"

"Well, I wouldn't say that," the Popsicle replica computer answered. "A popsicle is a popsicle, however great it may be—otherwise it wouldn't be a popsicle, would it? And all popsicles are friendly, otherwise they wouldn't be so beloved by all humankind and others. As to being Evil Toad's teacher, you can learn a lot from a popsicle. You of all people should know that, Freddie Nfbnm*."

"You know who I am?"

"I know most things."

"You had trouble with four times four," Fafner said.

". . . but I'm a little shaky in arithmetic."

"Great Popsicle computer replica, I desire to find the actual, original Great Popsicle. Where is it?" Freddie asked, very excited.

"Ask not!" the Popsicle replica said ominously.

"Why not?"

"Ask not!"

"You won't tell?"

"I'll tell if you ask, but I ask you, ask not!"

"Why do you ask me to ask not?"

"Ask not that either, if you know what's good for you!"

"But I want to know!" Freddie said.

The computer popsicle was silent.

"Don't I?" Freddie added.

"This is the last time I will warn you," the replica said. "Ask not!"

"And now you'll tell us?"

"Yes."

"So tell us!" Freddie shouted. The Popsicle replica

DANIEL PINKWATER

said nothing. Then Freddie added, ". . . won't you?"

"Don't blame me for what happens. Leave here. Take a left at the road. Go four metaparasangs. Turn left again at the statue of a blue-and-orange-striped cow's head. Then you're on a winding road. You go, oh, about eleven metaparasangs. You cross an interdimensional bridge. When you cross the bridge you will have left this plane of existence. You'll be in a monochromatic two-dimensional state. Follow the signs for Terre Haute. This will take you to the Interstate. When you get on the Interstate, turn off at the sign for Hell."

"We're going to Hell?"

"You're going beyond it. Take a right at the end of the ramp. You'll be in a three-dimensional state. Go about a metaparasang, past the Gates of Hell, and look for the Blue Moon Rest. It's a good place to have lunch. Ask Milly, the waitress, if her husband, Glugo, has a boat for rent. Then you have to find a wilderness guide. Maybe Glugo will take you himself. Then you're on your own."

"That's it?"

"Except one more thing, I have to tell you."

"What's that?"

"Don't go."

"Will we be in danger?"

"That is all I have to say on this subject."

"I say let's go!" Freddie said. "What do you say? Do you all want to come with me to find the Great Popsicle?"

"Well, never let it be said that I shrank from an adventure," Borgel said. "Melvin, are you up to this expedition?"

"Sure," I said. "If you want to go, I do, too."

"How about you, Fafner?" Borgel asked.

"I say, let's forget it. Ask the Popsicle if there's an amusement park around here."

"So you vote against going?" Borgel said.

"Emphatically," Fafner said.

"Well, it's too bad the vote wasn't unanimous—but of course, as a dog, you don't really have a vote. I just asked you out of politeness. We'll go. Maybe we'll find an amusement park another time."

"I hope sometime, in another life, I get to be a humanoid, and you have to be a dog," Fafner said.

"Unlikely," Borgel said. "Cheer up. I'll buy you a cheeseburger or something at that diner."

"Phooey on you," Fafner said.

"Now let me get this straight," Freddie said. "We leave here. Take a left at the road. Go four metaparasangs. Turn left again at the statue of a blue-and-orange-striped cow's head. Then we're on a winding road. We go, oh, about eleven metaparasangs. We cross an interdimensional bridge. When we cross the bridge we will have left this plane of existence. We'll be in a monochromatic two-dimensional state. Follow the signs for Terre Haute. This will take us to the Interstate. When we get on the Interstate, turn off at the sign for Hell.

"We take a right at the end of the ramp. We'll be in a three-dimensional state. Go about a metaparasang, past the Gates of Hell, and look for the Blue Moon Rest. Ask Milly, the waitress, if her husband, Glugo, has a boat for rent. Then we have to find a wilderness guide. Maybe Glugo will take us himself. Then we're on our own. Right?"

"Right," said the replica Popsicle computer. "But I wish you wouldn't."

20

"It's a long way to the far side of Hell," Borgel said. "I suggest we camp somewhere around here, and get a fresh start in the morning."

"Let's go now," Freddie said. "We can drive all night, and take a rest when we get there."

"I vote for starting in the morning," Fafner said. "Even though I'm only a dog and don't have a vote."

"We'll ask Hapless Toad if there's a good place to camp," Borgel said.

We found Hapless Toad painting a new sign. DOGS MUST BE KEPT ON LEASH it said.

"Mr. Toad, do you know of a place we can camp for the night?" Borgel asked.

"Try Toad's Campground, just up the road," Hapless Toad said.

"Any relation?"

"My cousin Witless Toad runs it. Tell him I sent you."

"Thanks," Borgel said. "We're sorry about the dog attacking you. He thought he was doing right."

"He bit a hole right through my pants," Hapless Toad said.

"I'm sure he's sorry," Borgel said. "By the way, any place around here we can buy some groceries?"

"Yep. Toad's Store. It's near the campground."

"Another relative?"

"Nope. The guy just happens to be named Toad—Nasty Ugly Horrible Little Toad. Not one of our Toads."

We stopped at Toad's Store. It was one of those country places that sells a little of everything. Only in this case the proprietor, Nasty Ugly Horrible Little Toad, had nothing edible to sell, except onions.

"Onions will be fine," Borgel said. "I was just in the mood for a mess of onions, barbequed over an open fire. How about the rest of you?"

"Nobody touches the bag of kibble, understood?" Fafner said.

"Onions sound fine to me," Freddie said.

We bought a whole bag.

Witless Toad's campground was okay. It was not much different from Gypsy Bill's. We found a nice spot under some trees, and Borgel dug a bunch of blankets out of the trunk of the Dorbzeldge.

"Let's see, a couple of us can bunk in the Dorbzeldge," Borgel said. "And we can make a couple of beds on the ground by gathering some soft branches and folding them under the blankets."

"I prefer to sleep in a tree," Freddie said.

"That's interesting," Borgel said. "Do you always sleep in a tree?"

"Whenever I can," Freddie said.

"Suit yourself," Borgel said.

We spent the rest of the afternoon gathering wood for the fire and setting up Borgel's portable kitchen. Borgel and I peeled and cut up onions, and skewered them on branches.

Night came on suddenly, and it got cool. We gathered around the fire, and cooked our onions-on-a-stick. It was sort of neat. I even liked the onions.

Borgel brewed some Norwegian vole-moss tea in his portable kettle, and we all sat around after supper, drinking tea, and enjoying being outside.

"By this time tomorrow, we may have found the Great Popsicle," Freddie said.

"I wonder if it will be anything like the stories," Borgel said.

"That reminds me," Freddie said. "You never told us the story about Grebitz."

"So I didn't," Borgel said. He got up and walked over to the trunk of the Dorbzeldge. After rummaging around for a while, he came back with a banjo. "Can you handle one of these?" he asked Freddie.

"In an emergency, I suppose I can do pretty well with one," Freddie said.

Borgel handed Freddie the banjo. "Well, let's do it right. You get started, and I'll chime in after a while."

Freddie hefted the banjo. "It's a nice one," he said.

"Be careful where you point it," Borgel said. "Start me off with something repetitive in a minor key."

Freddie clawed at the banjo, making a sort of sad, squeaking sound in his nose at the same time. Borgel took a swig of Norwegian vole-moss tea, and leaned back, his eyes closed. Then he began to speak.

"The true story of 'The Travels of Young Grebitz,'" Borgel said.

DANIEL PINKWATER

"This is the story of Grebitz, a skunkherd of pure heart, who ventured far to win the hand of Glossolalia, the daughter of Napnik the King, and of what he saw, and where he went, and what he learned, and how he came back, and what he ate, and what he thought, and how much the skunks missed him when he was gone. Also of the amazing thing he encountered, so strange he knew not what it was, and he knew not what to call it, and how he learned wisdom from the amazing thing and discovered its fearsome secret name."

"Was that the Popsicle?" Freddie asked.

"Keep playing," Borgel said. "And don't interrupt."

"Young Grebitz walked, on foot and alone. He left the pleasant fields he had known all his life. He left the skunks he had cared for. He left his friends, the other skunkherds of the country. He carried with him a leathern bottle of Hot and Spicy Oil, a potato, and his skunkherd's flute. Nothing else did he carry, for that was all he owned.

"Grebnitz entered the Great Forest, a place of terror, for here skunks would sometimes stray and never be found again. For many days, Grebnitz wandered in the forest, nibbling his potato, playing his flute, and listening to the calls of the forest birds. When night came, he would sleep on the leafy forest floor, and each night a strange dream would come to him.

"This is the dream young Grebitz would dream each night while he wandered in the forest: Grebitz would be on the very peak of a high mountain. Below him he would see fields and forests and rivers and all the things which existed.

As Grebnitz dreamed this dream, he would feel great excitement and happiness. Then, in his dream, the ghostly figure of a woman of great height, in billowing robes and wearing green basketball shoes, would appear.

"'Beware!' the woman would cry. 'Only the pure and simple may taste of the Great Wisdom!'

"'I am pure and simple!' Grebitz would say. Then, in his dream, the ghostly woman would bash Grebitz on the conk with a stick. He would feel a stinging chill, and then awake.

"Grebitz was puzzled as to what this dream might mean. Night after night in the Great Forest, the dream would come to him, and day after day he wandered.

"At last, Grebitz emerged from the forest. No one in his country had ever come so far. At the edge of the forest he met a giant. The giant was large and hairy and dirty, and smelled like a thousand angry skunks. 'Prepare to die!' the giant said to Grebitz.

"'Why? What did I do?' Grebitz asked the giant.

"'You didn't do anything. Just prepare to die, that's all.'

"Grebitz saw there was no way to defeat the giant. He tried to run away, but the giant overtook him. 'Now, *really* prepare to die,' the giant said.

"'Spare my life,' Grebitz said, 'and I will give you what's left of this potato.'

"'Ha!' the giant said. 'I'll get that anyway, after you're dead.'

"'Ha yourself,' Grebitz said. 'You may kill me, but you will never learn the secret of this bottle.' Grebitz held up his leathern bottle of Hot and Spicy Oil.

"'Who cares?' said the giant. 'And how come that bottle is made of leathern and not the usual stuff?'

"'Go ahead and kill me,' Grebitz said. 'I will die with the satisfaction that you will never know the secret.'

"'Fine,' said the giant. 'I'll kill you right now, since you're so satisfied.'

"'Fine by me. Kill away,' Grebitz said.

"'Fine,' said the giant.

"'Fine,' said Grebitz.

"'Probably there isn't any secret to that bottle anyway,' the giant said.

"'You'll never know, will you?' said Grebitz.

"'So what's in there anyway? Something magic?' the giant asked.

"'I thought you were going to kill me,' Grebitz said. 'Get on with it. I haven't got all day.'

"'I'll kill you when I'm good and ready,' the giant said. 'So what's in the bottle?'

"'I'm not telling,' said Grebitz.

"'You don't have to tell me the secret,' the giant said. 'Just what's in it.'

"'It's a magic elixir,' Grebitz said. 'You drink it and it gives you all sorts of powers.'

"'Boy, are you stupid!' the giant said. 'You gave the whole thing away.'

"'No I didn't,' said Grebitz.

"'Yes you did,' said the giant. 'Now I can kill you and drink the elixir. What a dope.'

"'It won't do you any good,' Grebitz said. 'I didn't tell you how much to drink. If you don't drink enough it won't do anything.'

"'I've had breakfasts that were brighter than you,' the giant said. 'Now you've told me everything.'

"'No I haven't,' Grebitz said.

"'Oh yes? You told me that it's a magic elixir that will give me all sorts of powers. Then you told me that if I don't drink enough, it won't do anything. Now, given that I am a giant, and about four times your size, I don't suppose it would be too much if I drank the whole thing, would it?'

"'Well . . .'

"'Here, give me that,' the giant said. He snatched the leathern bottle of Hot and Spicy Oil from Grebitz and drank it dry in one gulp. Then, naturally, he fell dead on the spot.

"'That's funny,' Grebitz said. 'It never does that to me.'"

"Is there a popsicle in this story?" Freddie interrupted.

"I'm getting to it," Borgel said.

"Well, my fingers are getting tired, that's all," Freddie said.

"Before Grebitz's amazed eyes, the dead giant changed into the woman in the flowing robes and green basketball shoes from his dream.

"'You have shown courage in facing the giant,' the woman said.

"'I didn't know it would kill him,' Grebitz said.

"'I know,' the mysterious woman said. 'If you had, you would not be a perfect idiot, and therefore would be unworthy to taste of the Great Wisdom.'

"Then she hit Grebitz on the conk with some sort of stick and he fell unconscious.

DANIEL PINKWATER

"When Grebitz awoke, he was in a meadow full of flowers. Birds sang, and the sun warmed him. He felt an inexpressible happiness. Everything was beautiful and serene.

"Then he saw something strange beyond belief. It was a think like no other thing he had ever seen. Grebitz did not know if it was a creature, or a strange flower, or an apparition. Whatever the thing was, it filled him with wonder and happiness. It was frolicking and gamboling among the flowers—a shining thing, which seemed to be made of colored ice. It had two tiny legs which looked as though they were sticks of wood, and when it came near to Grebitz, he felt a delightful coolness which seemed to come from the thing.

"He did not know why, but he experienced a great feeling of love for the wonderful object.

"'What can this miracle be called?' Grebitz asked aloud.

"The mysterious woman with the green basketball shoes appeared beside him.

"'It has many names,' the woman said. 'In the form you now witness, it is known as the Great Popsicle—and few humanoids have ever seen it.' Then she vanished.

"Grebitz wondered at the Great Popsicle for a long time. Finally, it pranced away and returned no more. Grebitz rose, and said, 'What an incredible experience. I think I'll continue my travels now.'"

"Wait! Is that the end of the story?" Freddie shouted.

"No, there's more," Borgel said. "But that's all there is about the Popsicle."

"I'm going to bed," Freddie said.

"Don't you want to hear the rest of it?" Borgel asked.

"No." Freddie climbed a tree, wrapped his ankles around a branch, and went to sleep, upside down like a bat.

21

"Do *you* want to hear the rest of the story?" Borgel asked me.

"Maybe another time," I said. "Interesting how Freddie's sleeping hanging upside down in a tree."

"That's not all that's interesting about him," Borgel said.

"What do you mean?"

"Freddie is not what he seems to be," Borgel said.

"You mean because he sleeps upside down in trees?"

"That, too. But I was thinking about the way he played the banjo."

"I thought he was pretty good," I said.

"There's something about the way he played it," Borgel said. "I don't exactly know what it was. Something I must have forgotten. Well . . . no matter. I'm sure it will come back to me. Meanwhile, are you having a nice adventure, Melvin?"

"Actually, I've never been on an adventure before, so I don't have anything to compare it to. But I guess it's okay."

"Well, we'll see some interesting things tomorrow," Borgel said. "Look, Fafner is asleep already. We should turn in and get our rest."

"Uncle Borgel," I said.

"Yetz?"

"I was just wondering . . . I mean . . . well, it's been a long time since we left home."

"There's no such thing as a long time. I thought I explained that to you. Time is neither long nor short. Remember the elliptical bagel with poppy seeds? The correct thing to say would be 'it's been an elliptical time since we left home.'"

"What I meant was, won't they all be worried about us?"

"Why should they be? We're okay, aren't we?"

"Yes, but we've been gone a long . . . I mean, an elliptical time . . . and . . ."

"Oho! Homesick, is it? Actually, they might not even know we're gone."

"Not know?"

"It's relative. While you have the impression that we've been traveling in time-space-and-the-other for quite a while, it may seem like a minute to the folks back home."

"Really?"

"Oh, absotoomley. Of course, it could work the other way. It might seem to them that we've been gone ninety or a hundred years. It's tricky."

"Really."

"Look, if you want to go home, just say the word. I don't want you to have a bad time."

"We can go home anytime we like?"

"I don't see why not," Uncle Borgel said.

I felt a lot better knowing that. "No, I want to go on and keep having an adventure," I said.

"On the other hand, I don't see why either," Borgel said. "But let's get some sleep. Plenty to do in the morning."

In the morning, after a breakfast of leftover onions, we

piled into the Dorbzeldge, and were on the road again.

"Where are we exactly?" I asked Borgel.

"What do you mean, where?" he asked. "We're on a country road, in the Dorbzeldge, looking for a statue of a blue-and-orange-striped cow's head."

"I mean, are we on Earth or some other planet? I never quite worked it out."

"You ever see anybody on Earth who looks like Hapless Toad?" Borgel asked.

"You mean the blue ears?"

"Right."

"No, I can't say that I have."

"So we're on some other planet—or some part of Earth we've never heard of—or a separate plane of existence. It's complicated."

"Explain it to me."

"Well, when you travel in time-space-and-the-other, it's hard to tell which one you're traveling in—or whether it's more than one."

"I don't get it," I said.

"Did you ever see a ghost?" Borgel asked.

"No."

"How about someone who seems to appear for a second and then disappear?"

"No."

"How about one of those soft ice-cream stands, Dairy Chill and so forth?"

"Sure. I've seen plenty of those," I said.

"All right. They're the best example anyway," Borgel said.

"All those places exist in another plane of existence. They just tend to appear in the one you usually live in."

"What do you mean another plane of existence?" I asked. I was really confused.

"A different world, which is as real as yours and which exists in the same space, but in a slightly different time. You know what is it a tuning fork?"

"Yes."

"Well, it makes sound by vibrating, right? Vibrating is shaking to and fro. If you look at one closely while it's vibrating, you can see the tines of the fork appearing to exist on the 'to' side, and on the 'fro' side. Now what if you could see the 'to' side of each vibration, but not the 'fro' side? What would happen then?"

"Um, it would seem to disappear and reappear really fast?"

"Prezacktly. So what you might think is a ghost, or someone who appears for a second and then disappears, is just someone who vibrates to and fro, only slowly. And a soft ice-cream stand—don't ask me why it's always them—vibrates to and fro very, very slowly."

"I don't understand," I said.

"I do," Fafner said.

"Look!" Freddie said. "There's the blue-and-orange-striped cow's head!"

We turned onto the winding road.

"Next we have to look for an interdimensional bridge," Freddie said.

"This will be interesting," Borgel said. "Now you'll see what it's like to go from one plane of existence to another."

Interesting was hardly the word for it. Terrifying would be a better word. Also stunning. Also insane. After doodling along the road, which twisted and turned like a snake for a number of hours, we came to the bridge.

It looked like an ordinary bridge. It didn't go over a river or anything—just a bridge. One of those metal highway bridges you see all the time. Except when we were about halfway across, we all turned from color to black and white.

So did everything else. Even stranger, everything became flat. Borgel was flat. Fafner was flat. Freddie was flat. What we, and the Dorbzeldge, and everything outside the Dorbzeldge looked like was cartoons. The daily black-and-white cartoons in the newspaper.

"This is weird! What's happening?" I shouted.

"We're in a two-dimensional state," Borgel said. "Don't try to think any deep thoughts, hee hee hee!"

"You look like a cartoon!" I said. "How can you drive in this flatness?"

"Actually, it's easier," Borgel said. "One less dimension to worry about."

"I hate this," I said.

"You're just used to being round," Borgel said. "It makes a nice change, actually."

"I feel like a place mat," Fafner said.

"You want to see something really unusual?" Borgel asked. He pulled over to the side of the road. "Come on, Fafner! Get out and chase me!"

Fafner and Borgel ran around the car. It was exactly like those old black-and-white cartoons they show on the local cable TV station. It was funny. Anyway, *I* thought it was funny.

Freddie was impatient. "Get back in the car!" he said. "We have a long way to go!"

By this time, Borgel and Fafner were out of breath from running and laughing. "Watch this!" Borgel said. He turned sideways quickly and almost disappeared.

"Hey! Look at this one!" Fafner shouted. He crawled under Borgel's feet. "I'm a rug!"

I jumped out of the car. "Look at me! I can fold myself!" And I did it. I bent over double and folded like a piece of paper.

"Very good. Very good," Freddie said. "Now let's go."

"You're certainly in a big hurry," Borgel said, getting back behind the wheel. "You should have more fun. You'll last longer."

"Bear right for Terre Haute!" Freddie shouted, pointing to a sign.

"I see it. I see it," Borgel said. "Now look for signs for the Interstate."

We passed black-and-white cartoon farms with what looked like drawings of houses and barns and animals.

Fafner seemed to enjoy being two-dimensional. "Look out for paper clips, Borgel!" he chortled. "You know, we could get there faster if we put ourselves in an envelope and mailed ourselves special delivery."

"Not funny," I said.

"Aw, go fold yourself," Fafner said.

When we finally got on the Interstate, we popped back

into three dimensions, and full color. I guess I had been starting to get used to being flat and monochrome, because it
seemed suddenly very crowded in the Dorbzeldge. For a few
minutes, I couldn't get used to taking up space, and I kept
bumping into things.

The Interstate was the old familiar blackness and void.
The road was the same glowing ribbon beneath us. In the distance there were occasional areas which glowed dimly, and
once in a while, a distant flash like lightning.

"Ah, the old Interstate," Borgel said. "So restful."

"Uncle Borgel?"

"Yaas?"

"Remember the big energy ball that chased us the other
time?"

"Sure."

"I think I see another one," I said.

"Nope. That's not another one of those energy monsters."

"What a relief!"

"It's the same one. I wonder if it's been following us all
this while."

This remark of Borgel's depressed me — especially as the
big peach-colored thing was not behind us but diagonally
ahead of us and approaching fast.

"It looks like it's going to get us!" I shouted.

"Oh no! I'm too beautiful to die!" Fafner shouted.

"Actually, it looks sort of bad," Uncle Borgel said. "About
the only thing I can think of doing is running off the
Interstate, which is pretty much always certain death, from
what I've been told."

"Can't we turn around and run the other way?" I asked.

"That would involve stopping," Borgel said. "By the time I did that, and got us turned around, it would be a lot closer, and it would overtake us before we built up speed. No, the best thing would be to swing off the Interstate, and hope we'd come around in an arc going the other way. Or, I could try the same thing, swinging around behind the energy ball— but, as I said, the chances of getting back on the road are almost nonexistent. I think we're probably doomed."

"I know what to do!" Freddie said. He had dug what looked like a potato out of his pocket, and was holding it up for us to see.

"Well, if you like," Borgel said. "But we'll barely have time to eat before it catches us."

"We aren't going to eat it," Freddie said. He seemed to be whispering to the potato thing. Then he casually tossed it out the window. It hovered in the void outside the Dorbzeldge for an instant, and then made a beeline for the glowing energy monster.

Suddenly the energy ball extinguished, like a light being switched off.

"All gone," Freddie said.

"How'd you do that?" I asked.

"Just a handy trick," Freddie said. "Something I picked up on my travels."

"I hope nobody but us saw you do that," Borgel said. "We aren't supposed to destroy things along the Interstate. We could get in serious trouble."

"We were already in serious trouble," Freddie said.

DANIEL PINKWATER

"True," Borgel said. "Do you have any more of those potatoes on you?"

"No, that was my only one," Freddie said.

"Good," Borgel said. "Weapons scare me."

"What did you mean, 'too beautiful to die'?" I asked Fafner.

"Did I say that?" Fafner asked.

"Amazing the conceit of some animals," I said.

22

The signs for Hell appeared along the Interstate long before we got to the turnoff. They said things like GO TO HELL! and SEE YOU IN HELL and STAY AT THE PRINCE OF DARKNESS MOTOR LODGE—BAR-B-QUES NIGHTLY.

Then there was big sign: HELL, NEXT EXIT.

Borgel turned the Dorbzeldge off the Interstate onto Good Intentions Boulevard. I have to say it. It was fantastic.

Never in my life had I seen so many electric signs, so many fast-food restaurants, motels, shopping malls, drive-in movies, used-car lots, roadside stands, billboards, miniature golf courses, and discount hardware stores.

The traffic was astounding. Vehicles of every imaginable description were progressing at a crawl, in three lanes, bumper to bumper. There were cars and buses, spacecraft, wagons drawn by animals, boats, strange machines I couldn't figure out, beings on bicycles, and thousands of people on skateboards.

I had seen a few strange aliens, mostly at Alfred's time-space root beer stand, but the sheer number and variety of weird-looking creatures along Good Intentions Boulevard was mind-blowing. There were seemingly intelligent life-forms ranging from the size of a chipmunk to one we saw as big as a blue whale. And species resembling humanoids, reptiles, birds, hunks of rock, and animated pizzas—scaly, slimy, hairy, smooth, lighter than air, glow-in-the-dark, little green men—they were all there, every kind of freak in any number of universes.

"It looks just like places in New Jersey," Freddie said.

"Only more so," Borgel said. "Hell is the most popular place there is."

A really enormous sign came into view. It was incredible. There were lights of every color. Little red animated devils ran all around the edges of it, and real fireworks exploded in the air above it. It was the greatest sign I ever saw. Letters twenty feet high flashed one message after another:

THIS IS IT!

HELL!

THE ORIGINAL—THE ONLY!

GET FRIED!

FREE ASBESTOS FOOTWEAR!

HELL!

The Gates of Hell, when we got to them, were even more impressive than the sign. Really fantastic. Made of metal, with all sorts of fancy sculpture on them. Inside, past the gates, there was a fireworks display going on, even better than the one above the sign. There was quite a smell of gunpowder.

Outside the Gates of Hell was a guy with horns! He was capering around and waving the cars in.

"Is that the actual devil?" I asked Borgel.

"Probably just a minor one," Borgel said. "I hear they have quite a few."

"What happens inside?" I asked.

"I'm not exactly sure," Borgel said. "But I know one thing about it."

"What's that?"

"If you didn't like it, you'd have a lot of trouble getting your money back."

We were hung up for quite a while, in front of the Gates of Hell, while traffic from the other direction made left turns in front of us. Most of the cars on Good Intentions Boulevard seemed to be going to Hell.

"Let's just go in for a while," Fafner said. "I want to see what goes on."

"Nah," Borgel said. "I always avoid cheap tourist attractions."

"Besides," Freddie said, "we have someplace important to go."

"It looks great!" Fafner said. "I wish I were going to Hell."

"May your wish be granted," I said.

Once we got past the Gates of Hell, traffic in our direction was much lighter, and we drove along at a reasonable speed. The roadside establishments were much the same, plenty of malls and drive-ins, and places that sold little cement statues—mostly of devils—the kind people put on their lawns.

After a while, we appeared to be getting into the outskirts of Hell. The junk architecture thinned out quite a bit, and we could barely smell the brimstone.

"Maybe we missed the Blue Moon Rest," Freddie said.

"Nah, I was looking carefully," Borgel said. "It ought to be coming up fairly soon now."

23

The Blue Moon Rest was a circular building, painted blue. It looked sort of old and beaten-up and friendly. There were a few assorted vehicles parked outside. We went in, and sat down at a table.

There wasn't a humanoid in the place. Various creatures of various shapes and sizes were munching, gnawing, sucking, gobbling, and absorbing plates of great-looking food. I realized that I hadn't been getting many balanced meals lately.

"We are going to eat something, aren't we?" I asked Borgel.

"Of course, Melvin," Borgel said. "After nothing but onions for the last day or so, I think we're all ready for something tasty."

In addition to the tables there was a counter. Behind the counter was an amorphoid fleshopod, flipping hamburgers. He was disgusting, but he didn't approach Alfred in that respect. He didn't affect my appetite one bit. There was a sign hanging above the counter:

OUR SPECIALITY: NO-CAL–NO-NUTE.

FOOD FOR ALL SPECIES.

The waitress came over. She was a fur-bearing Anthropoid from the Nofkis galaxy, Freddie told us. She looked as though she weighed about 450 pounds. Her fur was a light green color—except for which detail, she looked pretty much like any ape at home. She was wearing a button on her uniform that read, *I am the Gorilla of Your Dreams.* She smiled at us. I liked her. She seemed friendly.

"Know what you want, honeys?" the ape waitress asked.

"What's 'no-cal–no-nute,' miss?" Borgel asked.

"No calories, no nutritional content," the waitress said. "We can feed beings from anywhere. All the dishes we prepare are one hundred-percent cellulose. Fiber. Good for man and beast, and whatever. If you desire, we can give you nutrients on the side."

"So what is everything made with, wood chips?" Borgel said.

"I guess," the waitress said. "The maple pancakes are really good, and the okra is real oak."

"I guess I'll have that," Borgel said. "And give me a side of B-complex, some C, E, and trace minerals."

"One humanoid special," the waitress said. "How about you, sweetie?" she said to me.

"I'll have the same, I guess," I said.

"Nothing for me," Fafner said. "I'll have some kibble in the car," he whispered to Borgel.

"And a complimentary synthetic cookie-bone for Rover," the waitress said. "It's on the house, poochie. Enjoy."

"Just a pineburger for me," Freddie said. "And some iron filings on the side, with maybe some copper sulphate and a slice of lead."

The waitress raised one eyebrow as she wrote down Freddie's order on her pad. "The lead is extra, okay?" she asked.

"Fine," Freddie said.

"Turpentine shakes all around?"

"Just water," Borgel said.

"I'll try the shake," Freddie said.

"Sure you can digest all that?" Borgel asked Freddie. "You and I aren't so young anymore. You might have trouble sleeping."

"I crave minerals," Freddie said. To the waitress, he said, "Your name wouldn't happen to be Milly, would it?"

"That's me, shorty," the ape waitress said.

"I wanted to ask you a question," Freddie said.

"The answer is no, grandpa," Milly said. "I do not date customers. I'm a married gorilla."

"That wasn't it," Freddie said, blushing.

"Oh no?" Milly said. "I saw the way you were giving me the eye. There's no need to be embarrassed. I know I'm irresistably adorable."

"You certainly are," Borgel broke in. "But my companion just wanted to know if your husband, Glugo, has a boat available."

"Could be," Milly said. "Why don't you ask him yourself? Here's the number. The phone's over there." She scribbled a number on a page of her order pad and handed it to Freddie.

"I'll call him right now," Freddie said. "Excuse me." He went to use the telephone.

When Freddie was gone, Milly said to Borgel, "It's none of

my business, but how long have you known that little guy?"

"Not very long," Borgel said.

"Were you aware that he's a Grivnizoid?"

"A Grivnizoid?" Borgel asked.

"A native of the planet Grivnis," Milly said. "Now, I like to think I am not a prejudiced person, but those Grivnizoids can be very dangerous."

"How so?" Borgel asked.

"Well, let's just say they tend to be evil, power mad, untrustworthy, and abominably clever and sneaky. Of course, I could be wrong."

"But you think he's one?"

"How many little bald-headed men you know eat side orders of iron filings and lead?"

"Not many."

"I'd be careful if I were you," Milly said.

"Thanks," Borgel said.

Milly went to give our orders to the fleshopod.

"Do you think she's right?" I asked Borgel.

"She may just be a talkative waitress," Borgel said, "but I have had my doubts about Freddie Nfbnm*. We'll just keep this to ourselves, and Fafner—keep a sharp eye on him, understand?"

"Right, boss," Fafner said.

Freddie came back. "Glugo is going to meet us here," he said.

24

The no-cal–no-nute food was actually not bad. It tasted like regular fast-food such as you'd get at any roadside restaurant. Watching Freddie eat the iron filings and lead was a little strange, of course.

"My compliments to the chef!" he called to the Amorphoid Fleshopod behind the counter.

"Merci, monsieur," the fleshopod responded.

Milly came back. "Everything all right here?"

"First rate," Freddie said. "What's for dessert?"

"The maple-walnut ice cream is one hundred percent," Milly said.

"Let's have it," Freddie said.

"Four maple-walnuts," Milly said. "No, five—here comes my sweetie." An ape on a big motorcycle had just pulled up outside the Blue Moon Rest. "Hi, honey!" Milly said to the ape as he came in. He was a big upland gorilla, wearing a blue feed-cap with DON'T MONKEY WITH ME printed on the front.

"Hiya, toots," Glugo said. "Where's the bozo who wants the boat?"

"It's the little goon with the whiskers," Milly said. She gave Glugo a hug, and I could see her whisper something in his ear. "Sit down. I'll bring you all ice cream and coffeelike substance."

"So?" Glugo said, drumming his fingers on the table. "What can I do for you?"

"We were told you can supply us with a boat," Freddie said.

"For what purpose?" Glugo said.

"Well, we were told about a certain popsicle," Freddie said. "I'm very interested in popsicles."

"Who isn't?" Glugo said. "But you don't need a boat to find one. You can get popsicles everywhere."

"This is a certain particular rather unusual popsicle," Freddie said.

Milly brought the ice cream, which had a strange woody taste. The coffeelike substance was horrible, but I don't like coffee much anyway.

Glugo spooned in ice cream for a while, and drank coffeelike substance with a whistling slurp. "Hmm," he said. "I'm not sure I can help you. Who told you you'd need a boat to find this special popsicle?"

"We were talking to a computer built by a deceased genius named Evil Toad."

"Evil Toad?"

"That's right."

"And the computer he built said you should find me?"

"Yes."

"Mentioned me specifically by name?"

"It said we should ask Milly if you had a boat available. Also that we'd need a wilderness guide. The computer said maybe you'd take us yourself," Freddie said.

"That's different," Glugo said. "That Popsicle replica

knows everything Evil Toad knew and thinks everything he thought."

"So you know about the Great Popsicle replica and computer?" Freddie asked.

"Listen," Glugo said, "I helped build it—the statue part, not the computer. Evil Toad was my best friend. He saved my life once. Nursed me through a brain fever. Sat with me day and night while I raved deliriously and plucked at the covers. It's not an easy job taking care of a gorilla with brain fever. I don't forget a thing like that, even if Evil Toad is now just a statue of an ice-pop with an electronic brain. I didn't understand everything Evil thought and did, but if the computer sent you to me, I'll help you, no matter if . . ."

"No matter if what?" Borgel asked.

"Just no matter," Glugo said. "The Popsicle you're looking for lives in the big wilderness on the other side of the river. I'll take you there."

"Lives?" Borgel asked.

"Yes," Glugo said. "But it's shy and elusive. Not more than three beings alive have the skill to track it."

"Are you one of those three?" Freddie asked.

"I've seen it a few times," Glugo said.

"When can we go?" Freddie asked.

"How about right now?" Glugo said. "We can cross the river tonight, sleep on the far shore, and then go looking for the Popsicle. That all right with you geeks?"

"Fine with me," Borgel said. "By the way, what time is it anyway? Seems to me it's been night ever since we arrived."

"It's always night in the region of Hell," Glugo said. "But

you'll see daylight across the river. Milly!" he called to his wife. "Pack a bunch of lunches. I'm taking these slobs across the river tonight!"

"You'd better be careful," Milly said.

"I know what I'm doing," Glugo said.

A few minutes later, we were in the Dorbzeldge, following Glugo on his big motorcycle. He turned off Good Intentions Boulevard onto a winding road. We drove after him through the darkness until we came to a low building at the side of a wide dark river.

Glugo switched off his motor and we piled out of the Dorbzeldge.

"Boobs, this is the Styx, a famous river. Maybe you've heard of it," Glugo said.

"Where's the boat?" Freddie asked.

"Right over here," Glugo said. "You fellows don't mind doing some rowing, do you?"

Glugo pulled a flashlight out of his pocket, and showed us a very large boat tied up to a little dock.

"That's a Roman trireme!" Borgel said.

"Sort of huge, isn't it?" I asked.

"It's the only boat I've got," Glugo said. "The three of you will have your work cut out rowing. I assume the dog can't work an oar."

"Sorry," Fafner said. "That's a trick I never learned."

"The three of us have to row that big thing?" I asked. "What will you do?"

"I steer," Glugo said. "And crack the whip."

25

Rowing Glugo's Roman trireme across the Styx was no fun at all. Firstly, the thing was enormous and heavy. Pulling at my oar felt like the other end of the thing was stuck in semisolid glue. Also with three rowers—Freddie and I on one side and Borgel on the other—the boat tended to slew to one side.

It would have been a lot easier if Glugo had rowed, too, but he seemed to think it was important to stand at the bow and crack a big whip and holler, "Pull! Pull!" He said it was important to observe traditions.

By the time we bumped into the opposite shore, I was exhausted. Apparently, so were Freddie and Borgel, because we wrapped ourselves in the ratty blankets Glugo gave us and fell asleep immediately on the grassy riverbank.

When we woke up, it was dawn—on our side of the river. The other side, the Hell side, was shrouded by clouds as black as night. Our side was beautiful—a soft, misty morning. There were green hills and forest, and dewy meadows. I would have felt wonderful, waking up to such a morning, except for one thing—Glugo and the boat were gone!

The bags of no-cal–no-nute lunches Milly had packed were piled on top of a flat rock. On one of the bags, Glugo had written a note: Dear Goops, Remembered something I had to do. Look around and have fun. Maybe you'll even find what you're looking for. I'll come back in a day or two. Maybe three. Certainly no more than a week.

"How did he get the boat back across by himself?" I wondered out loud.

"My guess is he used the engine," Borgel said.

"The thing has an engine?" I asked.

"Well, something on board smelled of gasoline," Borgel said. "Didn't you notice?"

"I was so tired after a while, I didn't notice anything," I said. "Fafner! You didn't do any rowing! You weren't exhausted! Why didn't you keep watch?"

"Nobody told me to," Fafner said. "You guys all went to sleep, so I did, too."

"Some dog," I said.

"I didn't know," Fafner said. "What was I supposed to do, read that gorilla's mind?"

"Never mind," Freddie said. "The main thing is, we're here. I'm sure the gorilla will come back for us."

"What if he doesn't?" I asked.

"Maybe we won't need him," Freddie said. "Let's look for the Great Popsicle."

"I suggest we have some breakfast first," Borgel said. "Let's see what Milly packed for us."

Cold no-cal–no-nute hamburgers taste a little like pencils. The added nutrients taste like the graphite part. We didn't spend a long time eating breakfast.

"Now, about looking for the Popsicle," Borgel said. "I suggest we spread out. If anyone sees anything like a popsicle, whistle."

"I can't whistle," Fafner said.

"You go with Freddie," Borgel said. "See that nothing happens to him."

"I'll keep an eye on him," Fafner said.

"That's not necessary," Freddie said.

"Take the dog with you," Borgel said. "He needs the exercise. Besides, he might be useful if you run into danger. Melvin and I will go up that hill. You two can take a look in the forest."

"Fine with me," Freddie said. "We'll meet back here about noon to eat some lunch, and see if Glugo has returned."

Borgel and I started up the hill.

"Now that we're alone, there are a lot of questions I want to ask you," I said.

"Not yet," Borgel whispered. "Wait until we're farther away. Grivnizoids have excellent hearing."

"Then he *is* a Grivnizoid?"

"Shh!"

When Borgel thought we had gotten far enough away from Freddie and Fafner, he stopped and sat down on the grassy slope of the hill. "Now, I think we can speak freely," he said. "You wanted to ask questions?"

"I hardly know where to begin," I said. "Who or what is Freddie? What is this popsicle thing we're looking for? Is it real? Is it here? Why does Freddie want to find it so much? Why did Glugo leave us here, and is he coming back?"

"Ha! Good questions! I will answer them all at once, in no particular order. Get comfortable."

I got comfortable.

DANIEL PINKWATER

"First, the Popsicle. It is probably a real thing, but its form is provisional, okay?"

"Nope. Don't understand."

"It's complicated. Certain objects—we'll call them objects, but they're really complex phenomena involving energy, consciousness, time, matter, and other stuff we don't understand—these certain objects appear from time to time."

"What do they do? I mean what are they for?"

"They energize. You know the way our sun energizes our solar system? Everything depends on it. These objects—let's call them energy bundles—energize all sorts of things, maybe a galaxy, or many galaxies, or the known universe."

"Are there a lot of them?"

"There are twenty-six of them."

"How do you know that?"

"I know. Anyway, I think this Popsicle is one of them."

"But why is it a popsicle? I mean, when you think about it, that's sort of a stupid thing to be, isn't it?"

"No more stupid than anything else," Borgel said. "Why is the Sun a flaming gas-ball? Why not an enormous bowl of spaghetti? Why not a grizzly bear or a soft-drink machine? If all your life, the source of life and energy had been a huge blazing soft-drink machine, you'd be used to it. You wouldn't give it a second thought."

"I think it's better for it to be a star," I said.

"I do, too—but really, couldn't that just be because we're used to it? Anyway, I doubt the energy cluster is a popsicle all the time. It's probably one just for now, just for us."

"Why?"

"Maybe Evil Toad knew the answer to that. It's funny how interconnected things are. Someone's vision of something can affect the reality for others. I'll give a concrete example: You know who was it, Napoleon?"

"Yes, he was that French guy."

"Right. Here's a dime." Borgel handed me a dime. "Now, you may also remember that Napoleon was a little shrimp type, a shorty. You read that somewhere?"

"Yes."

"Now. Suppose someone was a time traveler and had the power to change Napoleon to an eight-foot giant."

"Is that possible?"

"Theoretically, sure. If someone did that, and Napoleon was an eight-foot giant, what do you suppose would happen?"

"He'd have to have all his suits lengthened?"

"Not only that. Also, nature would adjust to the change by giving him giant ancestors. That's a temporal adjustment. It's the way things work. Time is elliptical, you remember."

"The bagel?"

"Yes."

"I thought that was space."

"Space, time, it's all the same thing. If you change something here, it connects with things there—in time, in space, in the present, in the future, in the past."

"So why is it a popsicle?"

"I have no idea, but there's a reason, you can be sure of that—just we'll probably never know it. Next, Freddie. You wanted to know about Freddie."

"Yes. Is he a Grivnizoid?"

"I think it's likely. That ape waitress sees a lot of different life-forms, and she thought so. So, assuming he is one, what would he want with the Popsicle, you want to know. If the Popsicle really is one of the twenty-six immensely powerful energy bundles that maintain the shape and quality of reality, he'd want to get it so he could steal its power."

"Why would he do that?"

"So he can be absolute ruler of everything."

"Freddie?"

"Don't let appearances fool you. If Freddie is a Grivnizoid, he's in disguise. Grivnizoids are big scary fellows. They're just the sort who would want power over the whole universe, and more if possible."

"If he got it, that would be bad," I said.

"Bad for some. Good for Grivnizoids."

"Shouldn't we stop him? What if he finds it?" I asked Borgel.

"Well, I think it may not be so easy to get. Those powerful energy bundles must be very smart. Besides, I doubt that it's here."

"You do?"

"When we get to the top of this hill, I bet you my lunch, we'll find we're on an island. Can't get off. And Glugo . . ."

"Yes, what about Glugo?"

"He's probably gone for help. He certainly knows that Freddie is likely to try something dangerous. Glugo seemed to be a good ape—what do you think?"

It was just a few yards to the top of the hill. I ran ahead, and when I got there, I could see river on all sides.

"It *is* an island," I said.

Borgel arrived at the top of the hill. "See? What did I tell you? Glugo stranded us here, and he's probably getting in touch with someone with the authority to call Freddie off."

"Who can do that?"

"Oh, a number of people. Probably he'll get in touch with somebody like Rolzup, the Martian High Commissioner."

"I've heard of him," I said.

"I'm not surprised. He's a very important person."

"So why didn't you do something to stop Freddie yourself?" I asked Borgel.

"It's not my style," Borgel said. "Remember, Freddie is just doing what's normal—if you happen to be a Grivnizoid. I try not to judge people or interfere. Besides, I find that things usually work out pretty well if I leave them alone. I don't think there's any real danger."

"No danger? From what you've told me, not that I understand most of it, if Freddie could somehow steal the power of the Great Popsicle, he'd be the most powerful being in the universe!"

"At least."

"So why not dangerous?"

"Well, for one thing, Freddie isn't all that bad—oh, maybe ruthless and power mad and possibly a little cruel, but in a cute sort of way. What's more, who's to say he's going to find the Popsicle? We're on this island, and the Popsicle is probably all the way over on the far shore."

"What's that?" I asked.

"What?" Borgel asked.

"That thing down there," I said.

"You mean that thing romping in the grass?"

"Yes."

"That thing that is glowing with an amazing light?"

"Yes, that thing."

"Very pretty, isn't it?"

"What is it?"

"Looks a little like a popsicle."

"Are you sure?" I asked Borgel.

"It's hard to tell at this distance," Borgel said. "What we need is a pair of binoculars."

"But we don't have any," I said.

"I have a good pair, made by Carl Flutz," Borgel said. "Maybe I should just nip back and get them."

"Nip back where?" I asked. "Remember the Dorbzeldge is on the other side of the river."

"They're not in the Dorbzeldge. They're in my room. I think I'll get them. Wait here and watch that thing while I'm gone."

"Oh no! You've gone mushy in the head! You can't get your binoculars from your room! We're away off in time-space-and-the-other, remember?"

"Ah-ha! There are plenty of tricks you don't know," Borgel said. "Just watch this."

Borgel put one finger up his nose, another finger in his ear, and whistled shrilly. Then he vanished—just ceased to be—was gone—turned into thin air. I felt a sinking feeling. I thought maybe he'd been bilboked again. I didn't have time to get upset, because in a few seconds, there was another

Borgel   145 whistle, and he was back, with a pair of old field glasses.

"Just where I thought they were," Borgel said.

"Wait a second!" I shouted. "Where did you get those?"

"Where I said," Borgel said. "They were in my room."

"You just went back to your room, in our apartment, and came back here in, what, ten seconds?"

"Sure. I told you, there are tricks."

"Can I do that, too?"

"Why not?"

I was astonished. "So we could have gotten anywhere without driving in the Dorbzeldge?"

"Yes," Borgel said. "But what fun would that be? Here, I brought you some fig bars."

He handed me a cellophane bag of fig bars.

"Where is that thing?" Borgel asked, peering through the binoculars.

"I don't know. I forgot all about it," I said.

"Hmm. Seems to have gone out of sight," Borgel said. "Hand me a couple of fig bars, will you?"

Freddie and Fafner came puffing up the hill. "We heard a whistle," Freddie said.

"Where did you get the fig bars?" Fafner asked.

"Borgel found them," I said, handing him one.

"Well, did you see something?" Freddie asked.

"I thought I did," Borgel said, "but I don't see it now."

26

"What was it like, the thing you saw?" Freddie asked.

"Little," Borgel said.

"Couldn't have been the Great Popsicle," Freddie said. "It has to be huge. Remember the replica?"

"Oh yes," Borgel said. "That replica was pretty big, wasn't it?"

"I wish you'd take this search more seriously," Freddie said. "Look, we can see everything from up here. Nothing like a gigantic popsicle in sight. It must be in the forest. Say! We're on an island!"

"I was wondering when you'd notice," Borgel said.

"That makes it better," Freddie said. "If it's here, it can't get away from us. I'm going back to the forest. Who's coming with me?"

"Fafner, help Freddie," Borgel said.

"I'm tired," Fafner said.

"Go anyway. We'll look around here some more, and catch up with you."

Freddie and Fafner went down the hill toward the forest.

"Don't whistle unless you're sure!" Freddie called back.

"Ha!" Borgel said to me. "I'm not sure Freddie really knows what he's looking for."

"Why do you say that?" I asked.

"Well, there's no reason the Great Popsicle has to be

huge," he said. "If it's an entity of enormous power, as I suspect, it could be of atomic size, or as big as a world—or anything in between, anytime it likes. Similarly, if it wanted to get off this island, or eat this island, or turn this island into a fig bar, it could do it."

"Wow!" I said.

"That's what I meant when I said it might not be so easy to catch," Borgel said. "I think he's heard something about it, but maybe he doesn't really know what he's up against. It's a little like trying to catch an elephant with a butterfly net, which I have seen done once or twice, but it's not the best way."

"Would it do any of those things?" I asked.

"What things?"

"Turn this island into a fig bar, and things like that?"

"It could," Borgel said. "But would it? Here. Look through these. See whether you think it would."

"It's back?" I asked.

"Right over there," Borgel pointed. "Adjust the focus with the little knob in the middle."

We were lying prone, just below the crest of the hill. I steadied myself on my elbows and looked through the binoculars.

I had to scan around a bit, and then I saw it. There wasn't any doubt in my mind. It was something powerful—as powerful as the Sun, or a whole lot of suns—and it was a popsicle. It was sort of prancing around in the grass, as though it were playing. It was an orange popsicle, maybe a little larger than an ordinary one. It seemed to be alive, and—this is the unbelievable part—it was beautiful. I know that seems idiotic, to say a popsicle can be beautiful, but this one was. It was not that it was much different from thousands of popsicles I'd seen—except for the amazing light that seemed to come from it. It was beautiful in a way nothing I had ever seen or thought of was beautiful.

"Unusual, isn't it?" Borgel said.

I wanted to laugh. Or cry. I knew I could never figure out what was causing all these strong feelings in me. I wanted to stay there, looking at the shining Popsicle forever. It gave me shivers and made me feel warm, the way you feel when you're bathed with sunlight.

"Uncle Borgel, what? . . . I mean, why? . . . I mean, it's got some power. I can feel it. It isn't bad. It's good. I don't understand what I'm feeling."

"It's love, sonnyboy," Borgel said. "You're feeling what the Popsicle is putting forth. Energy and love, and a whole lot of it. That's why I never worry. It's impossible to persuade anybody of it until they see it for themselves, but most of the big things in the universe—like that beautiful little Popsicle— are like that."

"Most things in the universe love us?"

"That's what I've observed," Borgel said, thoughtfully nibbling a fig bar.

"Gee."

"Yeh, nice isn't it? Now wait. Pretty soon the Popsicle is going to be sure we don't have any hostile feelings."

"Then what?" I asked.

"Who knows? Wait and see."

We waited. Pretty soon the Popsicle came closer to us.

The closer it got, the more I liked it. It was wonderful watching the Popsicle move around in the grass. It was like dancing. When it came closer still, it was like dancing and music. Also like a light show. Also like hearing music. Wonderful music. It was also like riding a ride at an amusement park. The Popsicle was dancing all around us, but it felt as though we were moving, dancing with it.

I also felt that all of a sudden I knew a lot of things I never knew before, strange things that were hard to put into words. I felt that I was part of something larger than I could have even imagined a few minutes before—something that included everything and everyone that existed or had ever existed or ever would exist. I felt that the universe was wise, and as part of the universe, I was wise, too.

"This is the greatest thing that ever happened to me," I said to Borgel.

"You bet, sonnyboy," Borgel said. "What's more, once it starts happening, it never really stops."

"That's a little scary," I said. "About all I can do is sit here with my jaw hanging open. I don't know if I could handle it going on all the time."

"Oh, it doesn't go on all the time like this," Borgel said. "Most of the time, it's just a little vibration you're aware of— but you're always partly aware. Just being this close to something like that Popsicle is a little intense."

"And yet, we're able to carry on this normal conversation while all that power is going on," I said.

"We always do everything while all that power is going on," Borgel said. "Only most people don't notice it."

"How can they not notice it?" I asked. "It's like ten orchestra concerts, six fireworks displays, an earthquake, and a rock concert all at once."

"As I said, it isn't usually this obvious," Borgel said. "But it's pretty obvious. There is no limit to what most people don't notice. Look, it's moving away."

The Popsicle was skipping away into the distance. I really loved that Popsicle. I'd have thought I'd be sorry to see it go, but I wasn't. I somehow knew that it would always be with me in some way or other.

"Boy!" I said. "That's remarkable."

"I'm glad you got to experience it," Borgel said. "You'll be a better person now that you know a little more about how things really are."

"Freddie's mistaken if he thinks he can catch that thing," I said.

"Maybe we're mistaken about Freddie," Borgel said. "Anyway, you see why I'm not worried."

27

We sat on the top of the hill, nibbling the last of the fig bars. I was thinking about what I had seen and experienced. It was quiet and the sun was shining.

I was different than I had been before I saw the Popsicle. I wasn't a whole lot different—I still felt like me—but something had changed, I was sure of that. I noticed that things looked different to me. Colors were different. It was as if things had not been in full color before, and now they were. And I felt something inside me that I hadn't been aware of before. It was like a place in the middle of me, quiet and active both at once.

"So?" Borgel said. "Now do you understand everything?"

"I feel like I do," I said.

"Yetz?"

"But I don't."

"Good. Poifect. Maybe you have some questions?"

"Yes."

"What?"

"Is the Popsicle God?"

"Sure."

"It is?"

"Everything is. Everything is God."

"I knew that," I said. But now I knew it better. "So let me get it straight, just to be sure."

"Okay," Borgel said.

"The Popsicle is a . . . a . . ."

"Manifestation."

"Manifestation . . . of some sort of great power."

"Yep," Borgel said, shaking the last fig bar crumbs out of the cellophane bag into his mouth.

"You say there are a number of these."

"Correct. I heard there are twenty-six of them, but it doesn't matter. There could only be one, there could be more."

"It doesn't have to be a popsicle—it could appear as anything. It's just a popsicle sort of by accident."

"And because a popsicle is as good a way for us to see it as anything else."

"And this Popsicle sort of . . . well, watches over everything, and gives everything the power to work and exist and do stuff."

"Yaas," Borgel said, "I guess that's a good enough explanation."

"And it loves us."

"Certainly seems that way."

"Why?"

"Why?"

"Why does it love us?" I asked.

"Why not? I suppose that's just the sort of popsicle it is," Borgel said.

"It sure is neat," I said.

"I think so, too," Borgel said.

Fafner appeared. He seemed excited and out of breath.

"Fafner! Where's Freddie?" Borgel asked.

"He's in the forest," Fafner said.

"Something happened?"

"Hoo boy!" Fafner said.

"So why didn't you whistle? I told you to whistle."

"I told you, I can't whistle!" Fafner said. "I'm a dog, for Pete's sake!"

"You could have barked."

"Oh. Barked." Fafner looked embarrassed.

"Well, what is it?"

"He changed."

"Who changed? Freddie?" Borgel asked.

"Freddie. Changed."

"Changed how?"

"Changed all over," Fafner said. "He changed into a monster! A big one! A scary one!"

"No fooling!" Borgel said. "Did he change into something between an octopus and a gnarled old tree?"

"Yes! With eyestalks and really bad breath," Fafner said. "How did you know?"

"That's a Grivnizoid. That's how they look. They're good at disguising themselves—and you can see why they'd want to."

"Well, he's undisguised himself now," Fafner said.

"That must have surprised you," Borgel said. "I wonder why he did it."

"There's more," Fafner said.

"Tell us the more," Borgel said.

"We saw the Popsicle," Fafner said. "It was amazing! I tell

154   DANIEL PINKWATER

you, it was the nicest little Popsicle! I just loved it."

"We saw it, too," I said.

"Cutest, sweetest little Popsicle," Fafner said.

"Yeh, it's adorable," Borgel said. "How did Freddie like it?"

"Too much," Fafner said. "I think he may have eaten it."

"Whoops!" Borgel said.

28

"Oh no!" I shouted. "Then Freddie, a Grivnizoid, is the most powerful thing in the universe!"

"You're sure he ate it?" Borgel asked.

"Not sure," Fafner said. "I didn't want to get too close. In fact, I was busy running away. But it looked like that—and there were some very ugly noises."

"I'll bet there were," Borgel said.

"We're doomed," I said.

"Never say doomed," Borgel said.

"What should I say?" I asked.

"Say 'in terrible trouble,'" Borgel said. "But it remains to be seen whether we are. Let's go see."

"I was going to suggest we try to swim to shore," Fafner said.

"No, I think we'd better find out what's been going on," Borgel said.

We started down the hill. Near the beach we ran into Glugo, with about fifteen other apes.

"Glugo!" I shouted.

"Where's the little guy?" Glugo asked.

"We think he's a Grivnizoid," Borgel said.

"That's what I was afraid of," Glugo said. "That's why I went for help."

"Who are these apes?" Borgel asked.

"These are the members of the Greater Hades Motorcycle Club," Glugo said. "They're tough guys. I'll introduce you later. Now, we'd better find the Grivnizoid before he figures out that the Great Popsicle is on the far side of the river."

"There's a problem about that," Borgel said.

"What?"

"When last seen, the Popsicle was here, on the island."

"Zeus!" Glugo said, slapping his forehead with the palm of his hand. "Now we're in terrible trouble!"

"See?" Borgel said to me. To Glugo he said, "Fafner was the last one to see them. We were just going to have a look."

"Let's go!"

Borgel and Glugo and the members of the ape motorcycle club and I followed Fafner toward the forest. When we got there it was deathly quiet.

We followed Fafner, who was walking on tiptoe. We all walked on tiptoe, too, and whispered.

"This could be bad," Glugo whispered.

"Let's wait and see," Borgel whispered back.

"They were right around here somewhere," Fafner whispered.

There was nothing in sight.

"Spread out," Glugo whispered to the members of the G.H.M.C. "No, stay together—keep a sharp lookout and don't make any noise."

We tiptoed through the forest, keeping a sharp lookout and not making any noise.

Then we saw it! In a clearing, a little distance away,

we saw what had to be Freddie. My first Grivnizoid.

Keep in mind that in my travels in space and time, I had already encountered a Bloboform, an Amorphoid Fleshopod, and quite a number of life-forms which would appear to the average person to be scary, dangerous, and nauseating. The Grivnizoid beat them all. By a light year. It was huge. It was powerful-looking. It seemed alert, and it was built for combat.

"I have to tell you," Borgel whispered to Glugo, "Fafner thinks Freddie may have eaten the Popsicle."

"Buddha!" Glugo whispered between his teeth. "I shudder to think what that could mean for intelligent life-forms everywhere."

We were creeping closer to the monstrous thing. I didn't know why we were doing that. What we should have been doing would have been to run the other way as fast as we could. There wasn't any question that the Grivnizoid could eat the sixteen gorillas, Borgel, Fafner, and me for lunch. The only question was, was it powerful enough to have eaten the Popsicle?

"The only question is," Glugo said, "is it powerful enough to have eaten the Popsicle?"

"Let's find out," Borgel said. He stood up straight, walked directly toward the Grivnizoid, stopped just a few yards from it, and shouted, "Hey, Freddie! Did you eat the Popsicle?"

The Grivnizoid turned slowly toward Borgel. Only then did I see its face. I wished I hadn't. It moved almost like some enormous plant, or as though it were underwater. From deep within the huge body, I heard a faint voice I recognized as Freddie's.

DANIEL PINKWATER

"Yes," it said.

"That was your plan, all along?" Borgel asked.

"Yes."

"Why did you want to do it?" Borgel asked.

"To get . . . power," the Grivnizoid said haltingly.

"So? Now how do you feel?" Borgel asked.

"Funny . . . you . . . should . . . ask," the Grivnizoid said. "Ordinarily . . . I . . . can . . . digest . . . anything."

"And this time?"

"Uurrp," the Grivnizoid belched.

Borgel turned to the rest of us. "Come closer, gentlemen—and apes. I suggest we sit quietly and watch while Freddie digests his snack."

Glugo whispered in Borgel's ear, "It seems weak. Maybe this would be a good time to attack it."

"I strongly advise you to do no such thing," Borgel said. "Just sit down and watch for a while."

The apes, Borgel, Fafner, and I sat in a semicircle on the forest floor while Freddie the Grivnizoid appeared to be struggling with a monumental case of indigestion.

We said nothing. Now and then the Grivnizoid burped.

Time passed.

As we sat, watching, I had plenty of time to study Freddie in his Grivnizoid form. As I said, he was hideous, a complete departure from the form in which I'd known him up to now, which was on the cute side. The fact that as a Grivnizoid he was dealing with profound gastric distress didn't make his appearance any more pleasant.

And yet, I found I was getting used to him. After a time, I

even found that I didn't have to avert my eyes occasionally, or concentrate on not being sick. In fact, a little while later, I was amazed to realize that I was beginning to actually like his looks.

The apes seemed to be more comfortable, too. Their expressions had softened, and they were looking at Freddie with something approaching pleasure.

Fafner had gone to sleep, with a peaceful look on his face, and Borgel was quite calm, humming little tunes to himself.

"You know," I said to him, "this is crazy, but I can't help feeling that Freddie isn't such a bad guy."

"No, he really isn't," Borgel said. "Keep sitting a while, and you'll see something good."

Freddie was feeling better, I could tell. I was glad he was finally getting over his upset stomach. This struck me as weird because, after all, I had come to love the little Popsicle so much—but then, I loved Freddie, too. That last thought tripped me up. "Loved Freddie?" How truly bizarre.

But it was so. I realized the others were feeling the same thing.

Freddie was feeling fine now. He was up on his tentacles, sort of hopping around. It was grotesque, but at the same time, a pleasure to watch. He was also looking quite . . . well, pretty. There was a fascinating glow coming from him.

I got it. "Well, I'll be doggoned," I said to Borgel. "Freddie has turned into what the Popsicle was."

"Absotoomlutely," Borgel said. "What, you thought anything else could happen?"

Freddie was up and dancing now. It was the same dance

the Popsicle had done. Actually it was a little better, because Freddie, with all those tentacles, could do some moves the Popsicle couldn't. The apes had all caught on, too. It was the whole performance Borgel and I had seen on the hilltop, all over again.

"It's just as good as before!" I said to Borgel.

"Better," Borgel said. "Just think, now the wonderful energy thing is someone who was once a personal friend of ours."

"Hey, Freddie!" I shouted. "What does it feel like?"

But he was too involved in being a supremely powerful energy bundle to be able to answer, and soon after that, he pranced away into the forest.

Glugo and the members of the ape motorcycle club were deliriously happy.

"So," Glugo said. "We didn't need to protect the Popsicle after all."

"Nah," Borgel said. "It's more like the other way around."

"Well, come on back with us to the Blue Moon Rest," Glugo said. "We'll have a party."

The party was still going on when Borgel, Fafner, and I said good-bye to Milly, Glugo, and the G.H.M.C., and drove off in the Dorbzeldge.

In the Dorbzeldge I asked Borgel, "So Freddie will just go on being a Popsicle—I mean a whatever he is?"

"Probably for a long time," Borgel said. "Until he changes. Everything changes. One thing is sure—not many creatures will try to eat him."

"Was that what he wanted?" I asked. "I mean, when he

wanted to get the power of the Popsicle, did he know this would happen to him?"

"Probably not," Borgel said. "I always thought he didn't have a very clear idea of what the Popsicle was, but he does now, hee hee hee."

"I'm going to take a nap," I said.

"Good idea," Borgel said. "I'll drive awhile."

I slept right past the Gates of Hell, and the two-dimensional monochrome state of existence. In fact, I didn't wake up until we were in a place I recognized.

"Hey!" I said, "we're right near Hapless Toad's place."

"So we are," Borgel said. "Let's stop in and see him."

We drove up the long path through the forest until we came to the round building. Everything was the same, including Hapless Toad sleeping in his old car.

"Fifty zlotys to go in, and the dog stays in the car," he said.

"Hapless Toad, don't you remember us?" I asked.

"Sure I remember you," Hapless Toad said. "What do you think, that entitles you to a discount?"

"Why'd you want to see him again?" I asked Borgel.

"Well, I really wanted to see the replica," Borgel said.

We paid Hapless Toad our hundred zlotys and walked up to the building which housed the replica. The sign had been changed. It now read, THE GREAT GRIVNIZOID.

Inside was a life-size replica of Freddie.

"How is this possible?" I asked Borgel.

"Ask the Grivnizoid," Borgel said.

"How long have you been a Grivnizoid?" I asked the replica.

DANIEL PINKWATER

"I have always been a Grivnizoid," the computer replica said.

"But there used to be a statue of a popsicle here," I said.

"Is that a question?"

". . . wasn't there?" I added.

"Yes."

"So how come it's changed?"

"A temporal adjustment," the replica said. "You know that Napoleon was a little shrimpish guy, right? Well imagine that some being went back in time, and changed him to an eight-foot giant. Well, if that happened . . ."

"I get it," I said to Borgel. "Let's go."

Outside I said to Hapless Toad, "How do you like the replica now that it's a Grivnizoid?"

"It's always been a Grivnizoid," Hapless Toad said.

We got back into the Dorbzeldge.

"Well, where to next?" Borgel asked.

"Home!" Fafner said. "I've been missing all my favorite TV shows."

Borgel turned to me. "What do you say, Mr. Experienced Time Tourist; you ready to go home for a while?"

"For a while," I said.

YOBGORGLE

Mystery Monster of Lake Ontario

1

This is about the time I lived for two weeks in a motel in Rochester, New York, with my Uncle Mel, and what happened to me while I was there.

My parents had gone to Europe for six weeks. They had been talking about going since before I was born. My mother always said they would never really go. She said they just talked about it, but they never went. She said probably I'd be all grown up, and they'd be old and gray before they ever took a trip to Europe. Then they won a contest! My mother cut a coupon out of a newspaper, and sent it in with a label from a jar of low-calorie, low-cholesterol, imitation chicken fat, and they won the grand prize—six weeks in fourteen European countries, all expenses paid, deluxe air-conditioned buses, meals and tips included—for two. The second prize was a home videotape machine. I would have liked it better if they had won that, because I could have started a collection of science-fiction movies. But they won the trip, and off they went—and off I went, to spend six weeks with my Uncle Mel.

Which was not so bad. Uncle Mel isn't married, and he lives in an apartment about two blocks away from our house in Cliffside Park, New Jersey. So really nothing would be changed—I'd see my friends and do all the same things. The only difference would be that I'd live with my Uncle Mel, which meant that I could stay up late and have pizza and hamburgers just about every day. Also, Uncle Mel goes skeet shooting on weekends, and he said that he would take me with him and let me shoot his shotgun. So it promised to be a pretty good summer. And my parents had promised to bring me all kinds of good souvenirs from Europe. It would have been better, of course, if they'd won the videotape machine—but you can't have it all your way.

Then Uncle Mel found out that he was going to have to go to Rochester, New York, for two weeks to take a course. He has a job selling and installing these food vending machines. They have ones that sell coffee, and ones that sell ice cream, and ones that sell sandwiches, and lately, ones with little microwave ovens in them, so you can get a hot corned-beef sandwich wrapped in cellophane, or a frankfurter. Uncle Mel's company wanted him to go to Rochester, New York, to learn to operate a new type of machine that has freeze-dried chemical foods in it. When you push the button, after depositing your coins, the freeze-dried food, which is in little cellophane envelopes, gets water injected into the envelope, and then it gets mushed around, and then it gets microwaved. It all comes from space technology. So if you wanted, say, a bowl of chili with crackers, you'd deposit your coins, push the button for chili with crackers, and this cellophane envelope of reddish powder that has a shelf-life of sixty years, without refrigeration, gets injected, mixed, mushed, microwaved, and served up in a little styrofoam cup. Same thing with the crackers.

DANIEL PINKWATER

Uncle Mel lives on nothing but junk food. On his *birthday* he eats a Greaso-Whammy burger from McTavish's — that's his favorite fast-food chain. He hasn't eaten anything off a real plate in years — just cardboard and plastic — and even *he* can't stand the stuff that comes out of those machines. He says he doesn't know who eats it. Nobody knows, he says. They just come around every couple of months to fill up the machines, and some of the stuff has been sold.

Anyway, the new freeze-dried, mix, mush and microwave machine was supposed to be real complicated, and Uncle Mel was going to have to go up to Rochester, New York, where the factory is, and take a two-week course in how the thing was put together, and how to fix it, and how to work it. The company was going to pay all the expenses, his room, train fare, meals — the whole works.

Since my parents had already left when Uncle Mel got the news, he decided that he'd better take me along. "Eugene," he said, "have you ever wanted to see Rochester, New York?" I told him that it wasn't a place I had always longed to see — but I hadn't traveled much, and I was in favor of the idea. Uncle Mel said that was good, because I didn't have any choice anyhow.

We took the train. Uncle Mel said it was so that I could see the country. That was a lie. Actually, Uncle Mel is deathly afraid of airplanes, ever since he cut himself with one of those little plastic knives with serrated edges they give you with your meal on airplanes. Also, he hates airplane food. On the train, they have a sort of fast-food counter, and you can get a microwaved hamburger or a powdered scrambled-egg sandwich. Uncle Mel gets nervous when he doesn't have access to junk food. The fact is, the stuff they give you on airplanes is too classy for him.

The train ride was pretty good. We sat right next to the fast-food section, and by the time we got to Rochester, Uncle Mel had tried everything they had. The trip was supposed to take seven hours, but it took nine because they were repairing the tracks. Uncle Mel decided that the best thing they served was microwaved hot pastrami on a rye roll. He made notes about the junk food in a little book he always carries. Uncle Mel says that the best thing that can happen to you is to be really interested in your work. As a natural glutton and junk-food junkie, Uncle Mel is truly a happy man with the job he has.

I enjoyed the train ride. For a long time we ran right along the Hudson River. The conductor came through every now and then and told things about the places we were passing. He'd read up on the history of every place his train passed. He'd tell us that the big house on the right was built by colonel so-and-so in eighteen-oh-eight, and he died and left it to his sister, who married Mr. Such-and-such, and later it was bought by the famous Whooziz family who built the railroad.

It was interesting to listen to what the conductor said and look out the window. We went through a lot of forests and farmland and passed through little old-looking towns. I had brought a lot of comic books with me to read on the trip, but I didn't read one. I just looked out the windows and felt the rocking and rumbling of the train and counted the number of sandwiches Uncle Mel ate. He had eleven. There were nine kinds of sandwiches offered on the train, and he had two extra microwaved hot pastramis on rye rolls.

It was getting dark when we arrived in Rochester. We went straight to the motel. I couldn't tell much about the city from the taxi ride from the station. In the motel, I checked out the color TV while Uncle Mel went out to look for a fast-food place. He came back with a bunch of Greaso-Whammies in a paper bag, and some milk shakes. I ate a Greaso-Whammy. Uncle Mel ate three. Then we watched a movie about cowboys and went to sleep.

2

It was hot. It was already eighty-two degrees in Rochester when Uncle Mel and I went to McTavish's for breakfast. We both had eggs McTavish—a poached egg with olives and cheese on a taco shell. I had a cola. Uncle Mel had coffee. Then he asked me if I knew how to get back to the motel, gave me two dollars for lunch, told me he'd be back to take me out to supper at about six-thirty, and left for the factory where they make Mix-and-Mush Microwave Food Vendors.

I finished my cola and thought about what I'd like to do for the rest of the day. People were going to work, stopping into McTavish's for a fast breakfast. They got on and off of buses. Everybody looked sort of bleary-eyed, as though they hadn't slept well during the hot night. I went out into the street. There were a lot of tall buildings and people hurrying. The sun was bright. The sidewalks had this glittery stuff mixed in with the concrete, so that it was uncomfortable to keep your eyes down and uncomfortable to keep your eyes up. The day was going to be a scorcher, there was no doubt about it.

I wandered around the downtown area for a while. I looked in store windows and at the buildings. They were just buildings—nice, I suppose, but nothing very interesting. The best building in Rochester is this parking garage where the cars parks on spiral ramps. The whole thing looks like it's screwed into the ground. I wondered if they could really

172

make a building like that. When it got full of cars, they could just unscrew it a turn, and expose another level. There were two or three movie houses—I had considered going to a movie to get into the air-conditioning—but none of them were showing movies that a kid is allowed to see.

There was this underground thing, a sort of mall, I suppose, in the basement of one of the big office buildings. It had stores in it, and a weird thing like a clock or a sculpture that rotated slowly, and there were these cylinders that went around, and every hour they were supposed to open and you could see dolls representing different countries inside. It was altogether the dumbest-looking thing I've ever seen. Also in the underground mall there was a great big scale model of the White House on display—like a giant doll house. People were lined up to see it. It was sort of nice, I guess. I wasn't very interested. The only nice thing about the mall was that it was air-conditioned.

I walked around for a while, but I didn't see anybody my age—at least not on their own. There were kids with their mothers, going shopping, or going to the doctor—that sort of thing. Cliffside Park isn't far from New York City. You can see New York City across the river from some streets in Cliffside Park, and there's a bus that goes there—but I'm not allowed to go by myself. If I go to New York City, it's with some responsible adult, and it's on serious business of some kind. I don't get to hang out and meet any other kids. It was just the same in downtown Rochester. I hadn't really thought about it before I came, but it seemed entirely possible that I was going to be mostly alone for the whole two weeks.

I got tired of walking around the mall and went outside into the street. It was really hot! I looked at a clock on a building, and saw that it wasn't even ten o'clock yet. People were going to be falling dead from the heat before the day was over. I discovered that I was slightly lost. That wasn't much of a problem—just a matter of getting my bearings. There's a river running right through the middle of Rochester. It's called the Genesee River. It isn't much of a river compared to, say, the Hudson, but it makes it pretty much impossible to get lost in the middle of town. The motel we were staying at, a blue and white building, was right near the river.

After I found the river, I decided I'd go back to the motel. I was hot and bored. At least the motel room would be cool. I thought I might have a look at the comic books I had taken along on the train, and not read.

I'm a fairly fast reader, and it wasn't long before I finished all the comics. I had the TV running the whole time and flicked from channel to channel—there wasn't anything on. I made a trip to the soda machine, and the ice machine. I took a shower. It got to be noon. Lunch—that was something to do. I went outside to look for a place to eat. I didn't want to go to McTavish's because that was most likely where Uncle Mel was going to want to have supper. This trip to Rochester was turning out to be one big bore.

I thought that maybe I could get a model airplane kit to build in the motel room. That would keep me busy for a while. I had noticed a hobby section in a big department store I had walked through that morning. The truth is, I'm not all that crazy about building models—it's something I usually do when I'm sick in bed or there's absolutely nobody around to hang out with. I figured that I could probably put together at least twenty-five models while I was in Rochester. I thought about all this while I was walking around looking for a place to have lunch.

In among the modern buildings in downtown Rochester are some streets with real old buildings. I like the old buildings better than the new ones. They're smaller and darker and sort of friendlier. The new ones all look sort of dumb—except the spiral garage—I was getting to like that one better every time I saw it. In one of the streets with old buildings, I found a place called Bob's Beanery. It had a counter and stools and a tile floor and little hand-lettered signs all over the front of it telling what they had to eat that day. One of the signs said

BOB'S LAKE ONTARIO CHILI 65¢

SECOND BOWL FREE —

— CRACKERS AND BEVERAGE INCLUDED.

That looked like the best deal in the place. I studied the rest of the signs and couldn't find anything else that cheap. I went inside, climbed onto a counter stool, and asked for a bowl of Lake Ontario chili. I found out why they call it Lake Ontario chili. It was pretty watery. But it didn't taste too bad. I had the free second bowl, and a cola with it. There was one of those big electric fans in the place, the kind that stands on the floor and turns from side to side. Every time it turned in my direction it made little ripples on the surface of my Lake Ontario chili.

After lunch, I headed back toward the motel. I just couldn't think of anything else to do. This time I was walking on the opposite side of the street—the river side. Across this street, opposite the motel, was a big gray building. I hadn't paid much attention to it—I figured it was a post office or something like that. Now I noticed that it was the public library. I went up the stairs and through the door.

DANIEL PINKWATER

3

I had been in the Cliffside Park Public Library at home a few times. I went on a school trip there every year—they'd show us how to use the library and take us around on a sort of tour. Once I even checked out a couple of books and took them home. It's not that I don't read—I take a few books out of the school library, and I read comics, magazines, and sometimes the newspaper—I just never got around to using the public library much at home. The library at home is nothing like the one in Rochester, which, as I said, is a great big place, and looks like a post office.

I went through the doors into a sort of lobby, then through another doorway into a very large room. The ceiling was made out of little panels of glass, and daylight came through. It was very quiet. "The children's room is upstairs," a lady said to me. I went upstairs. I followed the signs that said CHILDREN'S ROOM.

The children's room was large, with lots of books, nice wood, tables and chairs, and a fireplace. Of course, there wasn't a fire going in it, because it was ninety-six degrees outside according to one of those temperature and time things on a big office building. No one was in the children's room at the time except for a lady sitting at a desk near the entrance. She noticed me coming in. "Did you know that there is a secret door in this room?" she said. "I'm not going to tell you where the secret door is or what is behind it," the lady at the desk said. "But you may look for the secret door and go through it."

I looked at the librarian. She didn't seem to be the sort of person who would play a trick on a kid. I looked around the room. It was a corner room—there were windows on two sides, so there wouldn't be a secret door there—there would be no place for it to lead.

Another wall ran along the hallway—so there would be no secret door there. That left the wall with the fireplace. I'd seen movies on TV where there is a secret door near the fireplace. Usually there is all sorts of fancy carving around the fireplace and the detective, or whoever it is in the movie, pushed a button that looks like part of the carving, and the secret door slides open. But this wasn't that sort of fireplace. There weren't any fancy carvings, just smooth stone. I sort of felt around the fireplace, but I couldn't find anything like a secret door. The other kind of secret door I've seen in movies is the kind where part of the bookshelves swings out on hinges. That made sense in a library. Sure enough, I saw some scratches on the floor in front of a section of bookshelves. When I got closer, I could see two hinges. I took hold of one of the shelves and pulled. The whole section of shelves swung out toward me, and revealed a low door—too low for a grown-up to go through without ducking.

The librarian had gotten up from her desk and come up behind me. "You've found the secret room," she said. "Shall we go in and see what is in it?" She ducked through the door, and I followed her. We entered a small room with a small

DANIEL PINKWATER

fireplace that backed up against the big one on the other side of the wall. There were some kid-sized chairs lined up in rows, and a grown-up sized stool off to one side of the fireplace. All around the room were glass cases with lots of dolls—strange ones, all sizes, and in different costumes.

"In the 1930s," the librarian said, "a school here in Rochester had a doll-exchange program with schools all over the world. The children here would send a typical American doll to a school in a foreign country, and the children there would send back a typical doll of their country. Later the whole collection was given to the library."

The dolls were sort of interesting, some of them; about the best ones were two Japanese dolls with all kinds of really lifelike details, elaborate clothing, hairdo, and so forth. I'm not all that interested in dolls, but some of these were very interesting, as I said before.

"We use this secret room as a story room," the librarian went on. "Of course, during the summer, we don't have story hours during the week. Sometimes, during the winter we have a fire in the fireplace."

"Would it be all right for me to come in here?" I asked the librarian. "I mean, if I wanted to, could I read in this room?"

"I don't see any reason why you shouldn't," the librarian said. "Of course, there aren't any reading tables in this room—but if you think you'd like to read here, please go right ahead."

I don't know why I asked her that. It wasn't such a special room—I mean, after you'd seen the dolls and had the experience of finding the secret door, it was just a room—but it was a secret room, and something about that appealed to me very much. It was just a nice place to be. And it wasn't as bright as the big children's room—the light that came through the window made the room seem as though it was cloudy outside, whereas actually it was blazing hot, and the sun made you squint.

The librarian went back to her desk, and I went out into the big children's room to find something to read. I closed the secret bookshelf door behind me. The librarian had told me to do that so that if any other kid came into the children's room for the first time, they could have the experience of looking for the secret door.

I found a book, an adventure story called *Howard Goldberg, Frontiersman*. It was a story about the first Orthodox Jewish Indian Scout and how he helped to open up the West in the early 1800s. I took the book into the secret room, settled down on the smooth, cool stone floor, and began to read. It was a pretty interesting book. It told about how Howard Goldberg ran away from home in Philadelphia, when he was just a young kid, to go out West and live with the Indians. He showed the Indians how to make bagels out of corn meal, and how to make pastrami from buffalo meat. He hunted bears and raccoons with the Indians, but he wouldn't eat them because they weren't kosher. Years later he met General Custer and told him he was making a big mistake, but nobody listened to him. It was a pretty good book, and it showed how people who belonged to different minorities helped build this country—for example, Howard Goldberg's best friend, who wasn't an Indian, was an Armenian prospector he met in Colorado.

By the time I finished the book, it was pretty late. I heard someone ringing a little bell, like a chime, and saying, "The library will close in fifteen minutes! The library will close in fifteen minutes!" I left the secret room, put my book on the corner of the librarian's desk, the way they told us to on our school trips to the library in Cliffside Park, and went outside.

4

I watched TV for a while, had a cola with ice from the ice machine, in one of the plastic glasses from the bathroom, and waited for Uncle Mel to come back. He arrived in a bad mood because he had had to sample all sorts of freeze-dried food from the mix-and-mush microwave machines at the factory. "I wouldn't feed that stuff to a cat," Uncle Mel said. "I don't know if I'm going to be able to eat my supper."

It was obvious that Uncle Mel was feeling under the weather, because he only had two Greaso-Whammies, a double order of french fries, and a double-thick shake at McTavish's that night. Then he wanted to go for a walk around downtown Rochester. At least it wasn't as hot as it had been earlier in the day. I had been all over the area, so I sort of took the lead and showed Uncle Mel what there was to see. He agreed that the spiral garage was the best thing in town.

"Did you find some things to do?" he wanted to know. I told him that I had spent the afternoon reading in the children's room of the public library. He thought that sounded like a good activity. I told him that it was O.K., but I hoped that I was going to find something else to do before I went through all the books in the place. Uncle Mel said that he would ask some of the guys at the factory if they knew of any interesting things for a kid to do. He also wanted to know if I'd like to come to the factory with him one day and see how everything was made. I wanted to know if I'd be expected to eat any of the slop from the freeze-dried, mix-and-mush microwave machine. "Well, you know, we have to be polite," Uncle Mel said. I told him I'd think it over.

We looked in a newspaper and found that a movie about a monster called Yobgorgle that's supposed to be real and lives in Lake Ontario was playing at a movie house in a shopping center not too far away. We took a taxi to the shopping center.

The movie was fair. It was a lot like the movie I saw one time about Bigfoot, the monster that's supposed to be real and lives in the North Woods. They had about fifteen seconds of film that might have been a sea monster, or it might have been a big fish or a guy in a monster suit or anything! They showed that fifteen seconds about ten times—regular speed, slow motion, extra slow motion, extra extra slow motion. In between they showed various people who claimed to have seen Yobgorgle, and they showed drawings that people who had supposedly seen Yobgorgle had made. Too bad none of the people who had seen Yobgorgle knew how to draw—all the drawings looked like a first-grader had done them, and all of them were different.

Then they showed professors in various laboratories talking about whether they thought Yobgorgle might really exist. There was this real heavy narration all through the movie: "DOES YARBORGLE EXIST? THIS MARINE BIOLOGIST, EQUIPPED WITH ALL THE MOST MODERN SCIENTIFIC DEVICES THINKS HE WILL FIND HIM." Then the movie showed this weirdo in a big rowboat with all kinds of ropes and nets and a thing for listening to fish, floating around in the lake.

Then the weirdo in the boat turned around to the camera, and took the pipe out of his mouth. The narrator said, "THIS MAN IS PROFESSOR AMBROSE McFWAIN OF THE PISCEAN DISCOVERY INSTITUTE IN ROCHESTER, NEW YORK. PROFESSOR McFWAIN TELLS OF HIS EXPERIENCES IN TRACKING THIS STRANGE MONSTER."

Professor Ambrose McFwain scratched his beard with the end of his pipe. "I think I may have actually heard Yobgorgle. One night I was rowing my research vessel in the vicinity of Irondequoit Bay. I had my earphones on, and the tape recorder attached to my supersonic listening device. I was recording the usual sounds of Lake Ontario on a summer evening. Then I heard something quite unusual. At first it sounded very much like a 1956 Chevy with bad valves that I used to own. Of course, there would be no way for a 1956 Chevy to be that far out in the lake.

"The sound was very clear and sounded as though it was near my boat. I took off my earphones and found that I could hear the sound much better. I was trolling a hydrophone—that's an underwater microphone—at fifteen feet, but this sound was coming from the surface! It was a very dark night. I couldn't see anything very clearly, but I thought I saw something dark on the surface of the water about fifty yards away. It sounded like a '56 Chevy, as I said, or a monster breathing. Those are the only two things it could have been. I reached for my special waterproof camera with infrared flash, but just as I got the thing up to my eye, I heard a splash, and the dark thing on the surface of the water disappeared. At the same moment, I flashed my picture. When it was developed, this is what I saw."

DANIEL PINKWATER

Professor Ambrose McFwain, of the Piscean Discovery Institute held up a snapshot—you couldn't make out anything but glare from the movie lights.

"As you can see," Professor Ambrose McFwain said, "the picture at first appears to be nothing but bubbles and lake mist, but if you look closely, you will see a faint red light— right here." He pointed with his pipe. "This could only be the tail light of a '56 Chevy or the eye of a monster. There is no explanation as to what a '56 Chevy would be doing that far out in the lake. So I believe the only reasonable explanation is that I had encountered some strange life-form in the lake. I believe that what I heard and almost saw and very nearly photographed that night was Yobgorgle."

Then the movie showed the fifteen seconds of film for the tenth time. Then it showed all of the people who had talked about their Yobgorgle experiences, and the drawings, and the shots of newspaper headlines, and the professors in their laboratories, and Ambrose McFwain in his rowboat, and the narrator said, "YOBGORGLE! IS IT A FOLKTALE OR IS IT A REALITY? WE HAVE SHOWN YOU THE FACTS—THE DECISION IS UP TO YOU."

Then the movie was over. Even with repeating everything four or five times, it still only ran a little over an hour and a half. Then there were four cartoons—old ones—and a short subject about boating in Australia, and the house lights came on.

Uncle Mel spent some time looking at the food vending machines in the lobby of the movie house while we waited for the taxi he had called to come and pick us up.

We got to McTavish's just before closing time. The movie apparently helped Uncle Mel get his appetite back because he got into some heavy cheeseburger eating. They were mopping up McTavish's when we left. We walked back to the motel.

Before going to sleep, we watched a talk show on television. One of the advertisements they ran in between was for the movie we'd just seen. The ad was a lot better than the movie—it had all the good stuff in the movie in it. Also the ad only took about thirty seconds, while the movie was about one hundred and eighty times as long, and didn't contain any more information.

DANIEL PINKWATER

5

The next morning, after eating my egg McTavish with Uncle Mel, I headed straight for the library. The day was going to be another scorcher, and I didn't feel like doing any exploring. I wanted to get inside the cool library as soon as possible.

The lady was sitting at the desk. She said hello to me. I asked her if she had any books about Yobgorgle. She didn't know what Yobgorgle was—I guess she didn't watch much television or go to the movies. I told her that Yobgorgle was a monster that lived in Lake Ontario.

The librarian said that she might have a book on sea monsters. I went with her, and together we looked it up in the card catalog.

"Here it is," she said. "*Great Sea Monsters I Have Known* by Professor Ambrose McFwain of the Piscean Discovery Institute, right here in Rochester."

It was by the same guy—the weird guy in the boat—the one with the beard that I had seen in the movie the night before! I took the book and went into the secret room to read it. It was a pretty interesting book, but Professor Ambrose McFwain didn't really give any proof for the things he said in it. He talked about the Loch Ness monster. He said he had seen it clear as you like, but when he tried to take its picture, he forgot and left the lens cap on his camera. Another monster he wrote about was Moby Dick, the great white whale.

He said that Moby Dick was real and that Herman Melville, who wrote the story about him, had seen him, but he didn't give any proof of that either. Then he went on to write about a monster called Ogo Pogo—no proof—and about his expedition to find Tieholtsodi. Tieholtsodi was a sea monster mentioned in Navajo Indian myths. According to the myths, Tieholtsodi lived in the Eastern Water.

Professor Ambrose McFwain figured out that the Navajos, when they said Eastern Water, meant Lake Michigan. So he went to Chicago and started asking people if they had ever heard anything about a monster living in the lake. He didn't get anywhere, but in Evanston, Illinois, he found a bunch of people who said they had seen a monster. They called it Knob Ears. Ambrose McFwain decided that this must be the same Tieholtsodi mentioned in the Navajo myths.

He hired a boat and a guide named Reynold, who claimed to have seen Knob Ears a number of times. They spent several days floating around Lake Michigan before dawn, looking for Knob Ears. This time Professor McFwain did find the monster and actually got his pictures.

But on the way home, Reynold, the guide, went crazy in the boat. He took off his shoes and stood up and started to dance around and mutter all sorts of strange things. As a result, the boat was swamped, the camera and film were lost, and Professor McFwain and Reynold arrived back at the dock very wet.

It seemed to me that Professor Ambrose McFwain had very little luck in his sea-monster tracking. But he kept at it.

DANIEL PINKWATER

He was determined. He said that the one greatest deed of his career would be finding Yobgorgle. He had moved to Rochester, New York, to be near Lake Ontario, and started the Piscean Discovery Institute, which was supposed to encourage all sincere sea-monster finders everywhere, but was primarily for the purpose of finding Yobgorgle.

I don't know if any of this would have been as interesting to me if I had read about it back home in Cliffside Park, but here in Rochester where the search for Yobgorgle was actually going on, after seeing the not-very-good movie about Yobgorgle, and then finding the book by Professor McFwain—I was getting sort of interested in the whole project. It hadn't taken long to read the book by Professor McFwain. There were lots of pictures—old ones of what people imagined sea monsters looked like—and there was very large type and a lot of white space. I looked at the clock in the big children's room when I had finished the book. It was only ten-thirty. I still had the whole day ahead of me. I really didn't feel like reading another book right away, so I put my copy of *Great Sea Monsters I Have Known* on the corner of the librarian's desk and went downstairs.

I stood for a while in the lobby of the library. It was too early to go to Bob's Beanery for lunch. The egg McTavish still lay in my stomach, like an undissolved glob of plastic. I didn't feel bored now so much as anxious. I wanted to do something, but I didn't know quite what it was. In the lobby of the library there was a telephone booth. Outside it on a slanting shelf was a telephone book. I looked up the Piscean Discovery Institute.

"See McFwain Foundation," read the telephone book.

I looked up the McFwain Foundation. "See McFwain Institute," it said in the telephone book.

I looked up the McFwain Institute. "See Professor Ambrose McFwain," it said.

I looked up Professor Ambrose McFwain. "See McFwain Toy Company," the book said.

I looked up the McFwain Toy Company. There was a telephone number. I went into the phone booth, dropped in a dime, and dialed the number.

The dime clicked. The number rang. Someone answered.

"Hello. E. J. Kupeckzky Thought Factory," the voice on the telephone said.

"Excuse me," I said. "I was calling the McFwain Toy Company."

"This is the McFwain Toy Company," the voice said.

"Oh—well, actually," I said, "I was calling the Piscean Discovery Institute."

"This is also the Piscean Discovery Institute," said the voice.

"Uh—I was wondering—I wanted to talk to Professor McFwain."

"You *are* talking to Professor McFwain. What can I do for you?"

I didn't really know what Professor Ambrose McFwain could do for me. I guessed he was a very busy man, what with the Piscean Discovery Institute, the McFwain Foundation, the McFwain Institute, the McFwain Toy Company, and the E. J. Kupeckzky Thought Factory to run. I didn't know what to say to him. For a second I thought of just hanging up, but that would have been too rude. "Uh—I was—uh—I read your book. . . ."

"Which one?"

"I read *Great Sea Monsters I Have Known*, and I saw that movie you're in. . . ."

"How'd you like the movie?"

"Well, uh, not too much. I thought it was pretty long and it just kept repeating the same information over and over again."

"Are you a fellow scientist?"

"Well, actually, I'm just a. . . ."

"Of course, you are," said Professor Ambrose McFwain. "Tell you what—I'd love to talk over scientific matters with you, but I'm just going to duck out for a bite. Why don't you join me for lunch? You know where the downtown branch of McTavish's is, don't you?"

"I had breakfast there," I said.

"I hope you don't mind eating there twice in one day," Professor Ambrose McFwain said.

"I expected to eat there twice today," I said.

"Good for you! You know what you like, and you stick with it. I'll meet you there in fifteen minutes." Then Professor Ambrose McFwain hung up.

6

I arrived at McTavish's in less than fifteen minutes. I went to the counter, got a Greaso-Junior and a thick shake, and sat down where I could see the door. I wondered why Professor Ambrose McFwain wanted to have lunch with me. Maybe he didn't realize that I was a kid. Maybe he just thought I was someone with a high voice. Maybe he thought I was a lady. That would be embarrassing. Maybe he thought he was going to have lunch with a lady. Sometimes people call up at home to try and sell my mother encyclopedias or home delivery of the newspaper, and they think I'm her. Uncle Mel says my voice will change later. I hope it doesn't change to a voice like his—it's higher than mine and sort of squeaky—no, whistley. Uncle Mel's voice sounds like a boat whistle.

I was thinking about all this stuff when Professor Ambrose McFwain came in. He looked just the way he had in the movie. I got up. "Excuse me, Professor McFwain," I said.

"Ah, you're the young man I'm supposed to have lunch with," Professor McFwain said. "I see you've gotten your food already—good idea, avoid the lunch rush—that's why I come here no later than eleven o'clock. I'll just get a few things and join you. I won't be a minute."

Professor Ambrose McFwain was back in a little while with a tray piled high with everything McTavish's sells. "This guy would get along fine with my Uncle Mel," I thought.

"I'm Eugene Winkleman," I said.

"Delighted," Professor Ambrose McFwain said, and dived into his tray of paper and plastic-wrapped junk food. While he ate, every now and then he'd say, "Mmmmmmmm," or "Aaaah!" or "Superb!"

When Professor McFwain had finished packing away a meal that would have been worthy of Uncle Mel, he rolled all the napkins and paper and plastic wrappers into a big ball between his palms. "Now," he said, "let's get down to business. I'll come straight to the point and tell you that there are no other candidates, and you've got the job as my assistant for two weeks, beginning tomorrow."

"The job as your assistant?" I was a little bewildered, but when he said it, I realized that somehow or other that *was* the sort of thing I had in mind.

"Yes, don't you want to help me find Yobgorgle?" Professor McFwain said. "It's been two weeks since I ran the newspaper ad for a volunteer to help me—and frankly, you're the first applicant."

"I'll have to ask Uncle Mel," I said.

"Who's Uncle Mel?"

"My uncle."

"Well, let's ask him."

Professor Ambrose McFwain gave me a card with the address of the McFwain Toy Company on it. "Just drop by at seven o'clock," he said. "If that's convenient for your uncle. We'll talk it over then." He looked at his watch. "Well, well, I've got to run. I've got an order for six thousand Yobgorgle dolls to get out."

"You sell Yobgorgle dolls?" I asked.

"Hottest new toy of the year," Professor Ambrose McFwain said.

"But nobody has ever seen Yobgorgle," I said.

"That's not true," Professor McFwain said. "Lots of people have seen Yobgorgle. It's just that nobody reliable has ever seen it. You and I are going to be the first reputable scientists to see it."

"I'm not a reputable scientist. I'm only a kid," I said.

"Never say that!" Professor McFwain said. "Mozart wrote great music when he was three. Thomas Edison invented all sorts of things when he was only a boy. And I myself invented the dill pickle when I was six years old. You never know what you can do until you try."

"You are the inventor of the dill pickle?" I asked.

"I have that honor," Professor Ambrose McFwain said.

"Wow!" I said.

"I thought you'd be impressed," Professor McFwain said. "I'll see you at seven tonight."

Professor Ambrose McFwain hurried out of McTavish's, still holding the ball of wrappers and napkins between his palms. He was obviously as crazy as a loon, but I liked him. He didn't make anything special of my being a kid—I mean, he treated me like a regular person.

I still had quite a bit of time until Uncle Mel came back to the motel. I decided that if I was going to be a scientist's assistant, I might as well do some extra reading, sort of research to prepare for my job.

I used the big card catalog downstairs in the adult

department. I found three books by Professor Ambrose McFwain, *How I Invented the Dill Pickle—and How the Idea Was Stolen from Me; My Expedition to the Lost Civilization of Waka-Waka*; and *The Research Scientist and Monster-Hunter's Handbook*.

The first two books were out, the librarian in the adult department told me, but they had *The Research Scientist and Monster-Hunter's Handbook*. I asked the librarian in the adult department if I could take the book upstairs and read it in the children's room. She said it would be all right.

I took the book upstairs into the secret room. One nice thing about Professor Ambrose McFwain's book—they were easy to read. This one had big print, lots of white space, and lots of pictures. The book was full of advice for monster-hunters and researchers. It started with a chapter about photography:

PHOTOGRAPHING MONSTERS

It is a good idea to take pictures of the various monsters you will be tracking. Any sort of camera will do, but certain rules should be observed. First, take film along. There is nothing as frustrating as coming upon a monster, hitherto unknown to science, in some uncharted place like the Arctic tundra, the Amazon River basin, or the Gobi Desert, only to discover that you don't have any film. The author has learned this "trick of the trade" from painful experience in all those places.

Next, the best camera in the world will not take a suitable picture if you forget to take the lens cap off. Learn from the tragic experience of this author—take off that lens cap!

Another thing which can go wrong with photographing monsters is to accidentally let your thumb or finger or beard get in the way of the lens when taking the picture. This, too, has happened to the author in the heat of the chase.

There is a lot that can go wrong with photographic equipment. Lack of film, leaving the lens cap on, getting one's thumb or beard in front of the lens—this will explain to the reader why there are so few pictures of monsters available.

The book went on with good advice like that for scientists and monster-hunters. There was a long chapter on what kind of shoes to wear when going after monsters (loose); what kind of bags to put your lunch in (waterproof); how to approach a monster in the wild (with caution). It was a very informative book. I liked it better than Professor McFwain's other book because it got right to the point and gave helpful suggestions. After reading it, I felt that I was really ready to help Professor McFwain look for the monster Yobgorgle.

When Uncle Mel got back to the motel that night, he was really bugged. "Guess what they made me eat from that horrible machine," he said. I couldn't guess. "Salad!" he said.

"Freeze-dried, reconstituted, mixed-and-mushed chef's salad! With Italian dressing! I thought I was going to die!"

"Did it taste like salad?" I asked.

"It tasted exactly like salad!" he said. "I hate salad!"

"I wonder how they do the lettuce," I said.

"It's an engineering miracle," Uncle Mel said.

"Look," I said, "I've been offered a part-time job, and I want to take it. It only lasts two weeks, so I could do it while we're here."

"A job? What sort of job?" Uncle Mel asked.

"It's helping a scientist—I think he may be a mad scientist—look for a sea monster that lives in Lake Ontario."

"It sounds educational," Uncle Mel said, "I guess your parents would approve."

"He wants us to come to his office at seven o'clock," I said. "He gave me a card with his address."

"O.K.," Uncle Mel said. "After supper. I really need a few Greaso-Whammies to get the taste of that salad out of my mouth."

7

Professor McFwain's office was in the basement of a building on North Water Street, right near the river. Uncle Mel asked the desk clerk at the motel how to get there, and we walked. It was just a couple of blocks from McTavish's. The rest of the building was a factory where they make clothes for fat guys. Uncle Mel, who must weigh two hundred and eighty pounds was glad to know about the factory. He said he might come back and get a suit.

There was a little sign near the steps to the basement door. It said McFWAIN TOY COMPANY, INC., and there was an arrow pointing down the stairs. At the bottom of the stairs were all kinds of waste paper and garbage that had blown down there. There was a metal door, painted gray with big round rivets in it, and a doorbell button. Uncle Mel pushed the button.

"Just a minute! I'm coming." I could hear Professor McFwain's voice from somewhere inside the building.

The door opened. There was Professor McFwain. He was wearing a fancy bathrobe with a dragon embroidered on the pocket. When he turned to lead us into the building, we could see that there was also a dragon embroidered on the back. The bathrobe was about five sizes too big for Professor McFwain. I guess it had been made in the fat guys' clothing factory upstairs.

"Welcome to my toy company, my research facility and my humble home," Professor McFwain said. "You see, I have a very economical arrangement with the company that owns this building. In return for my services as night watchman, I get the use of my basement apartment and offices free. I also get a fabulous discount on clothes. Unfortunately, size 50 is the smallest they make."

He took off the dragon bathrobe. Underneath it he was wearing the same suit I had seen him in earlier that day. "You must be Uncle Mel," Professor McFwain said. "Here, try this on. I think it may fit you."

Uncle Mel tried on the bathrobe. He was obviously delighted with it.

"Please take it as a present," Professor McFwain said. "It didn't cost me a penny—it's a sample they made up and decided not to manufacture. I have a friend in the design department who lets me have things like this. It's brand-new. If you don't like the color, there are five or six others upstairs."

"No, bright red is fine," Uncle Mel said, "I've always wanted a bathrobe like this."

"I'm delighted to have met someone who's . . . uh . . . substantial enough to wear it," Professor McFwain said. "Now, here we are at my quarters."

All this time Professor Ambrose McFwain had been leading us through all sorts of dimly lit corridors, storerooms, boiler rooms, and similar stuff that you find in basements. He opened a door on which there was a sign reading McFWAIN TOY CO. We entered a large room with a big wooden table in the middle and shelves along the walls. On the shelves were green plastic dolls looking a little like a dragon with a bushy beard and three eyes.

"These are the Yobgorgle dolls," Professor McFwain said. "I'm making a fortune selling them. I have them made up in a factory in Iceland, and they're shipped here, and I distribute them. There's such a demand for them that I've shipped every one I've got, except these few that I keep for samples. I'm presently waiting for more. They'll be arriving from Iceland in about two weeks, which gives me some time to go out looking for the real Yobgorgle. That's where young Eugene comes in. I need a bright young fellow to go along with me, help with the research, and handle the boat while I take a few pictures. It's an opportunity not many young boys get."

"Now I know who you are!" Uncle Mel said. "You were in that movie we saw last night! You were the guy in the boat!"

"Quite right," Professor Ambrose McFwain said. "Now, if you'll excuse me, I think I hear the doorbell. I took the liberty of calling out for five double-giant pizzas with everything. I thought we might munch while we talk. I'll go answer the door. You'll find some gallon bottles of root beer in that little refrigerator; and if you don't mind, please put some ice in those glasses. I'll be right back."

When Professor McFwain had gone, Uncle Mel said, "He seems to be a really fine man, Eugene. I think you can learn a lot working as his assistant."

Naturally, Uncle Mel and Professor McFwain hit it off beautifully. Two born eaters and guzzlers, they ate four and a half double-giant pizzas with everything while they talked, and consumed a gallon and three-quarters of root beer. Professor McFwain wanted to hear all about the freeze-dried, microwave, mix-and-mush machine; and Uncle Mel wanted to hear all about Professor McFwain's toy business, the stories (all of which I had read in his book) about his career as a monster-hunter, and different junk food places in Rochester.

While they talked, I looked at maps of the shoreline of Lake Ontario, which Professor McFwain had marked with X's to show places where Yobgorgle had been sighted.

"About this monster-hunting," Uncle Mel asked. "I don't suppose there's any danger? I wouldn't want Eugene's parents to get mad at me—not that I expect anything will happen to him."

"Danger?" said Professor McFwain. "Danger? Sir, monster-hunting is the most dangerous occupation there is—there's no use denying it. Of course, with me, the boy will be as safe as anyone could be when tracking something which, I believe, will turn out to be better than a hundred yards long, and goodness knows how wild. By the way, you haven't got any use for a fancy cowboy suit, have you? They have one upstairs that was made for a famous country and western singer, but he went on a diet and they never delivered it."

"What sort of cowboy suit is it?" Uncle Mel asked.

"Oh, it's terrific!" Ambrose McFwain said. "It has all sorts of fancy Indian embroidery, and a hat that goes with it, and everything. I could ask my friend if they want to get rid of it."

"Well, I have sort of always wanted a cowboy suit," Uncle Mel said. "Nothing too loud, you understand, just something I could wear to a party."

"This one will be perfect for you," Professor McFwain said. "And about that other matter—don't worry."

"Don't worry?"

"Don't worry."

"Well, Professor, I feel sure that Eugene will have a really valuable educational experience working with you," Uncle Mel said. "And if they feel they don't need the cowboy suit. . . ."

"I'll send it along with Eugene," Professor McFwain said.

I had been worried for a while that Uncle Mel might decide that monster-hunting was too dangerous an occupation for a kid and not give me permission to go. But he liked Professor McFwain too much—and apparently he wanted that cowboy suit. Ordinarily, Uncle Mel just wore these rumpled-looking gray suits. I never knew he was interested in clothes. Maybe it's hard for fat guys to get nice clothes.

Back in the motel room, Uncle Mel spent a lot of time looking at himself in the mirror, wearing the dragon bathrobe. Then he went out to an all-night drugstore and came back with a pipe. Then he spent a lot of time looking at himself in the mirror, wearing the dragon bathrobe and smoking the pipe. It stank up the room.

Professor McFwain had told me to turn up at his office early the next morning, so I went to bed. Uncle Mel was watching a late movie, and before I fell asleep I saw him get up every now and then and look at himself in his new pipe and bathrobe.

8

As soon as I had eaten my egg McTavish with Uncle Mel, I hurried right over to North Water Street to report to Professor Ambrose McFwain. When I arrived, the fat men's clothing factory was in full operation. I could hear different kinds of machinery, sewing machines and other stuff, all the way down the block. Trucks were pulled up to the loading dock, and fat employees were loading boxes on some trucks and unloading bolts of cloth from others, while fat truck drivers stood around drinking soda pop and telling jokes. It was a busy place.

I went down the basement stairs, and through the gray metal door—it was open. The basement of the fat men's clothing factory was cool and dim. I got a little lost, but finally I found Professor McFwain's office. He was sitting at the big conference table, eating a hero sandwich wrapped in cellophane.

"Ah! Eugene!" Professor McFwain said. "Are you ready to begin your exciting new career as a monster-hunter?"

"I certainly am, Professor," I said. "Are we going out after Yobgorgle right now?"

"Ah, the enthusiasm of the young!" Professor McFwain said. "There it is—in a nutshell—youth versus experience. Monster-hunting, like most other things, is ninety-eight percent preparation plus one percent action and one percent luck. I'm afraid that monster-hunting is not all glamor and flash like you've seen in the movies."

If he was thinking about the movie I'd seen about Yobgorgle with Uncle Mel the other night, it showed monster-hunting as one hundred percent talk, with no action and no luck.

"You see," Professor McFwain went on, "any fool can go out in the lake and just run into Yobgorgle by dumb luck. In fact, that's how every sighting of Yobgorgle so far has happened. Some ordinary citizen is out fishing or sailing for pleasure, and, bang, there's the monster. He gets scared, doesn't observe closely, tells his story in a disorganized fashion—and what do you have? Inconclusive data! But we are scientists. We have to prepare, prepare, prepare! When we find the monster, it won't come as a surprise. We'll be ready to take his picture, measure him, shake hands—or shake fins—with him, and say 'how do you do.' That's what we want. So we have to make sure that we are ready mentally, physically, and scientifically. Today, we are going to begin to assemble needed equipment."

Professor McFwain took another bite of his sandwich. "What we are going to do today, Eugene, is acquire a field research vehicle, which will serve as our traveling laboratory. It will allow us to transport the McFwain Institute research vessel from place to place, act as a portable photographic darkroom, and also enable us to go to drive-in restaurants in the suburbs. I have just such a machine in mind, and I've been waiting almost a year to buy it. And today is the only day in the year to do so."

DANIEL PINKWATER

"Why is that?" I asked Professor McFwain. "Do you believe in astrology, or something like that?"

"Certainly not!" he said. "I am a scientist. The reason that this is the only day in the year to buy our research vehicle, or any sort of a car or truck, is that this is the only day in the year when Colonel Ken Krenwinkle sells cars."

"Who is Colonel Ken Krenwinkle?" I asked.

"Colonel Krenwinkle is the richest man in Rochester. He may be the richest man in the United States or the richest man in the world—nobody knows how rich he is. To give you an idea of how rich he is, he once bought the entire State of Florida, because he liked an amusement park there. But later he got tired of it, and sold the whole state to real estate developers."

The Professor threw his sandwich wrapper in the wastebasket and unwrapped a big slice of cake. "What Colonel Ken Krenwinkle likes to do best is sell cars. He used to get in trouble by going to used car lots on Sundays, when they were closed, and pretending to be a salesman. He'd make all sorts of deals with people who came to look at the cars—selling them for a dollar or offering to give the people money to take the cars away—and he'd write up the deals on little slips of paper. Then on Monday morning, when the real used car dealer came to open his business, there would be lines of people thinking that they'd bought cars at bargain prices, waiting to pick up their purchases. Colonel Ken Krenwinkle was always getting sued by used car dealers."

Professor McFwain offered me a piece of the cake. I took it gladly. Then he continued: "Of course, the Colonel could buy his own used car lot, but he never did that. Maybe it came of being disappointed when he bought the State of Florida and then got tired of it. What Colonel Ken Krenwinkle does now, is buy a different used car lot every year on the same day—that is, he buys every car on the lot and then spends a day making deals. Quite a few people know about Colonel Ken Krenwinkle's strange hobby and take advantage of the unusual deals he makes. But they never know which used car lot he has bought—and since he appears in a disguise every year, there is no sure way to find out if he's really the one selling the cars on a given lot. Of course, the other used car dealers know which day of the year Colonel Ken Krenwinkle does his car-selling, so they all put on fake beards and dark glasses on that day and trot out all the old junkers they haven't been able to sell all year, and offer them at bargain prices. No one is ever sure if they're buying a fantastic bargain from Colonel Ken Krenwinkle or a cheap, but worthless, rusted-out hulk from a regular used car dealer. It's very exciting."

"And this is the day?"

"This is the day. What's more, I have pretty good information about which used car lot has been bought up by the real Colonel Ken Krenwinkle. And, as luck would have it, on that used car lot is the perfect research field vehicle for my purposes, a four-wheel drive, Hindustan-eight—a fine machine of Indian make, not seen very often in this country. So without further ado, let's go and see if we can buy it for a very low price."

"What kind of unusual deals does Colonel Ken Krenwinkle make?" I asked.

DANIEL PINKWATER

"Well, it varies from year to year," Professor McFwain said. "For example, once he sold a nearly brand-new, last year's model car, super deluxe, with air conditioning, stereo, whitewall tires, and all sorts of extras for $27.95. The unusual part of the deal was that the car came with, as an extra that you were required to buy, a stuffed gorilla tied to the roof with rope. The gorilla cost $12.00 extra. And the buyer had to sign a contract saying that he would leave the stuffed gorilla where it was. If he removed the gorilla, and Colonel Ken Krenwinkle found out about it, then the buyer would have to give back the car. Someone bought it, and you can see it sometimes around town with the stuffed gorilla tied to the roof. That is the sort of unusual deal Colonel Ken Krenwinkle makes.

"Another time, Colonel Ken Krenwinkle sold a car—and the buyer had to sign a paper promising to paint his house blue—Colonel Ken Krenwinkle supplied the paint. Another time, he sold a car with a huge sign on top saying DON'T EAT DUCKS! The buyer had to promise to leave the sign. But why are we sitting around here talking? Let's get going before the Hindustan is sold!"

Professor McFwain and I went outside and caught a bus. We got off in front of a used car lot, which had a big sign saying

RIDICULOUS ROOSMAN
THE SENTIMENTAL SRI LANKESE—
EVERY VEHICLE,
A TRANSPORT OF DELIGHT.

9

In the middle of the used car lot stood a man wearing a heavy winter overcoat, blue sunglasses, and a beard that was obviously a fake. When we got closer, it was apparent that his nose was made out of putty.

"Is that Colonel Ken Krenwinkle?" I whispered to Professor Ambrose McFwain.

"I believe it is," he whispered back. "But we'll only know for sure when he closes the deal. Just act natural and don't say anything."

"Ah, gentlemen," the man in the heavy overcoat, blue sunglasses, fake beard and putty nose said. "May I help you this beautiful morning?"

"Are you the proprietor?" Professor Ambrose McFwain asked.

"I am he. I am Ridiculous Roosman, the Sentimental Sri Lankese, from Sri Lanka, which used to be called Ceylon. My father and my father's father were dealers in fine used elephants. I have come here and sell the finest of second-hand cars in my beloved adopted country, sirs."

Ridiculous Roosman, the sentimental Sri Lankese, if that was really who he was, didn't sound like he came from Ceylon. Not that I know what a Ceylonese or a Sri Lankese is supposed to sound like, but this man had a regular American Southern accent, like someone from Georgia or Alabama.

"I noticed that Hindustan-eight panel truck," Professor Ambrose McFwain said. "Not to waste your time, I'm not really interested in buying it, but I thought it would be amusing if you'd show it to me and my young friend here."

"Think nothing of it," said Ridiculous Roosman. "I am here exclusively for your pleasure. If you wish to buy a fine car, naturally, that will make me the happiest man on earth—but if you would enjoy just looking, or throwing cold spaghetti in my face, or knocking me down and stamping on me—in fact, anything which would give you a moment's fleeting pleasure would bring me ultimate joy. You wish to see the Hindustan-eight. You shall see it. You may feel free to inspect it as minutely as you like. Kick it, hammer on it, set fire to it. Your slightest wish is my command."

While he was talking, Ridiculous Roosman was leading us to a little green truck with rusty bumpers. "This is a fine and, if I may so, a very rare vehicle," the sentimental Sri Lankese said. "Needless to say, it is in perfect running order—just listen to this. . . ."

Ridiculous Roosman reached inside the Hindustan-eight and pulled a wooden handle, which had a long cord attached to it, like the thing they use to start outboard motors. The cord was wound around a metal spool, which spun when he pulled the handle, and the motor began to cough and sputter. Clouds of black smoke poured out of the tailpipe and from under the hood.

"A masterpiece of engineering," the sentimental Sri Lankese said.

Professor McFwain walked around the truck, kicking the

tires, and grabbing at the fenders, which made a soft crunching noise when he rocked them back and forth and showered little reddish flakes of rust on the ground. "It seems to have had a bit of use," Professor McFwain said.

"No, that's the way they're built. This car will never rust any more than it has rusted already. They come from the factory pre-rusted."

"Oh, I didn't know that," Professor McFwain said. "How much are you asking for this machine?"

"Well, this is actually a collector's item," Ridiculous Roosman said. "There are only two or three of them in this country. I could sell this over the telephone to a collector in Oswego for $20,000, but because I like you very much, if you wish, it's yours for $19,500."

Professor McFwain made a face.

"Or," Ridiculous Roosman continued, "I could make the price a little lower, if you are interested in a special deal."

"Here it comes," Professor McFwain whispered to me.

"In the event that you will agree to certain conditions by which I can advertise my business, I will make a substantial reduction in the price."

"How much of a reduction?" Professor McFwain said.

"I'll sell you the automobile for $3.00, but there is a condition," the car dealer said.

"I accept your offer, Colonel Ken Krenwinkle," Professor McFwain said.

"Colonel? Colonel? I am no Colonel. In the Sri Lanka Jiujitsu Self-Defense Forces, I was only a private. I don't know what you're talking about."

"Excuse me," Professor McFwain said. "For a moment, I thought you were someone else. Now, what was the condition?"

"Now we're getting someplace," said Ridiculous Roosman. "You may purchase this magnificent Hindustan-eight motor vehicle for the full price of $3.00, if you will sign a legally binding agreement to wear this costume whenever you drive it."

Ridiculous Roosman reached into the back of the little green truck and brought out a big white feathery thing. "If you will agree to wear this chicken suit whenever you drive it, the machine is yours for $3.00. Try it on—let's see how you look in it."

Professor McFwain climbed into the chicken suit. "It's sort of comfortable, actually," he said. "I'll agree to the deal."

"Bravo!" Ridiculous Roosman said. "I knew you were a sport the minute I saw you. I'll get the papers for you to sign."

"Are you really going to drive around wearing that chicken suit?" I asked the Professor.

"It's not so bad," the Professor said, "the beak makes a sort of visor. It will keep the sun out of my eyes. Besides, it's not what you wear that's the important thing. It's who you are—inside."

The sentimental Sri Lankese came back with the papers for Professor Ambrose McFwain to sign. When the Professor had signed his name, the used car dealer got very excited. "Professor Ambrose McFwain! The very man I've been wanting to meet! You are the man who is going to find Yobgorgle, are you not?"

"That is my mission," Professor McFwain said, as he

handed over the $3.00. "Allow me to introduce Eugene Winkleman, my young assistant. Now, since we've concluded our deal, wouldn't you like to reveal your true identity?"

"Yes, of course. It's an honor to meet you, sir," said the used car salesman, pulling off his fake beard. "I am, as you have already guessed, Colonel Ken Krenwinkle, at your service." He shook hands with both of us. "You know, I truly admire the work you are doing. I'd be proud to offer you any help in my power, and also I'd like very much to go out looking for the monster with you."

"And so you shall!" Professor Ambrose McFwain said. "We will be proud to have you join our expedition."

"Oh, thank you," Colonel Ken Krenwinkle said. "Here is my card. I can always be reached through this telephone number."

"I'll be in touch with you within the week, never fear," Professor McFwain said.

The two men shook hands, Professor McFwain pulled down the visor of his chicken suit, and we both climbed into the Hindustand-eight. The Professor yanked the wooden handle to start the motor, put it into gear, and we rattled out into the street.

10

We were rumbling and rattling through the midday traffic. The Hindustan-eight was trailing black, oily smoke. "This is a truly magnificent machine," Professor McFwain said.

"It seems sort of crummy and beat-up to me," I said.

"That's only because you are not familiar with its unique design," Professor McFwain said. "This machine doesn't operate on conventional automotive principles; instead it is built along the lines of obscure Vedic philosophies of India. It's too complicated to understand unless you are well-versed in the wisdom of the East—but suffice it to say, this is the ideal car, the *only* car to have a real adventure in. And how about that Colonel Ken Krenwinkle? Isn't he a fine man? And a philanthropist—why he practically gave us the car. What a selfless contribution to science!"

"He made you wear the chicken suit," I said.

"You know, I rather like this chicken suit," Professor McFwain said. "You'd think it would be warm, but I get a nice breeze through the feathers."

"Professor McFwain," I said, "a lot of people are staring at us."

"You've got to expect that when you drive a classic car," he said. "Now, I'm famished after all that haggling. What say we motor out to Braddock Point and have a look for Yobgorgle or any signs thereof, and on the way we can stop at

Fred's Fat Pig, a really superior drive-in restaurant. They have a six-level super cheeseburger that is fit for a king."

Professor McFwain stepped on the accelerator, and the Hindustan-eight sort of threw itself forward—the car had a desperate way of moving, as though it were hurling itself off a cliff.

Professor McFwain evidently enjoyed driving, even though the car shuddered as though it was terrified, lurched, hesitated, and then lurched forward again. I wasn't sure if it was the Hindustan-eight or the way Professor McFwain drove—maybe a little of each.

As he drove, Professor Ambrose McFwain talked and chattered continuously. "Well, well, our expedition is taking shape, is it not? Now Colonel Ken Krenwinkle wants to join us—I trust him, don't you? I'll wager he's a good man in a tight place—military background—must have gotten that title somewhere. He's our man in case of a crisis. What about your uncle Mel? Do you think he'd like to join us? There can't be much to interest a man of his obvious taste and culture in Rochester of a weekend—maybe he'd like to come aboard on a part-time basis, when he's not engaged in his business activities."

I told Professor McFwain that I'd ask Uncle Mel if he would like to come along and look for Yobgorgle, and I reminded Professor McFwain about the cowboy suit, as Uncle Mel had asked me to.

"Oh, yes, the cowboy suit! That's all arranged. The factory says he can have it. If we get back this afternoon before my friend goes home, I'll send it along with you this very evening."

We arrived at Fred's Fat Pig. We pulled up outside and

DANIEL PINKWATER

Professor McFwain honked the horn. It was the first time I'd ever seen one of those horns that you honk by squeezing a rubber bulb. A waitress wearing a pig mask came out and gave us menus. When she walked away, I noticed that there was a curly pig's tail attached to the back of her uniform.

"This is a high-class place," Professor McFwain said.

The waitress in the pig mask and tail didn't seem to take any notice of the fact that the man she was serving was dressed in a chicken suit. I guess that people who are dressed up as animals start to take it for granted after a while.

We ate right in the car. The waitress fastened little metal trays to the windows, and we ate from them. As I ate my six-level cheeseburger, the thought crossed my mind that it would be more than a month before my mother got home and gave me some real food. I wondered how long a human being could survive on the stuff that Uncle Mel and Professor McFwain ate. They were alive, of course, but Uncle Mel was fat and Professor McFwain was crazy. I wondered if a steady diet of fast food had done that to them.

After our meal, Professor McFwain started up the Hindustan-eight, and we headed for Braddock Point on the shore of Lake Ontario. There wasn't much traffic on the way, but we got our share of attention from the drivers we passed (going the opposite way) and the drivers who passed us (going the same way). A kid and what looked like a giant chicken, in a little smoking trucklike car, was not the sort of sight encountered every day in the suburbs of Rochester, New York.

Braddock Point was nice. There was a kind of park there, and we had a good view of the lake. I had never seen a Great

Lake before. It looked like the ocean, which I have seen. In fact, the only difference between it and the ocean was that it was a lake, and not salty. It had waves and everything.

"And there he is, just waiting for us, taunting us because he knows we haven't got our boat, telescopes, and cameras," Professor McFwain said.

"Who? Yobgorgle?" I asked. I was getting excited.

"Who else?" Professor McFwain said. "It's uncanny—you go out without any equipment, and there he is—just as plain as day. But go after him with a recording device, a camera, or even a reliable witness . . . not a sign of him. It's almost as if he could read your mind."

"Where? Where is he? I didn't see anything!" I was looking as hard as I could in every direction. All I could see was empty lake, except for a boat way off in the distance. It looked like some kind of a work boat; it wasn't a pleasure craft.

"He's right out there," Professor McFwain said, pointing at the boat in the distance, "big as life and twice as ugly."

"All I see is that boat," I said.

"Now you're beginning to learn a few things about the craft of monster-hunting," Professor McFwain said. "To you or any other average, untrained person, that sea monster floating on the surface out there looks like an old fishing boat or a small freighter, but that's just because your eyes aren't accustomed to scanning for monsters. I can see him as plain as the nose on your face. I can almost count his scales. I can even tell that he's asleep. Oh, if we were only in our boat! What an opportunity to get close to him and snap a picture before he wakes up!"

"It looks just like a boat to me," I said. "I can even see smoke coming from it."

"Now that's interesting," Professor Ambrose McFwain said. "The reason you see smoke is because you expect to see it. When you see a boat, like the one you imagine you see, you expect to see smoke—so you see it. It isn't really there, you know."

I shaded my eyes with my hand. I squinted. It still looked like a boat. In fact, it looked more like a boat. I was pretty sure it *was* a boat, but I wanted to give Professor McFwain the benefit of the doubt, so I really tried to see it as a monster. But the more I looked, the more certain I was that it was a boat. I told Professor McFwain that I thought so.

"Well, there's no substitute for experience," Professor McFwain said. "You'll get to be able to distinguish a monster from a boat, I assure you, but it will take time. For now, you'll just have to trust me. Anyway, you've had your first look at Yobgorgle, even if you aren't ready to appreciate it, and I'd say that you were a pretty lucky young man. Now, let's head back for town. There's nothing more we can do here without equipment, drat it!"

We bumped along the road back to town in the Hindustan-eight. I was still not convinced that what we had seen was anything but a boat, but I decided that it would be best not to say anything more about it to Professor McFwain. He seemed very happy with his day's activity, and he hummed a tune as he drove.

11

Professor McFwain went upstairs into the fat men's clothing factory and brought down the cowboy suit for Uncle Mel. It was really something. It was blue, and it had all sorts of fancy embroidery and fringes and shiny stuff on it. He also had a big round box. I guessed that had the hat in it.

"Here, Eugene, take this to your uncle with my compliments," Professor McFwain said. "I'll let you go for the day— you've had enough excitement. I'll see you tomorrow."

The cowboy suit was on a hanger and covered by one of those clear plastic bags. I carried the cowboy suit by the hanger and the box with the hat in it by the string that was attached to it, and walked back to the motel.

Uncle Mel flipped when he saw the cowboy suit. He tore his clothes off and put it on right away. It fitted him pretty good, except for the hat, which was just a tiny bit too large. He didn't seem to notice; he looked in the mirror and smiled and smiled. All he said for about fifteen minutes was, "Wow!" over and over.

The telephone rang. It was Professor Ambrose McFwain. "I wanted to know if the suit fits," he said.

"It fits perfectly," Uncle Mel said. "I'm wearing it right now."

"And have you had your evening meal?" Professor McFwain asked.

"Not yet," Uncle Mel said. "I just got back from the factory."

"Well, I suggest you keep your fancy suit on," Professor McFwain said. "I've just gotten a call from Colonel Ken Krenwinkle, the multibillionaire, and he's invited me and you and Eugene to dine with him. So if it's all right with you, I'll pick you up in ten minutes."

Uncle Mel asked me if I wanted to eat with a multibillionaire. I said it was all right with me. He told Professor McFwain yes, and we went outside to wait for him.

After a few minutes the little green truck pulled up outside of the motel.

"Look!" Uncle Mel said. "There's a chicken driving that Hindustan-eight!"

I told him it was Professor McFwain.

"Get in! Get in!" Professor McFwain said. "We've got a long way to go, and we'll have to hurry if we don't want to be late."

Uncle Mel had some trouble getting into the little car. For one thing, he was too fat, and for another, the car wasn't high enough for him to sit in it wearing the light blue cowboy hat. He finally squeezed himself into the front seat and dragged the hat, which was somewhat crushed, in after him. He smoothed out the hat and put it on his lap. The little car leaned to the right.

"Slide over to the left as far as you can, Eugene," Professor McFwain said. "We have to trim ship—get better balance. This is good practice for when we're all out in the boat together."

"We're going out in a boat?" Uncle Mel asked.

"Yes," Professor McFwain said. "I forgot to tell you— you're invited to join the expedition to hunt for Yobgorgle. That is, if you would like that."

"Gosh!" Uncle Mel said. "I'm not sure. I mean, I've always sort of wanted to have an adventure, but I've never been in a boat, and I don't know . . . I'd feel sort of awkward."

"Of course, you couldn't go monster-hunting in that beautiful suit," Professor McFwain said. "If you decide to go with us, I could arrange with my friend at the factory to make you a beautiful safari suit with lots of little pockets and flaps on the shoulders and short pants."

"Would it have a hat with a leopardskin band like Victor Mature used to wear in the movies?" Uncle Mel asked.

"Imitation leopardskin."

"I think I'd like that," Uncle Mel said. "I'd like to join the expedition and go looking for the monster, but I could only come in the evening and on the weekend."

"We'll be looking for him mostly at night," Professor McFwain said, "so that won't be a problem."

"Incidentally, Professor," Uncle Mel said, "I notice you're wearing a chicken suit. Is there any particular reason for it?"

Professor Ambrose McFwain told Uncle Mel all about buying the Hindustan-eight from Colonel Ken Krenwinkle, and the condition that he wear the chicken suit at all times when driving it.

I had heard all this before, so I sat in the backseat, as far over to the left as I could get, and looked out the window. We had left the city and were driving through a forest. Every now

DANIEL PINKWATER

and then Professor Ambrose McFwain would slow down, as if he was looking for a landmark. All I could see was trees.

Professor McFwain was telling Uncle Mel how we had seen Yobgorgle out in the lake that day. I put in that it looked like a boat to me, but neither of them paid any attention. Uncle Mel was very interested in the sighting—almost as interested as he was in Professor McFwain's description of Fred's Fat Pig. Professor McFwain promised to take Uncle Mel there soon.

"How about after dinner tonight?" Uncle Mel asked.

"We'll see," said the Professor.

Professor McFwain seemed to be counting trees now. He was driving very slowly. He stopped in front of a particularly large tree and tooted the horn.

A door opened in the side of the tree, and an old man with white hair stepped out. "Yes, sir?" the old man said.

"Professor Ambrose McFwain and party to see Colonel Ken Krenwinkle," Professor McFwain said.

"One moment while I telephone, sir," the old man said. He stepped back into the tree. I guessed there was a telephone in there. He came out again in a minute. "It's all right, sir. I'll open the gate."

The old man went back into the tree again and must have pushed a button. Then the trees next to the big tree with the old man in it lifted up like a giant curtain! I never heard of any gate like that! They were fake trees, of course, and there must have been some giant machinery concealed in the woods to lift them like that. Professor McFwain threw the Hindustan-eight into gear, and we lurched forward.

It was twilight. I could just make out a long driveway through the trees. The Hindustan-eight's headlights flickered as we bounced along. The driveway led out of the forest, and I could see a vast lawn, with a big house in the middle of it, a long way off.

It took about five minutes to get to the end of the driveway. When we pulled up in front of the house, Colonel Ken Krenwinkle was standing in the doorway.

"Good evening, gentlemen," he said. "I'm so glad you could come on such short notice."

"We are honored," Professor McFwain said. "You've already met my assistant, Eugene Winkleman, the youngest doctoral candidate ever to attend Catatonic University, and this is Doctor Pierre Unclemel, a specialist in nutritional mechanics, who has consented to join our little expedition."

I must have looked startled, for Professor McFwain turned to us and whispered, "Never mind the fibs. It's polite to do that when dealing with rich people."

"The honor is mine," Colonel Ken Krenwinkle said. "Please come in. Dinner will be ready shortly."

We went into the house, which was bigger than the Rochester Public Library.

"Let's go right into the great hall," Colonel Ken Krenwinkle said. "We can have a glass of wine and get acquainted while we wait for our meal."

The great hall was just that. It was about the biggest room I've ever seen without basketball hoops. There was a giant table in the middle of it about a block long. On the walls there were big wooden plaques with trophies on them. In movies I've seen the trophies were usually lion's heads or elephants, and maybe there were suits of armor and old swords and battle-axes. On the walls of Colonel Ken Krenwinkle's great hall were the front ends of automobiles from just behind the windshield to the headlights. Each automobile was mounted on a polished wooden plaque, and there was a little brass nameplate at the bottom of the plaque. The cars were about fifteen feet above our heads. They looked small in the huge room. I recognized a Hindustan-eight and a few other cars I'd seen before. There were some smaller plaques with half-motorcycles and washing machines, drill presses, power lawn mowers, a popcorn vending machine from a movie house, a small cement mixer, and at the end of the great hall a forklift truck. The forklift was mounted with the two steel forks angled slightly downward, so it reminded me of an elephant. The brass nameplate underneath read, "Nafsu Motors Forklift, 44 horsepower, bagged in Utica, New York, 1962."

"As you can see from my trophies," Colonel Ken Krenwinkle said, "I don't go in for conventional game—in fact, I'm against taking the lives of wild animals—but stalking a wild forklift in the industrial parks of Utica, alone and unarmed in my modified Deuesenberg 16-cylinder safari car—that's another matter. That's true sport, gentlemen."

"I was admiring your 1952 Chrysler," Professor McFwain said.

"Ah, yes," Colonel Ken Krenwinkle said. "Bagged the blighter out west in Buffalo in '70. I had the devil of a time with that one, I don't mind telling you. I wounded the brute on my first pass, and it went berserk. Just as it charged, something went haywire with my magneto—I was stopped dead. Well, the only thing to do was to finish it off by hand. I climbed up on the hood, and just at the moment of impact, I jumped aboard, threw the monster into reverse, and ran it into a concrete embankment rear end first. It was a close one."

"Excuse me," I said. "I'm not sure I understand this. How do you go about hunting cars?"

"It's very simple, my young friend," Colonel Ken Krenwinkle said. "I locate the beast I wish to bag. Then my trusted shikaris, who have made arrangements with the owner, if any, set the throttle, get the thing in motion in a big field or other open space, and I give chase in the modified Deuesenberg. I try to finish the thing off with a clean collision. Then it's time to take photos, and off to the taxidermist to have the dents smoothed out, and up on the wall it goes."

All I could do was stare at the cars on the wall. I had never heard of anything like this.

12

The meal served at Colonel Ken Krenwinkle's house consisted of nothing but vegetable dishes. Colonel Ken Krenwinkle was a vegetarian. There were a number of different kinds of salads and some hot vegetable dishes and different kinds of grains. I liked everything, but Uncle Mel and Professor Ambrose McFwain just nibbled and pushed things around on their plates. I was pretty certain we'd be stopping at Fred's Fat Pig later on. They just weren't used to that kind of food.

During the meal, Colonel Ken Krenwinkle told us more about his adventures hunting automobiles and other machines. Professor McFwain told stories about monster-hunting expeditions in various parts of the world. Uncle Mel told about new developments in food vending machines. Colonel Ken Krenwinkle said he'd like to bag one of the new freeze-dried, mix-and-mush, microwave machines for his collection of trophies. Uncle Mel said he'd find out how much they cost, and if Colonel Ken Krenwinkle wanted, the factory could probably fix the machine up with wheels and a motor so the chase would be more sporting. Colonel Ken Krenwinkle told him to go ahead and arrange it, if he could.

Everybody agreed that when Professor McFwain had finished making arrangements, we would all go out on Lake Ontario looking for the monster, Yobgorgle. Professor

McFwain was going to get a safari suit for Uncle Mel at a wholesale price. Colonel Ken Krenwinkle already had a safari suit, and I didn't want one. Professor McFwain remarked that he found the chicken suit very comfortable and had gotten a lot of compliments wearing it.

"I'm glad you like it," Colonel Ken Krenwinkle said, "I had a very successful day, if I say so myself. I have three other gentlemen riding around in chicken suits in small foreign cars; a life-size papier-mâché cow mounted on top of a late model station wagon; a sedan with a loud speaker that plays a recording of 'West End Blues' with Louis Armstrong twenty-four hours a day; and two vans fully upholstered in fake fur on the outside. It's not the best day I ever had dealing in used cars, but it was a very good day."

We all agreed that Colonel Ken Krenwinkle had certainly done well.

After the meal, Colonel Ken Krenwinkle invited us to his den for cigars and coffee. Of course, I didn't have either. I had a cherry milk shake with real cherries in it. The grown-ups smoked cigars and sat in big green leather chairs. Colonel Ken Krenwinkle's study had a lot of portraits of ducks on the walls. These weren't the usual sort of pictures of ducks. I had seen them—I don't know where—maybe in a doctor's office, with ducks in flight or maybe a close-up of a couple of ducks. These were pictures of duck's heads. The ducks had nice expressions in the pictures. I never knew ducks had expressions.

"I see you're admiring my duck pictures," Colonel Ken Krenwinkle said. "I have a soft spot in my heart for ducks of

DANIEL PINKWATER

all kinds. Ducks are the major enthusiasm of my life, more so than sport, more so than making untold billions of dollars. You see, gentlemen, my mother died when I was very young, my father was away much of the time, and I was . . ." Here Colonel Ken Krenwinkle stopped speaking, overcome with emotion. "I was raised by a duck, bless her dear heart. I hope that none of you ever eats ducks, gentlemen."

Professor Ambrose McFwain and Uncle Mel both swore that they never ate ducks, which was probably true, since no fast-food chain that I know of serves ducks. I had never eaten duck either, as far as I could remember, so I told Colonel Ken Krenwinkle I would never eat duck in the future, if I could get out of it.

"Thank you, gentlemen," Colonel Ken Krenwinkle said. "I knew you were all good men. I'm proud to be associated with you."

Things got quiet for a while after Colonel Ken Krenwinkle's emotional speech about ducks. Then Professor McFwain suggested that we'd better be going. I was ready for that. I figured that the Professor and Uncle Mel would be needing some junk food by this time.

"So early?" Colonel Ken Krenwinkle said. "I had hoped you'd stay a little longer."

Professor McFwain reminded Colonel Ken Krenwinkle that I was but a youngster, and he and Uncle Mel were responsible for seeing to it that I got to bed at a decent hour.

When we went outside, the Hindustan-eight refused to start.

"Never mind," Colonel Ken Krenwinkle said. "Just leave

it here. My driver will fix it for you in the morning and deliver it to your office. I will drive you home, and I have something that may be of interest to show you en route. Just excuse me for a moment while I make the arrangements."

Colonel Ken Krenwinkle went into his house and gave some instructions to his staff. In a few moments two enormous cars pulled up in front of the house. One was a shiny black Rolls Royce, the other was the longest, highest car I have ever seen. It was greenish gray, and the paint was chipped and scratched. There were wire screens over the headlights.

"We will ride in the Rolls," Colonel Ken Krenwinkle said, "and my servant will follow in the safari car. I hope you don't mind if we make a short stop on the way. It won't take very long."

Professor McFwain and Uncle Mel said they didn't mind at all. They both glanced at their watches. They were worried that they'd get back to town after McTavish's had closed. With the Hindustan-eight out of commission, Fred's Fat Pig was no longer a possibility for that evening. I could read Uncle Mel's mind when it came to food, and Professor McFwain, though crazier in other ways, wasn't much different. I didn't care. I wasn't hungry, and I wanted to see what Colonel Ken Krenwinkle was going to show us on the way home.

He drove the Rolls Royce himself. It was a neat car! Now I know why they are so expensive. They're really nice to ride in.

Colonel Ken Krenwinkle drove fast through the night. The car had a stereo that played a tape of duck noises. "We're going to make a stop at the County Fair Ground in Henrietta, a suburb of Rochester," Colonel Ken Krenwinkle said. "Arrangements have been made for some time—I was just waiting for a fine night like this."

When we arrived at the deserted fair grounds, Colonel Ken Krenwinkle's servant jumped out of the safari car and ran off somewhere. In a few seconds, banks of floodlights switched on, revealing a little green car at the far end of the fair grounds.

"There it is!" Colonel Ken Krenwinkle said. He was very excited. "A 1969 Austin America in perfect condition. I had to search everywhere for it. Just stay here, you'll be perfectly safe."

Colonel Ken Krenwinkle jumped out of the Rolls Royce, and ran over to his modified Deuesenberg safari car, hopped in, and gunned the motor.

In the distance, the 1969 Austin America started with a puff of gray smoke. We could just see that there was someone behind the wheel. The Austin started moving, and Colonel Ken Krenwinkle's driver jumped out of the moving car and ran away. Colonel Ken Krenwinkle revved the motor of the modified Deuesenberg safari car but didn't move.

The Austin was picking up speed. It was weaving and turning and going in little circles. Then it straightened out and started moving toward us. It got closer. I was scared. I wanted to look over and see what Colonel Ken Krenwinkle was doing, but I couldn't take my eyes off the Austin speeding toward the three of us in the Rolls Royce.

The Austin wasn't more than thirty feet away when he heard a loud roar. Colonel Ken Krenwinkle had popped the clutch of his safari car, and was coming toward us in a cloud of dust. For a while it looked as if we were going to be hit by both the Austin and the Deuesenberg at the same time, but at the last moment, Colonel Ken Krenwinkle veered off to the left, just enough to miss us, and caught the Austin by the left front fender as he passed in front of it. The Austin spun around and began going in the other direction. Colonel Ken Krenwinkle was making a wide circle. He continued turning and caught the Austin amidships as he came around 180 degrees.

The Austin left the ground, flew sideways fifteen or twenty feet, and landed on its four wheels with a crash. It shuddered, and then was still. Colonel Ken Krenwinkle came to a stop a little to the right of the Austin, got out of his safari car, and walked over to the smoking wreck. His driver ran up with a camera and took a flash picture of him. Then he walked back to the Rolls Royce.

"Bravo! Bravo!" shouted Uncle Mel and the Professor, when Colonel Ken Krenwinkle returned to the Rolls Royce.

"Oh, it was nothing," Colonel Ken Krenwinkle said. "Not very dangerous, but I thought you might enjoy seeing how it's done."

When we got back to Rochester, McTavish's was already closed. The only place open was Bob's Beanery. Of course, Uncle Mel and Professor Ambrose McFwain didn't tell Colonel Ken Krenwinkle that they were going there. They didn't want him to know that they hadn't enjoyed his dinner. He dropped us all off in front of the motel, and we walked to Bob's Beanery.

13

Bob's Beanery looked sort of different at night. The neon lights in the window and the fluorescent lights on the ceiling made everything look greenish. There were a few people sitting at the counter and one guy sleeping with his head on his arms at one of the tables.

Uncle Mel, Professor McFwain, and I sat down at a table.

"This is nice. We'll get a nice breeze here," said Professor McFwain.

They ordered hamburgers. I ordered a cherry cola. It was very interesting that nobody in Bob's Beanery seemed to take any special notice of a man in a chicken suit and another in a very loud cowboy suit sitting in a lunchroom late at night. Either people in Rochester are very polite, or they're very hard to surprise.

"That was exciting," Uncle Mel said, "when Colonel Ken Krenwinkle went after the Austin."

"Yes, he's a brave man," Professor McFwain said. "He's just the sort of fellow one would want to face a monster with."

"I was thinking about that," Uncle Mel said. "I've never done anything brave. The only sort of hunting I've ever done is shooting clay pigeons. I wonder if *I'm* the sort of man one would want to face a monster with."

"Why, my dear fellow, of course you are," Professor McFwain said. "The only reason you've never done anything brave is you haven't had an opportunity. I can see you now, wearing your brand-new safari suit. . . ."

"And the hat with the imitation leopardskin band," Uncle Mel put in.

". . . and the hat with the imitation leopardskin band," Professor McFwain said. "What a dashing fellow you'll be!"

"I'll never know until I've tried," Uncle Mel said.

"That's right!" Professor McFwain said. "I've known brave men and adventurers on every continent—I can tell when a man has got the right stuff in him for daring deeds—and I'm sure you'll be just fine."

"Really?"

"Really. You'll see for yourself when we put out in the lake tomorrow night."

"Tomorrow night?" That took Uncle Mel and me by surprise. "Are we going out after Yobgorgle tomorrow night?" we both asked at once.

"I can't see any reason why not," Professor McFwain said. "I'll send a message to Colonel Ken Krenwinkle when his driver brings my car, and we'll meet at my office at eight o'clock sharp. Then we'll motor out to Irondequoit Bay with the research vessel in tow and put in a couple of hours of searching. Then a light snack, and another good day's work will be done—unless we find him, of course."

"What if we do find him?" I asked.

"Well, the main thing is to try to get pictures," Professor McFwain said. "After that, it's up to the monster."

"But will my safari suit be ready in time?" Uncle Mel wanted to know.

"Just leave that to me," Professor McFwain said. "It will be ready for you, hat and all, when you come to my office at eight. They turn them out like cupcakes. You'd never believe there were so many fat explorers."

"Do you want me to turn up in the morning?" I asked Professor Ambrose McFwain.

"Not necessary, my boy," he said. "I plan to sleep as late as possible in order to be fresh for our adventure in the evening. I suggest you do the same. Just come at eight o'clock with the others."

"I guess we'd better break this up so we can get some rest," Uncle Mel said.

"Good idea," said Professor McFwain. "We'll have one more round of double cheeseburgers and call it a night." He ordered two more double-deluxe cheeseburgers with everything.

"Two more doubles for the cowboy and the chicken!" the man behind the counter shouted into the kitchen.

14

The next day dragged on and on. I tried to sleep as late as I could, which wasn't very late. I was wide awake at dawn thinking about going out in the lake after Yobgorgle. I tried to go back to sleep and didn't go out to McTavish's for breakfast with Uncle Mel, but it didn't work. I got dressed and went outside into the street.

It was going to be some hot day—it was hot at nine in the morning. I didn't feel like going to McTavish's now that Uncle Mel wasn't with me, and I had a choice. Bob's Beanery had lost some of its charm too. I wandered around looking for a new place to eat. I found one. It was called Charlie's Health Food and Juice Bar. The thing that attracted me to it was the window display. There was a mechanical carrot about four feet tall, with arms and legs, who kept lowering himself into a giant juice-making machine. There was a sign that said COOLER INSIDE. I went inside. If it was cooler, it wasn't more than two degrees cooler. There was an electric fan, like the one in Bob's Beanery, but it just didn't seem to be able to do the job.

However, Charlie's Health Food and Juice Bar was truly a great place! They had carrot juice! I never had carrot juice before. Charlie—that was the guy who owned the place—told me that if you drink a whole lot of carrot juice you'll turn orange. I had three glasses—not enough to turn me orange. I

DANIEL PINKWATER

also had a couple of these nifty health-food muffins, with all kinds of grains and ground-up stuff and nuts in them. A really magnificent breakfast! I decided to eat in Charlie's Health Food and Juice Bar every morning. That meant eating without Uncle Mel—it wasn't the sort of place you could drag him into.

Charlie told me to come back for lunch. I said I would. Then I drifted over to the library. I went into the secret room and leafed through a book about a kid who gets involved with an old maniac and a bunch of talking lizards, but I really couldn't get interested. I was too nervous waiting for it to be time to meet Professor Ambrose McFwain and go out looking for the sea monster.

I ate my lunch in Charlie's place. He told me about bran and vitamin-B complex, and brewers' yeast. Charlie was an interesting guy. He knew a lot about food and what it does for you. More than ever, I wondered how Uncle Mel and Professor McFwain could stay alive, eating what they did. I asked Charlie. He said that sometimes your diet takes a long time to catch up with you.

I walked around and looked at the river and looked into store windows. I just couldn't get anything organized. Finally, it got too hot to be outside, and I went back to the motel and watched soap operas on television until Uncle Mel came home from work at the factory. He sent me over to Professor McFwain's to see if his safari suit was ready. He said he couldn't wait until eight o'clock.

Professor McFwain was sleeping on a folding cot in his office when I arrived. He didn't want to wake up; he just pointed to the suit, which was hanging from the doorknob in a plastic garment bag, and said, "See you at eight."

I brought the suit back to the motel. Uncle Mel was in the shower. He came out and put on the suit. After looking at himself in the mirror for a long time, he said, "Now let's go out and have some dinner."

"You're not going out in the street dressed like that?" I said.

"Why not?" Uncle Mel said.

It occurred to me that I had been seen in the street with a guy wearing a cowboy suit and a guy dressed up as a chicken. A fat man in a Jungle-Jim suit was no worse. We went out.

Even Uncle Mel likes a change once in a while, so we didn't go to McTavish's. We went to Burger-Chief, which was introducing a new Swiss-steak sandwich. Uncle Mel had read an advertisement in the newspaper and wanted to try it. It was close to uneatable. It was sort of a toy steak. It looked like a piece of meat, but I couldn't tell what it was. It was on a toy roll that looked like a real roll with a crust and little seeds, but it was all stamped from one piece of something or other. Uncle Mel didn't like the steak sandwich either. He only ate three. He says you can never be sure if you like something until you've had it three times.

Walking away from the Burger-Chief, Uncle Mel said that he felt a little sick. I wasn't surprised. I felt very sick, and I had only eaten about half of one of those plastic steaks.

It was almost eight when we arrived at the fat men's clothing factory. Colonel Ken Krenwinkle was already there, standing on the sidewalk with Professor McFwain. The research vessel was on a little trailer tied to the back of the

Hindustan-eight with a piece of rope. We all got into the car and drove out to the place where Professor McFwain intended to start the night's search.

We put the research vessel into the water. It was the same rowboat we had seen in the movie. Professor McFwain got in first, and then me, and then Colonel Ken Krenwinkle. The boat was sitting fairly low in the water. Uncle Mel got in. Colonel Ken Krenwinkle and Professor McFwain started to row. They didn't seem to be able to get the boat moving. The sky was still fairly light, and I could see the water glisten as it poured over the sides of the boat. It filled up in a few seconds and then slid out from under us. We floundered around for a few more seconds and then discovered we could stand up— the water was only about four feet deep.

We sloshed around for a while, trying to find the boat with our feet, but we couldn't seem to make contact with it. Besides it was getting dark. Finally, we all slogged out of the water, back to the Hindustan-eight.

Professor McFwain was mad. Uncle Mel was worried. He felt guilty about being the one to swamp the boat, and he was worried that his explorer suit might be ruined. Colonel Ken Krenwinkle seemed to be in good spirits, though. "Ah, yes," he said, "the frustrations and setbacks of the chase. This is what real adventure is all about. Now we'll have to use our wits—and improvise—and see what we can come up with!"

"I don't see what we can improvise," Professor McFwain said. "The McFwain Foundation research vessel appears to be lost. We can't go after a sea monster without a boat. What do you suggest in the way of improvising?"

"Well," said Colonel Ken Krenwinkle, "how about an eighty-two-foot yacht? My private craft is anchored about a hundred yards away. It was going to be a surprise. I had instructed my crew to follow us, and then when we were finished searching, we were all to go on board, take the research vessel in tow, and have some refreshments. I supposed we could search from the yacht."

"Well, it's not quite the same as the research vessel," Professor McFwain said.

"But it'll do in an emergency," Colonel Ken Krenwinkle said.

"You're right!" Professor McFwain said. "We have to use the resources at our disposal. Lead us to the yacht, Colonel."

Colonel Ken Krenwinkle took a little thing that looked like a transistor radio out of his pocket. He pulled out a telescoping antenna and pressed a red button. The little gadget made a continuous series of beeping noises, and out of the darkness came the biggest, whitest boat I've ever seen.

15

Colonel Ken Krenwinkle's boat was called *La Forza Materiale*. Professor McFwain asked him what the boat's name meant, and Colonel Ken Krenwinkle told him that he'd tell him later. As far as I know, he never did. The boat was really fancy. It had lots of polished wood and shiny brass and white paint. Everything was clean and smooth and shiny. The engine made a deep, even humming noise. It was some fancy boat.

"Professor McFwain," Colonel Ken Krenwinkle said, "I'd like you to meet the captain of *La Forza Materiale*, a great sailor and a fine gentleman. His name is Sinbad Weinstein. While you are aboard, Captain Sinbad Weinstein will take orders directly from you. Please treat this boat as your own research vessel."

Captain Sinbad Weinstein was a very tall fellow with a neatly trimmed beard and eyeglasses. He bowed to Professor McFwain and said, "It is a pleasure to meet you. I await your instructions."

Professor McFwain reached into his pocket and took out a bunch of little aluminum whistles. He distributed them to Colonel Ken Krenwinkle, Captain Sinbad Weinstein, Uncle Mel, and me. "I have more of these for your crew, Captain," he said. "These are ultra high-frequency dog whistles. Their sound is of too high a frequency for the human ear to hear.

Ordinarily, only dogs can hear them. However, I have perfected this, the McFwain high-frequency ear stopple." He showed us a pair of white plastic things that looked like badminton shuttlecocks. Professor McFwain sort of screwed one into each ear. They stuck out strangely, making him look like some sort of strange bird—all the more because he was still wearing his chicken suit, except for the headpiece, which had gotten lost, probably when the research vessel sank.

"With these," he said, "I will be able to hear the high-frequency whistles I have given to each of you. In this way, you will be able to signal me and, hopefully, not alarm the monster, if we are lucky enough to sight him."

I wondered how Professor Ambrose McFwain knew that Yobgorgle couldn't hear high-frequency sounds.

"What I propose is this," he went on. "We will darken ship as much as the law allows, leaving only the required red and green marker lights to prevent collision. Then we will position ourselves around the rail, each man looking in a different direction. I'm a little worried about the engine noise— I'll ask Captain Sinbad Weinstein to drift as much as possible. It would have been better in the McFwain Foundation Research vessel, with no engine, of course. If you think you've sighted the monster, you will blow your whistle. No one will hear it—but with my high-frequency ear stopples, I will hear it—and I will come running with my infrared camera for night photography and take pictures of the monster. We will begin with a two-hour watch, during which time no one will speak or make any noise at all."

"At the conclusion of the watch," Colonel Ken Kren-

DANIEL PINKWATER

winkle interrupted, "we can gather in the main cabin for some refreshments prepared by the ship's cook."

"Thank you," Professor McFwain said.

The two-hour watch began. My station was on the left side of the boat—the port side, Professor McFwain called it—toward the back, or stern. There were several crew members in white coats, who appeared and vanished silently, and one of them brought me a wood and canvas chair to sit in. We churned out toward the middle of the lake. After a while, the *La Forza Materiale*'s engines were switched off and the boat drifted silently. It had clouded over—no moon, no stars. The darkness was total, except for the dim glow of the boat's marker lights. Now and then I could see a light twinkling on shore. A lot of the time I couldn't see anything. I held up my hand in front of my face. I couldn't see it. I had never been in such darkness. The only sound was the water sloshing against the sides of the boat.

Sitting in my chair, I tried to look for Yobgorgle. It was hard to look for something when I couldn't see anything. After a while, I couldn't be sure if I was awake or asleep. I might have been dreaming. I actually had to feel my eyes from time to time to make sure they were open.

I liked being on the boat. I even liked the way the lake smelled, though it was not as fresh as I would have imagined. I liked the rocking sensation and the noises the water made. It was very peaceful.

A couple of times I heard someone cough softly or clear his throat. Except for that, there was no noise aboard the *La Forza Materiale*.

After a long time, the darkness got lighter. That is, I started seeing it as lighter. It was still totally dark. I still couldn't see anything. It was just my eyes getting more and more used to the darkness. Now, instead of blackness, I saw grayness. I couldn't see the water. It had been a long time since I had seen a light from shore. Either we were too far away to see any lights and the boat was drifting toward the middle of Lake Ontario, or I was facing away from shore.

I couldn't tell how much time had passed. I couldn't tell if I had been watching for Yobgorgle for an hour or for ten minutes.

Then I saw something. That is, I thought that maybe I saw something. I didn't actually *see* something. It was just a darker place in the darkness. It didn't have a shape. It didn't have a size. I couldn't tell how far or near it was. I wasn't even sure I was seeing it. I tried to open my eyes wide to see it better, but I couldn't be sure. It was there sometimes, and sometimes it wasn't.

I thought about blowing my whistle, but I wasn't sure there was anything out there. I decided to wait and see if it got any clearer. It did. It got closer. It got bigger. Soon I was sure that something was out there, floating near our boat. I thought that probably it was a small island—it was too large to be another boat. I still couldn't make out a definite shape, but there was *something* out there. I blew the whistle and kept blowing it until Professor McFwain, making no noise, came up behind me.

"Where?" he whispered.

"There," I whispered.

DANIEL PINKWATER

"Take my hand and point," he whispered.

I pointed his hand at the black mass. "Yes," Professor McFwain whispered. "I think I do see something."

I heard the camera click. I didn't see any light, because the camera had a special infrared light that you can't see without special glasses.

"That should do it," Professor McFwain whispered. "Now, I'll take one with the regular flash, just to make sure."

The light of the flashbulb seemed to last a long time. I was looking at the black mass, hoping I would get a glimpse of whatever it was when Professor McFwain snapped the picture.

I did get a glimpse of something. It was big—bigger than I had guessed—much bigger than *La Forza Materiale*. It was pink! There was something enormous and pink and rounded and shiny floating in the water about the distance of a city block from the boat.!

"I'll tell Captain Sinbad Weinstein to turn on the search-lights," Professor McFwain said aloud, "although I have no doubt that the flash scared him off. Still, we've got the pic-ture—if it only comes out this time—and you've seen him, Eugene, my boy. You and I have seen Yobgorgle!"

When the searchlights came on and made long, thin, gray cones through the blackness, the thing had *not* gone away! It was still there, shining pinkly in the searchlight's beams. It was unmistakable. Anybody could have seen in a moment that what we were looking at was an enormous, impossible, gigantic, floating pink pig!

16

Everybody gathered at the rail and stared at the thing. It was a pig—there was no mistaking it.

"And that," asked Colonel Ken Krenwinkle, "that is Yobgorgle?"

"I confess, I am as amazed as you are," Professor Ambrose McFwain said. "I had no idea that Yobgorgle was so . . . so . . . porciform."

"Porciform?" Uncle Mel said.

"Yes, shaped like a pig," Professor McFwain said. "This goes against all the rules of Monsterology. By rights, he should be like a scaly dragon or a walrus with three eyes—something bizarre. But, as you can see, he is just an ordinary-looking barnyard pig, fifteen or twenty times larger than normal."

"I should say that's nothing to be disappointed about," said Captain Sinbad Weinstein. "Pigs that size don't grow on trees."

"Of course, you're right," said Professor McFwain. "I'm just trying to get used to the idea. Captain, the monster doesn't seem to have noticed us. Do you think we can get a little closer?"

Captain Sinbad Weinstein started the engines as quietly as he could. We made slow progress in the direction of the monster. The floating pig gave no sign that it was aware of us.

"You'd think that the searchlights would have scared him," I said.

"He may be asleep," Uncle Mel said.

That was the only explanation. As we got closer and closer, the pig did not move. It was bigger than any of us had thought. It was considerably more than twenty times larger than an ordinary barnyard pig. I was getting a little nervous about being so close to anything that big.

Apparently Uncle Mel was having the same thought. "Don't you think we're close enough?" he asked. At this point, the pig was towering over us.

"Nonsense!" said Colonel Ken Krenwinkle. "This is the best sport I've had since I bagged the Mack truck in Herkimer County. I want to get close enough to touch the fellow!"

Professor McFwain didn't say anything. He was busy snapping pictures. Captain Sinbad Weinstein seemed perfectly happy in the wheelhouse. It was about this time that I noticed that the members of the crew of *La Forza Materiale* had lowered a lifeboat and were rowing away as fast as they could.

"Look!" I shouted. "The crew is running away!"

"Not so loud, boy!" Professor McFwain said. "We don't want to wake Yobgorgle up until we're right on top of him. Then I can get some action closeups."

"That crew is a cowardly lot," Colonel Ken Krenwinkle said. "I'm going to take something out of their wages for this, you can be sure."

"I wish the crew had told me what they were going to do," Uncle Mel said. "I would have gone with them. Don't you all think we've gotten close enough? Professor McFwain, you've gotten some really wonderful pictures. Let's go a little distance away so we can watch the monster. Maybe we'll get to see him feeding. Wouldn't you like to know what he eats?"

"I think he eats boats," I said. "Big ones. Please, let's get out of here."

"What's this?" Colonel Ken Krenwinkle said. "Let's not panic. The worst thing with big game is to let them know you're afraid of them—they can smell it. Look him in the eye—don't let him get the better of you."

We were close enough now to bounce a tennis ball off the pig's snout. He still hadn't moved or paid the least attention to us. I was hoping that maybe he was dead, when I realized that I could hear him breathing. He was breathing or snoring or maybe growling. It was a continuous grinding noise. It sounded more mechanical than piglike. Also, I could smell him. I don't have much experience with farm animals, but I know that pigs aren't supposed to smell like diesel fuel. This pig smelled like a truck—sort of a hot oil smell.

Then a voice came from the pig. "What ship are you?" the voice shouted.

Uncle Mel and Professor Ambrose McFwain and Colonel Ken Krenwinkle and Captain Sinbad Weinstein and I looked at each other.

"What ship, where from, and where bound?" the voice repeated.

"I am *La Forza Materiale*, out of Rochester, on a research expedition," Captain Sinbad Weinstein shouted through his cupped hands. "The crew has deserted. We're carrying a party of scientists and provisions for three days: imitation vegetarian hard salami, swiss cheese, whole wheat bread, pickles, cole slaw, celery tonic, mayonnaise, coffee, and non-dairy creamer; also five dozen assorted doughnuts and crullers."

Apparently this was some kind of nautical courtesy—when you meet another ship (or, in this case, a floating pig that talks to you) you're supposed to tell where you're from, what you're doing, and what you have on board.

"No corned beef?" asked the voice from the pig.

"No corned beef," Captain Sinbad Weinstein shouted. "Only what I told you. And what—uh—what pig are you?"

"I am the submarine *Flying Piggie*," the voice replied, "on a secret mission. I am the master of this vessel, Captain Van Straaten. If you wish, you may come aboard."

It was a submarine! It wasn't a real pig. It was a boat made to look just like a real pig, only much bigger. As we realized this, a hatch opened in the middle of the pig's back—just where the slot would be on a piggy bank—and a man climbed out. He was tall and wore a fancy sea captain's coat with gold braid at the cuffs. He had a great big gray beard.

"Gentlemen," the captain of the pig-submarine said, "you are the first people I have encountered after seven years of sailing this lake. Please honor me by coming on board and dining with me."

17

"We will be honored to come aboard, Captain Van Straaten," Captain Sinbad Weinstein said. "However, we can't all come at once. As I mentioned before, my crew has deserted, and at least one of us will have to stay aboard the *La Forza Materiale* to keep ship."

"That won't be necessary, Captain," said Captain Van Straaten. "Just tie up to the ring in the *Flying Piggie*'s nose. In this calm sea, there won't be any trouble. Meanwhile, I'll lower a ladder."

Captain Sinbad Weinstein tied a rope to the ring in the nose of the *Flying Piggie*, and Captain Van Straaten lowered a flexible ladder down the side of the pig-submarine. One by one, we went down the flight of stairs on the side of *La Forza Materiale* and clambered up the smooth pink side of the *Flying Piggie*. As each one of us got to the top of the ladder, Captain Van Staaten shook hands and introduced himself again. Then he directed each of us to climb into the hatch, down the ladder, and wait for him to join us.

I was the last one on board except for Captain Sinbad Weinstein, who was right behind me.

"I'll be down in a moment, gentlemen," Captain Van Staaten called down the ladder. "I just have to do a couple of things on deck, and then I'll give you a tour of the boat."

Uncle Mel, Professor Ambrose McFwain, Colonel Ken

Krenwinkle, Captain Sinbad Weinstein, and I were all gathered in a little room at the bottom of the ladder. There wasn't anything in the room. The walls were made of steel plate, painted gray. There was a bronze plaque attached to one of the walls:

Deutsches Unterseeschwimmschweinboot
FLIEGENDES SCHWEIN
In Dienst gestellt, 194__

I asked Professor McFwain if he could read the writing on the plaque. He said it was in German. It said, "German Underwaterswimmingpigboat, *Flying Piggie*, Commissioned, 194__."

Captain Van Straaten came down the ladder, fastening the hatch behind him. "Are you from Germany?" I asked him.

"No, I am Dutch," he said, "but my boat was built in Germany. It is an interesting story. Perhaps you gentlemen have noticed that this submarine looks exactly like a pig."

Everyone had noticed that.

"Well, this boat was built for the German Navy right at the close of World War II. They had the idea of building submarines to look like familiar barnyard animals. In this way, if sighted by a hostile ship, the sub would be taken for a pig out for a swim, and no further notice would be taken. At a great distance, the fact that the pig was nearly a city block long would go unnoticed."

"Brilliant," said Professor McFwain.

"Yes, it was a good idea," Captain Van Staaten continued, "but the German Navy never had a chance to try it out. The war ended before they could commission their first animal-shaped submarine, the *Flying Piggie*. In fact, the *Flying Piggie* was never even assembled. It was built in the Peugeot car works in occupied France, packed in thousands of boxes, and shipped by rail to the sea where it was supposed to be put together. Years after the war, I bought the submarine, still packed in thousands of boxes, from a French junk dealer named Sharnopol. In my spare time, I assembled the sub—by this time I had come to live in America—and finally launched it in Lake Ontario exactly fourteen years ago."

"Fourteen years ago was when the first reports of Yobgorgle started to come in!" Professor McFwain shouted.

"Yes, Professor McFwain, I know about your search for the monster Yobgorgle," Captain Van Staaten said. "There is a drive-in movie in a suburb of Rochester that has a screen facing the lake. I saw the movie in which you appear by periscope two weeks ago. I hope you are not disappointed to find that your sea monster is actually an electric boat."

"Well, really, this is about the biggest success of my career," Professor McFwain said. "I mean, even if the monster isn't a prehistoric creature, as least I've found *something*."

"But what are you doing in this boat?" Captain Sinbad Weinstein asked.

"I'll be happy to answer all of your questions at dinner," Captain Van Straaten said, "but now, I'd like to show you around my boat. I'm sure you'll find it interesting."

Captain Van Straaten had made a lot of improvements in

the design of the *Flying Piggie*. He had no crew. Everything was done by computer and electric motors. Also he had fixed up the crew's quarters into a really nice apartment for himself.

"Gentlemen, we are now in the midsection of the boat where the spareribs would be—just a little joke," Captain Van Straaten said. "If you will make yourselves comfortable, I will go and see about the dinner. There are brandy and cigars for those who use them. I'll be right back."

Captain Van Straaten stepped out of the room and closed the door behind him. We heard a loud click.

"Well, what an interesting boat," Colonel Ken Krenwinkle said.

"And what a nice man Captain Van Straaten is," Uncle Mel said.

"I think he's locked us in this room," I said.

18

Nobody seemed to pay any attention to what I'd said. Uncle Mel was spreading some cheese on a cracker he had found on a side table. Professor McFwain was munching little bits of salami. Colonel Ken Krenwinkle and Captain Sinbad Weinstein were lighting up cigars. I went to the door and tried it. "It's locked," I said.

"Eugene," Captain Sinbad Weinstein said, "submarines have watertight doors between compartments. It isn't locked, it's just hard to open. I'll show you." Captain Sinbad Weinstein went to the door and tried to turn the big wheel in the middle. "It's locked," he said.

There was a noise, a humming, vibrating sort of noise, and we felt one end of the room tilt downward. "Excuse me, Captain Weinstein," Colonel Ken Krenwinkle said. "Am I correct in assuming that Captain Van Straaten has started the engines, and this boat is under way?"

"Not only that, Colonel," said Captain Sinbad Weinstein. "I believe we're diving."

"Gentlemen, please do not be alarmed," we heard Captain Van Straaten's voice say—it was coming over a loud-speaker. "It has been necessary for me to cast off from your vessel and submerge. You are all perfectly safe. Please make yourselves comfortable, and I will rejoin you in a few moments and answer all your questions. By the way, in case you are considering an act of force, I should tell you that this submarine is extremely complicated to operate—it is unlike any other boat in the world, and I am the only person who knows how to operate it. If anything should happen to me, it is very unlikely that you would ever be able to get to the surface again."

"I should say that things are getting serious," Colonel Ken Krenwinkle said.

"Let's not be hasty," Professor Ambrose McFwain said. "Let's give Captain Van Straaten a chance to explain."

"Yes," said Captain Sinbad Weinstein. "After all, he is a ship's captain—he must be a gentleman."

"I want to get out of here," Uncle Mel said.

"So do I," I said.

Captain Van Straaten entered the room. "Ah, gentlemen, please excuse all these interruptions. Now we will be able to sit down and have something to eat and a nice talk. By the way, we're now cruising at forty knots at a depth of thirty feet."

"Good Lord!" said Captain Sinbad Weinstein. "That's terribly fast. Shouldn't you be at a porthole or a radar screen looking out for obstacles?"

"Not at all, Captain," said Captain Van Straaten. "As I told you, this is unlike any other boat in the world. It runs itself electronically. If an object should appear in our path, the *Flying Piggie* will automatically correct course and miss it. Now, please allow me to serve some food."

Captain Van Straaten opened a cupboard and took out various dishes of food and put them on the table. There was sliced roast beef, salad, two kinds of bread, pie and ice cream, wine, and a pitcher of milk. "Eat hearty, gentlemen," said Captain Van Straaten, helping us to food.

Uncle Mel took a big bite of roast beef and then screwed up his face in a strange expression. Professor Ambrose McFwain bit into a forkful of salad and stared at Uncle Mel.

"Good, isn't it?" Captain Van Straaten said. "Now I'm going to amaze you. Every single thing you're eating—everything, even the milk—is made entirely from fish. That's right—fish. This submarine was designed to be entirely self-sufficient for long periods of time. There's an incredibly efficient food-processing plant on board that can duplicate almost any taste and texture of food, using only the fish I net in my electrically operated fish-catcher."

I took a sip of milk. It tasted like fish. So did the roast beef. So did the salad and the bread. The idea of fish-flavored ice cream was too much for me, so I didn't try it.

"There are many more marvels aboard this boat, and I will tell you about all of them as the days go by," said Captain Van Straaten. "We'll have a wonderful time, don't you fear. I couldn't have asked for a more perfect crew."

"Crew?" we asked. "As the days go by?"

"Yes," said Captain Van Straaten. "I neglected to tell you that we will all be together for some considerable time— seven years at least—so we may as well be friendly."

"See here, Captain," said Colonel Ken Krenwinkle, half rising. "I think you'd better explain yourself."

"I shall be happy to explain everything," said Captain Van Straaten. "Kindly sit down and enjoy your cigar, which, by the way, is also a fish product."

Colonel Ken Krenwinkle took the cigar out of his mouth and stared at it.

"Now," said Captain Van Straaten, "kindly let me tell my story without interruption. If you have any questions when I've finished, I will be happy to answer them.

"Have you ever heard of the Flying Dutchman?" Captain Van Straaten said, lighting up a fish-cigar. "Well, I am that very person. In the version of the story you usually hear, the Flying Dutchman is captain of a cursed ship, doomed to sail the seas forever, never putting into port. Every seven years, he may touch land, but unless a woman will offer to marry him, even though it means her death, he has to continue sailing."

Captain Van Straaten took a long puff on the cigar. "That's the story most people know, and like most stories, it is not exactly accurate. In fact, I am sailing under a curse, and in fact, I do have to sail the seas—or in the present case, Lake Ontario—continually. However, I have no wish to get married, and if I did, it wouldn't make any difference to the curse, except that in addition to everything else, I'd have to drag a wife along with me. What's more, I can *never* touch land—not until the curse is lifted. You see, it's a lot more complicated than the usual story."

"Tell us more about this curse," Colonel Ken Krenwinkle said.

"Well, for one thing," said the Captain, "it is not the ship that is cursed—it is me. In the past six hundred years, I've been the captain of perhaps two dozen ships. As soon as I set foot on a ship, the curse takes over—that ship can never touch land. In order to escape the curse, I have to meet two conditions: first, I have to leave my ship and go directly to land. This might seem simple—I could just steer close to land and jump off—but in fact, no ship with me on board can come closer than five miles to any land, and I can't swim. Second, after getting ashore, if no one offers me a decent corned-beef sandwich within twenty-four hours, I have to put out to sea again. This makes going ashore in most parts of the world a futile exercise. You may ask why I don't jump off with a life-preserver and just paddle to shore. I tried that, but under the terms of the curse, anything that keeps me afloat is regarded as a ship. I spent two years floating around in a life-preserver until I finally got picked up by a ship, which then, of course, became my ship."

Uncle Mel interrupted Captain Van Straaten. "But what do you want with us? Why have you kidnapped us?"

"Because I'm lonely, man! Can't you understand that? I'm always losing crews, and then I have to sail around all by myself," Captain Van Straaten shouted. "Now that I have you jolly crewmen on board, we can have all sorts of fun. We can sing sea chanties and dance hornpipes and play games and sit around having discussions like this."

"So what," said the Flying Dutchman. "Who wants to sail forever? Do you think I like it?"

"But that isn't fair," I said.

"Of course not," Captain Van Straaten said. "But is it fair that I have to sail and sail and sail with nobody to talk to?" At this point he got very excited and rushed out of the room, locking the door behind him.

19

"Well, what do you think?" Colonel Ken Krenwinkle asked Professor Ambrose McFwain, when Captain Van Straaten had left. "Is he crazy or is he really the Flying Dutchman?"

"He is certainly crazy," Professor McFwain said, "and he may also be the Flying Dutchman. In any case, I suggest we try to be as pleasant as possible and keep him calm. He strikes me as the sort of person one doesn't want to stir up."

"What about the story that he put this submarine together from parts in little boxes?" I asked. "If that's true, then it doesn't fit his story about being cursed."

"I wouldn't say anything about it, Eugene," Professor McFwain said. "Just be friendly and go along with things. We'll have to wait and see what favorable opportunity develops."

Captain Van Straaten came back. "Excuse me, gentlemen," he said. "I suddenly remembered something I had to do. Now, let's continue our little chat." Captain Van Straaten looked strange—his eyes were red, and his beard was all messy. It looked as though he had been crying.

"Captain, you said you would show us the rest of this boat," Professor McFwain said.

"Yes," Captain Van Straaten said. "Do you all promise you won't try to take over my boat by force?"

We promised.

"Then I'll be happy to show you around," the Flying Dutchman said. "Please come this way."

We followed Captain Van Straaten down a long corridor. "These are the crew's quarters," he said. He showed us a small compartment hung with five hammocks. "I'm sorry the accommodations aren't more comfortable," said Captain Van Straaten, "but you are free to visit in my quarters, which are much nicer—and you can make fish-popcorn in the galley, and you can look through the periscope—oh, you'll have a good time on board the *Flying Piggie*, I promise you."

The idea of spending the rest of my life on a submarine and eating fish-popcorn didn't appeal to me at all, but I didn't say anything.

"Now this is the control room," Captain Van Straaten said. "As I explained to you before, the boat can be run electronically—that is, it can run itself—or I can steer her and control her. The only thing I can't make the boat do is get closer than five miles to any land—the curse, you know. But I can dive, run on the surface, stop, and go as fast as I like."

"Captain Van Straaten," Captain Sinbad Weinstein said, "you told us that the boat is now running at forty knots underwater. That's almost fifty miles per hour, land speed, and terribly fast for any sort of vessel—especially underwater."

"Oh, she can go much faster than that," Captain Van Staaten said. "In fact, I don't really know how fast she can go. I once had her up to ninety-three knots, and the engines weren't even working hard. She's the fastest pig afloat."

"That's way over a hundred miles an hour!" Captain Sinbad Weinstein said. "That's faster than anything but a

DANIEL PINKWATER

rocket-powered speedboat! What sort of engines does this boat have, and what do they run on?"

"They are special engines," Captain Van Straaten said, "and they run on fish-juice, which I process myself from my daily catch. As I told you the *Flying Piggie* is totally self-sufficient. As long as there are fish, she runs, and I have a thirty-day reserve of fish juice."

Captain Van Straaten led us to another compartment. "Now let me show you my traveling factory," he said. "This is where fish from Lake Ontario are converted into all the things I need for my very civilized life."

We were led into a room full of shining stainless steel pipes and vats with lots of dials and gauges and knobs and buttons.

"It looks very complicated," Captain Van Straaten said, "and it is, but it is simple to work. The *Flying Piggie* has automatic sensors located on the outside of her hull. When we encounter any fish, large or small—or any schools of fish—special nets shoot out from the sides of the boat and catch them. They are drawn into this factory-room and held for processing. If I am running low, on any stores—say cigars—I just punch these keys, and the supplies I need will appear on this screen."

Captain Van Straaten pressed keys on what looked like a typewriter keyboard. "See? Just as I thought—we're down to our last box of fish cigars. Notice the numbers and letters following the listing for cigars? That's a code. I just punch up that code, like this. . . ."

Captain Van Straaten typed out the series of numbers and letters that followed the word "cigars" on the screen. There was a hissing noise. Then there was a clanking noise, and various lights flashed on and off. After a minute or two, a stainless steel door opened in the side of a large boxlike thing, and let out a cloud of fishy-smelling steam. There in a stainless steel tray were a bunch of cigars, smelling of fish.

"You see!" cried Captain Van Straaten, "just like magic! Almost anything you want, except a decent corned-beef sandwich, can be had in this way. In time, I will teach you gentlemen to operate the fish synthesizer, and you can come in here and make whatever you desire."

Uncle Mel was really interested in the fish synthesizer. It was the most complicated machine he had ever seen that made bad-tasting food while you waited—and cigars, even! I could see he was very impressed.

"We also have a television on board," said Captain Van Straaten, "and radio, a small library, and a collection of phonograph records. The taste of whoever outfitted this boat ran to Spike Jones and modern French organ music. I hope that will suit you. In short, gentlemen, everything you need is here on the *Flying Piggie*. I know you will be very happy."

After saying this, Captain Van Straaten reached inside a jacket and took out a very large revolver. "Please don't be alarmed, gentlemen, but now I must ask you to go quietly to your quarters. It's time for lights out, you know. I regret that I will have to lock you in for the night. Just a formality, you understand. Now, march!"

Captain Van Straaten herded us into the little room with the hammocks. "I'll be letting you out at breakfast time. It's fish flakes and fish milk tomorrow—yummy! Good night." He closed the door and locked it.

20

"This will never do," said Colonel Ken Krenwinkle.

"No, indeed," said Professor Ambrose McFwain.

"We're prisoners!" said Uncle Mel.

"I don't want fish flakes for breakfast for the rest of my life," I said.

"I think that what Captain Van Straaten is doing is against the law," said Captain Sinbad Weinstein.

"I think we can overpower him and take that revolver away," said Colonel Ken Krenwinkle.

"We promised we wouldn't do that," Uncle Mel said.

"That was before he pulled a gun on us," Colonel Ken Krenwinkle said. "That's very bad manners, and we don't have to treat him like a gentleman after a trick like that."

"But, Colonel," Professor McFwain said, "even if we did overpower him, could we operate this submarine? Suppose we took away his revolver and tied him up. He might be very upset, and he might not be willing to tell us how to operate the boat. Don't forget, we're underwater."

"That's true," Colonel Ken Krenwinkle said. "Captain Sinbad Weinstein, can you operate this submarine?"

"It isn't like any other boat," Captain Sinbad Weinstein said. "Maybe if I had an instruction manual, or if Captain Van Straaten would give me lessons for a week or so . . ."

"In other words, we can't run the boat without Captain

261

Van Straaten, and as long as he's in charge, he'll keep us prisoners," said Uncle Mel.

"That seems to be the case," said Professor Ambrose McFwain.

"But Captain Van Straaten doesn't like being on this boat, really," I said. "He doesn't like it any more than we do. He just wants to keep us on board because he's lonely."

"That's true, Eugene," Professor McFwain said, "but it doesn't alter our predicament."

"Yes, it does," I said. "The only way for us to get off this boat is to take Captain Van Straaten with us. We have to figure out a way to break his curse."

"What Eugene says makes sense," Colonel Ken Krenwinkle said. "That is, assuming there really is a curse, and that Captain Van Straaten isn't just a garden-variety lunatic. But how are we going to break the curse? He has to get to land—and the boat is somehow magically programmed to get no closer than five miles to land. Captain Van Straaten can't swim, and any artificial aid, such as a life-preserver, is technically regarded as a ship under the terms of his curse. I assume that if we swam with him and kept him afloat, then we would be technically regarded as a ship and wouldn't be able to get closer than five miles from shore either.

"The second condition of lifting the curse," Colonel Ken Krenwinkle went on, "would be no problem, of course, if we land in the vicinity of Rochester. I happen to own a restaurant where the best corned-beef sandwiches in the state can be had, a little gourmet placed called Fred's Fat Pig."

"You own Fred's Fat Pig?" Uncle Mel and Professor McFwain shouted.

"Yes. I've owned it for years. I own all sorts of things," said Colonel Ken Krenwinkle.

Uncle Mel and Professor Ambrose McFwain looked at Colonel Ken Krenwinkle with admiration.

Captain Sinbad Weinstein spoke, "I think Eugene has hit upon the only solution. We must help Captain Van Straaten get free of his curse. The question is how to do that. I think I may have an idea. It may not work, and it may be dangerous, but it's worth a try. But first, I have to ask him some questions. Let's try and get him to talk to us."

We beat on the walls of the little room with our shoes, and shouted and screamed until we heard Captain Van Straaten's voice over the loudspeaker. "What is it? You woke me up with all that noise!"

"Captain Van Straaten, this is Captain Sinbad Weinstein," Captain Sinbad Weinstein said. "We are considering ways to help you break the curse, and we have to ask you some questions."

"Really?" Captain Van Straaten said. "I'll be right down to let you out. We'll go to the galley and make some fish-cocoa and talk it over."

Captain Van Straaten came to unlock the door of the crew's quarters wearing a really fancy bathrobe with gold embroidered dragons on it. It was five times as fancy as the bathrobe Professor McFwain had given Uncle Mel.

"Captain Van Straaten," Professor McFwain said, "you can dispense with that ugly revolver. We all agree to give our word to do nothing violent. Besides, we realize that without you to help us we can never get out of this submarine."

"Thank you," said Captain Van Straaten. "I would never have used the gun. It's just that so many crews have run away. Besides the gun is made of hard rubber anyway. It doesn't shoot."

In the galley, Captain Van Straaten served us mugs of hot fish-cocoa. It tasted like fish, of course.

Captain Sinbad Weinstein spoke. "Captain Van Straaten, please tell us exactly what the terms of your curse consist of."

DANIEL PINKWATER

21

"I'm flattered that you're interested in my story," Captain Van Straaten said, "but did you have to wake me up in the middle of the night to ask me that? Besides, I believe I already told you. I have to get to land, which is next to impossible; and once there, I have to be offered a decent corned-beef sandwich within twenty-four hours, or I have to steal a ship of some sort and put out to sea again."

"We're sorry to have awakened you," Professor McFwain said, "but we think that maybe we can help you—at least we want to."

"That's awfully nice of you," Captain Van Straaten said.

"Now tell us," Captain Sinbad Weinstein said, "exactly how the curse goes. Do you have a copy of it written down somewhere? What are the exact words of the curse?"

"Do you think I need to have the curse written down? I remember every word of it. Of course, it's in Dutch, but I can give you a rough translation. It goes like this:

As punishment for being a no-good, low-down, rotten so-and-so, Captain Seymour Van Straaten is cursed and shall forever sail the sea. No vessel with that miserable skunk on board shall ever float in waters closer than five miles from shore.

Only if that filthy creep can somehow get to land shall this curse be lifted, and then only if some kind soul will offer him a corned-beef sandwich on rye, with coleslaw and a pickle, of good quality within one day of his setting foot on land.

Let the fate of this worthless low-life be a lesson for all who break the sacred code of the sea.

"That's the curse?" Uncle Mel asked.

"Horrible, isn't it?" Captain Van Straaten said.

"The curse says 'No vessel shall ever *float* in waters closer than five miles from shore'?" Captain Sinbad Weinstein asked.

"That's what it says," Captain Van Straaten said. "I'm not sure it's good grammar, but that's what it says."

"Tell me," Captain Sinbad Weinstein said, "does this submarine have hydroplanes?"

"Of course, it does," Captain Van Straaten said. "Every submarine has hydroplanes."

"What are hydroplanes?" I asked.

"They're horizontal rudders. The sub uses them to dive and surface," Captain Van Straaten said. "They are rather like wings."

"Exactly!" said Captain Sinbad Weinstein. "And you told me that this submarine can go faster than 100 miles per hour, land speed."

"Oh, much faster," Captain Van Straaten said. "Goodness knows how fast she will go."

"Now," said Captain Sinbad Weinstein, "what would happen if we were to get going really fast on the surface—say, 150 miles per hour?"

"Well, the nose of the boat would rise up out of the water,

and she'd sort of skip along—flying almost," Captain Van Straaten said.

"That's called hydroplaning," Captain Sinbad Weinstein said. "In fact, the boat actually turns into a sort of airplane and is not really floating in the water, but skipping along above the surface—the whole hull is out of the water."

"And the curse says . . ." shouted Uncle Mel.

"The curse says floating," said Captain Sinbad Weinstein.

"Fantastic," said Professor McFwain. "Captain Van Straaten, do you think such a thing is possible, and do you think it would release you from the curse?"

"It would be worth a try," said Captain Van Straaten. "Except for one thing."

"And what is that?" Colonel Ken Krenwinkle asked.

"Well, I'd like to know what would happen when we hit the shore going maybe 160 or 170 knots," Captain Van Straaten said. "I expect we'd all be smashed to pieces."

"Not necessarily," said Captain Sinbad Weinstein. "Suppose we headed for a sandy, sloping beach. The nose of the boat is already up in the air. We'd just hydroplane through the shallow water and ride up onto the beach and skid to a stop. The soft sand would help us slow down."

"Unless we hit something hard first," I said.

"Well, the plan is not without risk," said Captain Van Straaten, "but it does seem worth a try. If it doesn't work out, I will just have to float around until I can get another ship. I'm immortal, you know—it goes with the curse."

"But we're not," Uncle Mel said.

"Well, then it's a greater risk for you," said Captain Van

Straaten. "I want you all to know that I really appreciate the sacrifice you may be making for me." Then he turned to Captain Sinbad Weinstein and said, "I say let's try it."

"I say let's talk it over some more," I said.

"The next thing to do is have a speed trial," Captain Sinbad Weinstein said. "Captain, let's take her up and see how fast she'll go."

"Excuse me," said Uncle Mel, "but I don't see why we all have to be on board for this landing. Couldn't you cruise around and find *La Forza Materiale* and put us back on board, and then make your high-speed run for shore?"

"I knew it!" shouted the Flying Dutchman. "This is all a trick to get off the *Flying Piggie!* I'm not going to surface, so there! Now get back to your room!" He began waving the pistol about.

"Captain Van Straaten, you have already told us that the gun is made of hard rubber," Colonel Ken Krenwinkle said. "Now, if we promise to stay on board will you try out Captain Sinbad Weinstein's idea?"

"Well, if you all promise . . ." Captain Van Straaten said.

"Of course, we promise," said Colonel Ken Krenwinkle, and then he turned to Uncle Mel. "Sir, I can see you have a lot to learn about adventuring. You will stick this out to the bitter end."

"That's what I'm afraid of," said Uncle Mel.

22

Captain Van Straaten took the *Flying Piggie* to the surface to make some speed trials with Captain Sinbad Weinstein. There wasn't room for more than two people in the little cockpit on top of the pig-submarine's back, so the rest of us had to wait down below. We could hear Captain Van Straaten and Captain Sinbad Weinstein shouting and screaming. "Whee!" "Let's go faster!" "Oh, boy!"

It wasn't very pleasant. Inside the submarine all we could feel was a terrible vibration, and all we could hear, except for the excited shouts of the two sea captains, was the roar of the engines.

"We're doing 180 knots!" we heard Captain Sinbad Weinstein shout.

"She's lifting! She's lifting!" Captain Van Straaten shouted. "We're airborne! We're flying!"

It felt to us as though the boat was going to rip apart. I felt sort of sick. Uncle Mel *was* sick. Professor McFwain and Colonel Ken Krenwinkle didn't seem too comfortable either. By the end of the speed trial, I was the only one who didn't look green, although I didn't feel exactly wonderful. I was sorry I had had my fish-cocoa.

Captain Van Straaten and Captain Sinbad Weinstein came down the ladder. They were very excited. "We can do it!" Captain Van Straaten said.

"She flies like a bird!" Captain Sinbad Weinstein said.

"Let's take her ashore right now!" Captain Van Straaten said.

"Why not!" said Captain Sinbad Weinstein.

"Don't you think it would be safer to wait for daylight?" Professor McFwain asked.

"There's no need," Captain Sinbad Weinstein said. "The fog has lifted and the night is clear. We can see the shore perfectly. I'll pilot her in from the bridge, and Captain Van Straaten can stay below and keep an eye on the engines. We don't want to run out of speed."

"Really, I don't see why we can't wait for morning," Uncle Mel said.

"Well, there is a reason," Captain Van Straaten said. "Something about the curse I forgot to tell you. You see, I am only able to surface for a few days every seven years. According to my calculations, starting tomorrow at dawn — which is only four hours away — we will have to go under for seven years. Of course, if you don't mind a short wait, we can make our landing seven years from now. I have a Scrabble set and a lot of other games to pass the time."

"Seven years may seem short to you, Captain," Colonel Ken Krenwinkle said, "but it is not short to me. I say let's go for the shore."

"Splendid," said Captain Sinbad Weinstein. "Now who wants to come up and watch from the bridge?"

"I do," I said. I don't know why I said it, except that I really needed some fresh air, and I knew that if I had to stay below during another 180-knot run, I was going to be sick.

"There's no time to lose," said Captain Van Straaten. "Eugene, go up top with Captain Sinbad Weinstein. I'll tend the engines."

"Captain, if this works, you shall have the finest corned-beef sandwich in the world within the hour," Colonel Ken Krenwinkle said.

I went up the ladder with Captain Sinbad Weinstein.

"See that white stretch of shoreline?" he asked me. "That's either a beach, or a concrete embankment. If it is a beach, we should slide right up it, nice as you please."

"What if it's a concrete embankment?" I asked.

"Then we'll be smashed to bits," Captain Sinbad Weinstein said. "But don't worry—I'm almost sure it's a beach." He spoke into a sort of tube that connected to the engine room. "Captain, you may give me full speed whenever you're ready."

The engines screamed, and we started forward. I never went so fast in my life. At first the nose of the *Flying Piggie* cut through the water, making two great mountains of spray on either side, but as we went faster and faster, the nose began to lift up, and the spray began to fall away from the pig-submarine.

"She's lifting! She's lifting!" Captain Sinbad Weinstein shouted.

The boat was rocking slightly from side to side. I could feel it losing contact with the water. Then we were sort of bouncing along. I remembered times I had skipped stones over the surface of water—that's what the *Flying Piggie* was doing, hopping along. Each hop was twenty or thirty feet at first; then the hops got longer. At last the motion of the boat became smooth again, except for a terrific vibration from the engines, and I knew we were actually flying over the water.

"Isn't this great, Eugene?" Captain Sinbad Weinstein shouted over the engine noise.

"Can you tell if that's a beach or a concrete wall yet?" I shouted back.

"Not yet," he shouted. "But don't worry—we still have time to turn away if we have to."

"It looks like a wall to me," I shouted.

"It's still too far to tell," Captain Sinbad Weinstein shouted.

"It's a wall! It's a wall!" I shouted.

"It's a beach!" Captain Sinbad Weinstein shouted.

"It's a wall!"

"It's a beach!"

"It's a beach *and* a wall!" I screamed. "It's a beach with a concrete wall running along in front of it!"

"I believe you're right," Captain Sinbad Weinstein said.

"Turn the boat! Turn the boat!" I screamed. I was really scared.

"It's too late for that, Eugene," Captain Sinbad Weinstein said. "If we start to turn now, we'll hit the wall at an angle, and that will be really bad. The only thing we can do is try to go over the wall and onto the beach. We might be able to do that—it depends how high the wall is." He shouted into the speaking tube, "Captain Van Straaten, open her up all the way. We have to clear an obstacle that might be as high as ten feet."

I could hear Captain Van Straaten laughing like a madman through the speaking tube. Suddenly the engines, which had been screaming all along, began to make a noise unlike anything I had ever heard before. I didn't so much hear it as feel it. It was too loud to hear. I felt as though I was inside the noise. The boat surged forward. My hair stood out straight behind me. I felt my nose pressing into my face. My teeth hurt. I felt pressure on my eyeballs. My vision got blurry.

"Now *this* is what I call fast," Captain Sinbad Weinstein said.

I couldn't hear him say it. I just saw him moving his lips, which were distorted by the force of our forward travel.

I could see the wall clearly now. It was solid concrete, and it looked as though it was fifteen or twenty feet high. We were doing 230 knots—over 280 miles per hour!

23

This is what a couple of fishermen who were camping out on the beach saw:

The *Flying Piggie*, which the fishermen thought was a gigantic swimming pig, came roaring along at over two hundred miles an hour. It cleared the concrete breakwater by a couple of inches, and belly whopped onto the sandy beach. On the beach it continued to travel at a slightly reduced speed—maybe a hundred and seventy-five miles per hour. It traveled the width of the beach, still losing momentum, and was not doing more than sixty when it crossed State Highway 18. Then it cut down sixty-four trees of all sizes, slid across an access road, and came to rest, only slightly damaged, in the parking lot of Fred's Fat Pig.

Captain Sinbad Weinstein and I were fine. We had just held on to the edge of the cockpit. The people below had been tossed around quite a bit, and the inside of the sub was a mess—but nobody was hurt.

Fred's Fat Pig was open all night, so there were some cooks and waitresses inside, but there were no customers in the place. The waitresses recognized Colonel Ken Krenwinkle and didn't seem especially surprised at having a giant pig crash into the parking lot. They knew all about Colonel Ken Krenwinkle's hobby of motor-vehicle hunting and probably thought the *Flying Piggie* had something to do with that.

Colonel Ken Krenwinkle ordered a corned-beef sandwich on rye, with coleslaw and a pickle, for the Flying Dutchman, who gleefully ate it with tartar sauce. Uncle Mel and Professor McFwain had a few dozen hamburgers to celebrate our safe landing.

Colonel Ken Krenwinkle telephoned his driver to come and pick everyone up. Professor McFwain was taken back to the fat men's clothing factory. Uncle Mel and I were taken back to the motel. Captains Van Straaten and Sinbad Weinstein were going to stay at Colonel Ken Krenwinkle's house. We were all going to meet again the next day at Fred's Fat Pig to have a celebration and discuss our adventure.

24

Captain Sinbad Weinstein and Captain Van Straaten had become good friends. They decided to convert the *Flying Piggie* into a restaurant and become partners with Colonel Ken Krenwinkle in running it as part of Fred's Fat Pig.

Colonel Ken Krenwinkle was delighted with the idea. He also offered Uncle Mel a job in a new company he wanted to start, which would make all kinds of fast foods, cigars, and other things out of fish, and sell them from vending machines in bus stations, bowling alleys, and other places like that. Uncle Mel took the job, which meant he'd be coming back to Rochester often to see his new friends. He said that sometimes I could come with him.

Professor McFwain applied for a patent on a toy pig that could swim through the water at 260 miles per hour. You've seen them—they're the most popular swimming pool toy since the inflatable shark.

The professor says that he's going to use some of the proceeds from his invention to mount an expedition to find Big Belly, the fabled giant horse of the Arctic Circle. I'm going with him. He says I'm the best assistant he's ever had.

I'm thinking about becoming a professional monster-hunter myself when I grow up.

The WORMS of KUKUMLIMA

1

My parents couldn't understand why I wanted to spend the summer working for my grandfather.

"Wouldn't you rather have fun with your friends?" they asked.

Certainly. I would have rather had fun with my friends—but the truth is, my friends aren't much fun. The summer before was all hanging around and maybe getting up a ball game once in a while. Once or twice we'd all manage to go somewhere, like the beach—and then it was time for school to start again, and nothing really had happened.

I wasn't going to get caught in that sort of summer again. Besides, kids who had jobs had a lot of status in the neighborhood. You were a big hero if you had a job. Mostly the jobs kids got were kid jobs, like working in a greaseburger stand, or dog walking, lawn mowing, baby-sitting. I was going to work full time for my grandfather and make a real salary. Besides, I like my grandfather. He's fun to spend time with. So the way I had it figured, I would have a better time with Grandpa than if I just hung out with the kids, I'd make a lot of money, and I'd be looked up to besides. It was a solid decision.

So the first Monday after school let out, I waited outside the house, and Grandpa picked me up in his very old Nash Metropolitan, and we went to work.

Like everything else about Grandpa, his car is a little strange. It's a two-seater. It isn't a sports car. It looks like an ordinary 1950s car, which is what it is, only it's sort of mini-size. It looks like a toy or a car in a cartoon. Grandpa says any car will last forever, if you change the oil a lot and never driver faster than thirty-five miles per hour. Grandpa's car tends to drift sideways a lot, and it makes black smoke. It's my favorite car.

That Monday morning, Grandpa and I chugged along, in his Nash Metropolitan, to Grandpa's business, The World Famous Salami Snap Company.

Nobody knows what a salami snap is—although everybody has seen them. They are the little metal fasteners on the ends of salamis. They hold the casing together. The casing used to be made of skin, but now they use paper or cellophane or plastic. The ends of salamis used to be tied with string. Now they use snaps. My grandfather is the inventor of the salami snap. Every salami snap in the world is either made by my grandfather or made by somebody who has to pay him five cents for every thousand salami snaps he makes.

Salami snaps are also used in the packaging of certain kinds of cheese and to close plastic bags.

My job was going to be helping my grandfather and his employee, Milton. There were a lot of things to do at The World Famous Salami Snap Company. There was the big machine that made the actual salami snaps. The machine had to be oiled and fed rolls of wire that it made into salami snaps. Then the snaps had to be weighed and packed in cardboard boxes of various sizes. The boxes had to be sealed, and labels with addresses had to be pasted on. Then the boxes had to be stacked by the door and loaded onto the truck that came every afternoon. The phone had to be answered. The cat had to be fed. The whole place had to be swept every day. Rolls of wire to make into salami snaps had to be unloaded from the delivery truck. And somebody had to go out for cups of coffee and sweet rolls, and lunch, and the newspaper.

I got to do a little of everything. It was a great job.

Both Milton and my grandfather are classical music freaks. There's a big old wooden radio in the ship that's always tuned to WZOT, the classical music station. Whenever WZOT plays something that Milton and my grandfather like a lot, they switch off the salami snap machine, and sit down and listen to the whole piece. Mostly, they like string quartets by Beethoven. When WZOT plays modern, weird-sounding music, Milton and my grandfather scream and groan and bang on the salami snap machine with hammers. Sometimes they call up the radio station and complain. The other thing they hate is the program every afternoon with this snobby-sounding guy who explains the music. They holler and talk back to the radio when he's on.

I was usually the one to go out for lunch. Most days, they'd send me to the Filipino cafeteria in the next block. I really got to like the food there. My favorite was fried squid. This sounds icky—but it's crunchy and chewy. The guy who owned the cafeteria made his own sausages and tied them with string. Grandpa thought he was old-fashioned.

Sometimes friends would drop by for a visit. I'd be sent out for cups of coffee and sweet rolls. The salami snap machine would be turned off, and we'd all sit down and have a chat. Sometimes we would play cards.

We'd play gin rummy for pennies. Grandpa would always reimburse whatever I lost. He said that playing cards was part of my job, so I didn't have to risk my own money. Most of Grandpa's friends had been playing cards for a long time. I never did get good enough to win.

When there wasn't anything to do, I could just sit around, listening to WZOT, or reading library books, or playing with the cat. I also had to water the plant. Grandpa had a Zitskisberry bush in the office, and it had to be watered every day.

2

I was really happy working for my grandfather at The World Famous Salami Snap Company. It looked like it was going to be a very nice summer, and I was going to put lots of money in the bank.

My parents never did catch on. They thought it was too bad that I was working instead of having a good time all summer. They didn't seem to understand that I found the salami snap business very interesting.

Things got to be a great deal more interesting when Sir Charles Pelicanstein turned up. Sir Charles Pelicanstein was an old friend of my grandfather's. Years before, Sir Charles and my grandfather had taken some trips together. They had gone to some unusual places in South America—up the Amazon, through the jungles, things like that.

Sir Charles Pelicanstein had continued to be an explorer and adventurer, while my grandfather settled down to invent the salami snap and became very rich.

My grandfather didn't act as though he were very rich. He drove around in his Nash Metropolitan, and he lived in a little apartment—but he had lots of money. Not only did he either make or receive royalties on every salami snap used all over the world, but he also held patents on the machines used to fasten the snaps on the ends of salamis. As if that weren't enough, my grandfather had also invented the little plastic thing that bunches together the plastic wrapper on loaves of bread. He was the main stockholder in The World Famous Little Plastic Thing Company.

So Grandpa had plenty of money.

Sir Charles Pelicanstein appeared one afternoon at The World Famous Salami Snap Company. He was really impressive, dressed in a white suit, with a big hat, and carrying a cane with a gold handle. I was sitting in the office reading a library book about famous chickens in history, when he came in.

"Young man," he said, "I am seeking my old friend, Seumas Finneganstein. My name is Sir Charles Pelicanstein. Kindly announce me."

"Sir Charles! Is it really you?" my grandfather shouted.

"Seumas, my old comrade!" Sir Charles said. They hugged each other.

"Sir Charles," Grandpa said, "this is my grandson, Ronald Donald Almondotter. And this is my friend and employee, Milton X. Mohammedstein. Milton X. Mohammedstein, Ronald Donald Almondotter, meet Sir Charles Pelicanstein." We all shook hands.

"Sir Charles and I were together in the Amazon jungle," Grandpa said.

"Your grandfather was the finest exploring partner I ever had in all my long years of adventuring," Sir Charles Pelicanstein said.

"Once, I saved Sir Charles's life," Grandpa said. "A twenty-six-foot anaconda had wrapped itself around Sir Charles's neck—four times. He was the color of Hungarian salami when I found him and unwound the beast."

"Another minute, and I would have been finished," Sir Charles Pelicanstein said. "I am in your debt forever, Seumas. In fact, for all these years, I've been trying to think of a way to repay you."

"That's not necessary," my grandfather said.

"Oh, yes, it is," Sir Charles Pelicanstein said. "It is necessary for my honor. I know that material things mean nothing to you—and so, offering you a mere fortune would not do the trick. Instead, I think I have finally found something of worth to offer you—an experience."

"An experience?" my grandfather asked.

"A great experience," said Sir Charles Pelicanstein. "As you know, I have explored and adventured in almost every part of the world. I have climbed all the important peaks in the Himalayas, descended deeper into the oceans than anyone else, made my way through the densest unmapped jungles, discovered the three deepest caverns on earth, and gone higher in a hot-air balloon than anyone before me. Also, I have discovered any number of formerly unknown species of animal, fish, and fowl. My contributions to science are well known. Most of these triumphs of exploration and discovery I have accomplished alone. All the credit goes to me.

"But all through the years, I have not forgotten you, Seumas, my old friend. I have always waited for the one great expedition, the one great glory to share with you. Now I have found it, and I have come to ask you to come with me on my greatest expedition—the search for the intelligent earthworm of Kukumlima!"

"The intelligent earthworm of Kukumlima?" Grandpa asked. "I've never heard of it."

"Few men have," Sir Charles Pelicanstein said. "Only in recent years have a few indistinct rumors filtered out of the remote regions of central Africa. Even the place, Kukumlima, is not known. It may be simply a name we are not familiar with for a place that is known—or it may be some totally unmapped and unexplored area. Such things are still possible, you know."

"I thought all of Africa had been mapped by now," I said. I had been reading some articles in the old *National Geographics* that Milton kept in the bathroom.

"Young Ronald Donald Almondotter, always remember this," said Sir Charles Pelicanstein. "The worst mistake a man of science can make is to assume that a thing is so simply because it is common knowledge or has been proven again and again. For example, if you were to throw a coin up in the air ninety-nine times, and it fell to the floor ninety-nine times, that would not be a reason to assume absolutely that it would not continue to rise straight up on the hundredth toss. You might expect it *probably* to fall to the floor on the hundredth toss—but you ought not to rule out the possibility of its doing something else. In the case of supposedly well-mapped and explored territory, there is much I know from firsthand experience. Aerial surveys, especially, are apt to go wrong. There are many magnetic mountains which confuse compasses. There are seemingly identical landmarks which can confuse observers. There are tricks of light, optical illusions, deliberate camouflages by native populations who don't want to be bothered. And I am obliged to say that there is often bribery, threats, foul play. Considering everything, one has every right to be skeptical about maps, unless one has made them oneself. Have you ever been to Los Angeles?"

I said that I hadn't.

"Well, how do you know that it's there?" Sir Charles asked.

"It's on all the maps," I said. "People talk about it. I just assume . . . "

"Aha! You assume!" Sir Charles said. "My point exactly! Let me tell you something surprising. There is no such place as Los Angeles—never has been. It is a fiction, a deception, a practical joke—and everybody believes it exists. Now, I ask you, if a geographical error of that magnitude can exist right here in this great country, is it so hard to believe that there may still be vast unexplored regions in Africa?"

I liked Sir Charles Pelicanstein. He was evidently crazy— but he had some interesting ideas. Besides, he took the trouble to argue with me. A lot of adults won't do that. I admitted that he had a point—that is, if it was true that Los Angeles didn't exist.

"Sir Charles Pelicanstein doesn't lie, boy," he said. "You can believe me—there is no such place as Los Angeles. Now, Seumas, my old friend, let me tell you about the intelligent earthworm of Kukumlima and the expedition I propose. I'm sure you'll find it interesting."

3

Sir Charles Pelicanstein said to my grandfather, "I suppose it's all right to speak in front of these two?"

"One is my own grandson," Grandpa said, "and the other has been my friend and worked for me for years."

"Of course," Sir Charles said. "I mean no offense—but what I am about to disclose is known to very few humans. I will begin.

"Years ago, a scientist named George Ngawa hit upon the idea that earthworms were actually extraterrestrials with abundant intelligence. Mr. Ngawa reasoned that earthworms appeared to be creatures of little intellect because they chose to appear so in the presence of earthpeople. Thus, they scored very poorly when tested under laboratory conditions. This sort of theory is all right as far as it goes, but how does one find proof with such an uncooperative creature?

"Mr. Ngawa founded the London Earthworm Society. Members of the society went around with medical stethoscopes, listening to the sounds earthworms made when they thought they were unobserved. A considerable amount of data was collected, and great numbers of recordings were made of the sounds made by earthworms. Many members of the London Earthworm Society believed that the sounds they had heard and collected represented a highly developed language with which earthworms communicate—but no human was able to understand a bit of it. For years, linguists, code experts, and philologists listened to the recordings of the earthworm language in the offices of the society. No progress was made.

"A wealthy member of the London Earthworm Society, Sir Noel Marsupial, left his entire fortune to further the research into the possible intelligence and language of earthworms. With the legacy of Sir Noel Marsupial, the London Earthworm Society became one of the richest private scientific organizations in the world. Years passed, George Ngawa passed away, and still no real progress was made in discovering the secret of the earthworm's language.

"However, through the years, the society collected a huge library on the subject of earthworms. Any report of any sort on the topic found its way to the society's archives. Earthworm researchers of every sort reported to the society and made use of the data it collected. But still, there was no progress in breaking the code of the worm noises.

"In recent years, with the advent of computer technology and other sophisticated scientific instruments, such as the worm electroencephalograph, for measuring brain-wave activity, it began to look as though the society might finally make an important breakthrough and find out what the earthworms were saying or thinking.

"Vast sums were spent in adapting and designing special equipment. New recordings were made, employing voiceprints and other modern techniques. Worm brain waves were monitored and recorded. One of the largest computers in the world was purchased and set to work decoding the worm noises. It took ten years to buy, design, and install the equipment, and six years to make all the computations.

"Finally, last year, the London Earthworm Society published its findings. After decades of work, enormous expense, and years of analysis, it was concluded, without a doubt, that earthworms are indeed as stupid as they appear to be.

"Mr. Ngawa's daughter, who had been running the society, was admitted to a nursing home. The society sold its computer and other equipment. The journal of the society, *Worm Words*, ceased publication, and a great many members resigned.

"However, the London Earthworm Society's great library was still intact. A few months ago, I was doing some general research there. I was simply curious as to whether the findings of the society might not have been mistaken. Remember Los Angeles! In going over their data, I found that based on what they had fed into the computer, the conclusion that earthworms were utterly stupid was inescapable. But—not all the data had been taken into consideration. Overlooked, behind a steam radiator, I found a handwritten report from a gem prospector in Africa. This unfortunate individual had the bad luck to step on a snake known as the green mamba and a few minutes later departed from this life. A considerate tribesman collected his papers and sent them to the coast. In some fashion, the part of his notes which dealt with earthworms found its way to the headquarters of the society, of which the prospector had been an associate member.

"The prospector, whose name was Gordon Whillikers, wrote about a variety of earthworm unknown to science.

These worms, he had observed in a place called Kukumlima. The singular thing about his report was mention of a particular worm which Whillikers had adopted as a pet. He named the worm Raymond and taught it to play chess!

"I went to the library of the Explorers' Society and found G. Whillikers's diary. Sure enough, there were several entries in which he mentions playing chess with Raymond. Most amazing, Raymond was able to beat Whillikers three games out of five!

"Now, it may be that Raymond is simply an extraordinarily intelligent earthworm—but it may also be that all the worms of Kukumlima are intelligent. I propose we go and find out."

4

"Go and find out? You mean go to Africa?" my grandfather asked.

"Of course!" Sir Charles Pelicanstein said. "It will be the greatest expedition of my career—and you will be a part of it. If we manage to find the place called Kukumlima, and if the intelligent earthworms are there, it will be one of the great discoveries of history."

"I can see that it would be very interesting," Grandpa said, "but is it as important as all that? I mean, a chess-playing earthworm—it isn't like going to the moon or something really special."

"That's just it! It is! It is really important!" Sir Charles Pelicanstein said. "Remember what George Ngawa first wanted to prove about earthworms. He wanted to prove that they were extraterrestrials! Beings from other planets! Imagine that! How would you like to be the first person to communicate with a being from another planet? Well, you wouldn't actually be the first because of Gordon Whillikers and Raymond—but you'd be one of the first! Wouldn't you call that important?"

"I suppose I would," Grandpa said, "but what made George Ngawa suspect that earthworms were from another planet in the first place?"

"Seumas, old friend, George Ngawa was a great man—a

293

scientist of the highest possible reputation. If he thought a thing was so, it is worthwhile at least to look into the matter."

"And you say that no one knows exactly where this Kukumlima place is located?" Grandpa asked.

"We know it is in Africa," Sir Charles said. "The name Kukumlima is Swahili for Hen Peak or Chicken Mountain. And Gordon Whillikers's notes turned up in Mombasa, having come from the interior—so it would make sense to begin our search in that part of Africa, that is, East Equatorial Africa. That's quite a bit to go on. I didn't have that much information when I found the Abominable Snowman."

"Did you actually find the Abominable Snowman?" I asked.

"I'm surprised that your grandfather has never told you about my Himalayan expedition," Sir Charles said. "Yes, I found the Abominable Snowman. It was the greatest triumph of my career—and also my greatest personal disappointment. I found the creature and took his picture as well—and yet, nobody ever believed me. That's what prejudice can do. Just because the Abominable Snowman didn't look the way people expected him to, they refused to believe the evidence of their own eyes. Look here!"

Sir Charles Pelicanstein opened his wallet and took out a small black-and-white snapshot. He handed it to me. The picture showed Sir Charles, standing with his arm around a very big hippie. The hippie had a beard and was wearing a headband and cutoff jeans. He was holding two fingers of one hand up to make a V. He was smiling and standing barefoot in the snow. He had very big feet.

DANIEL PINKWATER

"You see that?" Sir Charles asked. "That's him—the Abominable Snowman. This picture was taken by the abbot of Susila-Bubi monastery in Tibet—a highly respected man. All the Tibetans agreed that this was the real Abominable Snowman—but the scientific community and the press just made fun of me. They expected the Abominable Snowman to be a fur-covered monster, with fangs like a wolf, or a giant panda, or some rare species of snow-dwelling ape. When he turned out to look almost like a human, they insisted the whole thing was a hoax. Look at those feet! Did you ever see feet like that on a human being?

"It was a great disappointment to me. The Snowman was disappointed, too. He hasn't been seen since.

"Getting back to our expedition to Africa," Sir Charles said, "I propose we get everything ready and leave as soon as possible. Who knows how long it will be before someone else finds out about the earthworm somewhere in Africa, capable of playing chess, and maybe beats us to our goal?"

"It's been a long time since I did any expeditioning," my grandfather said. "The last time I went anywhere was a trip to Cleveland, Ohio, fifteen years ago, when my dear wife was still alive. I haven't taken a really rugged trip since you and I went bashing around the Amazon River basin all those years ago."

"It will all come back to you," Sir Charles said. "You were a great explorer. If you hadn't gotten involved in the salami game, you would have been as great as I am."

"Do you really think so?" Grandpa asked.

"Certainly," Sir Charles said. "I always thought you had the makings of a first-class adventurer."

"Well, I always wanted to go to Africa," Grandpa said.

"Then it's all settled!" Sir Charles said. "You'll come!"

"I'm not sure," Grandpa said. "I have to look after things here, at The World Famous Salami Snap Company."

"That's no problem," Milton said. "I can run this place with my eyes closed. You go to Africa with your friend and have a nice time looking for that earthworm. I'll take of everything here."

"That's right," I said. "Milton and I can take care of everything. You go ahead, if you want to."

"Do you really think I should?" Grandpa asked. "It would be fun, going on an expedition with my old friend."

"Sure."

"Go."

"I will! I'll go!" Grandpa said.

"That's the spirit!" Sir Charles Pelicanstein said. "There's only one minor detail to attend to. You see, when the London Earthworm Society got the bad news about earthworms being just as stupid as they seem to be, they gave away all their money. They gave to the Welsh Cat Protection Society. They don't have enough money to fund an expedition.

"So we'll have to look elsewhere for money. It may delay our departure for a few months while we collect all we need—but I'm afraid it can't be helped."

"That won't be necessary," Grandpa said. "You are forgetting that I am obscenely rich. I will finance the whole thing—on one condition."

"I accept your condition," Sir Charles said, "whatever it is. In the excitement of seeing you again after all these years, I had forgotten that you are, so to speak, disgustingly wealthy. Of course, now that you mention it, it would simplify things if you were to pay all expenses. By the way, what *is* the one condition?"

"The condition is this," my grandfather said. "I will pay all the costs of the expedition, provided that my grandson, Ronald Donald Almondotter, is invited to come along with us."

5

"Why do you want to go to Africa?" my parents said. "Wouldn't you rather stay home and have fun with your friends?"

"The boy is working for me," my grandfather said. "I am going to Africa, and he has to come along as my helper. I might get sick or suddenly become weak. You never know. I'm an old man."

"Seumas, you're as strong as an ox," my father said. "If I am half as healthy as you when I get to be your age, I'll be thrilled."

"Just the same, I think Ronald should come with me," Grandpa said. "He'll learn a lot. It's good for a young boy to travel and see things."

"But what could he learn on a trip to Africa?" my mother said. "I think he should stay here, and play baseball, and learn to adjust and get along with people."

"Fooey!" my grandfather said. "In Africa he can get along with all kinds of people he's never seen before. Ronald is coming with us, and that's all there is to say about it."

"Well, Daddy, I'll never understand why it has to be Africa," my mother said. "If you went to California, you could have a wonderful time. You could see lots of things in Los Angeles and go to Disneyland."

"First of all, daughter," my grandfather said, "there is no such place as Los Angeles. Second, I have no desire to go to

Disneyland, and I wouldn't take a child there if I did. Third, I want to say that you never cease to amaze me. How could you be the child of a great man like myself and have no imagination whatsoever?"

"Oh, Daddy, you're so eccentric," my mother said.

In the end they decided to let me go. My grandfather said he was going to leave all his money to a medical school in the hope that someday a way would be found to bring people like my parents to life.

The next day, we went down to the courthouse to get passports. Grandpa paid extra so we could get them the next day—usually it takes a couple of weeks. Then we went to see Grandpa's doctor.

Dr. Stonestein is the doctor Grandpa goes to. Not that he ever gets sick—he just likes to be examined and have medical tests done. It makes him happy when the doctor tells him that he's in perfect health and has the body of a young man. Dr. Stonestein believes in health food and vitamins. He insists that Grandpa is healthy because he eats lots of fresh vegetables and whole grains. Grandpa insists he's healthy because he eats salami every day. My mother won't go to Dr. Stonestein. She says he's deranged.

When we told Dr. Stonestein that we were going to Africa, he looked in some medical books to see what shots we'd need. It turned out that we needed about twenty of them. Actually, Dr. Stonestein said, we only absolutely had to have three or four—but if we were going into the interior, we'd better have everything, just to be on the safe side. We had shots for cholera, yellow fever, typhoid, the plague, tetanus, flu, and a whole bunch of others. I felt like a pincushion.

"Your arms will hurt like hell tomorrow," Dr. Stonestein said, "and you'll be sick as a dog." He also gave us some pills to take so we wouldn't get malaria. "These may make you sick, too," he said. Then he told us to watch out for tsetse flies, which can give you sleeping sickness, and he told us not to go swimming in fresh water because you can catch a horrible disease from the snails. "And of course, you're going to get food poisoning any number of times," he said. "Now have fun and enjoy your trip."

"That doctor is a sadist!" my grandfather said as we walked to the Nash Metropolitan, rubbing our arms. "He hates me because he can't stand seeing anyone so healthy. He's afraid if it gets to be popular, it will ruin his business. Now let's go to the explorers' supply shop to get our equipment. Sir Charles Pelicanstein is meeting us there."

I never knew there was a special store just for explorers. We drove into an old part of town, and Grandpa parked on a dark little side street. Over a dusty doorway hung a little sign; ADVENTURERS' OUTFITTERS, it said. Inside the door, we looked up the longest, steepest, creakiest flight of stairs I had ever seen. Instead of a handrail, there was a blue silk rope attached to the wall by stainless steel spikes, with round holes in the tops. Pasted to the walls were travel posters of the Alps. Painted on the risers of the steps every so often was the elevation above sea level. The bottom step was marked 5 FEET ABOVE SEA LEVEL. A little further up, it said 15 FEET; higher, it said 25 FEET, and so on. The top step was 75

FEET ABOVE SEA LEVEL. Using the hand rope, we hauled ourselves up the stairs.

At the top of the stairs was a door. We pushed it open and went through. There was Sir Charles Pelicanstein, having a cup of tea with a little man, with eyeglasses perched on top of his head.

"Pierre Pierre, this is Ronald Donald Almondotter, the grandson of Seumas Finneganstein. I believe you know Seumas."

"Yes, yes," Pierre Pierre said, shaking hands with both of us. "I know the inventor of the salami snap, which has saved the life of many a mountaineer."

I never did find out how the salami snap saved the lives of mountain climbers.

The shop was the most amazing place I'd ever seen. There was stuff everywhere. Coils and loops of red, blue, and yellow mountain-climbing rope hung from hooks in the walls. There were all kinds of strange-looking boots piled on tables and hung in bunches from the light fixtures. There were shelves with boxes and bundles and sacks of things. A large tent was set up in the middle of the room, and a collapsible kayak was suspended from the ceiling on wires. There were piles of aluminum cooking pots, bunches of alpenstocks, walking sticks and ski poles, rucksacks, pith helmets, shotguns, tools, portable stoves, field glasses, canteens, toboggans, diving masks, medical kits, and lots of things I couldn't identify. Wherever there wasn't mountain climbing and exploring gear there were photographs of people taken in jungles, on rafts, on snowy mountain peaks, riding on elephants.

"Sir Charles has already given me an idea of the sort of trek you are planning," Pierre Pierre said, "and I've made up a preliminary list of the things you'll need. Just look this over, and let me know if there's anything else you think should be included."

Pierre Pierre handled my grandfather five or six pages of lined yellow paper, covered with writing. I looked over Grandpa's shoulder. It seemed to me that we were going to buy at least three of everything in the place.

"Of course, it will be easier if you buy the tents and really big items when you get to Nairobi," Pierre Pierre said. "I've just listed a few of the items that will be hard to find when you get to Africa."

"This seems very complete to me," my grandfather said.

"Excellent," Pierre Pierre said. "Now, let me pour you cups of tea and begin taking measurements."

Pierre Pierre measured us up and down, fitted us with boots, and made a lot of notes on a pad of yellow lined paper. He said that it would take two days to put everything together and that all our equipment would be delivered to The World Famous Salami Snap Company.

I did take one thing away with me—a pocketknife with a scissors, saw, tweezers, magnifying glass, can opener, screwdriver, toothpick, file, compass, whistle, and sundial. It was the niftiest thing I ever owned, and it made me feel like a real explorer.

6

Grandpa said that he had a lot to do before we left. He had to make arrangements for The World Famous Little Plastic Thing Company to run smoothly in his absence. He told me I should take some time off and hang around with my parents because they weren't going to see me the rest of the summer.

I wanted to stay on at work. I knew it wasn't going to be easy to wait until it was time to leave for Africa, and I thought it would be better if I had something to do. But Grandpa insisted, and I was laid off.

I like my parents, but I've seen them every day of my life—how interesting could it be, hanging around the house? I knew we were just going to make each other nervous.

My father got to like the idea of the trip. He said it was a great opportunity for me. My mother spent a lot of time sewing name tapes into the big bundle of safari clothes that had come from Pierre Pierre. This included everything from underwear to a hat, and all of it was nifty beyond belief, especially the safari suits with pockets all over. I also got a pair of boots, my own first-aid kit, and a flashlight. And I already had the multipurpose pocketknife.

Both my parents had the idea that we were going on an ordinary vacation. Grandpa hadn't gone into much detail about the search for Kukumlima and the intelligent earthworm. This was partially because Sir Charles Pelicanstein had asked him to tell as few people as possible about the real purpose of our trip and partly because he didn't want to put too much strain on my parents. He assured them that the trip would be perfectly safe.

I hoped that wasn't true. I mean, what's the point of going to Africa if there isn't going to be any danger? I checked a bunch of books about Africa out of the library and read as much as I could. I got all the way through four books and read parts of three others. From my reading, I gathered that it was possible to get eaten, bitten by something poisonous, or even stabbed with a spear in Africa. Of course, not many tourists actually got eaten, fanged, or stabbed, but it was possible—and we were going where most tourists don't go. I was satisfied.

There was no point in telling the neighborhood kids that I was going to Africa. They would never have believed me. I decided I'd just disappear and send them all postcards, which would drive them crazy.

I spent so much time looking at myself in the mirror, wearing my new Jungle Jim outfit, that my mother had to iron everything twice—and I wore out a set of batteries, trying out the flashlight, and cut a sizable slice out of my thumb with the all-purpose knife.

It got harder and harder to fall asleep at night—and when I did, I dreamed about Africa.

Finally, my grandfather telephoned, and told me to come to The World Famous Salami Snap Company for a meeting with Sir Charles and himself.

When I got to The World Famous Salami Snap Company,

Sir Charles Pelicanstein and my grandfather were sitting in the office, drinking coffee from styrofoam cups and eating sweet rolls. "Ah, Ronald!" Sir Charles said. "I am just about to go over some preliminary plans for our expedition. Pull up a chair, and have a sweet roll, and I will begin."

I unwrapped a cinnamon danish and sat down.

"I would hate to think that anyone else might have the same idea we have and go out in search of Kukumlima and the intelligent earthworms. Gordon Whillikers's notes and journals are just where I found them. Anyone could come along and read them and decide to go off on an expedition like ours. Of course, I could have simply taken Whillikers's material away with me—but that would not be playing the game. All explorers adhere to a strict moral code. However, there is no need to call attention to our plans and activities. That is why I asked you to keep the purpose of our trip as secret as possible. I am not unknown by the public, and if we were to travel by ordinary commercial airlines, someone might recognize me and get curious.

"Therefore, I propose that we begin our travels in Africa in a very ordinary fashion, pretending to be regular tourists. To that end, I have contacted Baboon Safaris Limited, and requested that they take us on as clients. Baboon Safaris Limited is a well-known firm which arranges trips for tourists. They will supply a vehicle, a driver who knows the country, and accommodations, including tents and other equipment.

"Second, I have been in contact with a private, non-scheduled airline called Air Enterprise. It is operated by two brothers. I believe they are members of some obscure religious cult. They are vegetarians and appear to be good fellows, if a little odd. They have an airplane, and they are now standing by, waiting until they have enough cargo, passengers, and whatever else they may need. With your permission, I will tell them that we intend to go with them, and they will call us as soon as they are ready to go."

Grandpa said that he had no objection as long as the airplane would fly.

"Excellent," Sir Charles Pelicanstein said. "I will call Captain Roosman of Air Enterprise and tell him that we will be going with them. Now, stay close to your telephones for the next couple of days. Captain Roosman will call us all as soon as the plane is ready to take off, and then we will have to get there in a hurry. The captain said something about having to leave when the wind is favorable—but that was most probably a joke."

7

"Mr. Ronald Donald Almondotter?" the voice on the tele-phone asked. "This is Captain Roosman of Air Enterprise. We have a good breeze from the northeast, and it looks like a perfect night for a takeoff. Are you ready to fly with us?"

I said I was.

"Good. The Air Enterprise limousine will pick you up outside your house in fifteen minutes. Be ready! Then you will have time to relax in our VIP lounge—free instant coffee, candy bars, TV—until the rest of the passengers are collected, and then we're off on the luxury flight to Nairobi!"

It was eleven o'clock at night. I just had time to say good-bye to my parents, grab my duffel bag and my brand-new passport, and get outside in time to be picked up.

The Air Enterprise limousine was a white Plymouth station wagon with a cracked windshield. At the wheel was a small dark man in a blue uniform. Sticking out of the sleeves of his uniform were the striped sleeves of a pair of pajamas. Later, when we got out of the limousine, I noticed that pajama cuffs were hanging out of the legs of his trousers, too.

"I am Captain Rassman, the limousine driver," the lim-ousine driver said. "Now we will go to the VIP lounge at the airport, where you will have a good time with fellow world-travelers until it is time for the flagship to take off."

Captain Rassman ground the gears, and the station wagon lurched forward.

"This is a luxury flight you're taking," he said. "You get the best food—hot meatball sandwiches. And there's our elegant air-lounge."

We drove into the airport through a small gate marked EMERGENCY EXIT. We didn't go to the main terminal. We drove toward some small buildings at the far side of the airport. One of the buildings had a sign written in black crayon on a piece of a corrugated cardboard box. AIR ENTERPRISE, the sign said.

"Here's the VIP lounge," Captain Rassman said.

I was led into a small room. Grandpa was already there, drinking instant coffee from a paper cup. There was a counter with a pot of hot water, a jar of instant coffee, and five or six Hershey bars on it. There was also a black-and-white TV on one of those little stands, and a half dozen plastic chairs. In the corner of the VIP lounge was a folding cot. The sheets and blankets were messed up, as if someone had been sleeping in it.

"I must leave you alone," Captain Rassman said. "Captain Roosman is checking the plane—just the two of us are on duty tonight. I have to go and get Sir Charles Pelicanstein now. Watch any channel you like, have plenty of free instant coffee, eat the Hershey bars, sit in the chairs, and sleep in my bed. I'll be back in a little while."

Captain Rassman left.

"Nice boys," my grandfather said. "They really try to please."

I munched a Hershey bar and had a free instant coffee with lots of nondairy powdered creamer. Grandpa flipped the channels of the TV.

Captain Roosman came in. He looked exactly like Captain Rassman, except Captain Roosman didn't have any pajamas hanging out of his uniform.

"The Luxury Flagship Star Cruiser is all ready," Captain Roosman said. "As soon as the last passenger gets here, we can take off."

In a few minutes, the Air Enterprise limousine screeched to a stop, and Sir Charles Pelicanstein walked in. "Ah! You're both here! Good!" said Sir Charles. "Captain Roosman, we're ready when you are."

"Let's go before the wind changes and we have to turn the plane around," Captain Roosman said. "My copilot, Captain Rassman, will show you to the elegant air-lounge."

We all walked out onto the runway, carrying our bags. Captain Roosman pushed a wheelbarrow with the rest of our gear in it. The plane was exactly what I would have expected after seeing the limousine and the VIP lounge. It was a propeller-driven cargo plane, and it had rust spots.

"This is how we get into the flagship," Captain Rassman said. "Just grab this rope, and haul yourself up through the little hatch. I will throw your bags up after you."

One by one, we grabbed the rope that was dangling from the bottom of the plane and hauled ourselves through the hatch. The inside of the plane was full of boxes and bales of cargo, strapped to the inside of the fuselage with bands of webbing. The floor was made of wood.

One after another, our bags flew up through the hatch and thudded onto the floor. Then the rest of our gear came flying up through the hatch, and finally, Captain Rassman and Captain Roosman, sweating, clambered aboard.

"Now, Captain Rassman will show you to the fabulous air-lounge, while I go and try to start the engines," Captain Roosman said.

"No sitting in rows on the flagship," Captain Rassman said. "Here, in our deluxe air-lounge, you can sit around a table, and chat, or have a game of cards, and there is free ginger ale—with ice."

The air-lounge consisted of one of those kitchen tables— the ones with the chrome legs and the Formica top. Around the table were four kitchen chairs. The chrome legs of the table and the chairs were fastened to the floor with sheet-metal screws, and the four chairs had seat belts attached.

"For later, we have meatball sandwiches," Captain Rassman said. "See? Wrapped in aluminum foil. They'll stay hot for hours. Eat all the sandwiches. Captain Roosman and I are vegetarians, and we have bean sprouts in the cabin. Sit here. The ice is in that plastic bag. There are cups for the ginger ale—and the bottles are in this box. Have fun. Talk, play cards, eat. If you get tired, you can sleep on top of the boxes. I have to and help fly the plane now. I'll come back later, to see if you need anything."

"I'm sure we'll be just fine," Sir Charles said.

Before going forward to the cabin, Captain Rassman taped a sign to the wall. It was written in black crayon on a piece of corrugated cardboard. FASTEN SEAT BELTS, it said.

DANIEL PINKWATER

We fastened our seat belts.

The engines sputtered. Then they whined. Then they roared. The whole plane began to shake.

"We're moving," Sir Charles said.

We rattled along the ground. Through the one window, I could see the airport lights flashing past.

There were three or four bumps. After a little while, there was another bump. Then we felt a surging forward, and the ginger ale bottles clattered together.

"We're in the air!" Sir Charles said.

We could hear Captain Roosman and Captain Rassman cheering wildly in the cabin.

8

After a while, Captain Rassman came back and removed the sign that said FASTEN SEAT BELTS. "How about that take-off?" he said. "Smooth, wasn't it? Would anybody like to go forward and congratulate Capain Roosman?"

We said that we might go up to the cabin and congratulate Captain Roosman a little later—when we weren't feeling so sick. The airplane was rocking from side to side, like a rowboat in a choppy sea, and none of us was feeling very well.

"I almost forgot," Captain Rassman said. "On this deluxe flight, there is also music to delight the passengers." He handed us a small battery-powered cassette recorder and pushed the PLAY button. The machine played a tape of polka music. "Now, have a good time, luxury passengers," Captain Rassman said. "Feel free to come up and visit us in the cabin whenever you like. I will return to my duties now." He made his way up to the cabin somewhat unsteadily—the plane was lurching violently from side to side.

I got tired of sitting around the kitchen table with Grandpa and Sir Charles pretty soon and crawled on top of some cartons and tried to get some sleep.

Apparently I managed to fall asleep because when I woke up, the interior of the plane was flooded with brilliant sunlight coming through the window.

Grandpa and Sir Charles were sitting at the table, having a game of cards.

"Come have some breakfast," Grandpa said. "Cold meatball sandwiches and ginger ale are all we've got—it's a little unconventional, but it isn't too bad."

I slid off my bed on top of the cartons and went to the window. It was a beautiful clear morning. We were over the ocean. The water far below us sparkled in the sunlight.

"Are we nearly there?" I asked.

"Go and ask the crew," Sir Charles said. "The cabin is that way—right next to the toilet. You might have some trouble telling them apart."

I had gotten used to the pitching and rolling of the airplane while I slept. It was still wobbling wildly, but it didn't bother me so much. I went up to the cabin.

Captain Roosman and Captain Rassman were evidently having a good time flying the plane. They were laughing and chattering and pushing buttons and pulling levers. The cabin, in addition to all the things you'd expect to see in the cockpit of an airplane, had a lot of posters of rock bands and pinups of girls in bathing suits taped to the walls.

"Ah! Passengers up already?" Captain Roosman said when I came in. "Here is a hot breakfast drink." He handed me a thermos bottle, also three of those little individual-size boxes of cornflakes. "We should be sighting the coast of Africa soon," he said.

I took the thermos, which turned out to be full of hot chocolate, and the boxes of cornflakes back to the others. There wasn't any milk for the cornflakes, but they were a better breakfast, dry, than the soggy meatball sandwiches left over from the night before.

"You are certainly a good traveler, Ronald," Sir Charles said. "You slept right through the night. Your grandfather and I were able to take naps, but mostly we sat up, played cards, and talked to the crew. Did you know that we're flying by dead reckoning?"

"Dead reckoning?"

"Yes—almost nobody does it anymore. Captain Roosman and Captain Rassman are expert dead reckoners. They just take off in the direction of where they want to go—and get there without taking any trouble with positions of the stars, compasses, or any of that. If you're good at it, it's the surest way to navigate—no problems with confusing readings or faulty instruments."

"Are you saying that they are just guessing at our position?"

"Yes, but they're educated guesses," Sir Charles said. "They're really remarkable pilots, the old-fashioned kind."

I took my cup of hot chocolate over to the window and pulled up a box to sit on. I was a little worried. I wondered if Captain Roosman and Captain Rassman really knew what they were doing.

Captain Roosman stuck his head out of the cabin door. "If you all look out the window, you will see the coast of Africa coming up!" he shouted. "See? I told you we could do it!"

Sure enough, there was land. I had my doubts as to whether it was Africa. Flying by guessing, it could just as well have been anyplace—but at least we weren't over the ocean.

Captain Roosman came back. He was holding a piece of

paper. "Now comes the hard part," he said. "We had no doubts about finding Africa, big as it is—but finding Nairobi, which is relatively small, will take some real skill. See?" He showed us the piece of paper. It was a map of Africa, which appeared to have been torn out of a magazine, probably *National Geographic.*

"We think we're about here," Captain Roosman said, pointing to the map. "If that's so, then by heading in this direction, we should reach Nairobi in four or five hours. You can help us by keeping watch at the window. If you see anything like a big lake or a river—or a city—come up and tell us. If you see an ocean, that will mean we've gone too far—all the way across Africa to the Indian Ocean. But don't worry, it's easy to find Nairobi coming from the coast—if we don't run out of gas."

I sat at the window for hours—and got an idea of how enormous Africa is. I didn't see one landmark. There were some little rivers and some little towns—but nothing big enough to be shown on the map from *National Geographic.* As far as I was concerned, we were lost.

So I was amazed when Captain Rassman came back and taped up the FASTEN SEAT BELTS sign. "We're about to land at Embakasi Airport, Nairobi," he said with a big smile.

As we came in for our landing, I saw some giraffes through the window. They were running alongside the runway! It was as if the giraffes were there to welcome us.

Captain Roosman and Captain Rassman were hooting and screaming as we thumped and thudded onto the runway.

9

The moment I lowered myself out of the airplane, I knew that Africa was something special. I can't say just what it was—the way things smelled, the actual air I breathed—I knew I was in Africa. I could have told that I was if you blindfolded me.

Captain Roosman and Captain Rassman had borrowed a wheelbarrow somewhere and collected our luggage. Both of them were smiling from ear to ear. They were proud of themselves.

"Would you like us to wait?" Captain Roosman asked Sir Charles.

"Wait?"

"Yes, for the return flight."

"Well, you see," Sir Charles said, "we don't know when we'll be going back. It could be months from now."

"OK. We'll wait," Captain Roosman said. "This looks like a nice place, and you are our very favorite passengers, ever. It would spoil your trip to go home on just any airline. When you charter Air Enterprise, you charter the best."

Captain Roosman and Captain Rassman shook hands with us. "On the return flight," Captain Rassman said, very excited, "we are going to have a movie! We talked it over. Also there will be popcorn, made right on the plane! Won't that be great? And if the canned heat for the popcorn lasts, we're going to make cocoa!"

We told Captain Rassman it sounded fantastic, said good-bye, and went inside the airport terminal.

The first African I ever saw was the guy who checked us through customs. He was a big guy wearing a uniform. He had a nice smile—and he was black! That sounds silly—I mean, what color would you expect people in Africa to be? But this guy was really black. The people we call black at home are usually anywhere from light tan to chocolate brown; this guy's skin was like ink. "*Jambo, bwana*," he said to me, "welcome to Africa. *Jambo* means hello, and *bwana* means mister—so what I said to you means 'Hello, mister.'"

"*Jambo, bwana*," I said to the black guy. He smiled. I liked him. He had a nice voice. Also, he took time out from checking our baggage to teach me how to say hello.

We also had our passports looked at and stamped by another guy in a uniform. He was smiling, too. So far, everybody seemed glad we'd come. I was glad, too. There was a sort of friendly feeling in the air. I couldn't help feeling good.

"Let's find some transportation into town," Sir Charles said. "There should be some taxis in front of the airport."

"No need for a taxi, Sir Charles Pelicanstein," a voice said. "Baboon Safaris Limited has a vehicle waiting for you."

The voice came from a tall man in a white shirt. He was not just tall, but also fat. He wasn't black—he was more of a dark honey color. "I am Ali Tabu," the tall, fat, honey-colored man said. "I come from Ethiopia, and I am famous for having bad luck. I will drive you to your hotel now—and later I will take you to the office of Baboon Safaris Limited."

Ali Tabu gathered together a double armload of our bags

and proved his reputation for bad luck by instantly tripping and sending himself and our luggage sprawling all over the floor of the terminal.

Ali Tabu collected himself and led us to the Baboon Safaris Limited bus. This was a minibus painted to look like a baboon. The front of the bus was the baboon's face—the headlights were his eyes, and the tail lights were his rear.

Ali Tabu had us take seats in the bus and went back to get the rest of our stuff. Before he went back, he closed the door of the minibus on his finger and tripped on the steps to the terminal.

"I wonder how Baboon Safaris Limited knew when we would be arriving," Grandpa said.

"Most likely, they have a bus come to the airport every day," Sir Charles said, "to pick up any clients that happen to arrive."

"But Ali Tabu knew your name," I said.

Just then some people, Africans, walked past the window of the bus. "Hello, Sir Charles Pelicanstein," they said. "Welcome to Nairobi."

"Well, apparently my face is known to the people here," Sir Charles said. "That's not hard to understand. After all, I am a world famous adventurer. People in Africa are interested in adventurers. Also, they may have seen my movie about looking for sea monsters in Lake Ontario."

Ali Tabu came back, balancing the rest of our equipment, and shoved it into the bus. "Just one more minute, Sir Charles," he said. "I appear to have lost the keys to the bus somewhere in the terminal."

While we waited for Ali Tabu to find the keys, various people came up to the bus to say hello to us. They all seemed to know Sir Charles. Sir Charles was obviously pleased that he was so famous.

Ali Tabu finally came back with the keys. "Now we go," he said. He started the bus, and there was a hissing noise as one of the tires went flat.

Ali Tabu fixed the tire, and we began to drive toward Nairobi. In the distance, I could see giraffes—probably the same ones I had seen from the air. The airport is right near the Nairobi National Park. I felt very good and excited about being in Africa.

"You will notice what an excellent driver I am," Ali Tabu said. "I hope you will consider asking my employer to assign me as your regular driver when you go on safari."

Ali Tabu was stopped by a policeman when we reached the town and was given a ticket for making an illegal left turn.

"That sign wasn't there this morning," Ali Tabu said. "Everyone in Kenya knows what a superior driver I am. You would do very well to have me as your safari driver. Don't forget to ask my boss, Mr. Jiwe."

Ali Tabu came to a stop in front of Brunner's Hotel, crushing the bumper of a Volkswagen in the process. Then we walked up the steps to the entrance of the hotel. Ali Tabu tripped up the steps, dropping our bags. "Everything is all right," he said. "Don't worry about me. Now get settled in your hotel, and I will come back for you in a little while and take you to meet Mr. Jiwe."

There was a newsstand in the lobby of Brunner's Hotel.

Arranged in rows on one of those wire racks were copies of the *East African Standard*. Sir Charles's picture was right in the middle of the front page. The headline said FAMOUS EXPLORER. Printed below the headline was: Sir Charles Pelicanstein, World Famous Explorer and Adventurer Is Coming to Kenya To Begin the Greatest Expedition of His Career.

"I thought you wanted to keep this expedition a secret," Grandpa said.

"I did," Sir Charles said. "I can't understand how all this got in the papers."

We bought a paper. The story was sort of inaccurate and went on a lot about what a great man Sir Charles was, but it had most of the details right. It said that he was undertaking an expedition with some distinguished scientists and that expenses were being paid by the millionaire Seumas Finneganstein.

Then there was a whole paragraph about how the expedition was being flown to Kenya aboard a luxurious Air Enterprise flagship and how there was going to be deluxe cuisine, music, and lots of fun in the glamorous air-lounge.

"I'm starting to get an idea of who gave this story to the papers," Grandpa said.

"You mean Captain Roosman and Captain Rassman?" I asked.

"They could have called it in by radio," Grandpa said. "Sir Charles, do you think that the release of this news will have any effect on our expedition?"

"Well, of course it will," Sir Charles said. "We're

famous—celebrities. Everyone is going to want to know us. We may even be invited to visit the president of the country. We'll get plenty of free meals because of this, you bet."

"But, Sir Charles, you said that you were anxious to keep the expedition a secret," Grandpa said. "You were worried that a rival expedition might find the intelligent earthworm before we do."

"Yes, that was a concern of mine," Sir Charles said. "But there's no use crying over spilled milk."

We were shown to our rooms, which were small, clean, and plain. I washed up at the sink in my room (the bathroom was down the hall) and went downstairs to have tea with Sir Charles and Grandpa.

10

There was a nice room in Brunner's Hotel, a sort of lounge, where you could get tea and sandwiches. There were people sitting around reading the newspaper with Sir Charles's picture on the front page, talking and having drinks and cups of tea.

We had just finished our snack when Ali Tabu came in and sat down. The arm broke off his chair. "If you are all ready," he said, trying to put the arm back, "I can take you to the office of Baboon Safaris Limited to meet Mr. Jiwe now."

We piled into the bus and drove through the streets of Nairobi. Nairobi is a nice-looking city, with wide streets and big white buildings. Ali Tabu made an illegal left turn, and we found ourselves in an old section of town. There were raised sidewalks, something like the towns they always show in cowboy movies. There was a sort of roof over the sidewalk, and little shops and restaurants had their entrances under the roof.

Ali Tabu scraped up against the high curb in front of a sign that said BABOON SAFARIS LTD. "Go right in," Ali Tabu said. "Mr. Jiwe is waiting for you."

We went into a little office. An African, wearing a safari suit, was reading the *East African Standard*. He got up when we came in.

"Sir Charles, it is a pleasure to meet you," he said. "I am Mr. Jiwe, the director of Baboon Safaris Limited. We are ready to serve you in any way we can."

Sir Charles introduced Grandpa and me to Mr. Jiwe, and we all pulled chairs up to the desk.

"Now, I understood that you just wanted to take an ordinary tour," Mr. Jiwe said, "but the article in today's paper suggests that you have something a bit more elaborate in mind."

"Well, this unexpected publicity has changed things for us," Sir Charles said. "Our plan was to spend a week or so as ordinary tourists, just getting used to things and perhaps finding out something about the possible location of a place known as Kukumlima—you don't know of a place by that name, do you?"

Through the window, I could see Ali Tabu, polishing the minibus. He kept gesturing to me. I knew what he wanted. He was hoping we'd request him as our regular driver.

"No, I can't say that I've ever heard of a place called Kukumlima," Mr. Jiwe said, "and I know all of Africa pretty well."

Outside, the brakes of the minibus had somehow let go, and it had begun to roll. I saw Ali Tabu running after it, waving his polishing rag.

"The first thing you'll be wanting is an experienced and expert driver," Mr. Jiwe said.

We heard a crash. The minibus had found something to stop it.

"Yes, a driver," Sir Charles said. "The young man who picked us up at the airport seemed very eager to be assigned to us as our regular driver. Do you think he would be a good choice?"

It didn't surprise me that Sir Charles had said that. After all, he was the one who had picked out Air Enterprise to get us to Africa.

"Ali Tabu? He has rather bad luck, you know," Mr. Jiwe said.

"I'm not a superstitious man," Sir Charles said. "I'm a scientist."

"Still, I really don't like to send Ali Tabu out on long trips," Mr. Jiwe said. "It's not that he isn't a very nice chap—and his bad luck never seems to affect anyone but himself—but I just don't feel right about letting him take people into remote places. Ever since I sent him out with poor Mr. Whillikers . . ."

"Mr. Gordon Whillikers?" we all asked.

"Yes. Did you know poor Mr. Whillikers?" Mr. Jiwe asked.

"Not personally," Sir Charles said, "but we are interested in knowing what happened to him."

"There's not much to tell. Gordon Whillikers was a gem prospector. He came to me asking for a driver to take him into the bush. Whillikers had a complete outfit, everything he needed—but he was unable to drive. I suppose he had never learned. I assigned Ali Tabu to drive for him. They set out—and a few months later Ali Tabu came back alone. It's not the sort of thing a safari company wants talked about, you understand. I hope this won't reduce your confidence in us."

"Not at all, Mr. Jiwe," Sir Charles said. "These things

happen. We understand. And I have definitely decided that Ali Tabu is the man we want as our driver."

To Grandpa and me, Sir Charles whispered, "Don't show any special interest. This is a stroke of luck for us. If Ali Tabu was with Gordon Whillikers, then he probably knows where Kukumlima is. When we are alone with him, we'll question him, but carefully—he may not realize the significance of what he knows."

Just then, Ali Tabu came in. "Boss, the bus got away from me again. It will be in the shop for a couple of days."

"Never mind," Mr. Jiwe said. "I have an assignment for you. You are going to drive Sir Charles and his associates on their expedition."

"Oh, thank you, Mr. Jiwe," Ali Tabu said. "Thank you, Sir Charles, everyone! I won't let you down this time, I promise."

"Wait!" Mr. Jiwe said. "I can't allow this. At least, take another driver along. You'll probably need two vehicles anyway, a serious expedition like yours. I'm going to assign another driver. Ali Tabu, can you get in touch with Hassan?"

11

"Not Hassan!" Ali Tabu said. "If Hassan comes, he will want to run everything."

"Exactly," Mr. Jiwe said. "I don't mean to embarrass you, Ali Tabu, but you *have* lost a client. If you think about it, that's about the most serious mistake a safari driver can make. I'll feel much better about this expedition if Hassan is in charge. As for you—you can look upon this as a chance for you to redeem yourself. I expect nearly all—no, all—of these people to come back safe and sound. Now, what do you say?"

"Well, since you put it that way," Ali Tabu said, "I happen to know that Hassan is available. I met him in the second-hand comic book shop yesterday."

"Excellent," Mr. Jiwe said. "Go around to his house today and leave a message for him."

"Just who is Hassan?" Grandpa asked.

"Hassan is a truly excellent safari driver," Mr. Jiwe said. "He's equal to any emergency—even Ali Tabu. I will rest easy, knowing that Hassan is taking care of you."

"He sounds fine to us," Sir Charles said.

"Now, about arrangements," Mr. Jiwe said. "You can leave as soon as Hassan is ready—probably tomorrow. I will let you know."

"Perhaps you could come with us now and talk about the route we will take," Sir Charles said to Ali Tabu. "Maybe you know of a place where we can have a soft drink and a little chat."

"My favorite place is Wimpy's," Ali Tabu said, "but I usually go there only on special occasions."

"This is a special occasion!" Sir Charles said. "Come along."

We shook hands with Mr. Jiwe and went out with Ali Tabu to have a talk at Wimpy's.

Wimpy's is a hamburger place. It serves possibly the worst hamburgers I ever ate. The most horrible was something called the Kenya Burger, which is made with mutton, I think. The place was crowded and steamy with the smell of hamburgers. I had a pineapple milk shake. It was awful.

Ali Tabu ordered three double-deluxe Kenya Burgers. I suppose if you've never had anything better, you're apt to enjoy that sort of thing.

"I really appreciate this," Ali Tabu said. "I'm not a wealthy man, but fine cooking is my hobby. If I could afford it and didn't live in Kenya, I'd be a gourmet. On our safari, I'm going to do all the cooking."

Judging by the delight Ali Tabu was taking in his foul-smelling Kenya Burgers, I got the idea that the food throughout the trip was going to be up to Air Enterprise standards. "Well, we didn't come all this way to eat," I thought.

"Now, Ali Tabu," Sir Charles began, "we'd be very interested to learn something about your travels with Mr. Gordon Whillikers."

"Oh, gentlemen, I don't like to talk about that," Ali Tabu said. "It was the saddest experience of my life."

"Still, if you could make a special effort," Sir Charles said. "It isn't just idle curiosity that prompts me to ask. It is really important to us to learn about Mr. G. Whillikers."

"Please, do you want me to lose my appetite?" Ali Tabu asked. "I feel terribly bad about what happened to Mr. Whillikers. I just don't want to talk about it."

"Let me make myself clear," Sir Charles said. "It isn't necessary for you to talk about what happened to the unfortunate fellow—what we want to know is where you went with him."

"I went to a lot of places with him," Ali Tabu said, chewing. "He was looking for rubies and diamonds, you know."

"Now, Ali Tabu," Sir Charles said, making an effort to remain calm, "I don't want you to dwell on things which are upsetting to you—but didn't you take Gordon Whillikers to a place known as Kukumlima?"

"Do you think that's where he went?" Ali Tabu asked. "I never took him there. Maybe he went there after I . . . lost him."

"You weren't with him when he . . . ?"

"No. One night he wandered off—or I left him somewhere—I can't be sure. All I know is that one morning, I noticed that he wasn't with me." Ali Tabu started to cry. "Mr. Whillikers was a very quiet person. Sometimes he didn't say anything for a whole day. Sometimes he got sleepy and lay down and took a nap in the back of the truck. It was an honest mistake. I thought he was there. I looked everywhere for him."

"There there, man. Calm yourself. Here, take a sip of your pineapple milk shake," Sir Charles said. "So you never went to Kukumlima. Can you at least tell us where it was that you . . . that Mr. Whillikers became lost?"

"It was within a four-hundred-mile radius of Lake Manyara in Tanzania," Ali Tabu said. "Now, please can we talk about something else? Remembering all this tragedy is going to interfere with my digestion."

"Of course," Sir Charles said. "But just one more question. Would you be willing to take us to Lake Manyara? I mean, it wouldn't be too upsetting, would it?"

"I suppose not," Ali Tabu said. "Which reminds me, I have to go to Hassan's house and tell him that we have a safari to organize. I'd better go and do that now. Thanks for the gourmet snack."

12

Hassan turned out to be a dapper Pakistani. He had been born in Kenya and regarded himself as an African, although he still had a sort of Pakistani accent. He was wearing a sharply creased safari suit and a hat with the brim turned up at one side. He had a neatly trimmed mustache, and it was obvious that he felt that he was in charge of things.

Ali Tabu had already started out in the truck for Lake Manyara—he was going to meet us there. Hassan was taking the actual passengers, which, to his way of thinking, made him chief driver or head of the expedition, I don't know which.

After bundling us into the Land Rover, Hassan insisted we take a detour, which amounted to almost an hour, to meet his wife and family. It turned out that the real reason we had to go to Hassan's house, a little bungalow in the suburbs of Nairobi, was that he had forgotten his suitcase. His wife, who seemed relieved to be getting rid of him for a little while, also brought out his *panga*, which is a sort of African bowie knife, and a big bag of chicken sandwiches.

Under way at last, Hassan told us a lot of horrible jokes and puns. To get most of them, you had to understand Swahili or Urdu—but Hassan didn't mind that we didn't laugh too much. He appeared to tell the jokes for his own pleasure.

Even though Hassan was a cornball and never stopped talking, we all liked him. Sir Charles said that a cheerful fellow like that was worth three or four men of normal intelligence if the going got rough.

In addition to jokes, Hassan told us lots of stories about exciting adventures in the bush and narrow escapes he'd had. It was clear from his stories that he was fearless—but it usually appeared that the danger he bravely got out of, he had foolishly gotten himself into.

Looking out the windows of the Land Rover on the way to Lake Manyara, I got to see all kinds of African landscape. The farms right near Nairobi weren't so different from little farms anywhere, but as we rolled along, we began to see grass huts, and open country, and lots and lots of space and bright sunshine. I was never in a place that seemed so big and open and clean.

We crossed the border into Tanzania at Namanga. I had never crossed a border—by land anyway. In movies they always show a thing like a railroad crossing. There's a white barrier that goes up and down and a little house where the border guards stay. When you come up to the barrier, the border guards lift it, and you go through.

At the Kenya-Tanzania border they had something much more effective. It was a great big log with giant spikes sticking out of it, lying across the road. If you tried to drive over it, the thing would cut your tires to ribbons. After looking at our passports, the border guards dragged the log out of the road, and we drove through.

There's a very fancy hotel at Lake Manyara. That was

where we were going to meet Ali Tabu. The hotel sits on top of a cliff, and the lake is down below. The cliff is the western wall of the Great Rift Valley. This is a tremendous valley that cuts through half of Africa. Down below in the valley is Lake Manyara, which is a national park. If you stand at the edge of the cliff, eagles and vultures, sailing on updrafts of warm air, will pop into sight fifteen or twenty feet from the end of your nose.

I spent some time looking at the big birds—until it got dark. Then we ate and slept at the fancy hotel, waiting for Ali Tabu. He was late—hours and hours late. Hassan said he was most probably lost.

"Lost, strayed, or maybe went crazy, sold the truck, and went home to Ethiopia," Hassan said. "But please don't worry. Most probably he is lost. You know, I suppose, that Ali Tabu has unbelievably bad luck. Some say that his shoes are cursed. However, I will find out what has happened to him. All of you go and wash and rest and eat in the lovely dining room. I will do some detective work and report to you later."

I didn't really like the Lake Manyara Hotel. The trouble was—it was too nice. It didn't seem like Africa, really. It could have been a fancy resort anywhere. I knew that there were lions and elephants and all sorts of wonderful things just at the bottom of the cliff—but it didn't seem real. It was all sort of arranged. There were nice tourists, in nice clothes, having a good time, eating and talking. Later they'd have drinks and play cards and complain because there wasn't any television. The next day they'd be taken in cars to see the animals and take a picture to show the folks at home.

I couldn't quite understand why, but I didn't feel that it was right—this tourist resort. Sir Charles summed it up. "That's the dismal thing about being a tourist," he said. "The poor little creatures haven't anything to do. They buy their tickets, and here they are. It can't seem very real to them because they don't have to experience any inconvenience to be here—and they have no purpose except to stare at things. That's why we expeditioners have a better time. We take the country as it is—not as the hotel wallahs make it out to be."

I spent an uncomfortable night in the hotel. The bed was too soft.

In the morning, Ali Tabu had shown up.

"I hope there was no inconvenience," he said. "You see, I was driving along, and I came to this slippery place in the road. . . ."

"There is no need to explain, you hard-luck fellow, you," Hassan said. "Everybody knows about your constant mishaps."

"Quite so," Sir Charles said. "What matters is that you have arrived, and now we can make some plans for this expedition. Come in and have some breakfast, and we'll talk things over."

We all went into the hotel and ordered breakfast. Sir Charles cleared his throat and began to speak. "I think it is time to explain a few things about our expedition. Ali Tabu was the last person to see the unfortunate Mr. Gordon Whillikers. He claims to have lost him in the general vicinity of Lake Manyara—if you can call four hundred miles from this point in any direction the general vicinity. What you may not know is that Mr. Gordon Whillikers had found a place called Kukumlima before his sad accident. . . ."

At this point Ali Tabu looked as though he might cry.

"Now, Hassan," Sir Charles went on, "you have the reputation of being a very knowledgeable person about geography. Have you ever heard of Kukumlima?"

"Oh, boss, you are asking the right person," Hassan said. "There is no one in Africa who knows more than I do about remote places in the backcountry. I have been places where no civilized person has ever been. I have been to places where no person of any kind has ever been. I know this whole continent like the mustache on my face. When you ask Hassan if he knows of a place, you are asking someone who knows every little village, every stream and river—every tree almost. No, I have never heard of a place called Kukumlima."

"Somehow, I rather expected that you hadn't," Sir Charles said. "There is no doubt in my mind that Kukumlima is totally uncharted and unknown to any person. The problem before us is this—how do we go about finding it?"

"If you will permit me, bosses," Hassan said, "that is a simple matter. I mean to say that finding Kukumlima may not be a simple matter—who knows? Maybe it can't be found. But setting about finding it—starting to look for it—is the most simple thing in the world. There is only one way to begin looking for something that is unknown to ordinary men, unknown even to the most expert tracker in all of Africa— that is, myself. In matters of the unknown, it is necessary to consult a great wise man, a sharif, a holy person or a witch doctor. We have to ask a person of mysterious wisdom to guide us. That is how we have to do it."

"Very good," Sir Charles said. "I am no skeptic in matters like this. When I searched for the Abominable Snowman, mystic lamas of Tibet were a big help. The question is this — do we know of a person of great mysterious wisdom?"

"Oh, certainly, bosses," Hassan said. "The very wisest man in all of Africa can be found not far from here. I believe I can take you to him — and even arrange for you to get to see him. But you will have to bring him a present, is that understood?"

"Of course," Sir Charles said. "Who is this wise person?"

"It is Baba Pambazuka," Hassan said. "Oh, he is a great man, I tell you, bosses. It is a big inspiration just to talk with him. He is very old and knows many things that other men do not know. We can go to see him, but you must bring an appropriate present."

"That is fine with us," Sir Charles said. "What sort of present do you think we should bring him?"

Hassan thought for a while. "I have heard it said that Baba Pambazuka would very much like to have a pinball machine."

13

Anyone who thinks it's easy to find a pinball machine in East Africa ought to try it sometime. We had to go all the way back to Nairobi. It took a week there, looking and asking people all day long, before we finally found one. Covered by a dusty old sheet, it was in the storage room of a restaurant. The paint was peeling here and there, and the wooden legs of the machine had been eaten by ants a bit—but it worked, and it was for sale. Grandpa paid more than a thousand dollars for the machine, which he said was highway robbery. But Hassan kept assuring us that this was the perfect present to take to Baba Pambazuka—and that Baba Pambazuka was really the only person in Africa who could help us find Kukumlima.

As soon as we had loaded the pinball machine into the truck, we were off again, in the direction of Lake Manyara, to find Baba Pambazuka.

We stayed at the Lake Manyara Hotel again and drove around, asking various Bulu tribesmen if they knew where we could find Baba Pambazuka. Most of them said they'd never heard of him.

We looked for Baba Pambazuka, or anyone who had ever heard of Baba Pambazuka, for three days. We were beginning to wonder if there really was any such person as Baba Pambazuka.

"Oh, bosses," Hassan said, "please don't worry. Baba Pambazuka is a real person all right—and he's the only one who can help us to find Kukumlima. All we have to do is find Baba Pambazuka."

"As far as I can tell," Sir Charles said, "the only person ever to hear of Baba Pambazuka is you, Hassan. We've asked everybody for miles around, and none of them knows who he is."

"It's always that way with really wise people," Hassan said. "They don't go around advertising themselves. You don't find really, truly great men just hanging out in the road or giving speeches. You have to look for them."

We looked for Baba Pambazuka for another two days. At last, we got a clue. Someone said that he thought he lived somewhere near Babati. This was not much to go on, but it was more information than we'd gotten in five days, so we started off.

Not far from Babati, there was a sort of general store. You could buy almost anything there, from a road map to groceries, a pair of socks, or souvenirs for tourists. There were a lot of local Africans hanging around, talking and drinking Coca-Cola. It was a good place to get into a conversation or ask for information.

Grandpa approached a fellow who was sitting on the steps of the store, having a cigarette. "Excuse me," Grandpa said, "do you happen to know anything about a man called Baba Pambazuka?"

"Certainly," the man said. "What do you want to know about him?"

"Well, we'd like to know where we can find him," Grandpa said.

"You can find him sitting on the steps of this store," the man said.

"When?" Grandpa asked.

"When?" the man asked.

"When can we find him sitting on the steps of this store?" Grandpa asked.

"Now. Right now," the man said. "You can find him sitting on the steps of this store right at this very moment."

"You mean that you . . . ?"

"I am Pambazuka," the man said.

At that moment, I happened to look up and read the sign fastened over the door of the store.

PAMBAZUKA GENERAL MERCHANDISE

"We've been looking for you everywhere," Sir Charles said.

"I haven't been everywhere," Baba Pambazuka said. "I've been here. I've been here for more than fifteen years—that is, right here at this location. I've been right around here—in this neighborhood, so to speak—for about eighty years. When you have great wisdom, there's no particular reason to go running all over the place. Staying in one spot is best."

"Then you are Baba Pambazuka, the wise man?" Sir Charles asked.

"Going from place to place is tiring, and if you just stay still, everything that is supposed to happen to you will happen." Baba Pambazuka continued, "Of course, I traveled a

338   DANIEL PINKWATER

great deal when I was young. Until I was about forty, I went everywhere—but I stopped that. Staying put is best—or so I've found it."

If I was following what he was saying, Baba Pambazuka must have been at least a hundred and twenty years old. He didn't look any older than Grandpa.

"We came to see you about a matter of great importance to us," Sir Charles said.

"I've been as far as Cape Town. I went to Cairo, too," Baba Pambazuka went on. "I've never been to Europe—but I don't expect I've missed very much. Places are more or less the same—it's people that count."

"Baba Pambazuka," Hassan said, "these people have brought you a present."

"That's very kind," Baba Pambazuka said, "but I don't need anything. I'm a rich man. This is the only store for miles and miles around. Everybody comes here. I appreciate the thought—but I don't need anything. Besides, if you thought I was going to accept your gift and then let you ask me some hard questions, you're too late—years too late. I've retired from the wisdom business. No, no, if there's anything you need in the way of provisions, dry goods, Coca-Cola, I can help you—but I don't do wisdom anymore. Sorry."

"Baba, what these men have brought you is a pinball machine," Hassan said.

"Really?" Baba Pambazuka got up. "Let's have a look at it. Where did you find it? I've wanted a pinball machine for years, and I just can't seem to find one. Where is it? In the truck?"

Baba Pambazuka hurried over to it, and Ali Tabu and Hassan lifted the pinball machine out and placed it on the ground.

"It's a beauty!" Baba Pambazuka said. "It's like the one I played on in Cape Town eighty years ago. I'd like to buy it from you."

"It's not for sale," Hassan said, "but we would like to offer it to you as a gift."

Baba Pambazuka thought for a moment. "All right. I accept your gift. Now carry it inside, and take free Coca-Colas—and you may ask me any questions you wish."

14

"Go ahead and ask your questions," Baba Pambazuka said. "I can listen while I try out this machine."

Hassan and Ali Tabu had brought the machine into the back room of Baba Pambazuka's store. The room was fitted out as a sort of parlor, with comfortable chairs, a phonograph, and an icebox full of Coca-Colas, which Baba Pambazuka invited us to drink.

"I am Sir Charles Pelicanstein," Sir Charles said.

"I know that," Baba Pambazuka said. For someone who hadn't played pinball in eighty years, he was off to a good start. The machine was in good working order, and the lights flashed, and the bells rang, as Baba Pambazuka began piling up a score in the thousands. "I read about you in the newspaper," he said. "You and your party are looking for Kukumlima. You hope to find an intelligent earthworm."

"Yes, that's right," Sir Charles said.

"Drat!" Baba Pambazuka said.

TILT said the pinball machine.

He started another game.

"The problem is this," Sir Charles said. "No one seems to have any idea where this Kukumlima is. Hassan, here, tells us that if anybody can tell us how to get there, you can. Do you know how we can get to Kukumlima?"

"How did Mr. Gordon Whillikers find Kukumlima?" Baba Pambazuka asked.

"You know about Gordon Whillikers?" Sir Charles asked excitedly.

"Certainly," Baba Pambazuka answered. "I met him. He bought some supplies here—a nice chap. Does anybody know what happened to him?"

"I understand he stepped on a snake and went to meet his maker," Sir Charles said.

"Is that so?" said the baba.

"Baba, do you think you can help us?" Sir Charles asked.

"Certainly. Tomorrow I'll help you. Now go. You're distracting me from my game. Good-bye." Baba Pambazuka turned his full attention to the pinball machine. We could see that we were supposed to leave without another word.

As we filed out of the room, Baba Pambazuka said, "Drat!"

TILT said the pinball machine.

15

Baba Pambazuka was still fooling with the pinball machine when we came into the room the next day. He had run up a score of 90,000 points. The machine had evidently been made for export to Egypt years before, because there was a picture of Gamal Abdel Nasser, the former president of Egypt, on the backboard. If you got a score of 10,000 points, Nasser's nose would light up. If you got 50,000, his nose and ears would light up, and a bell would ring. If you got 100,000 points, Nasser's whole face would light up, and the machine would play the Egyptian national anthem. The baba was heading for his first score of 100,000 when we came in.

"I'll be with you in a little while," Baba Pambazuka said. "This is the best game I've played yet." Since we'd seen him last, the baba had developed some very subtle pinball moves. With easy grace, he manipulated the little levers and wiggled and shoved the machine, just enough to avoid lighting up the TILT sign. He made his 100,000—Nasser's face was illuminated from behind by light bulbs, and the bell rang continuously as a tinny recording played what I supposed was the national anthem of Egypt.

Baba Pambazuka turned to us, smiling broadly. "I must say, I like this gift you have brought me. Never before in my life have I been able to get a hundred thousand points. Now, please, have some free Coca-Colas, sit down, and we'll have our conversation."

We helped ourselves to Coca-Cola from the icebox and took seats around the room. Baba Pambazuka gave the pinball machine a pat and sat down with us.

"Now, you want to find Kukumlima, is that correct?" he began.

We said that it was.

"You know that very few men have ever gone to Kukumlima," Baba Pambazuka said. "In modern times, the only man to go there has been Mr. Whillikers. So the best person to ask about how to get there would be he."

"But Mr. Whillikers is dead," Sir Charles reminded the baba.

"Is that so?" Baba Pambazuka said. "Well, the best advice I can give you is as follows: First, you must understand that Kukumlima is a place of magic. You will not find it on any map. Not one person in fifty thousand will have ever heard the name. Even though all of Africa has been heavily charted, Kukumlima has somehow eluded discovery. There must be a reason for that."

At this point, Sir Charles looked at me significantly. He was remembering our first conversation, the one in which he told me about Los Angeles not being there.

Baba Pambazuka continued. "So we must assume that Kukumlima is, in some way, protected from casual visitors. What exactly it is that protects this place, we do not know— that is, I know, but I am not going to tell you. If you are meant to find out certain secrets, you will find them out. It is not my responsibility to tell you everything in advance—in fact, that would probably spoil your chances.

"You see, the only way in which you may be able to find Kukumlima will be to find it in exactly the same manner as Gordon Whillikers."

"And how did Gordon Whillikers find it?" Sir Charles asked.

"Mr. Whillikers found it by becoming utterly, totally, completely, and hopelessly lost," Baba Pambazuka said. "That is how to find the place—there is no other way. You must get yourselves lost—but it will not be that simple."

"It will be next to impossible," Hassan said. "I am the greatest tracker in Africa. I always know where I am."

"That is part of the problem," Baba Pambazuka said, "but there is even more. To become really, truly, perfectly lost is very difficult. You must not only lose your way, in terms of a map, but lose your direction, your intention. You must not only not know where you are—but not care where you are. And you must forget about what you are looking for. I should tell you that when I met Gordon Whillikers, he impressed me as being at least half crazy. It may be that he had an easier time getting lost because of that."

"Yes," Ali Tabu said. "I neglected to mention that Mr. Whillikers was crazy as a bedbug. It seemed disrespectful to say that, after what happened to him."

"And what was that?" the baba asked.

"He stepped on a mamba and died," Grandpa said.

"Is that so?" Baba Pambazuka said. "To continue . . . In your search for Kukumlima, you must become lost. You must become lost within as well as without. Also, you must conduct yourselves in a very peaceful manner while you are lost.

You may not hunt or kill any animal. You may not quarrel among yourselves or say anything depressing to dishearten the others. You must always be ready to help anyone in need you may meet. If you can do these things, it may be the Will of Mungu, which is our name for God, that you will find Kukumlima."

"What you suggest is nearly impossible," Sir Charles said. "To behave in a cheerful and moral fashion will not be hard for us, since we are all decent fellows—but to get lost, really lost, as you describe it, will be difficult, to say the least. Not only does Hassan know every inch of the country—but all of us know what we are looking for. How can we put it out of our minds?"

"Mungu will help you, if you are intended to find the place."

"I don't see how we can stop ourselves from thinking," I said.

"That is why so few people have ever found Kukumlima," the baba said. "And of course, you cannot really forget the intention of your search—but you may find that much of the time, you will be able to do so. I can assure you of this: Only at this moment when not one of you is thinking about Kukumlima, or where you are, or where you are going—only then will you actually find Kukumlima.

"Another thing I can tell you—you can take it as a good sign if you find the Elephant Portal."

"What is that?" Hassan asked.

"You'll know when you find it," Baba Pambazuka said. "Now, if you decide to continue your expedition, I think you had better buy a lot of provisions from me. You will need four or five times as much of everything as you are probably now carrying. Also, you will need many, many cans of petrol because you do not know how far you will have to go."

"Can you tell us nothing more?" Sir Charles asked.

"Nothing," said Baba Pambazuka, "except that I have everything you will need, if you decide to continue your journey, and, because I am so happy with my pinball machine, you may have a ten percent discount on all you buy."

"It seems there is nothing for us but to decide if we go on or not," Sir Charles said. "Well, what shall we do?"

"I came on this expedition to find Kukumlima," Grandpa said. "I am willing to go on."

"Me too," I said.

"I've never been lost," Hassan said. "It will be a novel experience."

"I'm certainly coming," Ali Tabu said. "I haven't had the chance yet to cook for all of you."

We all winced—except Ali Tabu, who was smiling.

16

By the time we had crammed all the stuff we bought from
Baba Pambazuka into the Land Rover and the old Bedford
truck, there was hardly room to squeeze our bodies in.

It was about midnight when we had loaded everything.
The idea had been to start off, trying to get lost, early the next
morning—but Hassan was eager to start right away. He said
he liked driving at night. Ali Tabu thought it was a good idea,
too, so we pulled away from Baba Pambazuka's store to the
sound of bells and the Egyptian national anthem.

Hassan drove all night and through much of the next day.
We made a number of stops, for meals and rest and to help
Ali Tabu. He had two flat tires, an engine breakdown, and
twice he drove off the road and had to be pushed. We all pre-
tended it was the fault of the very old truck, but we knew it
was Ali Tabu's usual bad luck.

Grandpa, Sir Charles, and I took naps as the little caravan
bounced and thumped along an unknown road. Hassan and
Ali Tabu never seemed to get tired. They drove for more than
twelve hours without sleep. It was early afternoon when we
came to a place that looked like a good camping spot. We
hadn't seen a car since the morning—and we hadn't even
seen a hut or a herdsman with cattle for hours.

There was a stream running nearby and a flat sandy
place. We unloaded our tents and went to work putting them

up. It took most of the afternoon. Ali Tabu got hit on the head by a falling tent pole, and had to go and sit down for a while. Hassan kept telling us that we were only having so much trouble because we weren't used to these particular tents, and once we'd had some practice, we'd be able to make camp in fifteen minutes.

It took something like six hours to finally get the tents and the folding cots, and the mosquito netting, and the portable field kitchen all put together.

Ali Tabu was feeling better from his bump on the head, and he went to work preparing supper. Hassan helped him get the portable stove fired up and then dragged some dead tree trunks together not far from the tents.

"We have to make a fire that will burn all night," he said. "That will keep the animals out of camp."

I didn't feel all that fine. I hadn't been able to get much sleep in the bouncing Land Rover, and I was tired after all the work getting the tents and everything set up. The camp didn't look so good. It looked as though a good wind would blow it away.

I had gotten a big splinter and had my fingers pinched setting up some of the folding furniture. Sir Charles was in a sullen, mumbling mood—unusual for him. He had a desperate look, as if he had finally realized just who made up this expedition, and there wasn't a hope of anything going right.

Hassan seemed cheerful as usual, working on placing bits of kindling here and there. He stepped back, finally, and looked at the giant pile of logs, wood, and tinder of all sizes. He appeared satisfied with it. In a grove of trees, maybe two hundred yards away, we heard a lion cough. Hassan flashed a smile at everybody and struck a match. In five minutes, the prettiest bonfire anyone ever saw was blazing and crackling away—just as the sun went down.

Ali Tabu was busy in the outdoor kitchen. He didn't want anyone to help him or come near him. I kept waiting for the inevitable scream, as he burned himself with hot grease or destroyed the meal he was making for the five of us—but nothing appeared to be going wrong. Then I realized that the disaster would consist of how the meal tasted, not how it got cooked.

I wasn't prepared to eat the best meal of my life, sitting in a creaky old camp chair, by a blazing bonfire, under a sky as black as ink, with stars as bright as light bulbs—but that's what happened. Ali Tabu could really cook. He was the best cook in Africa—maybe in the world. Everything he made— even if it was only a biscuit—was the best it could possibly be. The best biscuit. The best cup of coffee. He even made powdered eggs so we liked to eat them.

I watched everybody's face in the firelight. The tension and bad temper vanished as we ate the food Ali Tabu had prepared. Ali Tabu, his face shining with sweat, watched each of us as we ate the food. Nobody said anything for a long time— we were too busy eating. Then we broke into cheers and applause, and Ali Tabu beamed.

We sat for a long time, watching the fire. Now and then, we'd hear an animal noise, and Hassan would tell us what sort of animal was making it and something about the animal. The most interesting animal was the hyrax. A hyrax is

DANIEL PINKWATER

something that looks like a big guinea pig, maybe the size of a rabbit, but it's the only living relative of the elephant! Apparently, these little, round, fuzzy things have a lot in common with elephants when you take their skin off—and they scream in the night. At first the screams made us jump—they were sort of eerie. But after hearing what made that incredible noise, it got to be sort of funny. As Hassan explained it, they were romping around on a rocky outcropping, maybe sliding or jumping, and hollering the hyrax equivalent of *Whee!*

Those rocky outcroppings are called inselbergs. They suddenly poke up out of the level grassland, looking like the fake rocks you see in fish tanks. Leopards like to hang out on them because they get a long-distance view from them. They can be twenty or thirty feet high, mostly straight up, with a series of rounded tops, like hunched shoulders. Sometimes, on the next to highest shoulder, you see a leopard or a cheetah, watching.

Ali Tabu handed around cups of the best hot chocolate on earth, just when I was beginning to realize that I was getting sleepy. It finished me off. I stumbled to the tent I shared with Grandpa and flopped on my cot. As I fell asleep, I remember thinking that it was OK to let go, to close my eyes and lose part of that beautiful night, because when I woke up, I'd still be somewhere—I didn't know or want to know exactly where—in Africa, and there were days and weeks and maybe months more of this to come.

And when I woke up—it was true. I was still in African, and it was a beautiful morning. Ali Tabu was already up, and the field kitchen was working at high speed.

Hassan was showing something to Grandpa. I walked over and saw that he was pointing out lion tracks within ten feet of where I'd been sleeping.

"It's a good sign that the lions are so curious here," Hassan said. "When they come and sniff around at night, it means there haven't been many men around—otherwise, they are too bored to come and see."

Sir Charles appeared with a pair of field glasses slung from his shoulder. Apparently I was the last one to wake up. He had been climbing on an inselberg—first making a lot of noise in case of a late-sleeping leopard. He said the view was great—but he didn't say anything that would have suggested where we were.

There was a creeping, warm, silly happiness coming over me. In the cold, crisp early morning, we were far away from everything. We were going in no direction in particular, going no place in particular, looking for something by not looking for it—and taking all the time in the world. That was it! It was the endlessness of it! I knew that today was going to be just perfect-—and that tomorrow was going to be just as perfect. One day was free to run into another. It wasn't important to tell where we were, where we were going, or what day of the week it was. I tried to remember. Was it a Monday or a Tuesday? It didn't matter.

We would break camp and move on—or, if we felt like it, we would spend another night here, and go exploring in the forest, or climb the inselbergs and spend a lazy afternoon watching the game moving in the grasslands below us.

Lions and leopards would come snuffling around our

tents in the night. We would come upon majestic elephants taking their morning baths. There would be exciting close calls with rhinos and buffalo. We would go in search of some rare animal that Hassan suspected could be found nearby. Ali Tabu would amaze us day after day with his wonderful cooking.

And all this would happen, not in a week or ten days — not in a month — not on a Monday and a Tuesday and a Wednesday. It would just happen — as it was already happening. It was already just unrolling, as time unrolls. It was as plain and simple as the reality of living at home, and going to school, and all of that — only it was a much better reality. It was everyday life on safari — and that was all I wanted in this world.

17

We had been on safari for a week, or maybe it was ten days—or only five. It was hard to say how long we had been gone. Things were going better than I could have hoped. We had had any number of adventures—and there had been seemingly endless hours of just being quiet and enjoying wherever we happened to be. I had been chased by a spitting cobra, which put to rest the idea I'd always had that a snake will only attack you if you bother it.

We had seen some remarkable animals. Hassan had found kudu and bongo and a whole lot of game animals you don't see every day.

At night, we told our life stories. I knew all about everybody else's brothers and sisters, and mothers and fathers, and where they were born, and what it was like when they went to school. I even learned a lot I didn't know about my grandfather. Sir Charles's stories were the best, of course, and Hassan and Ali Tabu were very impressed with all his heroic deeds as an explorer.

I learned to drive the Land Rover and the truck. Grandpa finally convinced Ali Tabu to let him do some of the cooking. It turned out that Grandpa was a very able cook. He was no Ali Tabu, but he did a very good job. I did a bit of helping Grandpa with meals, and I was developing an interest in cooking, too.

Hassan seemed to have an unending supply of stories and information about the African bush and the animals we saw. He taught me a lot about tracking.

Something really surprising that happened to us was the ability to sense things before they turned up. The first thing I noticed was that my sense of smell was much keener than it had ever been before. We'd be driving along, looking for nothing in particular, and I'd sniff something—and think to myself "Rhino!" Then, in a few minutes, we'd see the rhino.

I was amazed that I could do that—but later, it got so that I'd think "Rhino!" and *then* I'd smell it. Grandpa and Sir Charles had the same experience. Our hearing got sharper, too, and our vision. I discovered that I was spotting things so far away, that I was sure I could never have seen them before coming to Africa.

And we became quieter. Maybe because of all there was to hear and see and smell in the bush, we found that we could go without making any noise or conversation for a long time and still find things very interesting.

One of the things we hadn't planned for was running out of gas. We had extra jerry cans strapped to the outside of the two vehicles, but to keep going, we would have to happen into some kind of town every so often. Naturally, if we got down to our last few gallons, we would have to had start looking for a place to get more—and that would have been against the spirit of our safari.

Magically, we never had to do that. Somehow, every time we were just about ready to break into the last reserve of gasoline, Hassan would accidentally route us through some little village with one gas pump.

Sometimes we'd read the name of the place off a sign, or someone would mention it in talking to us—but we were in such remote country that the names meant nothing to us, even to Ali Tabu. Of course, Hassan would know where we were then—but he'd soon forget. He said he had gotten the knack of simply putting things out of his mind.

After buying gas and maybe some fresh food, we'd rumble back into the bush and be lost again.

We never hit any big towns. I got to like the shabby little village center we would come through. There would be the gas pump and a little shack-store where they sold kerosene, a few pots and pans, and maybe a bolt or two of printed cloth—and that was the town.

The people were always friendly and wanted to talk to us, but they were usually sort of shy, too. So if we didn't do more than smile at them, we'd manage to keep them from asking questions. That way we ran less risk of finding out where we were.

We didn't even know what country we were in. We might have drifted across any number of borders any number of times. We didn't take any main roads, so we could easily have missed border guard stations.

The terrain changed as we fumbled along. Sometimes we were in open grasslands, sometimes mountains, and sometimes forests. We never saw any thick jungles like they always show in movies.

Sir Charles was growing a beard. Grandpa and Ali Tabu

DANIEL PINKWATER

had picked up flamingo feathers somewhere and stuck them in their hatbands. All of us were dusty and wrinkled. We were a rough-looking lot.

We had gotten to be expert at making camp and could set up in fifteen minutes, just as Hassan had predicted. We could break camp just as quickly. Everything was going smooth as silk.

18

One morning I woke up smelling elephants. I didn't so much smell them at first—I simply knew they were near. At first I thought I had been dreaming about elephants, and that the dream was staying with me—but then I knew that there were real elephants around.

Grandpa woke up at the same time. "Elephants!" he said. We unzipped the door of our tent and stepped outside. There were elephants nearby all right—hundreds of them. They were milling around on every side of our camp. The nearest one was no more than fifty feet away. There was no way to tell how many elephants there were. All we could see was elephants. It was as though a dusty gray forest had sprouted all around us overnight.

Hassan and Sir Charles and Ali Tabu appeared in the next instant. We'd all awakened at the same time. The elephants weren't making a sound. That's normal—elephants can be very silent or very noisy. Sometimes you can hear them crashing through the forest miles away. Other times they just appear, noiselessly, as this bunch had. But none of us had ever seen so many.

"Gentlemen, do not panic," Hassan said. "Let us quickly get some clothes or at least shoes on, and begin putting things in the truck. Ali Tabu and I will have the motors running quietly. If there is time, we will try to fold the tents and put them in the truck, too."

"If there is time before what?" I asked. I was feeling nervous.

"There may be no cause for concern," Hassan said. "The nice friendly elephants may simply disperse at any moment. On the other hand, they may begin to move in a group. Then we have to move with them—or squish."

"Squish?" Grandpa asked.

"Squish, I assure you," Hassan said. "So do not make any fast or sudden moves—and above all, do not shout or make loud noises. If possible, do not even think any loud or aggressive thoughts. Elephants are very sensitive."

It was like moving in a dream. Nobody spoke above a whisper—and not much was said. We silently and swiftly packed up our camp. It must have taken ten minutes to get everything stowed away in the truck—but it seemed like hours. All the time, the elephants shifted from foot to foot, and swung their trunks from side to side, and nodded their heads, and shuffled—all without making a sound.

We crept into the vehicles and closed the doors without slamming them. Then we sat in the morning light, looking at the dense wall of elephants which surrounded us. As usual, Hassan, Grandpa, and I were in the Land Rover, and Ali Tabu and Sir Charles were in the old Bedford truck.

Nothing happened for a long time. We sat there with the motors idling and watched the elephants. After a while, Ali Tabu carefully put the truck into gear and pulled up alongside us. He handed something through the window to Hassan. "Here is some coffee in a thermos flask left over from yesterday," he whispered, "and some biscuits. I'm sorry for such a poor breakfast, but it's better than nothing."

We sipped the coffee, and munched the biscuits, and looked at the elephants. It wasn't possible to count them accurately because they kept moving in front of one another. You couldn't see a single patch of daylight through the dense herd. I counted a hundred and fifty and then gave up.

"Did you ever see anything like this before?" Grandpa whispered to Hassan.

"Never in my life," Hassan said, "although I've heard stories about the old days when there were great herds. Elephants are very strange creatures—they have many ways about which men know nothing."

"You don't think they'd hurt us?" I asked.

"Elephants do whatever they please," Hassan said. "And although they don't often hurt people, it has been known to happen. More often, they just whack someone with their trunk or kick a car over out of annoyance or bad temper— they don't intend to do any harm."

This was hardly reassuring. It didn't make any difference to me if the elephant that stomped me flat was really angry or just a little annoyed—I'd be stomped just the same.

"What if we tried to scare them off by honking the horn?" Grandpa asked.

"The worst thing you could possibly do," Hassan said. "Elephants hate being honked at—it's the best way to get them annoyed at us."

"Then let's not do it," Grandpa said.

"Certainly not," Hassan said. "The only thing we can do is just sit here quietly. If the herd doesn't go away, but starts to move, we will try to move with them. Sooner or later, we will

DANIEL PINKWATER

make our way to the edge of the herd, and then we'll just drive away as if nothing had happened."

Ali Tabu leaned out of the cab of the truck. "They're beginning to move," he whispered.

It was true. The hundred-foot-wide circle which we had been in the middle of was getting lopsided. There were a lot of elephant heads behind us and a lot of elephant behinds ahead of us. The heads were getting closer, and the behinds were getting farther away.

"*Allah huakbar!*" Hassan said and eased the Land Rover into gear. We slowly moved off with the great herd.

19

As we drove, the elephants closed ranks around us. After a while there were elephants so close to us on every side that we couldn't see the tops of them—we just looked at legs and flanks and tails.

Ali Tabu was practically bumper to bumper behind us—and so we traveled at a steady fifteen miles per hour. The elephants kicked up a lot of dust, and we choked on it as we rolled along. It was almost as dark as night, and we had our headlights on, although they didn't help much.

Hassan's idea about making our way to the edge of the herd and then escaping seemed impossible. The elephants were keeping us closely hemmed in. We had to go where they went—there was no way out of it.

The silence of the early morning had worn off, and the elephants snorted and trumpeted to one another, and thundered along the ground, and bumped into each other with audible thumps. We relaxed a bit and felt comfortable talking out loud.

"Elephants don't normally travel in such a tight formation," Hassan said. "They usually string out in a loose file and pick up this and that to eat on the way."

"Why do you suppose they're moving in this compact crowd?" Grandpa asked.

"It can only be for one reason," Hassan said. "They want to make sure they don't lose their prisoners."

"That hardly seems possible," Grandpa said.

"I agree," Hassan said. "I wouldn't believe it myself, if I weren't seeing it."

We seemed to be going uphill. This went on for a number of hours. In all, we'd been traveling with the elephants for more than five hours without stopping. Everything was completely covered with dust. A few times, I had climbed out onto the hood of the Land Rover and wiped the windshield with my hat. We were getting pretty uncomfortable—being scared had worn off. I wished we could stop for a while or just get out into the open air.

I got my wish. All of a sudden, we had all the open air anyone could want—more. The elephants were all in front of us, and in back of us, and to the right of us. To the left of us was nothing. That is to say, to the left of us was a five-hundred-foot drop. All of a sudden we were traveling along the edge of a sheer cliff.

The elephants left enough room for the two vehicles—but not a foot too much. If even one elephant had decided to bump us over the edge, there wouldn't have been a thing we could have done to save ourselves.

Of course, we were able to breathe now—but we didn't feel that this cliff-edge development was much of an improvement. To make matters worse, the ridge we were driving along was inclined upwards. Every foot we traveled took us a few inches higher and made the fall we were worried about a bit more horrible.

I don't remember anyone talking or even breathing during the time we traveled along the cliff edge.

I don't know how long we skirted the edge of the cliff. It could have been ten minutes; it could have been an hour. All I know is that it was too long. I was ready to scream when the elephants moved over a bit and gave us a little room to get away from the brink.

Hassan and Ali Tabu took advantage of the extra space and moved over as close to the elephants as they dared. I felt a lot more comfortable and protected when the elephants began to close in on our left, and we were surrounded once again. This didn't last long, however, because the elephants soon came to a complete halt. We stopped with them.

Now the elephants started to draw in close to the two vehicles. They were close enough to touch. We could feel the heat from their bodies, and the smell of elephant was unpleasantly strong.

Then the elephants in front of us began to sidestep. A narrow passage opened between them—just wide enough for us to drive through. We began to drive through it—not by choice, but because the elephants to the rear of Ali Tabu's truck had started shoving it and bumping it with their heads. Ali Tabu's bumpers began smacking into us—and there was nothing to do but go forward.

As we went slowly through the sort of street made by the elephants, the space got a little wider, and we could see something ahead of us. It was a sheer outcropping of rock. There was an opening in the rock—like a doorway. As the elephants stepped back, we could see that the outline of the whole rock was something like an elephant in profile. The opening was the space under the elephant's belly.

"The Elephant Portal!" Grandpa gasped.

It was obvious that we were going to drive through the Elephant Portal. This was not our choice. In fact, we would never have done it if the elephants weren't forcing us. The reason for this was that we were still traveling up a fairly steep grade, and it looked as if the Elephant Portal might be the edge of the cliff that had scared us so badly a little while before. All we could see through the Elephant Portal was blue sky!

Nobody said anything about this. There was no point in saying anything. We all could see what the situation was. There was no stopping. The elephants were practically carrying us along. We were going through the portal—and if it meant falling hundreds of feet to death, that was what we would experience. We had nothing to say about it.

Actually, I did have something to say. As the Land Rover passed between the legs of the stone elephant, and I felt our front wheels hang for a moment in thin air on the other side, I said something.

Actually, I screamed it: "Mommmmmeeeee!"

20

We didn't fall to our deaths. Instead, the front wheels of the Land Rover crashed down, and we found ourselves hurtling down a steep and bumpy incline. After I got my breath—which took a while—I realized that we were descending an incredibly long flight of steps. The Bedford truck with Ali Tabu and Sir Charles was bucketing along after us.

Hassan was clutching the steering wheel and muttering to himself. It was obvious that all this was too strange for him. He was totally unable to figure any of it out. It wasn't as bad for me. Everything in Africa was still sufficiently new and strange to me to make this development only somewhat more incredible than a lot of other things I'd seen for the first time. But for Hassan, who knew the bush well, this was too odd to be tolerated. He was half crazy with puzzlement.

It took fifteen or twenty minutes to get to the bottom of the steps, going at high speed. We veered off, slowed down, and came to a stop. Hassan put his head down on the steering wheel and remained motionless for a while. Neither Grandpa nor I spoke or made any move to get out of the Land Rover. Ali Tabu and Sir Charles had pulled up nearby, and they sat in the truck, catching their breaths and settling down. The brakes of both vehicles were smoking. They'd had about all they could take—the same as we had.

Finally, Sir Charles alighted and walked over to the Land

Rover. He looked like he was walking on eggs. His knees were wobbling. When he got to the Land Rover, he just stood there for a while. He couldn't talk yet. I know, because I couldn't talk either. My tongue was stuck to the roof of my mouth, and my lips were dry as dust.

I unscrewed the cap of a canteen and took a swig of water. Then I handed the canteen out the window to Sir Charles. He took a sip. Grandpa and Hassan were starting to stir, and Ali Tabu was slowly climbing out of the truck.

"We're in a crater," Grandpa said.

"But what crater?" Hassan yelled. "It isn't Ngorongoro, or the Embagai Crater, or Ngurdoto Crater—or any crater I know of. And look! It's a big crater! By rights I should know about it—and I don't! How will we find our way out of here? And where will we get petrol? Oh, this is serious, I assure you!"

"Hassan, do you mean that you weren't really lost all this time?" Sir Charles asked.

"I was partly lost," Hassan said. "That is, I was lost whenever I remembered to be lost—but it is impossible for me to become truly lost, because I know all of equatorial Africa so well. Whenever we needed to buy petrol or get some supplies, I would just forget to remember to be lost. But now I am lost indeed, gentlemen. I have never been more lost."

By this time we had all climbed out of the Land Rover and were drinking from the canteen and having a look around. We were in a crater, all right—and it was a big one, as Hassan had said. It must have been miles across—we couldn't see the opposite rim. The crater rim was maybe a thousand feet above us—and there was the stairway we had come down. That was amazing. It was man-made; there was no doubt about it. It was straight and regular and made out of yellowish stone. At the top, the Elephant Portal looked for all the world like a big bull elephant standing guard. There was no sign of the elephant escort which had brought us to the portal.

The crater floor was green and grassy, with occasional clumps of trees. Obviously, with all that vegetation, there was plenty of water around. There was probably also plenty of animal life, although all we all saw at the moment were a couple of marabou storks in a tree.

Ali Tabu spoke. "Don't you see? We must be almost there! We must be near to Kukumlima! We are finally utterly and completely lost—and we have passed through the Elephant Portal. We have all but succeeded. Instead of worrying, you should be rejoicing, Hassan. Not to mention that we are still alive."

"It's true," Sir Charles said. "We are all here in one piece—and this is obviously where we meant to wind up all along. I suggest that we make camp right here and get some rest. We've had a very exhausting experience. Tomorrow, we'll start looking around this crater and find out what's here—besides us."

DANIEL PINKWATER

21

We were all dead tired. Somehow, we managed to get the tents up. The supplies in the truck were all in a jumble, but Ali Tabu fished out a tin of crackers and passed it around. I fell onto my cot and went to sleep with a half-munched cracker in my hand.

It was the best night's sleep I've ever had. The others said the same thing. For the first time since I had come to Africa, I slept as deeply as if I were in my bed at home—deeper. Usually, I had been sleeping lightly—half aware of the animal sounds and ready to jump out of bed in case of an emergency. There never had been one—at least nothing to get out of bed about—but things had happened. Lions had come into camp a number of times. I always slept through it, but some part of me knew they were there. Usually, I'd dream about lions, and in the morning, I'd find out they had been there. It got so I'd wake up knowing lions had been in camp before anybody told me or before I saw any footprints. So some part of me had been awake, taking note of what went on.

But this night was different. I slept like a stone. A lion could have climbed into bed with me, and I wouldn't have known anything about it.

I woke up feeling great. I felt better than great. I can't say how I felt. The first thing I did was notice how wonderful it is to breathe. Then I opened my eyes and looked at the sunlight making the roof of the tent glow. That was wonderful, too.

And then I stretched. It was wonderful to stretch. Each and every part of getting out of bed in the morning felt as if I were doing it for the first time—and it was all wonderful. I felt like singing. Somebody was already singing outside.

It was Ali Tabu. As usual, he was up before anybody else. He had gotten the supplies in the truck back in order, set up his little outdoor kitchen, and was cooking away.

The folding table and chairs were set up, and Hassan and Sir Charles were already having coffee and fresh-baked biscuits. Grandpa stumbled out of the tent after me, yawning and stretching and looking as if he were enjoying it.

Everybody was in an impossibly good mood. We sat at the table, which Ali Tabu had set up under an acacia tree, and ate our breakfast.

"About being near to Kukumlima," Sir Charles said, "I want to urge everybody to forget about it. After all—if we are close to it, we don't want to ruin our chances now by thinking about it."

"That's right," Ali Tabu said as he carried a plate of food to the table and sat down. "Now, more than ever, we must be vigilant and careful to forget all about it—also to forget where we may be, how to get home, and everything of that kind."

Hassan started to say something, and then thought better of it and continued to wolf his powdered eggs.

"I'd sort of like to look around this crater and see what's here," I said.

"We should do that," Grandpa said. "I find this a very interesting place."

"So do I," said Sir Charles.

"Look! Someone's coming!" Hassan said.

DANIEL PINKWATER

22

There *was* someone coming toward us. He wasn't exactly coming straight at us. He was moving through the tall grass in our general direction. He would take three steps in our direction, then a giant step to the side, then a step backwards, and three steps toward us again. Sometimes, he would spin around and face in the opposite direction and walk backwards.

As the man got closer, we could see that he was wearing a cardboard box for a hat, three pairs of glasses, and was dragging a piece of rope.

"It's a loony!" Hassan said.

Ali Tabu turned pale. He pointed unsteadily at the approaching figure. "It's . . . it's Gordon Whillikers!" he said—and then he fainted.

Sir Charles stuck his hand out and approached the man, walking stiffly. "G. Whillikers, I presume."

"Are you going to invite me to breakfast?" the loony asked.

"Yes, certainly," Sir Charles said. "Please sit down."

"Why is Ali Tabu asleep?" the loony asked.

"You recognize him?" Sir Charles asked. "Then you *are* Gordon Whillikers?"

"At first I thought *they* had come back," Gordon Whillikers said. "When I saw your camp, I thought it was *them*. Now I see that you are men like me. How is it that *they* allowed you to come here?"

Ali Tabu was recovering from his faint. He moaned a little and opened one eye. Then he spoke. "Mr. Whillikers! Are you alive? We all thought you were killed by a green mamba."

"I don't mean to be impolite," Gordon Whillikers said, "but this coffee is rather cold. Do you suppose we could have a fresh pot?"

Ali Tabu wandered off to make coffee. He was talking to himself. "Mr. Whillikers is alive! I am vindicated. I will take him back to Nairobi and show him to my boss. I have found my client. He did not die. My bad luck is over. People will no longer make fun of me. Now, no one will say that my shoes are cursed." Ali Tabu tripped over a root and fell flat on his face. "I am a fortunate man," he muttered.

"Ali Tabu," Gordon Whillikers called, "I'd like some scrambled eggs, if you have any, and some toast, and maybe some sliced pineapple, and whatever else is handy." Turning to us, he said, "I've missed his cooking. I've been living on nothing but crunchy granola for ever so long. That's all *they* gave me to eat. *They* think that's what humans like. You can't argue with *them*, you know. Once *they* get an idea—that's it. *They* are very inflexible."

"Who are *they*?" Grandpa asked. "You keep talking about *them*. We don't know who *they* are."

"*They*?" Gordon Whillikers said. "*They* are the masters of this place—but more to the point, who are *you*?"

"I beg your pardon," Sir Charles said. "I have forgotten to

introduce my companions and myself. I am Sir Charles Pelicanstein. This is my old friend, Seumas Finnneganstein, and this is his grandson, Ronald Donald Almondotter. Hassan Kapoora is our chief driver and guide, and of course, you know Ali Tabu."

"I am pleased to meet you all," said Gordon Whillikers, removing the crunchy granola box he used as a hat. "I am Gordon Whillikers, the first man in history to engage in business transactions with beings from another planet."

"What? What's that you say?" Sir Charles asked, very excited. "What did you say about beings from another planet?"

"Did I say something about beings from another planet?" Gordon Whillikers asked. "Imagine that. Well, you mustn't take things I say too seriously. I say all sorts of things without meaning to. I'm a loony, you know."

"But you did say something about beings from another planet," Grandpa said. "We'd like to know what you meant by that."

"I tell you, I just say things," Gordon Whillikers said. "I am one hundred percent certifiably insane. You don't want to take any notice of what a crazy person says, do you? By the way, what are you doing here on private property?"

"We came looking for you," Sir Charles said. "Well, since we all thought you were dead, we weren't looking for you exactly—but we were looking for Kukumlima. You see, your notes found their way back to England. We found out about Raymond, the intelligent earthworm you played chess with, and we came here as a scientific expedition. We had absolutely no luck in finding Kukumlima, until we met an old baba named Pambazuka. He told us how to find this place. I am correct in assuming that this crater is known as Kukumlima, am I not?"

"That Pambazuka! That old rascal! He's the one who sold *them* all those thousands of boxes of crunchy granola!" Gordon Whillikers said. "Did he tell you that? No, I'll bet he didn't. He's a shrewd fellow, that Pambazuka."

"You said that *they* are the masters of this place. You also said something about beings from another planet. This is all very unclear to us," Sir Charles said. "We'd appreciate it if you would explain just how you came to be here and what has happened since you came."

"Ah, my breakfast is ready," Gordon Whillikers said. "Please excuse me while I eat."

Gordon Whillikers ate, without saying another word, for almost an hour. He had second, third, and fourth helpings of everything. When he had finished he said, "I assume you brought plenty of food with you? Well, I have decided to allow you to stay here. If you will permit me to take my meals with you, I will take you all into my confidence and give you a quarter share in my business enterprise. Is that agreeable?"

"It might be, if you were to tell us what your business enterprise is," Sir Charles said.

"Very well," Gordon Whillikers said. "I will tell you everything. But first, isn't it getting very near to lunchtime?"

23

It was well into the afternoon when Gordon Whillikers finished eating his lunch, which was even more colossal than his breakfast. He sat back, burped, picked his teeth, and began his story.

"After I was accidentally separated from Ali Tabu, I came here. I found the place quite by accident. I was chased by a huge herd of elephants. It was a terrifying experience. The elephants chased me until I came to the head of that huge flight of stone steps. I ran down the steps and found myself in this crater. I tried to escape from the crater, but the only way out was up the steps. Each time I tried to climb them, I was met at the top by the elephants, who refused to let me pass.

"So I was stuck here and decided to make the best of it. The main problem was finding anything to eat. There isn't much game here—at least very little that you would want to make a meal of. I found some edible fruit and a source of fresh water, and made a little hut to live in.

"I lived in my hut, trying to make myself as comfortable as possible for a number of days. Then, one day, upon coming out of my hut in the morning, I found a box of crunchy granola. I was amazed. I had tramped all over the crater and found no sign of human life—and yet, here was the crunchy granola. I was grateful to have it, I can tell you, and ate the whole thing on the spot. The next morning, I found another box of crunchy granola. Someone was leaving this food for me—but who?

"As you may know, I am a trained geologist and gem prospector, and I had already noticed that this crater is probably the richest spot on earth for precious stones of all kinds. Look here."

Gordon Whillikers kicked around in the dirt under our folding table and picked up a pebble. He dunked it in his cup of tea and held it up to the light. It had a deep red color, and the light shone through it.

"That's a ruby, worth at least fifty thousand," he said. "I don't even bother with little stones like that." So saying, he tossed the ruby over his shoulder. Hassan made a dive for it.

"Of course, you can't eat rubies, diamonds, sapphires, emeralds, opals, or any of the other precious and semi-precious stones with which the floor of this crater is simply littered. Since I couldn't get out, the riches we are sitting on and walking over meant less and less to me. The most valuable thing I found every day was the mysterious box of crunchy granola left for me—by whom?

"I searched the crater again and again. I found nothing but precious stones. I can tell you, it was quite a strain for me, a lunatic, to have to deal with such mysterious goings-on. A sane man would have gone crazy—but I was fortunate in that respect. As Ali Tabu can tell you, I was already completely nuts. The only thing I feared was that I might suddenly go sane, in which case I would have never been able to endure the privation and uncertainty. Of course, if I had gone sane, the peculiar circumstances would have soon driven me crazy. So there was some comfort in that thought.

"When I met Raymond, I was given cause once more to be grateful that I was already a loony. Imagine the shock of seeing a huge, really enormous earthworm, coiled around my box of crunchy granola when I stepped out of my hut one morning. And then he spoke to me! Of course, being crazy already, I wasn't so surprised as glad for the company. Raymond turned out to be a nice person, if extremely disgusting in appearance, and we became friends.

"Raymond had a chessboard, and we got into the habit of playing every day. I was much happier, now that I had someone to talk to, although I still got nothing to eat but crunchy granola. It was Raymond, of course, who had brought me my box of the stuff every morning. As I got to know Raymond, he told me that he was an extraterrestrial from a planet called Bleeeegh—that's how it's pronounced—in a very distant solar system. The inhabitants of Bleeeegh are huge earthworms, naturally. Raymond was a sort of shepherd, staying in the crater to look after the elephant mice. You haven't seen any elephant mice. At the time, I hadn't seen any either, because they are entirely nocturnal and very shy. The inhabitants of Bleeeegh keep great herds of them and shear them of the one hair each elephant mouse grows each year. These hairs are spun into thread and made into a cloth which is highly prized on Bleeeegh.

"The Bleeeeghans have kept this crater as an elephant mouse ranch for centuries. Employing their advanced technology, they have more or less made the place invisible. As you must know, it isn't to be found on any map, and it's impossible to find on purpose. It's one of those geographical oddities—like Los Angeles, which does not exist.

"Elephant mice will not breed on Bleeeegh, so it is necessary for the Bleeeeghans to come here to obtain them. Raymond's job was to look after the elephant mice and collect numbers of them for a Bleeeeghan collecting ship which comes here from time to time.

"He was never able to get as many as the Bleeeeghans wanted because the elephant mice think he's a snake—their natural enemy—and run like mad whenever they see him. In case you're wondering why the Bleeeeghans don't just come here and snip the hairs off the mice, instead of transporting whole herds of them—they claim that the elephant mouse hair is of inferior quality unless it is grown in the frigid atmosphere of Bleeeegh.

"The Bleeeeghans suspected that elephant mice, which haven't ever seen humans, wouldn't be afraid of them. So they ascertained who was the wisest man in this part of the world—Baba Pambazuka—and communicated with him, probably through some agent or intermediary. Somehow, they got the impression that humans all love crunchy granola and that any human who was continually supplied with the stuff would be totally happy and content and willing to do anything for the beings who kept him supplied. Baba Pambazuka must have had plenty of the stuff on hand, because he sold them enough for ten lifetimes.

"By now, you must see what took place. Raymond offered me the job of looking after the elephant mice and collecting them. In return, I would get crunchy granola—and of course, I could have any pebbles, stones, and bits of this-and-that I cared to collect in the crater."

24

"All this talking is making me hungry," Gordon Whillikers said. "Ali Tabu, do you suppose I could have a little snack? A few sandwiches will be fine."

Ali Tabu made a stack of sandwiches, and Gordon Whillikers gobbled them down.

"Now, as I was saying," he said, wiping the crumbs off the front of his shirt, "I accepted Raymond's offer. After all, I was unable to get out of the crater. The walls are too steep and smooth to climb, and the herd of elephants stand guard at the head of the staircase. By the way, those aren't real elephants, you know. They're robots made by the Bleeeeghans. Probably you wondered why they didn't behave like regular elephants.

"Raymond showed me how to look after the elephant mice. I had to make sure they had enough food and keep track of where they were so I could deliver them to the Bleeeeghan collecting ship. Now that you're all here, I'll teach you to look after the elephant mice, too, so you can take a hand in running this place. And of course, you'll get a share of the gems."

"Mr. Whillikers," Sir Charles said, "did Raymond say how long you would have to work for the Bleeeeghans before you are permitted to leave this place?"

"Oh, yes, he told me that," Gordon Whillikers said. "Raymond said that I would never be allowed to leave this crater. I have to stay here forever. The Bleeeeghans don't want any more earthpeople to know about the existence of Kukumlima than is absolutely necessary."

"But how did your notes and journals find their way out of here?" Grandpa asked. "That is how we knew you were here—by reading your journals."

"Yes, that was a rare stroke of luck," Gordon Whillikers said. "Early in my stay here, when I had just known Raymond for a little while, I went to the top of the steps. The herd of robot elephants showed up, of course. They crowded around the big stone that looks like an elephant and threatened me. Of course, the robot elephants don't come down the steps into the crater. They just stand at the top and threaten. I had tied all my notes into a bundle and attached a long string woven out of grass to it. I whirled the thing around my head, as fast as I could, and let it fly over the heads of the robot elephants. I had the idea that if someone found it, maybe help would come, and I'd get out of here. Still, I didn't actually write anything like that—in case the Bleeeeghans found it. I didn't want them to get mad at me.

"Apparently, someone actually did find it, and you fellows have turned up. You will be a help. Now I'll have good food, while it lasts, and people to talk to, and people to help take care of the elephant mice. We're all here for the rest of our lives, you know."

"That remains to be seen," Sir Charles said. "First, I'd like to have a talk with Raymond, this big worm, or space creature, or whatever he is. Maybe we can arrive at an understanding of some sort."

"Oh, I know what you're thinking," Gordon Whillikers said. "You think that because I'm a loony, I haven't explored all the possible approaches to getting Raymond to let me go. Well, I assure you I have. I told you the Bleeeeghans are very inflexible. I'd be very glad if I could just get them to bring me something to eat other than crunchy granola—but I've had no luck at all. Anyway, Raymond isn't here anymore. He went home on the last collecting ship. I've been all by myself—until now."

"Then there's no one watching to see that you—that we—don't escape," Hassan said.

"No one but the herd of Bleeeeghan-made elephants," Gordon Whillikers said. "If you think you can sneak past them, you're welcome to try it. I'm sick of climbing all the way up those steps just to be insulted by a bunch of elephants who aren't even the real thing. They don't eat or sleep, or think, or anything, you see—they just chase people down the steps and keep them from coming back up.

"No, no, you're stuck here, just like me. Tomorrow I'll show you how to chop up grass into tiny pieces so it's easier for the elephant mice to eat. It's not so bad here. After the food you brought runs out, we'll still have crunchy granola to last us the rest of our lives. We can have a chess tournament."

"Grandpa," I said. "I don't want to stay in this crater for the rest of my life."

"You won't have to, Ronald Donald Almondotter, my grandson," Grandpa said. "We ought to be able to think our way out of this. It's like the old days in the Amazon jungle, isn't it, Charles?"

"That it is, Seumas," Sir Charles Pelicanstein said. "This is when adventuring gets to be interesting. Now, when things look bad, we old expeditioners can use our noodles, figure a way to escape, and leave this place in a blaze of glory. Yes, we'll get out of here, and the report of our exploits will thrill the whole world. This is the sort of thing you hope for when you're a world famous adventurer. How do you propose we get out, Seumas, old friend?"

"I propose we have a very careful look at everything in the crater," my grandfather said. "With all due respect, our friend Mr. Whillikers is crazy as a bedbug, and there may be something that he has missed."

"I take no offense," Gordon Whilliker said, "but even though I am unquestionably gaga, I doubt there is anything I have missed. Still, take a good look around, by all means. Just don't disturb the elephant mice."

"I'd like to see one of these elephant mice," I said.

"They're hard to see," Gordon Whillikers said, "because they're nocturnal, and shy, and very small—but I have trained one as a pet. I'll show you my pet elephant mouse, Ellis." Gordon Whillikers reached into his pocket and took out the tiniest creature I have ever seen that wasn't an insect. He put it on the table. It looked for all the world like a little, tiny, miniature elephant. It was shaped like an elephant. It had wrinkly grey skin like an elephant's, and a trunk like an elephant's. Growing out of the middle of its back was a single curly brown hair.

"Ellis is feeling a little confused," Gordon Whillikers said. "He's not used to being out in the daylight—that's why he seems a little stupid. Come nightfall, he's frisky as anything. You can all have pet elephant mice, too, if you like." Ellis, the elephant mouse, snuffled around the table, blinking. Even in his unfrisky state, he was the most interesting animal I had ever seen.

DANIEL PINKWATER

25

Gordon Whillikers stayed for supper.

The next morning Sir Charles, Grandpa, Hassan, Ali Tabu, and I set out to explore the crater. Gordon Whillikers didn't want to come along. He stayed in his hut, reading Hassan's comic books. Gordon Whillikers had told us that there weren't any dangerous animals in the crater. In fact, aside from some birds and insects, there were hardly any animals in the crater except for elephant mice.

We discovered that the Bedford truck had not survived the bumpy descent down the stone stairs. Hassan said the engine block was cracked. The truck was finished. The Land Rover would never be the same either. It would only go at about five miles per hour, which was just as well, as the brakes didn't work anymore. Also, it had a tendency to drift to the left. It reminded me of Grandpa's car at home.

We all jammed into the Land Rover and drove off. We'd drive for a while, stop, all get out and scatter, looking at everything. Then Grandpa would honk the horn of the Land Rover, and we'd all go back to it, report on anything of interest we had seen, and drive on for a while. Then we'd do it all over again.

For some time, we didn't find anything worth reporting—but as we covered more and more of the crater floor, we began to get a picture of the place we were in.

The crater walls were smooth and steep. They were made of some kind of grey, powdery lava. We tried carving steps into the walls with a shovel, but when we put our feet into them, they crumbled like sand. We also tried driving a long spike into the grey stuff, with the idea of working our way up the slope with ropes—but the spike came right out as soon as we put any weight on it. The walls were unclimbable, as Gordon Whillikers had said.

We also discovered that the volcano wasn't entirely dead. Now and then, we came across fissures, cracks in the crater floor, with hot, nasty-smelling clouds of gas coming out of them.

"It isn't out of the question that this volcano could erupt sometime," Sir Charles said.

"How likely is that?" Grandpa asked.

"Well, I'd say that we don't have to worry about it right this minute," Sir Charles said, "but on the other hand, I doubt that we'll have time to eat all of Mr. G. Whillikers's crunchy granola before the whole thing goes up like a Roman candle."

That gave us something to think about.

We also discovered a tree none of us had ever seen before. It was some unknown variety of rubber tree. Grandpa cut into the trunk of one, and the stickiest stuff I'd ever seen oozed out. You could roll it into a ball between your fingers, like rubber cement—but it was a thousand times stickier. It was next to impossible to get rid of the sticky stuff, but we discovered that if you took one of the leaves and rubbed it briskly between your hands, you'd get a coating of juice from the leaf, and then you could touch the sticky sap without

DANIEL PINKWATER

sticking to it. If it weren't for that discovery, we would have never been able to get the stuff off us. Unlike rubber cement, it never seemed to lose its stickiness, no matter how long you played with it.

"This is great stuff," Grandpa said. I could almost imagine all the inventions he could come up with using the sticky sap.

The other thing of interest we found was particularly surprising. We found something man-made. Well, it wasn't necessarily man-made—it was probably Bleeeeghan-made. It was a stack of big plastic bags. They were sort of like plastic garbage bags, except they were open at both ends—tubes made of some kind of very strong plastic, bigger than a man.

Later, Gordon Whillikers told us that the plastic tubes were used by the Bleeeeghans to transport the elephant mice. After Gordon Whillikers had rounded up a lot of them, the Bleeeeghans would stun them with a special ray, or sound wave, or something like that. The elephant mice would be unhurt—just in a state of trance or suspended animation. Then Gordon Whillikers would dump the hypnotized mice into the big plastic tubes, and the Bleeeeghans would load them on board the collecting ship. The tubes had to be open at the ends so the mice would have air to breathe.

"When do you expect the Bleeeeghans to come for their next load of elephant mice?" Grandpa asked Gordon Whillikers.

"I never know when they're going to arrive," Gordon Whillikers said. "And I've never seen their spaceship. They always come on a moonless night. I hear them singing, and I come out of my hut, and there they are. I help them collect the elephant mice. Then they send me back to my hut, and in the morning they're gone. Sometimes they leave additional boxes of crunchy granola—although as you can see, we're never going to run out." Next to Gordon Whillikers's hut was a mountain of boxes of crunchy granola, with some of those Bleeeeghan plastic tubes on top to keep the rain off. There was another pile of empty crunchy granola boxes almost as large.

"So the Bleeeeghans are only here for a few hours at a time?" Sir Charles asked.

"When Raymond was here with you," Grandpa asked, "where did he live, and what did he eat?"

"He lived all over," Gordon said. "He would just turn up suddenly anywhere in the crater. And he ate decayed leaves, like any earthworm, and dirt—he ate dirt, too."

"This is very interesting, isn't it, Seumas?" Sir Charles said.

"Yes," my grandfather said, "it is interesting, although I don't think we should discuss our observations just yet. Let's think things over independently for a while. Later, we can all put our heads together and share what we've figured out."

"I'd like to have a look at one of those Bleeeeghan earthworms," Sir Charles said.

"So would I," Grandpa said, "and if my guess is right, we'll have a look at them before very long."

I didn't know what Grandpa and Sir Charles were talking about. Obviously, they had some theory in mind that I hadn't gotten a clue about. Hassan and Ali Tabu were in the dark, too.

"I think Sir Charles and I are thinking along the same lines," Grandpa said. "Still, I don't want to discuss the matter, even with him. It will be best if we all just keep quiet and think our own thoughts for now. Later, if I'm right in what I suspect, I'll tell you all about it. For now, let's just have an interesting time and continue to observe this place. And if we should meet any earthworms, be polite, and don't ask too many questions."

Grandpa and Sir Charles wouldn't say another word on the subject—except to tell us that things looked as if they might prove very interesting in the near future.

26

Sir Charles consulted his pocket almanac. "There isn't going to be any moon tonight," he told Grandpa.

"In that case," Grandpa said, "I should be very much surprised if we fail to have a visit from the Bleeeeghan earthworms tonight."

I didn't understand how Grandpa could know that. He wasn't answering any questions either. He just told me that he wanted me to hide under a canvas tarpaulin when the sun went down. "And don't fall asleep," he told me. "At a certain point, I'm going to tell you to follow some earthworms. When I tell you that—or when I tap you on the head, which will be the signal—I want you to creep after them and not make a sound. This is very important. Do you think you can crawl after them without making the least noise?" I said I thought I could.

"Good," Grandpa said. "You will follow them—and if they should suddenly disappear at any point, just stop, and wait there for me—even if you have to wait all night."

I still didn't know how Grandpa knew the Bleeeeghan earthworms were going to turn up that night—and I didn't know why I had to creep after them in the darkness. Grandpa acted as if he were very sure of what he was doing. I supposed I was just going to have to do as he asked and find out why later.

Supper was a sort of feast—especially for Gordon

Whillikers. His appetite hadn't diminished, and he dove into third, fourth, and fifth helpings of Ali Tabu's cooking. All through the meal, Sir Charles and Grandpa asked him questions about the Bleeeghans, and between bites, he answered. Gordon Whillikers was crazier than usual this particular evening, and his replies didn't always make sense.

As the sun went down, Grandpa raised an eyebrow and jerked his thumb at the tarpaulin, which was spread untidily next to one of the tents. Without a word, I got up, and walked over to it, and crawled underneath. No one noticed me leaving the table or getting under the tarpaulin.

Peeking out under the edge of the tarpaulin, I could see the others in the light of the fire. I could hear the table conversation and the noise of Gordon Whillikers crunching and chewing and slobbering.

It wasn't very long before I heard something else, too. I heard singing. It was a little like a barbershop quartet, except that there wasn't any melody to speak of. The singing came from a long way off.

"It's *them!*" Gordon Whillikers said.

The people at the table listened for a long time, as the strange singing came closer. The Bleeeeghan earthworms had nice voices, but they didn't appear to be able to carry a tune. They sang random chords, of a kind, and one or two of them sang "Boom boom boom boom," in deep voices. It was the sort of music you can get tired of very quickly.

The singing got quite loud. The Bleeeeghans were near. Then the singing stopped. Just beyond the fire, I could make out five or six large, shadowy, earthwormy shapes. I couldn't say just how big they were, but the weaving shadows stood at least six feet above the ground. That meant that there was still a lot of earthworm not visible—maybe ten or fifteen feet. They were as big around as a man. I was glad it wasn't any lighter. I really didn't want to have a good look at these creatures.

"Whillikers!" a bass voice boomed. "Who are these people? Where did they come from? What are they doing here? Answer!"

"Ah, Raymond, my friend," Gordon Whillikers said, "these are human beings who came to the crater in the same way as myself. Allow me to introduce, Sir Charles Pelicanstein, Seumas Finneganstein, Hassan Kapoora, and Ali Tabu . . . and is that all? I thought there were more of us."

"No, that's everyone," Grandpa said before anyone could say anything about my being missing. Even from where I was hiding, I could see the wink he gave everyone. They all caught on, and no one said anything about me. Gordon Whillikers appeared faintly confused—probably he was thinking that he had imagined me.

"Have you explained everything to these newcomers?" the worm asked.

"Oh, yes," Gordon Whillikers said, "I told them everything."

"Good," said the worm. "Then you understand that as long as you work for us, you will have all the crunchy granola you will ever want. *Ummmm* good!"

"That's very kind," Sir Charles said. "We understand perfectly."

"Fine," said the worm. "Now let's begin our work. Whillikers, is everything ready?"

Gordon Whillikers said that everything was ready.

"Then summon the mice," said Raymond, the Bleeeeghan earthworm.

Gordon Whillikers reached into his pocket and took out Ellis, his pet elephant mouse, and set him on the ground. "Do your stuff, Ellis," he said. The little mouse stuck his trunk up into the air and did what I would call trumpeting if it were done by a real full-sized elephant. The sound that Ellis made was more of a whistle—actually, halfway between a whistle and a squeak.

In the distance, I heard a pitter-patter, like rain or a hailstorm. It was the sound of hundreds of tiny elephant mouse feet. It was coming closer. Then I felt as if my tarpaulin were being rained on. The miniature stampede had run right across the tarpaulin. The elephant mice hardly weighed anything.

Paying no attention to the humans gathered around or the Bleeeeghans in the darkness beyond the fire, the herd of elephant mice gathered around Ellis.

Then the Bleeeeghan worms all struck a chord. "*Hummmmm*," they hummed. As they sounded the chord, the little elephant mice all swooned and fell unconscious, including Ellis.

Gordon Whillikers carefully picked Ellis up and returned him to his pocket. "Ellis is a Judas-mouse," he explained. "The other elephant mice trust him and come when he calls them. Even though there are humans around and the possibility of danger, their instinct is so strong that they flock to him anyway when they hear his call. Now our good friends the Bleeeeghans have rendered them unconscious, and we can put them into the tubes. Let's have some help here."

Gordon Whillikers ran to get some of the Bleeeeghan collecting tubes, and Hassan, Ali Tabu, Sir Charles, and Grandpa helped him scoop the unconscious mice into them.

When the tubes were all filled, the Bleeghans slithered forward into the firelight. They were nasty-looking creatures without a doubt. One worm deftly spiraled the tip of its tail around each of the plastic tubes full of elephant mice, and another worm took a position at the opposite end of the tube, ready to push it along with its head.

"Now," Raymond said, "you will all retire to those tents— and remain there. I will stay behind until the others have gone and entertain you with a Bleeeeghan song. I am self-conscious about my singing, so please don't come out of the tents, or I will have to kill you. Into the tents, please."

Everyone crawled into the tents. I saw the teams of Bleeeeghan worms push and pull the tubes of sleeping mice off into the darkness. As they crawled, they began their weird singing. Raymond stayed behind, weaving in the firelight and singing "Boom boom boom boom."

After a half hour or so, he stopped singing. "I am going to have a rest," Raymond said. "Then I'll sing some more. Please stay in the tents, so I won't have to kill you."

Then he turned and began to slither away.

Grandpa's hand came from under the flap of the tent and tapped me sharply on the head. As silently as I could, I crawled out from under the tarpaulin, and like a worm myself, I slithered after Raymond.

27

My whole body was shaking as I silently crawled after Raymond. Sharp grasses pricked the palms of my hands, and although I felt very cold, I was sweating a lot.

Raymond made a fair amount of noise, crunching dry grass under his heavy body, and it wasn't hard to stay on his trail. He also gave off a peculiar odor, like moist earth.

As I crawled, I listened and sniffed. The thing I wanted to be certain not to do was catch up with him. It was pitch-black, and I couldn't see a thing.

After a while, I was able to hear the singing of the other Bleeeeghan earthworms in the distance. Raymond was going in the direction of their song. Soon, he began to sing himself. That made it easier to follow him, and his singing helped cover any noise I might accidentally make. I felt a little more comfortable once he began singing.

I can't say how long I followed him. It may have been as much as an hour. Raymond didn't move very fast, so we couldn't have covered much distance.

I noticed that the singing of the other Bleeeeghans was getting louder. We were catching up with them. Raymond's singing began to blend with the singing of the other worms. I could hear that they were all in a group together a very short distance ahead of me.

I had gotten over my fear. Tracking the worms in

the darkness wasn't all that hard. I felt almost secure.

Suddenly all my security went away as I felt something whish through the air, not a foot in front of my nose. I was certain of what it was. Raymond's tail had thrashed, almost touching me. I hadn't taken his great length into account, and while listening to and following the sound of the singing, coming from his head, I had almost crawled onto his tail. I fell back, feeling sick.

The worms weren't moving. The singing was quite loud. They were no more than fifteen yards ahead of me. I didn't dare move any closer, for fear of running into a tail.

Suddenly the singing began to get softer. At first, I heard all the worms, singing their tuneless harmony. Then one of the voices would suddenly become muffled, as though the worm whose voice it was had very quickly gotten a long way off. Then another voice would drop off suddenly, leaving fewer worm voices at full volume. This continued until there was only one voice clearly audible. I recognized it as Raymond's. Then Raymond was suddenly a long way off, too.

I could still hear the worm song—but it was muffled and moving away quickly. Something told me not to start after them. I knew I had to continue after them, or I'd lose them—but at the same time, something was keeping me from moving. Then I felt—or thought I felt—a slight vibration through my knees and fingertips. That was it! They had all gone underground! Soon I wasn't sure if I could hear them or not. Then I was sure I couldn't hear them.

I sat in the darkness, closed in by it, and waited. I felt frightened again. I almost missed the worm song. Now I was alone. And what if they should come back at me, silently? My breathing sounded very loud to me, and I tried to make it quieter. I was shivering.

I must have fallen asleep, sitting there, because the next thing I remember was being bathed in the white beam of a flashlight and hearing Grandpa's voice: "Brave boy! Did you follow them until they disappeared?"

"They went underground," I said, "maybe fifty feet from here."

"Good!" Grandpa said. "Just as I expected. Now, all we have to do is wait. Here, Ronald Donald Almondotter, my grandson, we've brought an extra blanket. Let's make ourselves comfortable and wait for dawn."

Sir Charles Pelicanstein, Hassan, Gordon Whillikers, and Ali Tabu had come with Grandpa, and we all sat down on the ground and wrapped ourselves in blankets. Hassan quietly gathered together some twigs and branches, with the aid of the flashlight, and soon there was a crackling campfire to warm us. Typically, Ali Tabu had brought two thermos flasks of hot chocolate and some sandwiches, most of which Gordon Whillikers ate.

So we sat, quite cozily, around the campfire, sipping the hot chocolate from two cups, which we passed around, and talking quietly.

"Mr. Finneganstein," Hassan said, "I am nearly crazy with curiosity. Evidently, Sir Charles and yourself have figured out something about these extraterrestrial earthworms which has escaped the rest of us. Won't you please tell us what you've discovered?"

28

"Yes," Grandpa said, "I think it is time we made things a bit clearer to you all. While we sit here and wait for it to get light, Sir Charles and I will tell you what we have theorized about our Bleeeeghan friends. First of all, Hassan, you are mistaken in referring to these worms as extraterrestrials. They do not come from another planet—at least not in the recent past. As Ronald Donald Almondotter, my grandson, has discovered, they live beneath the earth of this very crater. It may be that they originally came from another planet, but no spaceship comes here to take away the poor elephant mice."

"How did you know that?" I asked.

"Elementary, my dear boy," Sir Charles said. "When Mr. Gordon Whillikers here described the manner of the earthworms' coming—in the dark of night, never letting him see the spaceship, making him stay inside until they had gone—all this suggested some deception. The obvious conclusion was that the worms never left the crater."

"Also," Grandpa added, "the information that Raymond, when he spent more time aboveground, ate what worms always eat—decayed leaves and dirt—also suggested that this might be his home. Besides, they're *earth*worms, aren't they? With the exception of being a great deal larger than any other earthworms and having high IQs and the power of speech, they're no different from any other earthworm."

"Of course, all this was guesswork on our part," Sir Charles said. "None of these features would constitute positive proof—but Seumas and I have that infallible explorer's instinct. You might say that we made an educated guess."

"How did you know that the worms would appear tonight?" Hassan asked.

"That's quite simple," Grandpa said. "We had been chased down here by the elephants, with whom the worms appear to have some sort of agreement. They're real elephants, by the way, not robots—the smell should have told you that. It seemed likely that in some fashion, the worms knew of the elephants' having forced us into the crater. Perhaps the elephants report to them. Most likely the worms pay the elephants with crunchy granola, which elephants really *do* love.

"Then the worms waited for us to become acquainted with Mr. G. Whillikers, so he could tell us the same tall tale the worms had told him. By the second night, the worms could safely appear to us, sure that we would be sufficiently impressed to refrain from asking too many questions or inspecting them too closely."

"Why wouldn't they want that?" Ali Tabu asked.

"For one thing," said Sir Charles, "the worms didn't want us to think about the fact that they are blind. All worms are. They like to appear only on moonless nights, because then they are not at a disadvantage—we can't see any more than they can. And the worms apparently do not want it known that they live under the floor of this crater."

"Then the worms sing to keep in contact with one another!" I said.

"Good boy!" Grandpa said. "That's it exactly. And what we will do when it gets light is search for and mark the place where the worms have gone underground. No doubt, there are many entrances to their network of tunnels, but this will be the main or largest one, since they dragged the poor elephant mice with them tonight."

"What do you suppose they do with the elephant mice?" Gordon Whillikers asked. "Do you think they weave cloth out of their hairs, as they told me?"

"I'm afraid not," Sir Charles said. "Our guess is that they make quite a different use of the elephant mice. Since the elephant mice are totally nocturnal and can see in the dark, and since they have those useful little trunks, like genuine elephants, they would be quite useful underground, wouldn't you say?"

"But what use could the giant worms have for the little elephant mice?" Hassan asked.

"They must enslave them," Sir Charles said. "The worms must force the mice to dig their tunnels for them and bring them food. We've already seen that they seem to be able to control them by making certain sounds."

"Oh, the poor mice," Gordon Whillikers said. "Raymond always told me that they were very well taken care of on Bleeeegh. It can't be very nice being a slave underground."

"I'm sure it isn't," Sir Charles said, "and the fact that they constantly come back to the surface for more mice suggests that many of the little creatures do not survive very long down there."

"Awful!" Gordon Whillikers said.

"Now what about the story Raymond told Gordon Whillikers about this place being made invisible by Bleeeeghan technology?" Hassan asked.

"That's just a coincidence," Sir Charles said. "As some of you know, I am a world authority on places which appear not to exist—and do—and places which are generally thought to exist—and do not."

"Like Los Angeles?" Ali Tabu asked.

"So, you've heard about that," Sir Charles said.

"What are we going to do about all this?" I asked my grandfather.

"We are going to free the elephant mice, escape from this crater, and go home," he said.

"But how can we do that?" Gordon Whillikers asked. "Haven't you seen that there is no possible escape from this place? And won't the worms try to stop us?"

"Calm yourself, my dear loony," Grandpa said. "We will certainly escape, and if we confine our activities to the hours of daylight, there will be nothing the worms can do to stop us. Consider—a big, slow-moving, blind worm. It has no teeth. It can't catch us by running after us. I suppose it could give one a good thump if it actually managed to get near enough—but for the most part, they are harmless."

"You don't know that," Hassan said. "They might have other powers we don't know about."

"That's true, of course," said Grandpa, "but somehow, I don't think so. If they had other powers, they would have shown them or at least talked about them to scare us. I think they're just big worms and nothing to be afraid of."

"This still doesn't tell us how we're going to free the mice and get out of here," Gordon Whillikers said.

"Let's take one step at a time," Sir Charles said, "and the first step is to find the entrance to the worm tunnels. I think it's starting to get light. We'll be able to begin looking soon."

DANIEL PINKWATER

29

It was easy to find the worm hole. The grass was pressed down by the weight of the worms' bodies, forming long furrows which led to a big rock that jutted diagonally out of the ground. In the shelter of this rock was a sort of cavelike hole. I was the one who found it.

Hassan pushed a long stick into the ground, next to the rock, and tied his handkerchief to it. That was so we'd be able to find it easily later.

"Now," Grandpa said, "we've got a lot to do. Let's get busy. We're leaving this crater today."

Grandpa hurried us back to the camp. I wanted to ask questions, but he said that there was no time to talk. There was too much to do.

Gordon Whillikers was sent to his hut to put together whatever he wanted to take out of the crater. Grandpa and Sir Charles trotted over to the Bedford truck and rummaged around, looking for pieces of rope and tools. Hassan and Ali Tabu and I were sent to collect a whole lot of the sticky, rubbery sap that came from those strange trees.

We spent the whole morning collecting the stuff. It was hard work. The stuff flowed out of the cuts we made in the tree trunks easily enough — but it was so sticky that we had trouble handling it. Grandpa had told us to make the stuff up into blobs as big as our heads — and he said that we were to make two blobs for each person in the crater.

After a lot of trouble, we finally managed to get a dozen blobs into the back of the Land Rover. We took the precaution of smearing everything with juice from the leaves, so we would be able to get the blobs out again without too much trouble.

We arrived back at camp just as Gordon Whillikers came up, puffing and panting. He was dragging a huge bag that was evidently very heavy. It turned out that the bag was full of precious gems.

"You can't take all that," Sir Charles said.

"What?" Gordon Whillikers shouted. "These are my very best diamonds, rubies, and emeralds!"

"We are going to have to travel light," Grandpa said. "Just take five or ten of the best stones, and put them in your pockets."

"Awww, gee! That's no fair," Gordon Whillikers said.

"Please, we have a lot to do," Grandpa said. "And by the way, do you have Ellis with you?"

"Yes," Gordon Whillikers said. "He's right here."

"Well, hold on to him," Grandpa said. "We are going to need him later."

Gordon Whillikers opened his bag of gems. "Well, any one of these will allow me to live like a king for the rest of my life," he said. "I can buy my own lunatic asylum and live in it. I suppose ten will be enough. Here, you other gentlemen—please help yourselves! Take any ten stones, with my compliments."

We all helped ourselves. I put ten diamonds nearly as big as walnuts in my pocket.

"Now, everybody!" Sir Charles called. "Take some of

DANIEL PINKWATER

these rope harnesses, and come with us. We have to go and collect some volcanic gases."

Grandpa and Sir Charles had made six tangled things out of bits of rope. They also had some of the plastic tubes the worms used to transport elephant mice. Grandpa also had a cardboard box, which I recognized as the kind we used to pack size 3 salami snaps in.

Carrying this weird assortment of gear, we all went off on foot to the place where the volcanic gas escaped from fissures in the crater floor.

"It's a good thing I always take some samples of our salami snaps with me," Grandpa said. "It would be better if I also had a portable salami snap fastener, but a pair of pliers will do."

Slowly, I began to get the idea. The rope harnesses were for attaching ourselves to the balloons Grandpa and Sir Charles were going to make.

This is how it worked. First, Grandpa would put a salami snap on one gathered end of a tube. That would give us a big bag. Then we would sort of drape the rope harness over the bag and hold the open end over the fissure out of which gas was leaking. It was lighter-than-air gas, and it was all we could do to keep the bag right side up while Grandpa fastened a second salami snap on the other end. That would give us our balloon, with ropes crisscrossing around it and two loops of rope hanging down below.

The balloons really wanted to float upward. It took all six of us to wrestle each balloon to a big, sturdy baobab tree, where we could tether it—each balloon to its own tree.

It got easier after the first couple of balloons, and it didn't take very long to get all six made up. Then Grandpa wanted us to move each balloon to a baobab near the base of the crater wall.

When we had gotten that done, we all went back to camp.

By this time, we were all feeling tired and more than a little hungry. Hassan slapped some sandwiches together, and we took a break.

"By now you all can see the foolproof method of ascending the crater wall I've devised," Grandpa said. "We will unlace our boots and jam them into the blobs we've collected. The boots are unlaced, so we can kick them off, in case of an emergency. Then we loop our arms through the ropes on the balloons and push off from the trees in the direction of the crater wall. If the balloons should fail, we can still keep going upward with the footblobs. If the footblobs fail, we've still got the balloons—although it's risky to go floating free in one of those things. I know the World Famous Salami snaps will never leak—but I don't know how strong the plastic is. At any rate—if you should find yourself floating outside the crater and want to come down, just poke a tiny hole in the balloon with your knife. If I had time, I would have invented a valve for a more controllable descent—but we've got to free the mice and be out of here today."

"Why the hurry?" Hassan asked. "We've got everything under control. We could leave tomorrow or the next day."

"I don't think so," said Sir Charles. "Perhaps you noticed that far fewer of the fissures were issuing gases today, and didn't any of you notice the little earth tremors this morning? And where are all the birds? This volcano is going to erupt, and we don't know when—but I'll bet it's soon. If you don't believe me, look!"

We looked—a dense gray cloud seemed to be passing over the floor of the crater. As it came nearer, we heard the thundering of tiny feet. It was a vast herd of elephant mice—in broad daylight—on their way out of the crater.

"Keep your pocket buttoned, Gordon Whillikers," Grandpa said. "We don't want Ellis to escape just yet."

"Grandpa," I said, "if the elephant mice know that the volcano is going to erupt, won't the worms know it too?"

"They may," Grandpa said, "but then again they may not. Probably there are earth tremors here all the time. In any case, we are going to free the mice and get out of here. The worms will have to take care of themselves."

"If you think this volcano may erupt, I say let's get busy and leave as soon as possible," Ali Tabu said.

"Fine," Sir Charles said. "If you're all ready, we'll proceed."

30

"We've noticed that the elephant mice, while normally very shy, will ignore everything around them when they are very intent on something—like that group that passed right by our camp on their way out of the crater. Also, remember how fearlessly the mice came into our camp last night when little Ellis gave his call. What we propose to do is very simple. We will take Ellis to the mouth of the worm tunnel, and you, Mr. G. Whillikers, will get him to give his call. Hopefully, this will have the effect of making the elephant mice below-ground drop whatever they are doing and make for the exit.

"Once in daylight, the mice will follow their natural instincts and flee the crater. We will be doing the same thing. No doubt, the worms will come in hot pursuit of their slaves—but I don't think that will cause any trouble for us.

"You, Ronald Donald Almondotter, my grandson, will not come to the worm tunnel with us. Instead, you will drive the Land Rover, full of footblobs, to the place where the balloons are fastened to the trees. After we have gotten little Ellis to give the signal to his comrades, we will make our way to the Land Rover as quickly as we can. Then each man will unlace his boots and jam each one into a footblob.

"Carrying the footblobs by the boot tops, he will then run to a tree and slip his arms into the loops hanging from a balloon. Then he will slip his footblobs on, cut the rope by which the balloon is attached to the tree, and push himself off in the direction of the crater wall. We will meet at the top and make our plans."

Everyone else went off to the worm hole to have Ellis summon the rest of the elephant mice. I drove the creaky and damaged old Land Rover to the place where the balloons were fastened. The old thing barely made it. I could have walked there just as fast—but not with a dozen sticky foot-blobs.

The balloons were in good condition. Hassan had tied them to the trees with a special African tracker's knot that never comes loose. The footblobs were lined up in the back of the Land Rover. All I had to do was wait. Grandpa's plan sounded perfect. He had taken everything into considera-tion—and if he wasn't wrong about anything, it would all go off perfectly.

Even though they were a good way off, too far for me to hear anything, I knew pretty well when little Ellis had given his call. I knew this because shortly thereafter, I found out what Grandpa had been wrong about. He had been wrong about the worms being slow, and he had been wrong about the worms being harmless. And none of us had given any thought to just how many worms there might be.

All of a sudden, gigantic, angry worms began popping out of the ground—everywhere! Seeing these monsters in broad daylight was not pleasant. They were, most of them, fully twenty feet long and must have weighed close to a half ton. Blind, and furious, they weaved from side to side and made the most frightening bellowing noise imaginable.

It seemed to me that the noise they were making was all that saved me from being smashed. There was such a racket that the worms appeared confused and turned this way and that, striking like snakes. The head of an earthworm is relatively tough and dense — it is used for pushing dirt out of the way and burrowing. These monster, giant worms were thrusting their heads forward with enough force almost to tip over the Land Rover. I know this because one of them did make contact and gave me a terrible jolt — but he was too worked up to stay and keep it up, and went off, striking and punching with his nose at the air in a hundred different directions.

So the worms weren't exactly an accurate threat. They slammed away at everything and nothing in a random fashion. But they were still dangerous. For one thing, they covered the ground at a pretty impressive rate. You could easily outrun one — but then you were in danger of running into another one as you escaped. And they kept popping up out of the ground! That was the most disturbing thing. I imagined Grandpa running along and suddenly being faced with a thousand-pound, angry, blind worm, striking out everywhere. I half expected one to bash up through the floorboards of the Land Rover.

I was pretty frightened. There must have been forty or fifty worms in my general vicinity. I kept thinking, what if something had happened to Grandpa and the others? What if they had been overpowered by worms and dragged underground, like the poor elephant mice? I'd never see any of them again.

I was getting pretty worked up. The sight of all those worms wasn't doing my nerves any good. I thought I might go crazy if things went on a little bit longer.

Then I saw Grandpa and the others. They were trotting along, dodging worms. Grandpa was laughing! Hassan had a long stick, and when a worm got too close, he'd give it a good whack. Then the worm would spin around, to strike at wherever the whack had come from, but by that time, Hassan and Ali Tabu and Grandpa and Sir Charles and Gordon Whillikers would have run past.

"Oh, *hee hee hee!*" Grandpa laughed. "*Whee!* This is fun! Now, every man, unlace his boots, and prepare his footblobs! Come on, boy!" he shouted at me. "Don't just sit there in the truck! Come out here and dodge worms with us! Isn't this great, Charles? That little Ellis did his job, didn't he? You should have been there, Ronald, my boy—it went like clockwork!"

31

"Every man grab a pair of footblobs and head for the trees!" Grandpa shouted. "Remember to push off hard in the direction of the crater wall!"

I jumped out of the Land Rover and ran around to the back. I opened the door and handed two footblobs to each man as he ran up. Then I grabbed the last pair and started for the trees where our balloons were tethered.

The worms appeared confused. They had fallen back and become less active. It was only a few yards to the trees, and it looked as though it was going to be easy. Then the worms started humming. They all hummed the same note. As they hummed, they began to shift their positions. Each worm managed to touch tail and nose to the tail and nose of another worm. They were forming a circle—and we were in the middle of it.

"Quick!" Sir Charles shouted. "To the trees before they can complete the circle!"

We were too late. There were worms on every side of us.

Hassan rushed forward, whacking with his stick. He tried to break through the ring of worms. One of the worms, I think it was Raymond, poked Hassan in the stomach with his nose and sent him tumbling backwards. Gordon Whillikers and Ali Tabu ran forward and picked Hassan up. The wind was knocked out of him, and he was looking green.

The humming got louder. Involuntarily, we grouped closer together in the middle of the circle. The worms were moving closer, closing in on us. Each worm swept the ground in front of him with his nose, making sure that not one of us escaped.

It would only be a very few minutes until the worms were on top of us. It didn't look like we were going to be able to get away from them.

A large group of stampeding elephant mice ran right through the circle, on their way to the crater wall. I thought I recognized Ellis in the lead. The elephant mice could scamper right up the wall, and I remember wishing I could, too.

The mice ran between, under, over, and on top of the worms as they passed. The arrival of the mice gave us an extra minute or two, as the worms appeared momentarily distracted by the little creatures, trumpeting and galloping right past them. But the worms didn't break the circle. We were still caught, and there was no way out.

"All we can do is wait, and be ready to run like mad," Sir Charles said. "If you see an opening, go through it—it's every man for himself—and don't hesitate! The instant you see daylight between the worms, go for it! Don't stop to think."

We were all crouching—ready to run—but the worms didn't make any mistakes. They moved closer and closer, snuffling along the ground. They'd be on us in a minute.

Then the ground began to wobble under our feet. It was rolling like the surface of the ocean. From somewhere in the crater we heard a loud noise, sounding like gurgling and grinding—something like a stopped-up drain or a gigantic pencil sharpener. It was hard to stay on one's feet. An earthquake!

The worms were thrown into a state of confusion. Some continued to move toward us. Others stuck their noses straight up into the air and listened to the grinding, gurgling sound. Others became frightened or disoriented and moved off in the opposite direction. There were plenty of gaps in the circle.

"Now! Now! Run for it!" Sir Charles shouted.

We ran. It was a weird sensation. It was like running across a trampoline in high wind. The ground was bouncing and rolling under my feet. Sometimes, I'd take a step forward and be thrown in the opposite direction. Sometimes, I'd be thrown off my feet. Once I fell against a worm, who was so busy being confused that he didn't do anything about it. I picked myself up, ran around his tail, and continued to make for the trees.

It was like a nightmare. The trees were very close, but it seemed to be taking forever to reach them. The trees themselves were swaying dangerously, and the balloons attached to them were bobbing wildly.

Reaching the trees was hard enough. Getting hold of the ropes dangling from the balloons was next to impossible. I jumped and grabbed again and again, trying to get hold of the loops of rope which seemed to be hanging just beyond my fingertips. Every time, I missed them, sometimes just brushing them with my fingers. All this time, I had my foot-blobs in one hand, holding them carefully by the boot tops, so the blobs wouldn't get stuck together. It was so frustrating I was starting to cry.

"Put on the footblobs, and walk up the tree!" someone shouted. It was Hassan. I looked around. Hassan was the only one in position, his arms through the loops of rope, his footblobs on his feet, his knife in his hand, ready to cut loose.

I put on my footblobs and walked up the tree trunk. I found you had to give a little wiggle to your foot to make the blob come loose. Actually, I didn't walk up the trunk for the first couple of steps. I sort of shinnied up and then got hold of one of the balloon ropes. After that, it was easy to make my way up the tree and get my arms into the rope loops.

I looked around at the others. Everyone else was in place, too.

"Knives ready?" Grandpa shouted.

We all brandished our knives.

"Now remember to push off hard, with your arms, in the direction of the crater wall," Grandpa shouted. "There seems to be a wind with us, too, so we should all make it."

There was a wind, a fairly strong one, blowing from the middle of the crater, which was usually windless. This wind carried ashes and a burning smell. The earth tremors were continuing, but they were less severe. There were plenty of worms nearby, but they appeared not to have gotten organized yet.

"Now, unstick your footblobs from the trees!" Grandpa shouted.

We all did it.

"Get a good hold of a branch with one hand, and cut the rope attaching the balloon with the other—hold on tight now!"

I cut the rope. The balloon tugged upward, hurting my left shoulder slightly.

"Put your knives away, and grab hold with the other hand!" Grandpa shouted.

We did that.

"Now! Push off in the direction of the crater wall!"

I pushed. The balloon bobbed upwards. I hung from the loops by my armpits. I thought I was going to go straight up and out of sight. I started to feel sick. Then I saw the gray, cindery crater wall coming up at me fast. It looked as if it were going to smash me to bits. I screamed and stuck my feet out toward it.

THUD! I was stuck to the wall and being stretched out of shape by the balloon.

"Walk!" Grandpa shouted.

I unstuck one foot and put it against the crater wall a little higher than the other. Then I unstuck the other foot and moved it up. Then I did it again.

"Walk!" Grandpa shouted.

I was walking.

DANIEL PINKWATER

32

It didn't take long to get the knack of the footblob-and-balloon method of locomotion. The balloon wanted to go straight up—and that had to be watched out for. The main thing was to make sure that one foot was securely stuck to the crater wall at all times. A couple of times, I started to lose contact and had to scramble wildly to get a foot stuck again. The best way to proceed, I discovered, was to kick forward with the foot you wanted to move—as if you were kicking a football. This would get the footblob to break loose from the slope and move the foot forward. Then you could bring the other foot up, make sure both were sticking, and kick out with the other leg.

Once I got used to it, it was easier than walking. Because the balloon was propelling me upward, I made rapid progress. I noticed that the others were climbing fast, too.

There wasn't much talking after Sir Charles said, "The volcano is erupting." We mostly worked hard at getting to the rim of the crater as fast as we could. I took one look over my shoulder and saw a dark column of smoke coming from the center of the crater. After that, I concentrated on climbing.

We climbed about two thousand feet in minutes. We all arrived at the rim of the crater at about the same time. The rim was rather flat and about fifteen yards wide.

"Let's take a breather," Sir Charles said, "and have a look at things."

Down in the middle of the crater, we could see the beginnings of a brand-new volcano. There was a good deal of smoke coming up and lava flowing down the sides of a cone that had not been there before.

We could make out the shapes of a lot of giant worms in the crater. They seemed to be just sitting around, waiting to be covered with lava. Obviously, they couldn't get up the sides of the crater.

"Kukumlima seems to be erupting in a very dignified and reserved manner," Sir Charles said. "Some volcanoes just go up—*whoosh*. There isn't time to put your hat on. This one is going rather slowly."

"What will happen?" I asked. "Will the whole crater fill up with lava?"

"That's one possibility," Sir Charles said, "or it could really let go, and go *whoosh*, any second. As a volcanologist, my guess is that it will just bubble along for a day or two and then go dormant again. When it cools, the worms will have a nice mountain in the middle of their crater. Of course, there's no telling when it will erupt again."

I hoped Sir Charles was right. Even though the worms were nasty, dishonest, and extremely disgusting to look at, I hoped they wouldn't get swallowed up by burning lava. I hoped this mainly because I didn't want to think about what they'd look like squirming and melting.

"It seems to me," Hassan said, "that the next order of business is how to get away from here."

"You're quite right," Sir Charles said. "For one thing, I could be wrong, and if Kukumlima decided to erupt in a big

　　　　　　　DANIEL PINKWATER

way, we don't want to be anywhere near it. Also, we seem to have no food or water. We should try to cover as much distance as we can before we start getting weak."

We went to the far side of the crater rim and looked down. The outside of the cone looked even worse than the inside. It was smooth and steep, and about halfway down a thick forest began. This forest, which was more like a jungle, extended in all directions until it was obscured by a thick ring of clouds.

"I'll bet that ring of clouds is always there," Hassan said. "That's probably why nobody ever saw this crater from the air. You'd have to be practically right over it."

"I think the climb down would be a lot harder than the climb up," Ali Tabu said.

"Yes," I said, "and when we got down there, where would we be?"

"It could be worse," Sir Charles said. "What if there's some natural—or unnatural—barrier beyond those clouds. Remember, this place never seems to get found—there must be a reason."

"So what you're saying . . ." Grandpa said.

". . . is that probably the safest way to get out of here is straight up," Sir Charles said.

A few minutes later, we all joined hands, kicked off our boots, and the footblobs with them, and rose swiftly into the air.

As we went up, Grandpa explained his ideas about how to manage the strange lighter-than-air craft we'd become. "If we seem to be going too high," he said, "one of us will make a tiny hole in his balloon. When enough of the gas has escaped, we can patch it with some of the sticky stuff we made the footblobs out of—my pockets are full of it. I even threw away my diamonds so I could take more of it."

"You threw away your diamonds?" Gordon Whillikers asked.

"The blob stuff is more valuable than diamonds," Grandpa said. "If we are still too high, after making the blob repair, another one of us will puncture his balloon. Of course, when we want to land we will puncture balloons, one after the other, until we begin to descend at a nice, easy rate. Now, let's try to grab some loose ends of rope and tie the balloons together. I'm getting tired of holding hands."

After a little while, we had fastened the six balloons in a circle. It must have looked like a giant flying doughnut. Hanging from the loops of rope under our arms wasn't the most comfortable thing in the world, but it beat being caught in a volcanic eruption or being clubbed to death by angry giant worms.

Kukumlima was getting smaller and smaller beneath us. As we got higher, we could see beyond the ring of clouds. Hassan said that—taking into account that he was getting an aerial view, which he wasn't used to—he couldn't get a clue from the countryside as to where we were. One thing was certain—there were no towns or farms or houses. We were lost, and maybe three or four thousand feet up in the air.

"I've been in worse spots," Sir Charles said. "We're picking up a good wind now—it's sure to take us somewhere."

33

The wind took us out over a desert. Where there hadn't been a sign of human life before, now there wasn't a sign of any kind of life.

"I love desert scenery," Sir Charles said. "It's so peaceful."

"If we land down there, *we'll* be very peaceful before long," Hassan said.

"Well then, let's not land there," Sir Charles said. "We'll just float past it. After all, how big can a desert be?"

"If that's the Sahara, which I think it might be," Hassan said, "it's more than three million square miles big—and there are few enough oases that we might not see one. So we may just die of thirst and hunger up here."

"Don't be so depressing, Hassan," Grandpa said. "Besides, I think this sticky stuff is good to eat—although I'd hate to waste any."

We drifted on for two or three hours. All we saw below us was desert. I was getting pretty uncomfortable hanging there, and I scrambled around, put my legs through the loops, and hung upside down for a while, just for a change. The others were getting tired and sore, too, and everyone was fidgeting around, trying to find some way to hang comfortably from the balloons.

It was dry and uncomfortable—but most of all, boring—

hanging around in the sky. I wished we could go down and walk around for a while, and then come back up—but of course, that was impossible, since we'd have no more gas to fill the balloons with. If we had a long enough rope, we could have lowered someone, and that person could have tethered the balloons—to what? There weren't any trees. Besides, we didn't have a rope.

"I always thought ballooning would be more interesting than this," I said.

"I wonder how the worms are doing," Gordon Whillikers said.

"I wish I had a peach," my grandfather said, "or a nectarine."

"I wish that airplane would come over here and find us," Ali Tabu said.

"Airplane! What airplane?" we all asked.

Ali Tabu had wonderful eyes. None of the rest of us could see the plane. Sir Charles had brought along his binoculars. He looked through them. "Yes! There's a plane, and it's coming this way!"

"Shout! Wave your arms!" I said. "Let's make sure they don't miss us!"

"There's no need for that," Grandpa said. "If they see us at all, they'll think we're a UFO, and they'll be right over to have a look."

Grandpa was right. The plane made straight for us. As it got closer, I could see it clearly. It had a lot of rust spots on it. There was something familiar about it.

The plane made a pass quite close to us and a little

DANIEL PINKWATER

beneath us. It was close enough for us to see the pilot's face.

It was Captain Roosman!

Or Captain Rassman—I had a hard time telling them apart.

The plane made a second pass. This time both Captain Roosman and Captain Rassman were crowding against the window, waving and smiling. I had a horrible thought. Having said hello, they might just fly off about their business, thinking that we were where we wanted to be. It would be just like them. I began shouting hysterically and pointing at the ground.

Captain Roosman and Captain Rassman made another pass. This time they pointed at the ground and scratched their heads. They didn't understand the signal.

We all began shouting and pointing to the ground and gesticulating like lunatics. Three passes later, Captain Roosman and Captain Rassman were all smiles. They'd caught on. We wanted them to land. They headed the plane for the smooth desert floor below.

We punctured three of the balloons and began a slow descent. It took awhile. By the time we were almost to the ground, the Air Enterprise plane had long since taxied to a standstill. Captain Roosman and Captain Rassman were standing on the wing, waving to us.

We landed about a mile away from the plane, but we had a very good idea of where it was. We couldn't see it—just sand. It took more than half an hour to walk through the sand to the plane. When we got there, we were thirsty. I was thirstier than I had ever been in my life.

Captain Roosman and Captain Rassman gave us cups of water.

"What a coincidence!" Captain Roosman said. "We were just on a routine flight to test new equipment—we have a toaster oven now. Would anybody like a grilled cheese sandwich?"

34

We had a big party at Wimpy's in Nairobi. Captain Roosman and Captain Rassman were our guests.

At the party we told the story of our adventures. Also, each of us gave three of the precious gems he'd brought from the Kukumlima crater to Roosman and Rassman, to show our gratitude for having our lives saved.

"We're rich men!" Captain Roosman said.

"Now we can have a soda fountain installed in the airplane!" Captain Rassman said.

Of course, Grandpa hadn't brought any gems with him. He had thrown his away in order to have more room in his pockets for the sticky blob stuff.

Gordon Whillikers suggested that we each give Grandpa one of our gems.

"I will accept them," Grandpa said, "but not as a gift. I will take them in exchange for stock in my new company."

"What new company is that?" Sir Charles asked.

"After we fly home—on Air Enterprise, of course," Grandpa said, "I'm going to have the sticky blob stuff analyzed. Then we'll know how to manufacture it. You, gentlemen, are all stockholders in The World Famous Sticky Footblob Company."

The SNARKOUT BOYS & the BACONBURG HORROR

The moon rises. The leaves tremble in the night wind. Dark covers the city. I wait in my place of hiding.

I am changing. I feel my bones and sinews shift and move in the first light of the full moon. My nose gets longer. My skin tingles as fur sprouts everywhere. I become aware of a thousand things unseen and unheard by humans. I smell things. I feel things on the tips of my hairs. In parks and cemeteries and vacant lots, rat and raccoon, cat and opossum—the little children of the night—begin to stir. Now and then they catch a scent of me on the breeze and shiver in their skins.

My teeth are fangs now. My nails have turned hard and horny, and black and sharp. Far beneath me, the city turns to slumber. I crouch beneath the water tank, high atop the city's tallest building. Faintly, I hear my little brothers, the zoo wolves, raise their voices in greeting to the enormous autumn moon.

Few creatures, and fewer humans, dream that I exist—and those who know me, know me only as a frightened dream, an imagined flitting dark moment. I am invisible. My cunning and instinct protect me from the sight of men—but I will move among them. I will lurk beneath their windows, race their cars on darkened streets, lope through the open places, and climb the high buildings.

The moon is well into the sky now. The light in the houses are going out. It is almost time for me to begin my running. I tear my civics textbook in two. The binding makes a satisfying snapping sound. I distribute the pages into the night air. They flutter toward earth.

Now I am ready to scamper down the exterior of the tall building, to run, to cavort, perhaps to terrify those with the wit to see—or almost see—to sense my nearness.

I rise up on my haunches and announce myself to the night. I give the ancient cry—the howl of the wolfman.

DANIEL PINKWATER

For more than a year, my friend Winston Bongo and I have been snarking out together.

Snarking is the art of sneaking out of the house when your parents are sleeping, and having an adventure late at night. The adventure usually includes or consists of going to the movies at the Snark Theater, from which the art of Snarking takes its name. The Snark is open all night 365 days a year, and it has a different double bill every twenty-four hours.

Winston and I began snarking together in our first week of high school, and kept it up all through our freshman year. In the summer we snarked out nightly. As we entered our second year of high school, we had both become highly expert world-class snarkers.

There's a box in the lobby of the Snark into which you can put a slip of paper with the name of any movie ever made, and the Snark will try to get the movie and show it. They usually get it—and they will send you a free pass to see the movie—if the one you've requested is one they've never shown before. Theoretically, someone who knows a lot about movies could go to the Snark free any number of times. If you write your birthday on a slip of paper and put it in the box, the Snark will send you a free pass on your birthday too.

It's more than a movie house. It's a way of life.

It costs fifty cents to get in if you have identification

showing that you are a college student. Our I.D.'s are fakes. Nobody really cares.

We're not the only kids in town who snark out. When you snark regularly, you begin to recognize some faces around the soda machine and develop a nodding acquaintance with some unusual people. You don't get into friendships with other snarkers very quickly. Many people who snark are introverts—quiet types. You may run into someone fifty times before you have a conversation of a dozen words.

Winston and I have one friend we meet at the Snark—a girl named Rat. Her real name is Bentley Saunders Harrison Matthews. We call her Rat. So does her family. She likes the name.

Rat doesn't snark out with us—that is, she doesn't make a date to meet on a street corner and go down to the Snark the way Winston and I do. She's more of an independent solo snarker.

"If I'm there, I'm there," Rat says. When Rat turns up at the Snark, we find her sitting in an aisle seat, hunched down, her legs twisted around each other, chewing her knuckles. Draped over two seats next to her will be her oversized red jacket, which she says is just like a jacket James Dean had. Without taking her eyes off the screen, Rat will punch one of us in the hip with a bony knuckle as we move down the aisle, and motion us to the two saved seats.

The movie could be anything—*Sabu the Elephant Boy*, Doris Day, or *The Cabinet of Dr. Caligari*—Rat doesn't miss a single second. I don't think she even blinks. If you talk during the movie she'll give you a sharp poke. This applies to strangers nearby as well as to Winston and me.

Rat is skinny and wiry. When she hits you it hurts. There are some not-so-nice characters who go to the Snark and try to creep on people, boys as well as girls. Rat just gives them a rap when they start with her, and the creepers change their seats. The fact is, Rat is tougher than us, and we both know it. So does she.

I can count on the fingers of one hand the number of times Rat has spoken while the film is running. Therefore it was noteworthy when she spoke to us during a movie with Laird Cregar, one of her favorite actors. What she said was also unprecedented: "If you guys are willing to skip the second feature, I'd like you to come with me. There's something I want to show you."

Missing the second feature was no sacrifice. It had Charlton Heston in it. Almost all the movies on Winston's list of the worst movies in history have Charlton Heston—or Jeff Chandler. If Rat had not been present, we would have enjoyed the film by making obscene remarks about the actors and talking back to the screen, like the rest of the audience. However, with our friend present, we would have had no choice but to sit through it, silently suffering.

When the Laird Cregar movie was over, we followed Rat up the aisle and out of the movie house. "I think you'll be interested in this place I found," she said.

Rat led us through dark streets for a number of blocks. We were in a run-down and scuzzy part of town a little to the north of the Snark. It was an area Winston and I did not know well.

We went down a street which had a partially bombed-out appearance. Most of the stores were boarded up, and there were lights in only a few of the buildings above the store fronts. We stopped in front of a store that looked deserted at first, it was so dark inside. Then we saw candles burning through the plate glass windows, and we smelled something spicy, like cinnamon. Lettered on the window of the store were the words DHARMA BUNS COFFEE HOUSE.

"This is it," Rat said.

"This is what?" I asked.

"It's a coffee house," Rat said. "It's been here for years. There used to be all sorts of stuff like this around here—and beatniks—my uncle told me about it."

Rat's uncle, Flipping Hades Terwilliger, was someone we knew fairly well. Winston and I had helped find him once when he was kidnapped, and on other occasions had searched for him when he was merely lost. Uncle Flipping is the sort of person apt to get lost and kidnapped. If they ever have organized competitions for the weird, Uncle Flipping is my pick for World's Heavyweight Champion.

"So? What's so good about this?" Winston asked.

"Idiot! Poets hang out here," Rat said impatiently.

"Big deal," Winston said. "What I want to know is, have you been here before? I mean, does it cost much to get in? I don't want to spend a lot of money."

"Well, you just sort of go in, and you order coffee, and you sit around, and all the great artists and poets and people

DANIEL PINKWATER

like that are there—and it's just a neat place, that's all," Rat said.

I had the impression that she'd never been inside this Dharma Buns Coffee House. What was more, she was a little nervous about going in alone, and that was why she wanted us with her. This was not in keeping with her character as it was expressed around the Snark Theater.

"So, do you want to go in or what?" Winston asked.

"Makes no difference to me," Rat said.

She wanted to go into the coffee house, all right, and Winston knew it. He was just enjoying the unusual spectacle of Rat at a disadvantage.

"Who knows how much they charge in there?" Winston said. "A cup of coffee probably costs two dollars. I've only got a little more than two dollars, and I expect to snark out twice more this week. I'm not sure I want to go into any expensive clip joint."

"Look, it will be my treat, all right?" Rat hissed. "Now do you want to go in or not?"

"I never say no to a free drink," Winston said, "but are you sure you wouldn't rather go to the Hasty Tasty?"

The Hasty Tasty was an extra-greasy spoon across the street from the Snark. It was where we'd usually go for a root beer or a stale doughnut.

Rat glared.

"If we go in, are you going to get us something to eat too?" Winston asked Rat. "It smells like they have pastry or cinnamon buns or something."

He was pushing it. I took pity on Rat, and probably also

saved Winston from getting a lump on the head. "Let's go in already," I said. "I'm tired of standing around in the street."

We went from the darkness of the street into the darker darkness of the Dharma Buns Coffee House and an utterly different world.

It took a little while to get used to the darkness inside the Dharma Buns Coffee House. We sort of felt our way to a table made from one of those giant wooden spools they use for electric cable. There were some rickety chairs around the table. We sat down.

The only light in the place came from a candle on each table. The candles were stuck in old wine bottles with drippings of colored wax down the sides. The walls were hung with paintings, stuffed animal heads, signs, busted musical instruments, a suit of armor, and all kinds of junk.

At the other tables was an assortment of strange people. Most of the men had beards or big moustaches, and the women had on clothing which looked as though it had been made from tablecloths and bedspreads. There were a lot of sandals in evidence.

A stereo was playing loud jazz. Some people were playing chess. There was a lot of talking going on.

It was a much more interesting place than the Hasty Tasty. I was glad we had come, even if coffee did cost two dollars.

A waitress came over. She was dressed all in black, and had pale, almost white makeup all over her face—even her lips.

"Can I get you anything?" the waitress asked.

Winston likes to appear sophisticated. He leaned back in his chair and asked, "What have you got?"

"Coffee," said the waitress, "and cinnamon buns."

She didn't so much say the words as breathe them. It sounded tragic, as though she were saying "death" instead of coffee, and "disaster" instead of cinnamon buns.

"We'll have three coffees," Rat said.

"Three coffees," the waitress said, as if she were saying "the end of mankind." She went to get the coffee.

"Is she weird!" Winston said.

"Shut up," Rat said.

The jazz record finished, and this guy got up to sing. He had a guitar. Someone had switched on a spotlight. The singer sat on a stool, in the light of the spot. Nobody introduced him. He sang the longest and most boring song I'd ever heard. It was about a maritime disaster on the Great Lakes. The song told about the wreck of a freighter called the *Hortense Matilda McAllister* in 1957. All five crew members got wet—nobody drowned—because the boat sank at the dock in Toledo, Ohio. The singer had a lot of trouble with rhymes because of the name of the boat. There were about sixty stanzas, all more or less the same. The guitar playing was diabolical. The crowd seemed to like it—at least they listened attentively.

During the song the waitress came by with our coffees. "Six dollars," she said the way you'd tell someone that his best friend had died. Rat shelled out.

In my opinion the coffee at the Hasty Tasty was better. Winston said that probably the coffee in hell was better. Rat told us to be quiet—she was listening to the song.

As I feared, the folksinger did an encore. It was a sort of

sad love ballad. I can't describe it other than to say that I'd rather be shot through the head than listen to it again. Rat liked it even better than the first song. Winston was sorry we hadn't stayed and watched Charlton Heston.

Rat was getting annoyed. Obviously she liked the Dharma Buns Coffee House and everything about it. She was close to socking Winston in the head, but she hadn't done so yet because we were in a classy grown-up place, and she didn't want to appear to be nothing but an insignificant high school sophomore.

Things began to look up. The folksinger left. He was replaced by a poet named Jonathan Quicksilver. He launched right into a poem.

THE STOP LIGHT ON THE CORNER
OF FIFTH AND SNARK

IS WHANGING

    BANGING

      CLANGING IN THE WIND

OH JAMES DEAN   WHERE ARE YOU   NOW

SQUASHED

IN

YOUR

PORSCHE

JUST WHEN WE NEED

YOU

AND

THE MUSCLEBOUND CRUM-BUMS

THREATEN TO BEAT ME UP

JUST

CAUSE

I'M

WEIRD

*

440

It was better than the folk song. For one thing, it was a lot shorter. Also, Quicksilver had no guitar. I was sort of impressed. I had never seen a poet before. He did some more poems.

                    HOPALONG CASSIDY
                              YOU USED TO BE A BIG DEAL
        YOU   AND YOUR HORSE
                              TONY   EVERYBODY
LOVED   YOU   THEN THEY FORGOT ABOUT YOU
                  AND IF THEY REMEMBERED YOU
                  THEY REMEMBERED YOU AS A PUNK
                  COWBOY ACTOR IN A BLACK SUIT
                              BUT I NEVER FORGOT YOU
                              HOPALONG
                  AND I GOT A BLACK SUIT TOO

                  AND IF I HAD A HORSE I'D CALL HIM
                  TONY
                  NO
                  THAT WAS SOME OTHER COWBOY'S HORSE
WELL

                  YOU KNOW WHAT I MEAN
                              RIGHT?

                              *

<pre>
                          I'M REAL SENSITIVE
I MEAN
                          I FEEL THINGS
                          BUT DOES ANYBODY NOTICE ?
DO THOSE CHICKS NOTICE?
                          AND ARE THEY NICE TO ME?
                          HA!

                              THEY THINK I'M SOME KIND
OF CREEP
              WHEN I'M DEAD
                      AND MY POEMS ARE FAMOUS
THEY'LL BE SORRY
              THEY'LL WISH THEY WERE A LOT NICER TO ME

BUT IT WILL BE TOO LATE
              THEN
</pre>

*

Rat had come completely unglued. It so happened that she loved James Dean and had long since decided to dedicate her life to his memory—so when Quicksilver read that first poem in which he was mentioned, Rat decided that Quicksilver was great. The poem had also alluded to James Dean's death, an event she could hardly stand to think about—so she was in an emotional state—and when Quicksilver came over to our table to sell us an autographed book of poems, Rat handed over $6.95 without a second's hesitation.

Quicksilver also accepted a cup of coffee, which Winston offered, and Rat paid for. This evening of culture was costing her plenty, but she didn't seem to care that she was going through money like a fiend. She was really happy to be talking to a live poet.

She was also impressed with Quicksilver's appearance, which was singular. He was the littlest, scrawniest, palest guy possible. He was dressed all in black, and he had a big black cowboy hat, and carried a thick notebook. I supposed he had his newest poems in it. He had one of the biggest schnozzolas I'd ever seen—with freckles. His honker was as big as his head, almost. He was an admirable guy. I have to say it.

Rat's eyeglasses were shining in the candlelight. She was really taken with Quicksilver. For the first time in the more than a year I'd known her, I didn't have the vague feeling she might slug somebody at any moment.

Quicksilver sat around with us for a while and told us how jealous the other poets were of his work and lifestyle. I found out that he worked days in a Ms. Doughnut—that's a chain of roadside stands the trademark of which is this girl doughnut. They make them fresh, but they taste stale—I've never been able to understand it. Quicksilver told us they had a secret formula.

There was a scream from the kitchen. The waitress, the one in black with the white face, came out. She was hollering that something huge and dark and fast-moving had whisked through and frightened her.

"Sounds like a werewolf to me," Quicksilver said, "I'm

going."

He was gone in two seconds. So was everybody else in the place. There was nothing for us to do but get up and go home — so we did.

DANIEL PINKWATER

Winston Bongo and Walter Galt attended Genghis Khan High School. Rat was a student at George Armstrong Custer High School. Therefore the three snarkers did not have the opportunity to see one another every day and discuss, among other things, the events of the night before. Some days might pass before they would meet.

Each night's adventure would end in the same way—Rat would abruptly leave the two boys on a street corner. Rarely would she allow them to walk her home. Rat liked to think over the movies she had seen as she walked. If Walter and Winston were with her she would have had to talk.

On the night the three had visited the Dharma Buns Coffee House, when the place suddenly emptied and the snark artists had wandered out into the street, Rat was not inclined to hear a single word from her friends. The experience of sitting in the coffee house, and what she thought about it, were things she wanted to keep to herself for the moment. "I'm going," she said, and was gone. Walter and Winston were used to this kind of leave-taking, and waved and grunted, which was all there was time for. Rat was across the street and around the corner, leaving the boys to find their own way out of the neighborhood.

Rat had a lot to think about on her way home. What she thought about was the way it had been in the Dharma Buns

Coffee House, the feel of the warm mug in her hand, the darkness, the people sitting at the tables, and the poetry. It was the poetry she wanted to think about most. This was entirely different from the stuff in the literature book—as she had hoped it would be. This was not like the poetry Mrs. Starkley, the English teacher, made the class read:

> St. Agnes' Eve—Ah, bitter chill it was!
> The owl, for all his feathers, was a-cold;
> The hare limp'd trembling through the frozen grass,
> And silent was the flock in wooly fold—

Rat didn't actively dislike that sort of thing, but she didn't like it very much either. Mrs. Starkley made sure that Rat and the others would not actually enjoy poems. The impression Rat had was that Mrs. Starkley wanted to make sure her students showed the proper respect for poetry—but they were not supposed to like it. This was Rat's impression. She did not know for sure that Mrs. Starkley hated poetry.

Mrs. Starkley hated poetry. What Mrs. Starkley did not hate—but, in fact, loved—was Tuesday night wrestling on cable TV. She was a big fan. Her favorite wrestler was the Mighty Gorilla. The Mighty Gorilla was the uncle of Winston Bongo.

Mrs. Starkley never suspected that one of her students, Rat, was friends with Winston Bongo, the nephew of the wrestler she, Mrs. Starkley, most admired, and that she, Rat, had often eaten meals with him (The Mighty Gorilla). If Mrs. Starkley had known this, she would have thought about

DANIEL PINKWATER

it quite a bit. Mrs. Starkley had a color picture of the Mighty Gorilla which she had cut out of a magazine. The color picture was taped to the door of the refrigerator. Mr. Starkley, Mrs. Starkely's husband, said that it, the picture, ruined his appetite. Mrs. Starkley said that would do him good, fat as he was. Mr. Starkley was not even as fat as the Mighty Gorilla.

Rat was thinking about any of this. She did not even know that Mrs. Starkley was a wrestling fan. Rat was thinking about the poems of Jonathan Quicksilver. She was carrying the thin book that contained every poem he had ever written. The first thing Rat was going to do when she got home was read every one of those poems.

When she reached her street, the windows of all the houses were dark. The only illumination came from the streetlights. Rat's house was an old and big one, set back from the street behind an iron fence that was overgrown with vines. As she reached the gate, she thought she saw a large shadow flit before her. She was startled—and then decided it had only been a bat interrupting the light from the street-lamp in front of her house. She also felt a cold chill, and had the momentary sensation of being watched by someone or something crouching in the shubbery.

Rat was not easily frightened. The werewolf scare at Dharma Buns Coffee House had meant nothing to her. She was unfrightened now. She let herself into the darkened house without making a sound.

A pair of eyes watched from the bushes.

I ran, I loped through night streets. I jumped over cars. I smelled something. Coffee. Cinnamon. I went to investigate. A kitchen. A girl dressed in black. She screamed. I liked it. The others left. The place was empty. The spotlight still burned. I took my place. I said my poem. The empty room resounded. The walls heard my words. They were disgusted.

I ate a cinnamon roll. I was disgusted. I ran outside. In the street, another girl. The one with yellow hair tinged with green. Rat. She was known to me. She walked. I followed. She thought. She skulked in shadow.

She arrived at her house. I lurked. She went in. I went away. Back to the place of the poem. I said my poem again.

The cream for the coffee curdled. The cinnamon rolls turned moldy.

I said my poem again. The spotlight turned a sickly brownish-green.

I left the place. I returned to the streets and the moon.

I had a nice time.

"So what do you think about the werewolf?" I asked Winston Bongo as we walked home that night.

"It makes no sense to me," Winston said. "I suppose those beatniks are plenty superstitious."

"So you don't think there could be anything . . ."

Winston gave me an exasperated look. "I have an open mind," he said, "but I didn't see a werewolf or anything else. All I saw was that weird chick who waits on tables get all excited, and then the skinny poet hollered that it was a were-wolf, and everybody scrammed. Just panic—that's all I saw."

"Yeah—well, that's what I think too," I said, "not that there couldn't be any such thing as a werewolf."

"I'm not saying I know for sure," Winston said, "I'm just saying that I, personally, have never seen one—and I didn't see one tonight either. What's more, I don't think anybody else did."

"I saw something," I said.

"You what?"

"I saw something—at least I think I may have. It was like a big shadow—just before Quicksilver hollered and cleared the place out. It was standing in the kitchen door. I just caught it out of the corner of my eye."

"You probably imagined it," Winston said.

"Probably. Only I don't think I imagined it."
"Sure you did. Besides, it's so dark in there anyway."
"Yeah—I guess."
We both walked a lot faster.

DANIEL PINKWATER

Rat headed for school. There was a strong wind coming off the lake. Particles of dust stung her face. Wastepaper and dead leaves swirled along the pavement. A bit of paper, a portion of a page from a paperback book, wrapped itself around her knee and was held there by the wind.

She plucked at the paper, grasped it for a moment, and let it go. Her eyes had fallen on the fragment—she had almost read the words—then it was gone. It tumbled in air, plastered itself against a tree, and then continued on its way. It read:

> This is the story of a werewolf in a great city in the present time. It is the story of the hopes and dreams of a boy whose future is limited to biting strangers and running through the streets. It is the story of a soul on fire, a youth of pure heart and low morals. It is the story of one who knows not what he does.

The page was the beginning of *The Sorrows of Young Werewolf* by K.E. Kelman, PH., a romantic account of the life of a werewolf. The book had been reviewed as a monstrosity, and was banned in most cities. Even that did not help its sales.

Of course, Rat knew nothing about any of this.

Breakfast with my parents—ah, bitter dull it was! The scrambled eggs and bacon were a-cold. My mother, while she ate, smoked cigarettes—and this was the boring story my father told:

"So you see, Walter, what with avocados costing as much as they did, even back in those days, I wondered just who you had to be to get them at wholesale prices, and where they were to be gotten. Well, it turned out that there's a big wholesale vegetable market way over on the west side—and anybody at all can buy there, as long as you buy in lots of a full case at a time. All this takes place early in the morning—more like the middle of the night. Well, I went over there on my bicycle, and I got a whole case of ripe avacados, and brought the thing home balanced on the handlebars. Of course I had more avocados than the family could eat before they (the avocados) started to rot, so it occurred to me to see if anyone in the neighborhood might want to buy some. They did. My prices were lower than the grocery store's, and my avocados had been picked out by an expert. Well, that's how I got started on my first avocado route when I was only fourteen."

This wasn't the first time I had heard the story of my father's avocado route. It has to be understood, my father is not a bad guy. What's more, he knows quite a lot of interesting stuff—the only trouble with him is that, if left to choose his own topics he will invariably choose to tell stories about avocados. My mother, for her part, seems to like these stories. I guess that's why they got married in the first place.

Saturday morning breakfast can go on and on, and the safest thing to do is to get my father started on a topic other than avocados. You want him talking, you see, because it distracts from my mother's cooking. My father believes in my mother's cooking. He says it will prepare me for life. He says his mother cooked just like my mother, and that nothing in this world frightens him. To keep him from starting another avocado story, I thought it might be wise to ask him a question.

"Say, Dad, what do you know about werewolves?" I asked.

My father brightened up. I knew at once that I had hit pay dirt. He leaned back in his chair and looked up at the ceiling.

"What do I know about werewolves?" he said. "Let's see, I ought to know something about werewolves." I had struck the mother lode, I could tell. Obviously, he knew plenty about werewolves. I was going to get through breakfast without another word about avocados, and I'd have lots of information with which to astound Winston Bongo later.

"Now, by a werewolf, I assume you mean a lycanthrope, a person who turns into a wolf. This is all legendary, of course, although many people still believe in them. The Greeks told stories about wolf men. Their name for one was *lycanthropos*. The Romans called your werewolf *versipellis*, which means turnskin—which was also an early English name for a werewolf—because his skin changes, you see. In

French it's *loup-garou*, in German *wahrwolf*, and in Russian it's *volkodlak*. Werewolves seem to appear in almost every culture. The Navajos had 'em—and there's an African tradition of leopard men, which is the same sort of thing.

"There are a lot of different versions of how someone gets to be a werewolf. In some traditions the werewolf is a sorcerer or magician who deliberately changes himself into a wolf for whatever reason—just for fun, I suppose. However, in most versions of the story the person becomes a wolf by accident. A bite from another werewolf will do it, or coming upon werewolf flowers in the light of the full moon. There's a gypsy legend which goes like this:

> *Even a man who is pure in heart*
> *and says his prayers by night*
> *can become a wolf when the wolfbane blooms*
> *and the autumn moon is bright.*

"These days, most people know about werewolfery from the movies. My favorite is *The Werewolf of London*. You may have seen it at the Snark."

At this point, my father winked at my mother. I always deny that I snark out. It is part of the sport. My parents know that I snark out, but haven't actually gotten any proof. I insist that they insist irrationally that I snark, which of course I do, and they know I do—but there's no other way. My father always tries to trick me into admitting that I am a snarker. That was the intention of his remark about my having possibly seen *The Werewolf of London* at the Snark.

"I beg your pardon," I said, "I don't know what you mean."

"Well, never mind," my father said, "in *The Werewolf of London*, this outstanding English botanist goes to Tibet in search of a rare flower called *marifesa*. The marifesa blooms only by moonlight. The botanist is attacked by a werewolf who, for some reason, is looking for the same plant. The botanist gets bitten, thinks nothing of it, finds the flower, and brings it back to England. There, he intends to bring the flower to bloom by means of synthetic moonlight.

"He is visited by a Japanese scientist who, in actuality, is the very werewolf that attacked the botanist in Tibet. It turns out that the juice of the marifesa, squeezed onto the skin, is an antidote to the effects of werewolfism. Now, I got interested in the marifesa myself. I wondered if it was a real flower, or just something made up for the movie. I did a little research at the Blueberry Library, and what do you think I found out? Not only is there such a plant as the marifesa, but it's a distant relative of—guess what?"

I felt a sinking sensation.

"No fooling," my father said, "the marifesa is a member of the same family as the avocado. Isn't that interesting? Then I found out that there are just hundreds of Asian relatives of the avocado I never knew about."

It was hopeless. He was off again. Throughout this story, my mother had smoked cigarettes and listened with what appeared to be real interest. It was hard for me to believe that I was really the child of these people.

The phone rang. I ran to answer it. It was Winston Bongo

calling to tell me to be outside in ten minutes. He had something he wanted to show me.

I told my parents I had to go out, and that I was sorry I couldn't stay and hear more about Asian relatives of the avocado.

"That's all right," my father said, "it is not your fault, my son."

I went downstairs to wait for Winston. There wasn't any sign of him in the street. Then I heard a noise like a soul in torment. It was a clicking and wheezing sound with a sort of low-pitched throbbing behind it. From around the corner came the thing that was making the noise. Winston was inside the thing. He pulled up in front of the apartment building. The thing made a high, piercing squeal, and then a loud thump.

"What is it?" I asked.

"It's a car!" Winston shouted over the clicking and wheezing of the motor.

"But just barely," I said. "Whose is it?"

"It's mine!" Winston said. "Get in—I'll take you for a ride."

I got in, first undoing the striped necktie that held the door shut. "Just knot that securely, and we'll be off," Winston said.

He put the car in gear, making a noise like a bunch of marbles being shaken in a can. The car shook all over, and then seemed to try to move forward. In a few seconds, it was clear that we were rolling. When we worked up to a brisk walking pace, Winston shot his arm out the window and merged into traffic. There was a lot of shouting and horn honking from the other drivers.

The car was unlike anything I'd ever seen. There was liberal rust inside and out, and sections of the body were covered with wide swatches of that gray metallic tape that sticks to anything. The seats were lumpy and covered with what appeared to be an old bedspread. A lot of wires hung down under the dashboard, and one of the dashboard knobs had been replaced by a pink eraser with a screw through it.

"You probably don't know what this is," Winston said. "It's a classic European luxury car—a Peugeot 403 Super Grand Luxe Extra—probably a 1958 or '59—my uncle doesn't remember."

"Is that where you got the car, from your uncle?"

"That's right. He gave it to me. All I had to come up with was money for insurance. What a great car this is!"

Winston's uncle was the Mighty Gorilla, a professional wrestler. He was a very cultured man, and had spent a lot of time in Europe, where, I assumed, he had gotten the luxury car.

"It's sort of past its prime, isn't it?" I asked.

"Oh, you mean because it looks a little beaten-up," Winston said, "that has nothing to do with the machinery. It has been neglected—for example, it stood half under water in a field for a couple of years—but these cars were built to take a beating. Listen to that engine!"

I listened to the engine. It sounded like a kitchen stove rolling down a hill.

In fact, we were trying to go up a hill—and not a very steep one. There was a line of cars behind us, honking.

"I didn't know you even had your license," I said.

"I just got it," Winston said. "My uncle was saving this car to give to me as soon as I was legal. Just hand me that window crank—I'm feeling a little chilly." There was only one crank handle for the two front windows. I pulled it out of the door and handed it to Winston, who fitted it into the little hole and rolled up his window

"What do you say we motor over to Rat's house?" he asked.

We hadn't seen Rat for a while. She hadn't shown up at the Snark lately, and had missed a rare screening of *The Terror of Tiny Town*, a western with an all-midget cast.

Rat's family is rich. They have a butler. They always call their butlers Heinz, and their butlers always wear Chinese robes. Nobody has ever explained why this is so. Heinz answered the door.

"Miss Rat is in her soundproof room," Heinz said. Rat's soundproof room is in the basement. She hangs out there, playing the most powerful monophonic hi-fi set in the state. There's a push-button, like a doorbell, that flashes a light inside the room—Rat wouldn't be able to hear anyone knocking.

When Rat opened the door, Winston said, "Come outside. There's something we want you to see."

Rat followed us into the street. "A Peugeot!" she said. "It's a '58 Super Grand Luxe Extra with independent transverse leaf-spring suspension, rack-and-pinion steering, sixty-four horsepower, and a maximum speed of eighty-one miles per hour. Not a bad set of wheels—whose is it?"

"It's mine," Winston said, "my uncle gave it to me."

"You ought to be able to get about twenty-six miles per gallon with this baby," Rat said, "if you've got it tuned properly. Open the hood and start it up."

Rat knows a lot about cars. Winston had forgotten that,

and looked a little depressed thinking that Rat knew more about his new car than he did. He opened the hood and started the engine. Rat pulled a multiblade Swiss knife out of her pocket and unfolded the small screwdriver. She listened to the engine, then reached in with the knife and did something. The engine sounded smoother at once.

"That was way out of adjustment," Rat said. "It should run a lot better now. You ought to leave it here for a few hours sometime—I'll go over it for you and get it running perfectly. Right now, why don't we go someplace? What do you say?"

Winston was obviously bugged. It must have pleased him that his car was running better, but the fact that Rat knew all about his car while Winston basically knew how to start the thing made him a little uncomfortable.

"We came over to take you for a ride," Winston said, "that was our intention in the first place. Is there anywhere in particular you'd like to go?"

"Let's drive out to Hamfat," Rat said.

Hamfat is a classy suburb where rich people live. I had driven through it maybe once or twice while going somewhere with my parents, but I didn't know anything about it.

"Hamfat is pretty far," Winston said.

"If the car breaks down, I can probably fix it," Rat said.

"Why do you want to go to Hamfat?" I asked Rat.

"I just want to go there," Rat said. "I've never been."

"I've never been either," Winston said. "We may as well go."

"May as well," I said.

We piled into the Peugeot and rumbled off toward the suburbs.

I sat in the back seat. Rat sat up front with Winston so she could listen to the engine. When she had listened to the engine enough, she wanted to play the radio. Winston told her it didn't work. She dove under the dashboard and fooled with some of the wires. In a minute or two, she had the radio playing. Rat found a New Wave/Country station and settled back in her seat, her arm out the window, beating time on the side of the car.

Grand Avenue takes you right out of Baconburg and into the suburbs. You pass through Porkington and Trottersville, and then you arrive in Hamfat. Starting in Trottersville, the road is lined on both sides with discount gas stations, fast-food restaurants, and stores with big parking lots. All the stores have huge signs you're supposed to see a mile away, except there are other signs sticking up in front of them— KIELBASA MART, FUDGE GIANT, SOCK CITY, UNDERWEAR WORLD, UNPAINTED SURGICAL APPLIANCE OUTLET, and CLAMS ARE US.

In the distance we saw a sign in the shape of a gigantic doughnut with skinny arms and legs which ended in feet wearing big Minnie Mouse shoes. The doughnut had a crown on top and a lady's face. "Hey!" Rat said. "There's Ms. Doughnut, where Quicksilver, the poet, works. Let's stop in and see if he's there."

"Aha!" Winston said. "So that's why you wanted to come out here!"

"No," Rat said. "I just happened to remember that Quicksilver works at the doughnut place."

"And you just happened to remember that the doughnut place is out here in Hamfat," Winston said. "We know you've got a crush on that skinny poet, and think the sun shines out of his earholes."

"Slow down," Rat said, "you'll go right past it."

"I haven't got enough money for a doughnut," Winston said.

"I'll buy you one," Rat said.

"I want a cup of coffee too," Winston said.

"Okay, you can have a cup of coffee."

"Walter wants a doughnut."

"Fine," Rat said, "Walter can have a doughnut too, you creep."

"Walter wants a cup of coffee," Winston said.

"Pull in there, you miserable mooch," Rat said.

"I will buy you and Walter a doughnut and a cup of coffee each."

"I'm not a mooch," Winston said. "It isn't my idea to stop at Ms. Doughnut and visit your boyfriend—but if we're going in there, I don't want to stand around like a fool and not buy anything."

"Quicksilver is not my boyfriend," Rat said. "I am faithful to the memory of James Dean, as you know very well. You can quit with that sort of remark or the free doughnuts are off, see?"

"I'm not charging you anything to ride in my car," Winston said as he turned into the Ms. Doughnut parking lot.

Rat turned around in her seat. "Why are you his friend?" she asked me.

"He gets people to buy me doughnuts," I said.

"Cretins!" Rat said.

Jonathan Quicksilver was alone behind the counter. There were a couple of customers at the far end, dunking. It was pretty quiet. Two or three flies were buzzing around the racks of doughnuts. Quicksilver didn't remember us.

"Hi!" Rat said.

"Hi!" the poet said.

"She thinks you're wonderful," Winston said.

"You know my work?" Quicksilver asked.

"Oh, yes," Rat said. "I've read every poem in your book *I Am Cool*."

"All *RIGHT!*" the poet said. "What will you three cultured beings have?"

Rat ordered a toasted-coconut doughnut and a light coffee. Winston ordered a mint doughnut and black coffee. I asked for a chocolate-covered, orange-marmalade filled doughnut and a coffee with double cream and double sugar.

Quicksilver filled our orders. "No charge for poetry lovers," he said in a whisper. "The boss isn't here."

"Hey, thanks, Mr. Quicksilver," Winston said. "We sure do love your poems."

"Seconds are on the house, if you can eat 'em," Quicksilver said.

"This guy is a prince," Winston said to me with his mouth full.

"What are you sensitive souls doing out here in the wasteland?" Quicksilver asked. By wasteland, I assumed he meant the suburb of Hamfat, which I was starting to like. For instance, there isn't a Ms. Doughnut in the city of Baconburg.

"We came to see you," Rat said.

Winston winked at me. "We came to pay homage to your genius," he said.

"Well, it's about time somebody did," Jonathan Quicksilver said. "Some of the other poets, who are jealous of me, you know, have been telling my fans that I work in the Ms. Doughnut all the way out in Swinesburg, twenty miles in the other direction. The poetry lovers go out there—can't find me—get upset—eat doughnuts—get sick—and finally are turned against me and my poems."

"That's a filthy shame!" Winston said.

"Those other poets are supposed to be my friends," Quicksilver said. "All they want to do is destroy me. You guys want to hear my newest poem?"

"Oh, yes!" Rat said. She was really enthusiastic. Jonathan Quicksilver poured some extra coffee into her cup.

"Okay, here goes," he said.

THE WORLD OWES ME A LIVING 'CAUSE I'M SHORT

HEY

　　　　　I DIDN'T ASK TO BE

　　　　　　　　SHORT

　　　　　NOBODY

　　　　　SAID TO ME

　　　　　　　　　　　　HEY

　　　　　　　　　　DO YOU

　　　　　　　　　WANT TO BE

　　　　　　　　　A

　　　　　　　　　SHRIMP

IF THEY HAD

　　　　　　I WOULD HAVE SAID

　　　　　　　　　NO

　　　　　　　　　　　　I WANT TO BE TALL

AND I DON'T WANT TO

　　　　　　　　WORK

　　　　　　　　EITHER

　　　　　　　　　*

"God! That's beautiful!" Rat said.

"It is, isn't it?" Quicksilver said. "Any more doughnuts here?"

Winston had a mocha pistachio whole wheat, and I had a peppermint-stick guava with powdered sugar. Rat passed up a second doughnut, and was content just to gaze at Quicksilver with love and admiration.

After a while, Winston and I found her drooling on the skinny poet a little sickening—also we were feeling a bit queasy from the doughnuts. We wanted to get out of the doughnut shop, but Rat was going to have to be dragged away.

"Mr. Quicksilver," Winston asked, "can you suggest anything we ought to do while we're out here—in the wasteland?"

"Why don't you visit my guru?" Quicksilver asked. "He's always good for a few inspiring words of wisdom."

"You have a guru?" I asked.

"Yes, indeedy," Quicksilver said, "the Honorable Lama Lumpo Smythe-Finkel."

"The Honorable Lama Lumpo Smythe-Finkel?"

"My spiritual guide and teacher. You can usually find him at the mall on Saturdays—look for a guy with a long white beard and a saintly expression. He's the best."

"We'll look him up," Winston said.

"Give him my regards," Quicksilver said.

The Grand Mall was not what we expected. It was a couple of miles past the Ms. Doughnut where Quicksilver worked. We almost went right past it. All of us had been to the Mega-Mall in Swinesburg. That mall is huge. You can spend the whole day there and not see all the stores. There must be thirty places to buy jeans there. There are big trees growing indoors, a fountain as big as a swimming pool, Santa Claus at Christmas and the Easter Bunny at Easter. It's your regular, splendid, flashy, modern mall.

My father told me that untold thousands of dollars had been spent designing the Mega-Mall so that people shopping there would feel a certain way. He said they were intended to feel slightly fatigued and out-of-place and unimportant. He said that psychologists had been consulted about the lights, colors, the height of the ceilings, everything. The idea is that if you feel uncomfortable in just the right degree, you'll spend more money.

He said that just by making the lights flicker at a certain frequency, the designers of the mall could induce the average person to spend 11.3 percent more than if he was in his right mind.

My father didn't like the Mega-Mall because he felt there should have been a first-class greengrocer in a place as well planned as that.

The Grand Mall was completely unlike the Mega-Mall. The first thing we noticed was that there were hardly any people in it. There were a few shoppers walking around, but no huge crowds. Also, there were no vast bunches of kids hanging out the way there always are at the Mega-Mall. What was more, about half the spaces for stores had no stores in them.

There were iron gates across the fronts of the non-stores. Some of them still had signs up, left over from the last occupants: PROFESSOR POPCORN, THE JEANS GIANT, GORDON'S MODERN ORGANS, PHIL'S HOUSE OF FERRETS, FASHIONS OF GUAM, and BUGWORLD. It may have been that Bugworld sold bugs to people who collect bugs—or maybe it sold exterminator's supplies—roach traps and things like that. In any event, Bugworld was out of business.

The Grand Mall did not appear to have been designed by psychologists who wanted to make people spend more money. The people we saw there looked depressed, but they didn't appear to be spending anything. They drifted along, and the storekeepers were doing a lot of leaning and yawning.

We liked the place. The trees were small and obviously made of plastic, and the ceilings were low. There was a cheap linoleum in different colors and patterns on the floor, and the whole place was sort of grimy. It was a mall you could feel comfortable in.

The stores that were still in business were all sort of uninteresting. There were a couple of gift and card shops—the sort of place I never go into. There was a wood-burning stove store—nothing doing there. There was a health food store with an unhealthy-looking guy behind the counter. There was a dinky video arcade with about five machines—two of them out of order—and nobody playing. There was a frozen yogurt place. Winston and I took note of that in case the effects of the doughnuts should wear off. Rat will not eat yogurt. She says that if God had intended for us to eat spoiled milk He wouldn't have let us invent refrigerators.

All in all, at first glance, there was nothing of interest about the Grand Mall. What we liked about it was its very crumminess. We had been looking out for the Honorable Lama Lumpo Smythe-Finkel, Jonathan Quicksilver's guru. We'd had no luck finding him. Then we discovered the only interesting place in the Grand Mall, and the honorable lama, both at once.

What we discovered was a bookstore. The sign outside said HOWLING FROG—BOOKS OF THE WEIRD, and inside there was, in addition to a fat bald-headed guy behind the counter, a man with a flowing snowy-white beard.

"Welcome to Howling Frog—Books of the Weird," the fat bald guy said. "I am Howling Frog, the owner, general manager, clerk, stock boy, and janitor—and this is my good friend and spiritual guide, the Honorable Lama Lumpo Smythe-Finkel."

The guy's name was Howling Frog! Never in all my life had I heard such a neat name. I was afraid I was being impolite, but I had to ask, "Excuse me, your name . . . it's . . . I mean . . . are you by any chance an Indian?"

"So far as I know I am not," Howling Frog said, "neither East Indian, West Indian, nor Amerindian am I—although I have the greatest respect and admiration for all those peoples. Why do you ask?"

"It's just your name," I said, "it's such an unusual name."

"It's the name my father, the late Phineas Frog, gave me," Howling Frog said. "The Frogs, from whom I have the honor to be descended, are an illustrious family, mentioned often in American history—and Howling is a traditional name going back to my great-great-great grandfather, Howling Frog, who fought in the War of 1812, and later went out west to Illinois, where he was known as Yellow Dog Howling Frog. His son, Yowling Howling Frog, knew Dan'l Boone. There have been Howling Frogs around for a long time."

"Well, it's a name I never heard before," I said.

"Old American name," Howling Frog said.

"I'll take your word for it," I said.

"You can do so. A Frog never lies."

"What sort of bookstore is this?" Rat asked. She had been looking around while I talked with Howling Frog.

"What sort? What sort of bookstore is this? Lama, she wants to know what sort of bookstore this is. Why you sweet little girl, this is the finest sort of bookstore there is—just the finest there is, that's all."

Winston and I both got alert when Howling Frog called Rat a sweet little girl. Nobody had ever addressed her like that to my knowledge, and it didn't seem to Winston or me that she was apt to like it. Rat had no problem about talking back to adults, and using some pretty outrageous language too. Apparently Howling Frog had made a big hit with her, because she didn't even snarl when he called her a sweet little girl. She just listened as he went on with his explanation.

"Book of the Weird is the bookstore in which you can find those books you never dreamed of finding, books you never knew existed. I have books about unheard-of places, seldom visited and practically unknown. I have books dealing with miraculous events and strange occurrences. I have books on obscure topics, such as knot-worship in fifteenth-century Switzerland, and how to tell a person's character by the shapes of his ears. And I specialize in scary books about ghosts, vampires, poltergeists, banshees, time travelers, voodooists, cultists, and Republican presidential candidates."

"Anything about werewolves?" I asked.

"I've got the best werewolf section in town," Howling Frog said.

"I'd like to have a look at it," I said.

"Too scary for kids," Howling Frog said. "What do you say, Lama?"

"Maybe not for these kids," the Honorable Lama Lumpo Smythe-Finkel said.

"Jonathan Quicksilver said to say hello to you," Winston said.

"My disciple?" the lama asked, all excited. "He's a great poet, did you know that?"

"We know," Rat said. "We've heard him read his poems."

"Ever hear this one?" the lama asked. "It's a beaut!"

THERE'S

        SOMETHING

            FLOATING

                 IN

                 MY

                   MILK

UGH

          WHAT IS IT

            OH

            PLEASE

            GOD

                DON'T

             LET

            IT

         BE

       A

    MOUSE

      CAUSE

        I

           ALREADY

                DRANK

                SOME

         *

"That's a great one, isn't it?"

"It sure is," Rat said. "That's in his book."

"I've got copies right here," Howling Frog said. "He's the sort of poet my customers like."

"You asked about werewolves," the lama said. "Why?"

"Why?"

"Why?"

"Why did I ask about werewolves?"

"Yes. Why did you ask about werewolves?"

"I'm just curious about them," I said. "My father and I were talking about werewolves this morning."

"Incredible!" Lama Lumpo Smythe-Finkel said.

"It is?"

"Yes. It is. It's incredible that you should mention werewolves just at this moment."

"Sure. I can see that. I can see that it would be . . . incredible . . . I mean . . . why is it incredible?"

"Why?"

"Why incredible that I should mention werewolves just at this moment."

"I'll tell you why," the lama said. "It's incredible because at this very moment I am having a strong psychic experience having to do with a werewolf."

"You are?"

"The strongest. I am getting werewolf signals plain as day. You know, as an official lama of the Serious Hat Order of Tibet and New Jersey, it is part of my job to be psychic as a bug. I read the future, read minds, get all sorts of telepathic promptings— the works. Right now I am getting powerful werewolf signals."

"Really?"

"You bet."

"Oh, this is very interesting," Howling Frog said. "I just love it when the lama goes all telepathic."

"What are the werewolf signals like?" I asked the lama.

"It's fairly horrible," the lama said. "Are you sure you want to know?"

"Yes, tell us," Rat said.

"Someone in this room is going to have dealing with a werewolf in the near future."

"Who? Which one in this room?" Howling Frog asked.

"I can't be sure," Lama Lumpo Smythe-Finkel said. "All I know is that it isn't me, for which I'm thankful—werewolves aren't nice."

"I guess not," Howling Frog said, "and you don't know which of us it is—the one who's going to meet the you-know-what."

"It might be all of you, for all I know," the lama said. "It's a nasty business."

"When is this likely to happen?" Howling Frog asked.

"It could be any minute—I don't know."

"I think I'll close up early today," Howling Frog said. "Here's a book for you kids—no charge."

Howling Frog handed us a book. Its title was *Coping with Werewolves*.

"Can you give me a ride back to my yurt?" the lama asked.

"Of course, Lama," Howling Frog said. "See you kids another time."

Howling Frog hustled us out of the store and closed the folding metal gate and locked it. He and the lama hurried down the mall and out of sight.

We looked at each other, a little worried. Speaking for myself, I can't say that I especially believed the Honorable Lama Lumpo Smythe-Finkel. After all, he was just some bearded old bozo hanging out in a bookstore for twinkies interested in strange topics. On the other hand, he seemed sort of sure of himself, as though he knew what he was talking about.

"Those guys are crazy, right?" I said.

"Right."

"Crazy."

Winston and Rat agreed with me. Those guys were crazy. "Besides," Winston said, breaking into my thoughts, "you mentioned werewolves first. If you hadn't said anything about them, and *then* the lama had brought the subject up, that would be different."

"You think he's a fake then?"

"Sure," Winston said, "all those lamas are fakes."

"Ugh," Rat said. "Look, it's Scott Feldman."

You could see right away that Scott Feldman was a creep. He was incredibly, unbelievably neat and tidy. His hair was neatly combed, he had eyeglasses of which the lenses were singularly clean, and the frames appeared to have been polished. His sweater looked brand-new and it was tucked into the waistband of his trousers, which were spotless and had sharp creases down the front of each leg. He was leaning against a wall, with his hands in his pockets in such a way that he didn't wrinkle his pants, and he had the sole of one new-looking shoe against the wall. He was easy to hate. Scott Feldman had the most amazing and unusual expression I'd ever seen—a sort of hypnotic stare. It made you numb and turned your stomach.

Evidently, Rat knew Scott Feldman from school. He called her Miss Matthews.

"Hello, Miss Matthews," Scott Feldman said. "I am delighted and surprised to see you here in the mall. I am Scott Feldman, your classmate, in case you don't remember me."

"I remember you," Rat said.

"Thank you," Scott Feldman said. Then, extending his hand, he said to me, "I am Scott Feldman, I am pleased to make your acquaintance."

I shook hands with Scott Feldman. "Walter Galt," I said.

Then Scott Feldman did the same thing—introduced

himself to Winston and shook hands with him. Then he offered a compliment to Rat: "You are looking very pretty today, Miss Matthews."

"You want me to punch your face?" Rat said, in her prettiest voice.

"Hey! No violence, please!" Scott Feldman said. "I don't like to fight or get my clothes dirty. Otherwise," he said, sort of winking at Winston and me, "I am a regular guy."

To Rat he said, "Perhaps you will remember that I called you on the telephone once."

"You called me on the telephone about fifteen times," Rat said, "and I told you fifteen times that I don't want to go with you to the zoo to see the snakes at feeding time."

"You missed a treat," Scott Feldman said.

"You're a bizzarro," Rat said.

"No, I'm not," Scott Feldman said, "I'm a regular highly intelligent high school student with many interests and a healthy admiration for you, Miss Matthews."

"I'm getting a frozen yogurt," I said. "Anybody else want a yogurt?"

"I don't eat yogurt," Scott Feldman said. "Yogurt, like milk, cheese, and all other dairy products, is a mucus-producing food. It isn't good to have too much mucus."

"Maybe I'll skip the yogurt," I said, and to Rat, "your friend is fairly disgusting."

"Don't call him that!" Rat said. "Don't call him my friend. I can't help who I go to school with."

"I think she likes me quite a lot," Scott Feldman said. "I'm the cutest and best-dressed boy in school."

"Let's kill him," Winston said. It was the first thing he'd said since meeting Scott Feldman.

"I assume you're only kidding," Scott Feldman said, "but just in case, I think it only fair to tell you that I have studied Subi-waza with the Subi-waza master of New Jersey. It's the deadliest martial art. I took a course by mail, and I am now a lethal weapon."

"Only kidding, of course," Winston said, and then he whispered to me, "I mean it, let's kill him."

"Did you know that Bugworld has moved?" Scott Feldman asked.

I wasn't surprised to learn that Scott Feldman had an interest in bugs. He was what I would have pictured as the typical customer at Bugworld.

"How did you get all the way out here, Scott?" Rat asked.

"I took the shoppers' bus this morning," Scott Feldman said. "Now that I'm here, and Bugworld's not open, I have to wait three more hours for a bus to take me back—you didn't come in a car, did you?"

Rat said no, and I said yes, both at the same time. Scott Feldman chose to hear my reply. "Good! I can ride back with you kids."

"That will be ducky," Winston said.

ANOTHER MYSTERIOUS OUTBREAK OF VIOLENCE STRUCK THE BACONBURG AREA LAST NIGHT. . . . MILTON PAPESCU OF HAMFAT SURPRISED SOMEONE—OR SOMETHING—IN THE ACT OF WRECKING HIS 1978 CHEVROLET MALIBU. . . . WHEN MR. PAPESCU CAME OUT OF THE SHPILKIE TOWER, BACONBURG'S TALLEST BUILDING, WHERE HE HAD BEEN WORKING LATE IN HIS OFFICE, HE FOUND THAT SOMETHING WAS RIPPING THE DOOR OFF HIS CAR. . . . PAPESCU SHOUTED, AND A LARGE, DARK, INDIS-TINCT SHAPE LOPED OFF AT HIGH SPEED. PAPESCU WAS DIS-TRAUGHT . . . .

(Shot of Papescu—owner of wrecked car)

Papescu: I COULDN'T SAY IT WAS HUMAN . . . IF IT WAS A HUMAN IT WAS A VERY BIG ONE. . . . I HOLLERED, "HEY! STOP THAT!" AND THIS THING. . . . I DON'T KNOW WHAT IT WAS. . . . I WAS LOOKING RIGHT AT IT, BUT SOMEHOW I CAN'T REMEMBER WHAT I SAW. . . . I EVEN REMEMBER KNOWING THAT I WOULDN'T BE ABLE TO SAY WHAT I SAW. . . . THIS SOUNDS CRAZY, BUT I THINK I WAS HYPNOTIZED BY THAT THING. . . . ANYWAY, WHEN I HOLLERED, IT LOOKED UP. . . . THEN IT SORT OF LOPED OFF.

Voice of interviewer: LOPED?

Papescu: YOU KNOW, LOPED. . . . IT LOPED OFF, AND I WAS LEFT WITH MY CAR IN THE SHAPE YOU SEE IT IN.

(Shot of car with Papescu's voice over)

IT'S A MESS. . . . THE DOOR IS RIPPED OFF. . . . THE STEERING

480

WHEEL IS BENT DOUBLE. . . . THE UPHOLSTERY IS ALL TORN UP, AND THE INSIDE HAS THIS FUNNY SMELL . . . LIKE . . .

Voice of interviewer: LIKE WHAT?

Papescu: IT SMELLS LIKE DOG SPIT. . . . YOU KNOW, DROOL. . . . I HAVE THIS GIANT SCHNAUZER, AND HIS DROOL SMELLS A LITTLE LIKE THAT, ONLY NOT SO STRONG.

Voice of interviewer: ANOTHER ACT OF UNEXPLAINED VANDALISM IN OUR AREA. . . . BACK TO YOU, BOB.

(Shot of Bob Pontoon, newscaster, in studio)

Bob: THIS IS THE FIFTEENTH INCIDENT OF VANDALISM IN THE GREATER BACONBURG AREA THIS YEAR. . . . NINE CARS HAVE BEEN WRECKED. . . . POWER POLES HAVE BEEN KNOCKED DOWN. . . . AND THE STATUE OF FREE ENTERPRISE IN FRONT OF BACONBURG CITY HALL IS MISSING. . . . IN FIVE INSTANCES SOMEONE OR SOMETHING WAS SEEN. . . . AN AMORPHOUS DARK SHAPE, WHICH COULD NOT BE PROPERLY DESCRIBED OR REMEMBERED. . . . IN EVERY CASE, THE EVENTS HAVE TAKEN PLACE DURING A FULL MOON.

BACONBURG AND AREA POLICE ARE STUMPED.

(Shot of Police Chief Cloney)

Cloney: THIS THING HAS GOT US STUMPED.

Bob: LOCAL AUTHORITIES HAVE BEEN SWAMPED BY SUGGESTIONS FROM MEMBERS OF THE PUBLIC AS TO WHAT IS CAUSING THESE BIZARRE EVENTS. . . . EVERYTHING FROM SUNSPOTS TO AN EXTRATERRESTRIAL TO THE WRATH OF GOD TO A WEREWOLF HAS BEEN SUGGESTED. . . .

WHAT IS BEHIND THESE MYSTERIOUS DESTRUCTIVE ACTS? TUNE IN TO OUR SPECIAL BROADCAST FOLLOWING THE ELEVEN O'CLOCK NEWS.

(Shot of Papescu's ruined car with announcer's voice over)
WATCH "THE BACONBURG HORROR" TONIGHT AT 11:30.
(Shot of Bob Pontoon)

Bob: AND THAT'S ALL THE NEWS OF BACONBURG. . . . STAY TUNED TO CHANNEL 52 FOR NEWS AS IT HAPPENS. SEE YOU AT 11:00 AND 11:30 WITH THE FULL STORY OF "THE BACONBURG HORROR."

(Cut to deodorant commercial)

DANIEL PINKWATER

The ride home was fairly ghastly. Scott Feldman talked about good grooming and personal hygiene. Winston and Rat moaned and ground their teeth. I looked through the book Howling Frog had given us, *Coping with Werewolves*. It was by someone named K.E. Kelman, PH. PH. Stands for phantomologist, it turns out. This guy, K.E. Kelman, PH., claimed to have had vast experience with werewolves in all parts of the world. He said that werewolves were generally misunderstood creatures—so what if they bite someone once in a while? Dogs do that, and they are considered man's best friend.

K.E. Kelman, PH., went on to tell anecdotes about werewolves he had known. He told about the singing werewolf of Budapest, and the time he ate supper with a werewolf in Kazakhstan.

Kelman also claimed that many famous people were, in reality, werewolves. He said that Beethoven was one, also Dostoevsky, and Queen Victoria, Thomas Jefferson, Sigmund Freud, Mozart, Martin Luther, and Walter Cronkite.

I didn't get to read the whole book—I just skipped around. Also, I kept getting distracted by Scott Feldman's running commentary on the use of shoe trees and the responsibility of teenagers to help their families by taking care of their clothes.

After a while, Rat and Winston became openly insulting, and told Scott to shove his shoe trees and so forth. It didn't have the slightest effect. The only way to deal with Scott Feldman would have been to render him unconscious. Rat was talking about doing that when we arrived at Scott's house and dropped him off.

"I certainly had a good time," Scott Feldman said. "I hope we can do this again very soon."

"Just as soon as it snows in hell, Scott," Winston said.

"Or even sooner," Scott said.

"Get knotted," Rat said.

"And it was a special pleasure getting to see you again, Miss Matthews," Scott Feldman said.

"Step on the gas," Rat said to Winston.

Our next stop was Rat's house. "Let me take that book," she said to me. Rat hadn't shown any interest in the book or the werewolf topic until now. I handed her the book.

"I want to read it next," I said.

She got out of the car. "It was almost fun," she said.

DANIEL PINKWATER

The scene is the great council chamber of the Baconburg City Hall. The curtains are drawn, and a group of men is gathered around a table, lit by a single lamp. Their faces are grim. The mayor and the city council, the chief of police, representatives from the military, the FBI, and the state and federal governments are present. Dr. Bogenswerfer, Professor of Classical Lycanthropy at the University of Baconburg, is speaking.

"Gentlemen, I have given this matter prolonged and careful thought. I have consulted my books, and I have sought the opinions of my learned colleagues. I am sure. I can safely stake my professional reputation on my conclusions in this matter. What we have here, confronting us in the greater Baconburg area, are manifestations of the activity of a werewolf!

"Ordinary measures will be of no avail, for the werewolf stalks by night, and is all but invisible to the human eye. He is fleet of foot and vile-tempered. No person—and more to the point—no property is safe when one of these moon-crazed creatures is about. It is a werewolf, gentlemen, and you may quote me."

Professor Bogenswerfer sits down. Mayor Beesley speaks.

"If you are so sure it's a werewolf—and nobody else has come up with a better explanation—can you tell us how to deal with it?"

Dr. Bogenswerfer speaks.

"As to knowing how to deal with it—that is out of my line. As a classical lycanthropist, it is within the purview of my specialty to know what has been written and said about werewolves in the past. I am also acquainted with all the means of discerning a werewolf—although this is the first time I've ever had to consider a real one—and I know a lot of werewolf poetry by heart. However, as to what to do with one—I haven't a clue.

"However, there is one man—a shabby sort of scholar, if you know what I mean—who has had some experience with the actual thing. I mean, this fellow is a terrible writer, full of vague sentiment and odd-sounding ideas, but he has, I believe, seen a werewolf, and knows what to do with one. Perhaps you would be interested in contacting him. He can't tell you much about the history of lycanthropy—but he might possibly tell you how to get the werewolf to stop pulling the doors off automobiles."

"Who is this man, and where can we find him?"

"His name is K.E. Kelman, PH. His credentials, while not the very best, are nonetheless authentic. As to where he can be found—there I cannot help you. I don't even know if Professor Kelman is still alive. The last I heard of him was that he had delivered a paper on the best way to remove werewolf-spit at the University of Kuala Lumpur."

DANIEL PINKWATER

The man from the FBI speaks. "If this K.E. Kelman, PH., still lives on Earth, we can find him."

"Good," says Mayor Beesley. "Do so. It may be the best chance we have."

She walks in beauty like a bat
A lizard, monster, or a ghoul;
This one with hair of green, this Rat;
She is the neatest girl in school.

She has an underground lair. Good idea. It is very silent. Another good idea. The windows are covered with cork. An extremely good idea. No sound from the outside can get in. What a good idea! No sound from the inside can get out. A really wonderful idea!

It's difficult to get into the lair. The door is locked. It would be too obvious to pull it off its hinges. Once I am inside I might reveal myself to her—wouldn't that be fun? And if she screams, no one will hear. And if she tells the story, who would believe it? Perhaps I will tell her my poem.

I've never told my poem to a living human—who lived.

It turned out that my mother knew Jonathan Quicksilver slightly. She was going to high school at night, and so was he. My mother had never finished high school. She quit in her senior year to go to Peru and help harvest the avocados. That was where she met my father.

Jonathan Quicksilver was doing high school at night, in order to get to be a citizen. It turns out he was from some-place in Europe. My mother didn't know where—just some little country in the Carpathian Mountains was all she remembered. I was surprised, because Quicksilver didn't speak with an accent. Anyway, he was in her civics class.

All of this came up when I was telling my parents about my day in Hamfat, and the things I had seen in the suburbs.

My father, predictably, latched onto the weirdest part of the story. He was very interested in knowing what I thought of the Honorable Lama Lumpo Smythe-Finkel. He asked a lot of questions. I suggested that he come out to the Grand Mall with me sometime and meet the lama—I had the impression he was there every Saturday. My father reminded me that he couldn't make it—he was taking a course in auto mechanics, which met on Saturdays. He belonged to a Honda Civic car owners' club, and every Saturday morning, after breakfast, he left the house with his Honda Civic textbook and his bag of tools.

"So what was your impression of the honorable lama, son?" my father asked. "These holy men from the East can be very amazing, I believe."

"I think the lama comes from New Jersey," I said, "and my impression of him was that he probably didn't know what he was talking about."

My father looked disappointed. "Sometimes these fellows are very deep," he said, "appearances can be deceiving."

"My friends Winston and Rat thought he was a schnook too," I said.

"Really, you ought to keep an open mind," my father said, "some of these fellows have really amazing mystical powers."

"I don't think this one had any more mystical powers than you have," I said.

"Aum? Is that so?" my father asked.

... and so, after so many years, and so many adventures with our friends the werewolves, the author has come to think of the lycanthrope as just another misunderstood soul. Werewolves abound in every society, and are slowly starting to gain acceptance as being loyal, clean, thrifty, reverent, trustworthy, and honest—good family people—and possessed of a sense of humor.

The author hopes that the reader of this little book will try to show some understanding the next time he meets a werewolf—and even in the unlikely event that there should be a bit of tooth-play, to remember that this is just the werewolf's way of saying "I like you." So, dear reader, the next time something big and furry and horrible gets you by the leg, just remember the old lycanthropian greeting, "*Grrrrrrrrrowf!*" You may be at the beginning of a beautiful friendship.

Rat was reading from Professor Kelman's book, *Coping with Werewolves*. As she read the book she became aware of a strange sensation—it was as though someone was in the room with her. At first she dismissed it as mere imagination, but the feeling persisted, and grew stronger.

After a while, Rat felt as though she wanted to scream—she didn't know why.

Just as Rat lost her nerve, and flew through the door of her soundproof chamber, she had the briefest look at . . . something . . . nothing . . . a thick place in the air . . . a shadow where there shouldn't have been a shadow.

"That's good enough for me," Rat said. She picked up the phone in the hall and dialed Walter Galt's number.

"Walter," she said into the receiver, "get Winston and meet me at the Dharma Buns in an hour. We've got werewolf trouble."

Rat was waiting for us when we arrived at the Dharma Buns Coffee House. "Have a seat," she said, "I've ordered coffee."

"What's up?" I asked.

"Plenty," Rat said. "I think there's a werewolf around."

"That's what a lot of people have been saying," Winston said, "what makes you think it's so?"

"It was in my room," Rat said.

Winston and I looked at each other. "It was in your room? And you saw it?"

"I didn't exactly see it," Rat said. "I sort of sensed it—and I did see something. That is, I failed to see something. It was a weird sensation. It was like this—imagine that you know I'm sitting here, and all of a sudden you can't see me, but you sort of can see the space I'm sitting in. It's hard to explain."

"That's how it was when I sort of saw something the first night we ever came here," I said.

"You saw something that night?"

"Sort of . . . it was when Quicksilver hollered werewolf and everybody cleared out. I sort of saw something standing in the kitchen door. Winston said it was nothing."

"Winston is a bugwit," Rat said, looking at Winston. "You probably did see something—sort of."

"You know, the fact that everybody sitting around this place ran without a second's hesitation is interesting," I said.

493

"It's as if they all believed in werewolves, and had maybe had some experience with them—I mean, we didn't get up and run, but they all did."

"Here comes the waitress, the one who screamed," Winston said. "Let's ask her what she knows."

The depressed-looking waitress with the white makeup was bringing our coffee.

"Say," Winston said. "Remember the night when you saw something in the kitchen, and let out a scream?"

"Oh, yes, the werewolf," the waitress said, "it took me by surprise."

"How did you know it was a werewolf?" Winston asked.

"What else could it have been?" the waitress said.

"Have you ever seen a werewolf before?" Rat asked.

"Have you ever seen a live mastodon?" the waitress asked.

"No."

"But if one walked in here right now, you wouldn't have any doubts about what it was, would you?"

"No, I guess not."

"Well, there you are," the waitress said. She collected for the coffee and left.

"She's no help," Winston said.

"Of course not," Rat said, "werewolves are fast and tricky—I just got finished reading that book about them. What we need is a real werewolf expert."

"How about the Honorable Lama Lumpo Smythe-Finkel?" I suggested. "He seems to know something about them."

"We need somebody with a scientific approach," Rat said.

"I think we ought to get in touch with the guy who wrote the book, K.E. Kelman, PH."

"The phantomologist?"

"Why not? If we've got a real werewolf running around loose, he should be interested, and we need some help. I, personally, do not want the thing turning up in my room anymore. Maybe K.E. Kelman, PH., can get rid of the thing for us."

"That makes sense to me," I said. "How do we go about finding the guy?"

"That shouldn't be much of a problem," Rat said.

Federal Bureau of Investigation
Missing Scientist Division
Dillinger Office Building
Washington, D.C.

The Honorable Lance Beesley
Mayor, City of Baconburg
City Hall
Baconburg

Dear Mayor Beesley:

Pursuant to your request, this office has undertaken exhaustive measures to maximize the location potential of one K.E. Kelman, PH.

We have optimized collateral assistance with our corresponding agencies in other countries, and have substantiated the financial refurbishment of various non-agency informational sources as well.

We are happy to report to you that our undertaking has been a consistent penetration of all informational matrices to be considered in relation to the parameters of our assignment.

All agency, non-agency, and peripheral personnel participating in the project have demonstrated maximum inter-cooperation and professionalism.

We feel certain that our output has been exhaustive and mega-effective.

K.E. Kelman, PH., either does not exist, does not exist in any form correlative to documentation provided this agency, or has ceased to exist, or never existed. In short, we can't find him.

Your FBI stands ready to serve you in any meaningful way within the purview of our constitutional responsibility.

Yours truly,

A. Platt Fleischkopf
Agent

"Good news," Rat said: "K.E. Kelman, PH., lives right here in Baconburg."

"How do you know that?" I asked her.

"I looked him up in the phone book," she said. "He lives on Talbot Court, which is not far from Bignose's Cafeteria. I thought we might call him up, and ask him to meet us there."

"Good idea," Winston said, "that way, if he's too weird, we can just run."

"That's not the idea at all," Rat said. "I just thought it would be sort of polite, and businesslike, if we bought him a cup of coffee and a pastry."

"Now, this was your idea," Winston said.

"Right, right . . . save your breath," Rat said. "I'm paying for the coffee and pastry, you impossibly cheap slob, so spare me the usual whining and carrying on."

Winston does always whine and carry on when money is about to be spent. I, for my part, am willing to pay for my own refreshments, but Winston will never allow that. I suppose if I paid for myself it would call even more attention to the fact that Winston exploits Rat just because she's rich. In return for always buying him coffee and food, Rat gets to constantly remind Winston that he's a pathological cheapskate. They have a kind of symbiosis, I suppose. I get the best deal of all— free eats, and nothing on my conscience.

"So call him up," Rat said. "Here's a dime."

"Why me?" Winston asked.

"So you won't be useless," Rat said. "Now call."

Winston dialed. We had been standing in the street outside the Snark Theater, near a pay phone. "Uh, is this K.E. Kelman, PH.?" Winston said into the phone. Apparently it was. "This is about a werewolf," Winston said. "No, it isn't a joke. We want to talk to you about a werewolf. My friends and I. Yes. Do you know Bignose's Cafeteria on Lower North Aufzoo Street? Sure, we can be there in ten minutes—maybe fifteen. Okay" Winston replaced the receiver. "He wants to meet us right away," he said.

It was just a short drive to Lower North Aufzoo Street, where Bignose's Cafeteria was. I was happy to be going there. It was a place I'd first visited the time Rat's uncle, a mad scientist named Flipping Hades Terwilliger, had disappeared, and we were looking for him. Bignose's is the only place I know in Baconburg where you can get Napoleons—that's a really fantastic pastry, at least the ones Bignose serves are fantastic.

The Peugeot had been parked across the street from the Snark, where we'd caught the early evening show—Murnau's *Sunrise* and *Gidget Gets Sick*, a couple of classics.

We found another good parking place outside of Bignose's. Winston was very particular about where he parked—it had to be under a streetlight. "There are a lot of thieves who specialize in classic cars," he said.

When we entered Bignose's the place was empty. Bignose was there, of course—he's unmistakable with the nose—and there was the lady who runs the cash register. There was no sign of K.E. Kelman, PH., or anybody else. There wasn't even anybody in the street outside.

"Hello, kids," Bignose said, "I haven't seen you for a while—you want the usual?"

Winston looked at Rat. Rat said nothing. "You having something?" he asked her.

"I don't think so," Rat said. "I had a big supper."

Winston thought for a while. I happened to know that he loved Bignose's Napoleons better than anything. "Well, I'm going to have a Napoleon and a cup of coffee," Winston said to Bignose.

"Who's paying?" Rat asked.

Winston hesitated. It was clear from Rat's expression that she wasn't offering to pay for Winston's snack.

"Me. I'm paying," Winston said.

"In that case, make it three, Bignose—three Napoleons and three coffees. Thanks, Winston."

"That will be three-seventy-five," Bignose said.

Winston looked confused. He was trapped. Rat had trapped him. "That's what women are," he said to me, "exploiters and leeches." He paid Bignose and we carried our Napoleons and coffees to a table.

Winston was bugged. I was happy. I had yet to pay for my own food when I went anywhere with these two. "Shouldn't we have gotten a coffee and a Napoleon for K.E. Kelman, PH.?" I asked.

"Wait to see if he shows up," Winston said. "He's already late."

"I've been waiting for ten minutes," a voice from somewhere said, "and I would like a coffee, extra light, and a Napoleon, if the young man would be so kind."

We looked around. The place was still empty. "Who said that?" Winston asked.

"You are the parties who wish to meet with K.E. Kelman, are you not?" the voice said. This time we were able to locate it. It was coming from under the table.

"Are you under the table?" Rat asked.

"Yes, I am under the table. And now I am coming out," the voice said. A tall man in a raincoat appeared from under the table, pulled up a chair, and sat down.

"And you are K.E. Kelman, PH.?" Rat asked.

"I am he," the man in the raincoat said. "Now don't let me stop you from enjoying your pastry—just dig in, and I'll start in on mine as soon as the young man brings it to me."

Winston went to the counter to get K.E. Kelman, PH., his Napoleon and coffee.

"Why were you under the table?" I asked.

"I have my reasons," K.E. Kelman, PH., said, "but let's not talk about me. Why did you want to meet me?"

"You said something about a werewolf when you called," K.E. Kelman, PH., said. He was delicately working through his Napoleon. His beard was full, but neatly trimmed. He was bald on top and had shoulder-length hair. He kept his raincoat on, and buttoned, and he had a monstrous furled umbrella hooked over the back of his chair. There wasn't a sign of rain—and it hadn't rained for days.

"Yes," Rat said, "I'm pretty sure I sort of saw it."

"Not surprising," K.E. Kelman, PH., said. "There's one around these days. Quite a few people have had encounters with him."

"How do you know it's a him?" Rat asked.

"Quite so," K.E. Kelman, PH., said, "him or her . . . although female werewolves are rare indeed. I'd be pleased and delighted if this one should turn out to be a lady."

"Woman," Rat said.

"Oh, quit it already," Winston said.

"Take back what you said about women being exploiters and leeches," Rat said.

"Anything to stop the feminist rhetoric," Winston said. "It kills conversation. I take back what I said."

"As I was saying," K.E. Kelman continued, "there's a werewolf about. All the reports point to the same thing. The astrological conditions are right. It's the right time of year.

503

There hasn't been a werewolf in this vicinity for more than thirty years—which means one is overdue. And my mother says she's been getting pains in her left big toe."

"Your mother?"

"My mother, Mrs. Lydia L. Kelman, is the finest little werewolf predictor in the state. By the way, you haven't introduced yourselves."

"I am Bentley Saunders Harrison Matthews," Rat said, "but you may call me Rat. This is Walter Galt, and this is our host, Winston Bongo."

"I didn't know I was going to have to pay for everything," Winston said.

"I'm pleased to meet all of you," K.E. Kelman, PH., said. "Now about this werewolf—what exactly is it you want me to do? Do you want to be introduced to the werewolf, or what?"

"Well . . . we want to get rid of it," Rat said.

"Get rid of it? Why?"

"I mean, it's a werewolf, isn't it?" Rat said.

"So I believe," K.E. Kelman, PH., said, "but has it done you any harm?"

"It was in my room!" Rat said.

"Probably it likes you," said the phantomologist. "Couldn't you think of it as a big friendly dog which is also a human being at times, and potentially very dangerous?"

"No!" Rat said. "I do not want anything of the kind turning up in my room. It's creepy."

"Well, I suppose I'll have to get my mother to werewolf-proof your room."

"Your mother?"

"Oh, yes. Mother is a whiz at that sort of thing. She'll come around and werewolf-proof your room for you. It doesn't cost a thing. Mother is rather old, you see, and she just does things like that to keep busy. If you'll give me your address and telephone number, I'll have Mother get in touch with you. She'll do the werewolf-proofing, and that will be the end of your troubles—and we won't have had to bother the poor werewolf."

"How do I know this will work?" Rat asked.

"My mother, before she retired, was known professionally as Lydia LaZonga—I trust that name means something to you." K.E. Kelman raised his eyebrows.

"As a matter of fact it doesn't," Rat said.

"Lydia LaZonga was known, in her day, as the world's foremost ghost finder, spook chaser, hoodoo remover, and general, all around, freestyle psychic. That is my mommy."

"Gee," Winston said.

"You may well say gee, young man. Mommy is the best."

"I suppose we should give it a try," Rat said.

"You won't be sorry," said K.E. Kelman, PH.

THE BACONBURG HORROR STRIKES AGAIN! LATE LAST NIGHT, SOMEONE OR SOMETHING BROKE INTO THE PORKINGTON FREE LIBRARY AND MADE A HORRIBLE MESS OF THE POETRY SECTION. BOOKS WERE STREWN EVERYWHERE, AND BOOKSHELVES WERE OVERTURNED. THE CARD CATALOGS WERE TURNED UPSIDE DOWN, AND MANY OF THE CARDS APPEAR TO HAVE TOOTH MARKS ON THEM.

HAVOC WAS PLAYED WITH THE RUBBER STAMPS, AND THERE WAS ONE UNUSUAL CLUE—IN THE FOYER OF THE LIBRARY, WRITTEN WITH WHAT APPEARS TO HAVE BEEN A CLAW PRESSED REPEATEDLY AGAINST A RUBBER STAMP INK PAD, WAS THIS PHRASE:

"I wander'd lonely as a shroud . . ."

PORKINGTON POLICE FORENSIC EXPERTS ARE STUDYING THE CLUE.

RUMORS THAT THE BACONBURG HORROR IS A WEREWOLF OR SOME SIMILAR SUPERNATURAL THING CONTINUE TO CIRCULATE. MAYOR LANCE BEESLEY, WHEN ASKED FOR COMMENT, SAID . . .

(Shot of Mayor Beesley) "NOTHING OF THE KIND. WE HAVE HAD EXTENSIVE CONSULTATION WITH THE FBI, CRIMINAL EXPERTS OF EVERY KIND, AND PROFESSOR BOGENSWERFER OF THE UNIVERSITY. WE ARE CERTAIN THAT NO SUCH THING AS A WEREWOLF EXISTS. THESE ACTS OF LAWLESSNESS ARE THOSE OF AN ORDINARY PERSON WITH A SICK MIND, AND WE WILL

APPREHEND HIM VERY SOON. THERE IS NOTHING TO WORRY ABOUT. YOUR PUBLIC SERVANTS ARE ON THE JOB."

(Bob Pontoon in the studio) THAT'S THE LASTEST ON THE BACONBURG HORROR. KEEP TUNED FOR LATE-BREAKING BULLETINS AS THEY HAPPEN.

(Cut to commercial for home burglar alarms)

(Cut to commercial for stainless steel window shutters)

(Cut to commercial for mad dog repellent)

(Cut to commercial for discount flights to Australia)

(Bob Pontoon in studio) AND THAT'S ALL THE NEWS OF BACONBURG. . . . SEE YOU TOMORROW.

The Dharma Buns Coffee House is nearly empty, as are all places where people have been accustomed to gather at night. The panic surrounding the mysterious events connected with the so-called Baconburg Horror is at its peak. People have taken to locking themselves in after dark.

So it is that Jonathan Quicksilver has a scanty audience for his newest poem:

I COME FROM OLD TRANSYLVANEE

WHEN I WAS JUST A

LITTLE

BOY

AND

MY

OLD

TRANSYLVANEE

MOMMEE

SAID

TO

ME

SON

SHE

SAID

LOOK OUT FOR
THEM
WEREWOLF
HE
TAKE
A BIG BITE
OUT YOU TOOSHEE
HE
PULL
YOU
LEG
OFF
YOU
AND BEAT
YOU
ON
YOU
HEAD WITH
IT.
WEREWOLF IS NO JOKE
MY
LITTLE
SONNEE
SO MAYBE
BETTER WE
EMIGRATE OUTTA
THIS
PLACE
*

Even though this will later be regarded as Quicksilver's finest poem, it finds no favor with the audience. This is often the case with great Art.

"Big deal. Big phantomologist. Five whole dollars I spent in that place, and what's the result? His mommy is going to werewolf-proof your silly room." Winston was utterly disgusted.

"Well, I was sort of hoping for something a little more conclusive myself," Rat said.

"I had a good time," I said.

"Shut up," Rat and Winston said.

"Look," I said, "maybe Lydia LaZonga, or whatever her name is, can really do something for you."

"Maybe, but I doubt it," Rat said.

"It's your best bet," I said.

"It's all I've got," Rat said, "and it seems like nothing. Now I've got to go home and wonder if that weird thing is going to turn up again."

"K.E. Kelman, PH., didn't seem to be too worried," I said.

"K.E. Kelman, PH., is a dingdong!" Rat said. "He likes werewolves! He thinks they're cute! He wishes a werewolf would turn up in *his* room!"

"Now, am I correct in assuming that the werewolf didn't turn up in your bedroom, but in the soundproof room in the basement where you hang out all the time, is that right?" Winston asked.

"So?"

511

"So don't go down there. If the werewolf turns up upstairs, you can give out with a holler and wake up the house. From all accounts it seems to run away whenever anybody sees it."

"So you think the werewolf is shy, do you?" Rat asked.

"It keeps moving," Winston said.

"That's not very much comfort," Rat said.

"That's the best I can do," Winston said. "Unless you would like Walter and me to come and spend the night with you."

"Excellent idea," Rat said.

Winston leered.

"Spare me the juvenile sexual innuendo," Rat said. "Anybody who isn't identical to James Dean in every respect tries to get fresh with me, he dies. But I do want you guys to spend the night in my soundproof room."

"Why?" I asked.

"To see if the werewolf comes back," Rat said, "and grab him or scare him away, or protect me from him. I haven't mentioned this before, but I don't think this was the first time he's been near my house."

"Two pizzas," Winston said.

"I beg your pardon," Rat said.

"Two Pete's Pizzas—special super size with double everything, or you sleep alone," Winston said.

"I intend to sleep alone anyway," Rat said, "in my bedroom, as you suggested."

"You want the two of us to wait in your soundproof room for the werewolf to show up?" I asked.

"And a cheesecake," Winston said, "the large size with blueberries. If you expect us to wait up all night for some werewolf, we've got to have something to snack on."

"Wait a minute," I said.

"Shut up," Winston said. "And we can play your hi-fi."

"Nobody touches my hi-fi," Rat said.

"So forget it," Winston said.

"Right," I said.

"You'll handle the records by the edges?" Rat asked.

"What do you take me for?" Winston responded.

"And you won't fiddle with the needle?"

"Hey," I said.

"Is it a deal or not?" Winston asked.

"Deal," Rat said.

"What?" I said.

Hail to thee writhe spirit!
Bitten thou never wert—

No more alone. I will have a friend. There will be another to cavort beneath the moon. A nip, a nibble, a little bite, snap! A flower of a special kind presented in the light of the moon.

And then . . .

And then . . .

A transformation, a realization! I will wait. I will wait. I will put the bite on this one.

And then . . .

And then . . .

She will be like me!

The Honorable Lama Lumpo Smythe-Finkel sits in meditation in an upstairs room in his suburban yurt. He chants the ancient chants, counts his breaths, turns his eyes inward. He holds his hands in a complicated gesture, the mudra of the venerable Serious Hat sect. As he sits, the material universe recedes. An invisible galaxy revolves around him. His body is suffused with light. He levitates slightly, hovering an inch above the carpet.

It is an ordinary session, such as he has every night after watching the rerun of *Mary Tyler Moore*.

This time something unforeseen, something unimagined, something amazing happens.

From the ceiling of the room in which he sits there falls into his arms, outstretched in the posture of supplication, a book! A real book!

It is exactly the size and weight and shape of *Kenkyusha's Japanese-English Dictionary* — but it is another book.

The lama looks at the book in amazement. In over two years of meditating, nothing like this has ever happened.

He reads the title, stamped in finest gold on the front cover:

The Lycanthropicon

He opens the book. He reads.

"Oh my!" the lama says aloud. "Oh my goodness! Oh!"

The book dematerializes. It is suddenly thin air. It is no more.

"Oh my!" the lama says. "Oh! Oh boy! Oh! Oh! Wow!"

He rushes downstairs to use the telephone.

Rat has one of the finest record collections I've ever seen. Under ordinary circumstances I would have been delighted to have a whole night with Winston, two giant pizzas, and a cheesecake in her soundproof room. When you listen to records with Rat, it is very much her choice as to what will be played. There were records in her collection which we had heard only once—or only heard snatches of. Staying all night and watching for the werewolf provided Winston and me with a chance to hear whatever we wanted.

On the other hand, I had a hard time really enjoying myself. I kept thinking about the fact that should the werewolf show up, there was no way to summon help. We could holler our heads off in that room, and nobody would hear a thing. We'd phoned home to say that we were staying over at Rat's house. There was no problem with our respective parents—although it felt funny to us to be making an excuse for staying away from home all night that wasn't a lie. We didn't say anything about waiting up for a werewolf—it was really none of their business.

The first thing Winston wanted to do was eat a lot. Once that was taken care of, he selected some records he wanted to play. I myself didn't have any preference. I was worried about what would happen if the werewolf showed up.

The first record that Winston played was one of Lord

Buckley. Lord Buckley is one of the most revolutionary and amazing people ever to live. Rat had once played us a single cut from her Lord Buckley record. It knocked us out. Lord Buckley was this hipster back sometime in history—maybe the 1950s or '60s. He was like a comedian, but what he did was also like jazz.

Listening to Lord Buckley straightened my wig—that is, I got a lot calmer about the likelihood of a werewolf turning up, and I even got involved with the pizza. Winston's next choice was a record of blues by Blind Lemon—also great. Then we listened to *Don Giovanni* by Mozart. Winston has eclectic tastes.

At one point I thought I heard a scratching at the door. Except for that, nothing happened. When Rat came to check on us in the morning, we were in a good mood and ready to have breakfast with Rat's family.

DANIEL PINKWATER

While Winston Bongo and Walter Galt were sitting up all night in Rat's soundproof room, eating giant pizzas and cheesecake and listening to records—while Rat was sleeping in her bed—while all the city was quiet—a strange meeting was taking place in a nearly deserted all-night diner on the edge of town.

The Honorable Lama Lumpo Smythe-Finkel, the bookseller Howling Frog, and another man, who kept the collar of his coat turned up, and the brim of his hat turned down, sat at a booth at the far end of the Deadly Nightshade Diner—We Never Close. The men spoke in hushed tones and consumed plates of french fries with catsup.

If one had been sitting in the booth next to the one occupied by the three men (which no one was) one might have heard a whispered word or two. If one had been situated inside the napkin dispenser on the table (which no one could have been) one might have heard the Honorable Lama Lumpo Smythe-Finkel speak these words:

"In all my two years as a mystic lama and meditator, nothing this amazing has ever happened to me. It is as though I had been singled out, chosen from among all mankind to receive this vital information."

If one were a spoon on the table (which no one could possibly be), or if a spoon were a sensate thing with ears and a mind (which spoons are not), one might have heard the bookseller, Howling Frog, say:

"If the lama's information, which is of the nature of a mystical revelation, is true, the situation is one of great seriousness and danger. We thought it best to consult with you at once."

If one were the coat collar of the stranger with the slouch hat (which would be utterly ridiculous) one might, with great difficulty, have heard him say in the lowest possible whisper:

"Yes, yes, you acted correctly. I only hope it is not too late."

"Do you think it is possible that it is too late?" asks the bookseller in a voice so low that even the spoon can hardly hear him.

"What are you going to do?" asks the lama in an urgent whisper.

"You know my methods," says the stranger, more to his coat collar than to his companions. "I prefer not to reveal anything until I have more facts at my disposal."

"But you will help in this matter . . . ?" says the lama.

"I would be a swine not to," says the stranger.

Lydia LaZonga showed up. Rat called us to say that K.E. Kelman's mother was on her way over. We arrived two minutes before she did.

Heinz, the butler, let her in. She was about four feet tall, sort of fat, and wore a flowered print dress.

"Sonny tells me you're having a problem, dearie," Lydia LaZonga said. "Is it a hoodoo?"

"It's a werewolf," Rat said.

"Is that all? I thought it was something really complicated. Ordinarily this is my day to go marketing—if I'd known it was only a werewolf I wouldn't have called in such a hurry. Still, as long as I'm here . . . which one of you is the werewolf?"

"It isn't any of us," Rat said, "it's just this werewolf . . . at least I'm pretty sure it's a werewolf. I sort of saw it. It was in my room."

"I'll require a root beer, dearie," Lydia LaZonga said.

Rat sent Heinz to get a root beer for Kelman's mother. He brought it on a tray.

"I'll just take a sip of this," Lydia LaZonga said, "and we'll get to work."

Lydia LaZonga sipped her root beer. "I'm going to go into a trance now," she said. "Don't be frightened."

This was all taking place in Rat's soundproof room. That

521

was a good thing, it turned out, because Lydia LaZonga gave out with a howl that would have scared the whole neighborhood. Then she began running around the room at top speed, hooting and yowling and waving her arms. After she did that for five or six minutes, she stood stock still, vibrated for a while, spun around three or four times, jumped straight up in the air, and collapsed on the floor.

It was a good thing Lydia LaZonga had warned us not to be frightened—not that we weren't frightened. For a second I was afraid the old lady had dropped dead.

"That was a good one," Lydia LaZonga said, "and I'm glad I came. This is a much more interesting case than I first thought."

"Is my room werewolf-proof now?" Rat asked.

"Of course, dearie," Lydia LaZonga said, "but I don't think it's going to do you much good."

"Why not?" Rat asked.

"Because I don't think there's been a real werewolf here," the hoodoo lady said.

"No?"

"No. Oh, something has been here, all right—and I suppose someone without any real experience might think it was a werewolf—but I don't feel any real werewolf vibrations."

"What do you feel?"

"Something extremely strange and evil," Lydia LaZonga said. "It isn't any of the usual kinds of haunts—I know all about those. It isn't a hoodoo, or a poltergeist, or a banshee, or a ghost, or any of the things one ordinarily encounters. The signal I'm picking up is of a human being—but not just any human being. This would be some sort of malevolent genius. Whoever this is must be the veritable Napoleon of Crime."

Winston, Rat, and I looked at each other. Wallace Nussbaum! Wallace Nussbaum, the Napoleon of Crime, was the one who had kidnapped Rat's Uncle Flipping that time. As far as we knew he was in prison—but Lydia LaZonga's description fit him perfectly. Could she mean Nussbaum? Had she somehow picked up some sort of psychic signal from the smartest, meanest, trickiest criminal genius on earth?

"Yes, I would say it was a sort of master criminal. Understand that this very brilliant criminal is *not* the one who was here—and someone or something *was* definitely here. It's strange, but I'm getting pictures of an orangutan specially trained for evil purposes, and somebody's uncle having been kidnapped—does any of that make sense to any of you?"

It made sense. Wallace Nussbaum had used stolen orangutans trained to do his bidding as henchmen—and he had kidnapped Rat's Uncle Flipping, of course.

"What was here, I cannot say. It was like a werewolf—but it was not a werewolf. Werewolves are really good at heart— Sonny is quite fond of them, you know. The psychic emanations I'm getting are closer to those of a zombie—very rare in these parts—but it isn't a zombie either. Oh, it's very unusual. I'm glad I came. And then there's the sense of that very evil, very bright person. What he has to do with all of this, I don't know. Yes, it's a wonderful case. Well, good-bye now. I'm happy to have met you nice young people."

"That's all? You're just going?" Rat asked.

"For the present," Lydia LaZonga said, "there's nothing more for me to do here, dearie."

"So it's not a werewolf—but it's like a werewolf—it's more like a zombie, but it isn't a zombie."

"That's right, dearie. Good-bye."

And Lydia LaZonga was gone.

DANIEL PINKWATER

Is it possible that the master criminal Wallace Nussbaum is somehow involved in all this?

Anything is possible.

"I'm really confused," Rat said. "If Lydia LaZonga is anything but a fake or a looney, then what turned up here is something other than a werewolf (which I never believed in anyhow until just lately). She says it's sort of like a zombie. I don't know that much about zombies, but on the whole, I think I'd prefer a werewolf. On top of all that, she says she thinks a super criminal is involved. The only one I know about is Wallace Nussbaum."

Winston spoke. "Isn't Wallace Nussbaum still in jail?"

"As far as I know, he is," Rat said. "They reopened Devil's Island just for him."

"Well, then, it can't be Wallace Nussbaum," I said. "It's impossible to escape from Devil's Island."

SUPER-CRIMINAL WALLACE NUSSBAUM HAS APPARENTLY ESCAPED FROM DEVIL'S ISLAND. IT WAS BELIEVED THAT THE FORMER FRENCH PENAL COLONY, CLOSED IN THE LATE 1940s AND REOPENED FOR THE EXPRESS PURPOSE OF IMPRISONING NUSSBAUM, WAS ESCAPE-PROOF—HOWEVER, THERE IS NO SIGN OF THE ONE AND ONLY INMATE. THE ONE HUNDRED AND FORTY-ONE GUARDS HAVE SEARCHED THE ISLAND THREE TIMES, AND REPORT THAT NUSSBAUM CANNOT BE FOUND.

IN A STATEMENT TO THE PRESS, CAPTAIN DE BOLDIEU, COMMANDANT OF THE PRISON, SAID, "I SUPPOSE IT IS TOO MUCH TO HOPE THAT A SHARK HAS EATEN THE TERRIBLE FELLOW. NO, I THINK HE HAS GOTTEN CLEAN AWAY. I FEEL SO SILLY."

LAW ENFORCEMENT OFFICIALS THE WORLD OVER HAVE ECHOED THE SENTIMENTS OF THE SILLY FRENCHMAN. IT SEEMS MOST LIKELY THAT NUSSBAUM HAS ESCAPED ONCE MORE, AND A WORLDWIDE CRIME WAVE IS EXPECTED.

IN THE LOCAL NEWS, THE BACONBURG HORROR HAS STRUCK AGAIN. EXTENSIVE DAMAGE WAS DONE TO THE PAVEMENT OUTSIDE BACONBURG CITY HALL. THE SIDEWALK HAS BEEN RIPPED UP ALL ALONG ONE SIDE OF NIBITZ STREET. TOOTHMARKS ARE CLEARLY DISCERNIBLE IN THE CONCRETE. THERE IS CONSIDERABLE PANIC AMONG THE CITIZENS. MAYOR BEESLEY IS VACATIONING IN THE BAHAMAS, AND WAS UNAVAILABLE FOR COMMENT.

Lydia LaZonga is speaking on the telephone: "Sonny, I have to talk to you right away. Meet me at the Deadly Nightshade Diner—We Never Close in one hour."

The Honorable Lama Lumpo Smythe-Finkel is speaking on the telephone: "Frog, I've thought more about what I told you—and the other one. Let's meet again at the Deadly Nightshade Diner—We Never Close—say, in one hour?"

Jonathan Quicksilver, the avant-garde poet, felt hungry. He
had been preoccupied with worry that jealous fellow poets
were circulating werewolf rumors to keep his audiences small
at the Dharma Buns Coffee House. For days he had eaten
nothing but horrible doughnuts. Thinking that perhaps some
superior nutrition might help him work up a poem or two, he
left his room on the edge of town and headed for the nearest
diner.

"Look, we're letting this get to us," Winston said. "What we need is some recreation. Let's go for a spin in the car—maybe we'll wind up at a diner or something."

The world's greatest detective whacked his Dunhill against the heel of his shoe. "Now, Doctor," he said to his companion, "I think a brisk walk to the Deadly Nightshade Diner— We Never Close will do us both good. What's more, I feel a bit peckish, and could do with a serving of their excellent raisin toast."

Scott Feldman and his father, Phelps Feldman, are on their way home. Mr. Feldman has picked up his son at the dancing academy where young Scott is taking samba lessons. They decide to drop in at the Deadly Nightshade Diner—We Never Close for some tapioca pudding and Postum.

I stalk the streets. I run and jump. I howl and yell. I . . .
where is everybody?

It is an age long past. A time before our grandfathers' time. In a capital of eastern Europe a level of elegance and grace exists, unknown to dwellers in western lands. Dashing officers and graceful ladies dance the *hüpisch*. Gleaming horses draw elegant carriages. Everywhere is heard the clink of glasses and the cry *"Wupski!"* as the genteel and decorous citizens celebrate the carrot-wine vintage. Scholars and artists collide in the streets. Trade prospers. Culture flourishes. Time stands still.

It is within this happy, carefree moment in history that the first recorded ancestor of an illustrious family descends from a remote mountain village to seek his fortune in the great city. Hubertus Baolungpinski, a self-taught chef and genius, opens a modest eating house, the Transylvanian Mushroom—We Never Close. Baolungpinski works hard, and soon become a celebrated restaurateur, famous for his foot-long borgelnuskies.

Generations later, a proud tradition continues. On the edge of the city of Baconburg, a descendant of the first Baolungpinksi, Gus Bowlingpin, operates an establishment cherished by gourmets, the Deadly Nightshade Diner—We Never Close.

Unprepossessing, simple, a bit filthy, this great restaurant caters to a clientele which knows that a really superior rice pudding is worth enduring a little inconvenience—and is not stampeded by the germ theory and other unworthy ideas of a corrupt and cynical age.

It is here, among old-world surroundings and the sights and smells associated with great food, that the elite of Baconburg gather to enjoy raisin toast, California cheeseburgers, and the spécialité de la maison, the jitterbug—a scoop of creamy mashed potato atop a slice of magnificent meatloaf—not too hot and not too cold—beneath which is a slice of fresh and nutritious Wonder bread, all of this deliciousness topped with yummy brown gravy—a dish fit for the most discerning palate.

It is a busy evening at the Deadly Nightshade Diner—We Never Close. In the booths patrons converse in cultured tones.

"I tell you, Frog—and Mr. Sigerson—this has me very worried. Why was I selected to receive this amazing information? What can it mean? Who is this evil person? What can we do?" It is the Honorable Lama Lumpo Smythe-Finkel speaking to his friend the bookseller Howling Frog, and to Osgood Sigerson, the world's greatest private detective. Another man is present, Dr. Ormond Sacker, Sigerson's companion and biographer.

Osgood Sigerson speaks: "I am not one to doubt the events which befall the faithful. I believe that a book—or something which you took to be a book—fell from the ceiling during your meditation. As to the message you read in that miraculous book, I have given it much thought. Just tell my friend Dr. Sacker what you read."

"Gladly," says the lama. "It was in the form of a poem. It was unclear to me what the meaning was—but I had a feeling of unutterable horror when I read the words. They were these:

> "A man who is a wolf—
> A wolf who is a man—
> Revealed thus is the meaning of this rhyme.
> It is not a wolfman, nor a manwolf—
> Not as such—
> It's the work of the Napoleon of Crime."

"Amazing, Sigerson!" Dr. Sacker exclaims. "The meaning is perfectly clear—and, may I say, it makes my skin crawl!"

"And what do you take the meaning to be, old fellow?" the great detective asks.

"Why, there is some terrible crime afoot which involves fine pastry—namely Napoleons!" says the good doctor.

"You are improving, old chap," says Sigerson. "That is exactly the meaning I give the poem. Good for you!"

"Yes, but I was thinking," says the lama, "couldn't the phrase 'Napoleon of Crime,' pertain to a person—say a person who was an outstanding criminal? You know, one might say 'the Einstein of Crime,' or 'the Leonardo da Vinci of Crime,' meaning a major criminal genius."

"Ah, Lama," says Sigerson, "it is best to leave these things to the professional criminologist—still, your idea is not without merit. It is rather intriguing—but . . . no, I hardly think so—I mean, a pastry is hardly the same thing

DANIEL PINKWATER

as Einstein or Leonardo da Vinci, is it? I mean, to say that one is 'the pastry of crime,' it's rather ridiculous, what?"

"I was thinking of Bonaparte," says the lama.

"Of which?"

"Of Napoleon Bonaparte—thought by many to have been the greatest man in Europe at one time—not the pastry—the emperor of France," the lama explains.

"Oh," says the great detective. "Of course. Ah. Hum. Mmm. Hmmm. I'll have to smoke my pipe and think about this for a while."

In another booth, another conversation:

"Sonny," Lydia Kelman, also known as Lydia LaZonga, says to her son, K.E. Kelman, PH., "this is a very unusual case. My psychic powers tell me that we are not dealing with a werewolf—which is old hat for both of us—but some kind of evil genius. I'm afraid he means to do some harm."

"Mommy, are you going to finish that seven-layer cake?" asks the phantomologist.

"I'm afraid those nice children may be in some sort of danger," says Lydia LaZonga, "and yes, I am going to finish my cake—I'm just resting."

In another booth:

"This is good tapioca pudding, isn't it, Daddy?"

"It certainly is, son. I always say there's nothing like tapioca pudding late at night to make one feel tickety-poo."

"I'm making progress in my samba lessons."

"That's excellent, son."

In another booth, Jonathan Quicksilver, the poet, writes on a napkin:

<pre>
          THAT WEREWOLF   BOY
                    IT
                 REALLY
                  BUGS
                   ME
                I KNOW
             THAT   IT
                         HAS SOMETHING AGAINST
                              ME
                 PERSONALLY

                  WOW
                        *
</pre>

In another booth:

"So then James Dean says to Hitler, 'I'm going to wipe the floor with you,' and Hitler says, 'Ach, you sniveling degenerate amerikanischer film actor—mit one hand tied behind my back, I can make wiener schnitzel of you,' and then James Dean says . . . Heinz!"

Heinz, the butler, has appeared in the Deadly Nightshade Diner—We Never Close. "Miss Rat," says Heinz, "I am sorry to disturb you with your friends, but your Uncle Flipping requests that you come home at once. He says it is something important. I have brought the car."

Rat departs with Heinz, leaving Walter Galt and Winston Bongo alone in the booth. "She sure loves James Dean," Walter says.

"By Jove! You're right, Lama!" the great detective shouts.

"How could I have been so blind! It is not the Napoleon of Crime, meaning the pastry of crime—it is the Napoleon of Crime, meaning the world's nastiest and most brilliant criminal! Wallace Nussbaum!"

"I'm getting a psychic wave," says Lydia LaZonga. "A name is coming to me. I can see it plainly—it is . . . Wallace Nussbaum."

"Say, Walter," Winston Bongo says, "remember when Uncle Flipping was kidnapped that time?"

"Sure," says Walter Galt.

"Well, when we found him and rescued him from Wallace Nussbaum, the master criminal, didn't Nussbaum turn out to actually be—"

"Heinz the butler!" Walter shouts.

"And Nussbaum is supposedly on Devil's Island, but just a few minutes ago, Heinz was in here."

"That is funny, isn't it?"

"Rat never said anything—and her family never said anything. You don't suppose they'd allow Heinz to be around, knowing that he was Nussbaum?"

"It wouldn't make sense."

"It must be something we missed."

"You mean Heinz's twin, or something like that."

"Yes, something like that."

"Must be."

"Funny though."

"I really like tapioca pudding, Daddy."

"So do I, son."

"REALLY   BUGS   ME   WOW"

"Sacker, if ever I seem to grow too sure of myself—if ever I am too cocky—too smartypants—just whisper one word in my ear."

"What word is that, Sigerson?"

"Nussbaum—or Napoleon—or better, Lama—no, Nussbaum is better—whisper Nussbaum."

"You want me to whisper Nussbaum?"

"That's right."

"Nussbaum."

"No, not now, you idiot—when I'm too cocky, whisper Nussbaum."

"Not now?"

"No—wait until I am too sure of myself—*then* whisper Nussbaum."

"How will I know?"

"Know what?"

"When you want me to whisper Nussbaum."

"It's not when I want you to whisper Nussbaum—it's when I'm getting too sure of myself—then you whisper Nussbaum to remind me of what a fool I was about the message in the lama's book."

"Nussbaum."

"No! Not now!"

"On the other hand, Rat's family is pretty crazy."

"That's true."

"If by some chance the Heinz who was just in here is the same Heinz they've always had."

"Then he would be Nussbaum."

"Unless we missed something."

"You know," Howling Frog said, "we ought to come back here on Thursday. That's when they have borgelnuskies."

"No fooling, the foot-long ones?" asked Osgood Sigerson, the world's greatest detective.

"The very best," said the bookseller.

"But what does this Wallace Nussbaum, this Napoleon of Crime—meaning Napoleon Bonaparte, not the pastry—have to do with the werewolf?" the Honorable Lama Lumpo Smythe-Finkel asked.

"I like borgelnuskies with coleslaw and lots of mustard," said Dr. Ormond Sacker, the friend and biographer of the great sleuth.

"So do I," said Sigerson, "and grilled onions—what was that you said, Lama?"

"I was wondering what the criminal genius had to do with a werewolf."

"Who says he has anything to do with a werewolf?" asked the detective. "And root beer—you can' t have borgelnuskies without root beer by the pitcher."

"It's in the poem—the poem that was revealed to me in the book—you remember:

> "A *man who is a wolf*—
> A *wolf who is a man*—"

"Ah, yes," said Osgood Sigerson:

> *"It is not a wolfman, nor a manwolf—*
> *Not as such—*
> *It's the work of the Napoleon of Crime.*

"It still makes me think of the pastry—although I have no doubt that the Nussbaum interpretation is the correct one. What was the question?"

"What is the connection?" asked the lama, speaking slowly. "The connection between the master criminal and the werewolf?"

"Ah, well, that is what we have to find out, isn't it, Lama? That is where I come in. That is where I get to use my unusual powers of reasoning, isn't it? That's where all the fun starts."

"You have a suspicion, Sigerson?" asked Dr. Sacker.

"You know my methods, Sacker," the detective replied. "I prefer to remain silent until I have something conclusive with which to amaze you. There's no chance of getting a borgelnuskie today, do you suppose, Frog?"

"No, he only makes them on Thursdays."

"Pity."

"Look," said Walter Galt, "isn't that Osgood Sigerson sitting over there with Howling Frog and the Honorable Lama Lumpo Smythe-Finkel?"

"It is," said Winston Bongo. "We haven't seen him since we helped him solve the disappearance of Rat's Uncle Flipping."

DANIEL PINKWATER

"Let's go over and say hello."

The two boys approached the booth in which the great detective was sitting. "Mr. Sigerson, do you remember us?" said Walter.

"I should say I do!" replied the detective. "It's Larry and Jerry, the Bloomsbury Burglars. Still at large, but not for long. Dr. Sacker, I trust you have your weapon with you. Hands up, the two of you—Dr. Sacker has you covered with an Indian fruit bat. I must say I like your nerve—walking right up to me like this. I'll just put the darbies on you and march you to the police station. Put out your wrists. This is a good night's work indeed."

"We're not burglars," Winston said. "We're Winston Bongo and Walter Galt. We helped you rescue Flipping Hades Terwilliger the time he was kidnapped by Wallace Nussbaum."

"These confounded bifocals," said Osgood Sigerson. "Of course you are. You know, you look exactly like a couple of burglars. Come join us. Doctor, slide over and make some room for these two fine young men. Do you boys come here often? Have you ever eaten the borgelnuskies?"

"We have them all the time," Winston said.

"Really? Any good?" asked Sigerson.

"I like them," said Winston.

"Well, we'll have to come back on Thursday, and that's that," said Sigerson. "You remember my colleague, Dr. Sacker—and these gentlemen are . . ."

"We've already met," said Howling Frog. "And how is Miss Rat, your young lady friend?"

"She was here a little while ago," Walter said. "She left with her butler, Heinz—in fact, there was a question we were discussing which you might help us with, Mr. Sigerson."

"I'm always happy to make things clear for the young."

"Well, when we caught Nussbaum that time . . ."

Howling Frog and the lama exchanged surprised glances.

" . . . didn't it turn out that he was actually Heinz the butler?"

"I lose track of details once a case is finished," said Sigerson. "Doctor, what do you recall of the matter?"

"Yes," Dr. Sacker said. "I seem to remember that Nussbaum was masquerading as the family butler."

"Well, Heinz has been around ever since, just as if nothing had happened. Everybody in Rat's family seemed so unconcerned that we just never gave it a thought. We assumed that it was Heinz's twin or something—besides, Wallace Nussbaum went to Devil's Island, from which nobody has ever escaped. But we were just wondering what the story was."

A voice from the next booth was raised in a mournful wail, "But Wallace Nussbaum *has* escaped from Devil's Island. It was in the paper this morning!" It was the poet Jonathan Quicksilver who spoke.

"This is the poet Jonathan Quicksilver," Winston said. "Quicksilver, this is Osgood Sigerson, the world's greatest detective, and his friend and biographer, Dr. Ormond Sacker, and this is Howling Frog the bookseller—and I believe you know the Honorable Lama Lumpo Smythe-Finkel."

"Guru!" said Quicksilver.

"My son," said the lama, patting Quicksilver on the head.

"Squeeze over and make some room for the poet," said Sigerson. "Now, what did you say about Nussbaum escaping from Devil's Island?"

"It was in the *Baconburg Free Press* this morning," the poet said. "He got away and didn't leave a trace. I'm considering writing a poem about it."

"This gets more interesting by the minute," said Sigerson.

"But what does it have to do with a werewolf?" asked the lama.

"I'll tell you what it has to do with a werewolf," someone said. Standing by the booth was Lydia LaZonga Kelman, and her son, K.E. Kelman, PH.

Walter did the honors. "Lydia LaZonga Kelman and K.E. Kelman, PH., this is Osgood Sigerson, Dr. Ormond Sacker, his friend and biographer, the Honorable Lama Lumpo Smythe-Finkel, Jonathan Quicksilver, and Howling Frog."

"We've met," said Howling Frog. "These good folks are customers of mine."

"Come sit down," said Sigerson. "Everybody move over and make room. Shall we order some more raisin toast?"

"You said you would tell us what Wallace Nussbaum had to do with a werewolf," said the lama.

"I will," said Lydia LaZonga. "First of all, you must understand that I am psychic."

"Who isn't?" said the lama.

"I have had a vision in connection with a werewolf investigation I recently made, and the name Wallace Nussbaum came to me."

"Most interesting," said Osgood Sigerson.

"May my father and I sit with you?" asked Scott Feldman.

"Why not?" said the world's greatest detective. "Everybody move over."

DANIEL PINKWATER

It was good and crowded in the booth. Osgood Sigerson ordered raisin toast for everybody, and a pitcher of root beer. I could hardly work an arm free to get at my food.

Lydia LaZonga was speaking. "When I visited Rat, the friend of these two boys, it was a routine job—a werewolf-proofing. What I discovered was far from routine. I got the most confusing vibrations, didn't I, Sonny?"

"Mommy was really a mess after she left that place," K.E. Kelman, PH., said, "I had to take her to the Zen Chiropractor for a treatment."

"That's right," said Lydia LaZonga Kelman. "What I received in my psychic trance was this—it isn't a real were-wolf. It's like a werewolf—but it isn't a werewolf. For a little while I thought it was a zombie—but it wasn't a zombie. And I also got strong sensations relating to some sort of fiend, or master criminal. I just a little while ago received the name Wallace Nussbaum. Well, gentlemen, this is what I think: Wallace Nussbaum has taken over the mind of someone, and has turned that person into a sort of pseudo-lycanthrope. Possibly the person has no idea that he or she is acting on instructions from this Nussbaum."

"Sigerson! This is hideous!" Dr. Ormond Sacker shouted.

"It is indeed," said the great detective. "It makes Nussbaum's unauthorized use of hypnotized orangutans seem like a harmless prank. Madam, do you believe this pseudo-werewolf has the same powers as a real one?"

"At least," said Lydia LaZonga. "The psychic emanations I picked up indicated a very powerful presence indeed."

"And it's ruining my life!" moaned Jonathan Quicksilver. "People are afraid to be in the streets after dark, and my audiences at the Dharma Buns Coffee House have dwindled away to almost nothing!"

"You seem very up-to-date on the subject of werewolves," said Sigerson. "How do you know so much?"

"I read a book about them," said the poet.

"I wrote that book," said K.E. Kelman, PH., "and it's quite true, werewolves can cause a lot of trouble, although we shouldn't blame them too much—high spirits and all that, you know."

"I can assure you," said Lydia LaZonga, "if any werewolf can be a source of trouble, this artificially created one can— it's a regular monster of a werewolf."

"It is that," said someone standing in the aisle of the Deadly Nightshade Diner—We Never Close. "My hypno-simulated werewolf is the most energetic creature on this planet—and it is just in the testing stage. Wait until I have made some improvements and have turned a few hundred thousand of them loose. Things will be very amusing, I promise you."

"Who is that man, Daddy?" Scott Feldman asked.

We all looked at the person who was speaking. "Heinz!" Winston shouted.

"Not Heinz. Heinz, my bionic accomplice, is guarding

my hostage—your friend Rat. I am Wallace Nussbaum. . . . Ah, ah, ah! Dr. Sacker, I know you have an Indian fruit bat at the ready beneath the table—but I caution you to take a moment's thought. My Heinz android has instructions to do something really unpleasant to Miss Rat if I do not emerge from this diner in five minutes."

"Remain calm, Sacker," Osgood Sigerson said, "Nussbaum has us where he wants us. Nussbaum, I warn you, release the girl or I will have vengeance—you know I mean what I say."

"Miss Rat will be released unharmed, Sigerson—if I am permitted to leave this place, and none of you try to follow me; otherwise it will just be too bad. I only wanted to come here and taunt you in person, you silly detective. I have escaped from Devil's Island. I have been harassing this city with a lycanthrope of my own making since even before I escaped. And I am going to create many more such werewolves now that I am free, and dominate the world—and there isn't a single thing you can do about it, Sigerson. Now, how does that make you feel—pretty frustrated, I'll bet. *Nyah na na nyah nyah!*" Nussbaum thumbed his nose at Osgood Sigerson.

"You may taunt me all you like, Nussbaum . . ."

"Thanks, I will." Nussbaum stuck out his tongue and made rude gestures at Sigerson.

" . . . but you will never prosper in your evil plans." Osgood Sigerson was obviously furious, but spoke in calm and measured tones.

"We'll see about that, Mr. World's Greatest Detective,"

the evil Nussbaum said. "Now I'm going—and remember what I said. If any of you follow me, Rat's head will be about the size of a Ping-Pong ball in less time than it takes to tell."

Nussbaum was gone. "Quick, Sigerson! Follow him!" Dr. Ormond Sacker shouted.

"No, old fellow. You heard his threats—I believe he would carry them out. We will just sit here and finish our raisin toast."

"But, Sigerson!"

"Not to worry. Our old friend the Mighty Gorilla—the uncle of Winston here—is lurking in the shadows with instructions from me."

Outside the Deadly Nightshade Diner—We Never Close, the Mighty Gorilla, professional wrestler, crouched in the bushes and watched. He watched Heinz, the butler, emerge from the diner with Rat, and drive off in the direction of Rat's home. He watched Wallace Nussbaum emerge from a sleek limousine and enter the diner. He watched Wallace Nussbaum emerge from the diner and speed away in the limousine, apparently driven by a large ape.

And, while the Mighty Gorilla watched, someone—or something—watched him.

They are in the diner. I am outside. One crouches in the bushes. I crouch too. He is big. He watches. One comes out. It is Rat. My favorite. Her butler is with her. They go. My master comes. He goes in. I watch. The big one watches. My master comes out. He goes. The big one watches. I watch too.

"What is Scott Feldman doing here?" I thought to myself.

"This is exciting," Scott Feldman said.

"It sure is," said Phelps Feldman, his father, "and this is good raisin toast too."

"What wimps," I thought.

"Sigerson," Dr. Sacker said, "do you think that fiend will keep his word and release Rat?"

"I think Miss Rat is not in the slightest danger," Osgood Sigerson said.

"You do?"

"Elementary, my dear Sacker. Just take this dime, young Mr. Bongo, and telephone your friend Rat at her home."

"Do you think she'll be there already?" Winston asked.

"I think she hasn't been anywhere else," Sigerson said. "When she answers, tell her that I am here, and to tell Heinz—and that I want them both to come here at once—now, who would like some french fries? I'm having some."

Winston went to the pay telephone at the end of the diner. I went with him. "Hello, may I speak to Rat, please?" he said into the receiver. Apparently Rat came to the phone in a few seconds, because he said, "Rat? Is that you? Osgood Sigerson the detective is here . . . at the Deadly Nightshade Diner—We Never Close. He wants you to tell Heinz that he's here, and then come down here with Heinz as soon as you can." He hung up the receiver and turned to me. "She's home," he said.

When we got back to the booth everybody was nibbling french fries that Osgood Sigerson had ordered. "I take it the young woman was at home?" Sigerson said.

"She's coming right down here . . . with Heinz," Winston said.

"But Sigerson, if this Heinz is really an android or robot created by Nussbaum, as he said—isn't it dangerous to have told it that you are here?"

"My dear friend, I assure you Heinz is not an android or a bionic butler. You see, androids cannot pronounce their R's or L's, and they make a buzzing noise when they try to pronounce their Z's. To place an android butler in a household wherein a person named Rat lives—and someone named Flipping—would be folly. And to name the android Heinz would be another giveaway. You boys are frequently guests in the house—have you ever noticed that Heinz addresses your friend as Llat, or her uncle as Frrriping?"

We said that we hadn't.

"So many of the parts are made in Asia, you see," said Sigerson, "it's just a little problem of pronunciation that never got worked out. Now, who wants Nesselrode pie?"

The Mighty Gorilla entered the diner.

Mrs. Starkley, Rat's English teacher, who was sitting in a booth near the entrance, took one look and fainted. Later, she would revive and ask the Mighty Gorilla for his autograph.

"Everybody squeeze over and make room for the Mighty Gorilla," Osgood Sigerson said. "Mr. Mighty Gorilla, make your report."

"I waited outside," the world-famous wrestler said. "Rat left with Heinz, the butler. They drove off in the direction of Rat's house. A little while later, Wallace Nussbaum turned up. I could have tackled him, but you told me not to reveal myself on any account."

"Quite right, too," Sigerson said. "We've a werewolf to catch—and capturing Nussbaus, dear as that thought is to my heart, is of secondary importance. Pray continue."

"In a little while, Nussbaum came out of the diner and drove off in a limousine. I couldn't tell for certain, but the driver seemed not to be human."

"An unfortunate orangutan trapped in Nussbaum's power, no doubt," Sigerson said. "And the direction in which Nussbaum drove?"

"Opposite to that taken by Rat," the Mighty Gorilla said.

"So Nussbaum was bluffing, as I thought—still, I couldn't take a chance."

"This is exciting, isn't it, Daddy?" Scott Feldman said.

"Do you mean we might have grabbed Nussbaum when he was here?" Dr. Ormond Sacker asked.

"We might have," said the great detective, "but what if he actually was holding Rat captive? Nussbaum is not above kidnapping, as Rat's Uncle Flipping knows very well. Strange that we haven't seen Flipping this night—no doubt he'll turn up before this case is over. Ah, Miss Rat! And Heinz! Make room, everybody. Kindly join us, the two of you.

"And now, let's clear up the matter of Heinz's identity. Heinz, tell these people your real name."

"My real name," said the butler, "is Nussbaum."

"No, Doctor, there's no need to go for your stuffed Indian fruit bat. Tell us your first name."

"My first name is Heinrich."

"Quite so—Heinrich Nussbaum. And you are the identical twin of . . ."

"Wallace Nussbaum."

"So there you have it. Heinz the butler is the identical twin of Wallace Nussbaum. I summoned Mr. Heinrich Nussbaum from Peru to take the place of his brother in the Matthews home when it turned out that his evil twin, Wallace Nussbaum, had been masquerading as the family butler."

"I hate my brother. He's so evil," Heinrich Nussbaum said.

"Of course you do," said Sigerson. "I desired Heinrich here to take his brother's place in order that he might keep watch over the family. Mr. Heinrich Nussbaum is a member of the Peruvian police, and is fully trained."

DANIEL PINKWATER

"It is my dearest wish to bring my evil brother to justice and to remove the terrible blot on the Nussbaum name," Heinrich Nussbaum said.

"Perfectly understandable," Sigerson said. "The family was sworn to secrecy in this matter—and was instructed to behave as if this man was the same butler they'd always had—and, identical as he is to the other Nussbaum—"

"But only in appearance," Heinrich Nussbaum put in.

"But only in appearance—the family soon more or less forgot that this was another Heinz in place of the one who had proved so disloyal to them."

"When we were young, he used to steal my girlfriends," Heinrich Nussbaum said.

"And what have you observed which might be of help to us in thwarting your brother's evil plans?" Sigerson asked.

"Well, nothing, really—but I certainly do want you to thwart him. I hope you thwart him good."

Turning to Rat, Sigerson asked, "How's your Uncle Flipping been?"

"He hasn't been around much lately," Rat said. "He's been working on a new project—he's a mad scientist, you know."

"What is the nature of this new project?" asked Sigerson.

"It's a way of programming information into foodstuffs," Rat said. "Uncle Flipping first got the idea when he absent-mindedly put a tortilla into the disk drive of his computer—he was eating tacos as he worked. Uncle Flipping wondered if it might be possible to load the tortilla with information from the computer which would be released directly into the brain when the tortilla was eaten. He experimented with pizza, saltines, and pancakes. Then he made an adapted disk drive machine out of a toaster and tried whole-wheat bread, bagels, and frozen waffles.

"None of the experiments worked. Uncle Flipping also tried eating standard computer disks—and that had no effect either. He decided that he had to find an edible substance which also was able to retain magnetic information, which, in turn could be ingested directly into the brain.

"Finally Uncle Flipping discovered something which looked as though it might work—an Asian relative of the avocado that has magnetic properties. Uncle Flipping had decided that the best use for this invention—if he should ever get it to work—would be to make a breakfast cereal that would contain the contents of an entire high school textbook. So, for example, a pupil eating breakfast would ingest the contents of his or her civics textbook at a single sitting."

"And has your uncle made much progress with this project?" Osgood Sigerson asked.

"Who knows?" Rat said.

"And the plant which gave him so much hope—the Asian relative of the avocado—would the name of that plant be marifesa, by any chance?"

"Something like that," Rat said.

"Most interesting," said Sigerson.

"Sigerson! What does all this mean?" Dr. Ormond Sacker asked excitedly.

"Simply this, old fellow," the great detective replied, "we now see the connection between Nussbaum's presence in this city, the phenomenon of a werewolf, and the work of Flipping Hades Terwilliger."

"What is the connection?"

"I'm not prepared to reveal that as yet—but I will tell you this. The marifesa plant has something to do with were-wolfery—I saw a movie all about it."

"That's all?" asked Dr. Sacker.

"That's all for the moment."

"But what about Terwilliger's project—his plan to make it possible for people to ingest information with their food?"

"I suppose it's a good idea. It will save time reading."

"Sigerson, it's dangerous!"

"What is? What's dangerous? Where?"

"Flipping Hades Terwilliger's plan! It's very dangerous! Suppose instead of the contents of a civics textbook—suppose some evil individual, like Wallace Nussbaum, should inject some horrible doctrine or bizarre mode of behavior into—let's say tapioca pudding. Everyone who ate the stuff would instantly become a slave—and we know how dearly Wallace Nussbaum wants to enslave the population of Earth."

Phelps and Scott Feldman looked at each other. "You don't suppose he'd put it into tapioca pudding?" Phelps asked.

"That's not the point!" Dr. Ormond Sacker said. "The point is that Flipping Hades Terwilliger is doing experiments which might lead to something like that."

"And they have to do with marifesa plants!" K.E. Kelman put in.

"And marifesa plants have to do with werewolfian matters," Lydia LaZonga said.

"And we're after a werewolf," said Sigerson. "It all begins to fit together, doesn't it?"

"You know," Heinrich Nussbaum said, "in the last letter I received from Mommy Nussbaum, down in Lima, she hinted that Wallace may have found a way to enslave the mind of another individual, and to cause that individual to behave like a werewolf—and in fact to be a werewolf to all intents and purposes, except that the individual is not a real werewolf— that is remains a werewolf only as long as my evil brother's influence continues. These were just hints, you understand. Mommy always brags about Wallace when she writes to me. I wonder if she brags about me when she writes to him."

"Did Mommy Nussbaum indicate how Wallace planned to do this?"

"This is all reading between the lines, you understand. If Mommy knew for certain about any of Wallace's criminal activities, she would tell me, because I am a policeman, you know. I think she may have mentioned that he intends to introduce something into the food of his victims."

"Aha!"

"Aha, Sigerson?" Dr. Ormond Sacker asked.

"Aha, definitely," said Osgood Sigerson. "It seems very likely that we now know how Wallace Nussbaum has gained control over the poor devil who is popularly known as the Baconburg Horror. The question to be answered now is, into what food has Nussbaum introduced the lycanthropy-causing marifesa and, of course, who is eating it?"

"I think I can be of some help," said Phelps Feldman. "I am a graduate chemist—and only last week I was reading something about the marifesa in *Avocados Today.*"

"My father reads that magazine," Walter Galt said.

"The marifesa, both in its flower and in the avocadolike fruit, has a very strong and distinctive flavor—so if it were introduced into a food, that food would have to have a very strong flavor indeed to disguise its taste."

"Ooooh! Daddy is helping to solve the crime," Scott Feldman said.

"Shut up, son," Phelps Feldman said.

"Something with a very strong flavor, eh?" Sigerson said. "What would you suggest as a suitable foodstuff for the introduction of marifesa?"

"Only two things occur to me," Phelps Feldman said. "One is Chef Chow's Hot and Spicy Oil undiluted and by the glassful, and the other is . . . borgelnuskies. I should add that the essential properties of the marifesa are volatile and unstable. If indeed this Wallace Nussbaum is making a werewolf of someone by feeding them marifesa, the dose would have to be repeated every few days—or at the least every week."

"Most helpful, Mr. Feldman," Sigerson said. "So, we have a theory that Wallace Nussbaum, possibly taking a clue from spying on the scientific work of Flipping Hades Terwilliger, may have created his werewolf by feeding someone a decoction of the plant marifesa. We further theorize that the dose would have to be sustained on a weekly basis—and still further we hypothesize that a suitable vehicle for the administration of this dose would be the delicacy borgelnuskies, which are available where in this city?"

"This is the only place that serves them," Winston said.

"And it serves them once a week!" said Sigerson. "It all fits. If we are not going in the wrong direction entirely, it would seem that our werewolf is a regular customer of the Deadly Nightshade Diner—We Never Close."

"This suggests that the management of this diner may have some connection with the crime," Dr. Ormond Sacker said. "Could they possibly be putting this devilish substance in all the borgelnuskies?"

"A possibility," Sigerson said. "I take it everyone here is a habitual borgelnuskie eater."

"Except us," Phelps Feldman said, "in our family we believe that borgelnuskies lead to shortness."

"I, of course, move from place to place, and alas, have no regular source of borgelnuskies," said the detective, "but many of you eat the borgelnuskies on Thursdays, do you not?"

"Whenever possible," K.E. Kelman said.

"And the rest of you?"

"Yes."

"And the hippermost citizens of Baconburg?"

"Yes."

"A bit of a puzzle," Osgood Sigerson mused. "Either the Nussbaumian pseudo-werewolf is the only one getting the special borgelnuskies—or he is getting them somewhere other than here—or we're barking up the wrong tree altogether. Now, Mr. Feldman, perhaps you would favor us with your opinion—what would you suggest as an antidote to the effects of the marifesa?"

"Well, as I said, the essential nature of the plant is unstable and volatile—if the dose were discontinued, my guess would be that the effects would wear off in short order."

"Yes, yes. This is quite enough for one night's work," Osgood Sigerson said. "Doctor, we have quite a bit of investigating to do. I propose that we agree to meet here again on Thursday. After enjoying a nutritious meal of borgelnuskies, we will go and catch the werewolf. What do you all say to that?"

"It won't be so easy to catch the werewolf," Jonathan Quicksilver said. "Werewolves are strong and fast and nasty."

"Catching the werewolf is no problem for Mommy and me," said K.E. Kelman, PH. "It's finding the werewolf that usually gives us the most trouble."

"Oh, I think we'll have little difficulty finding the werewolf," Osgood Sigerson said, "and once that's done, I can deal with Wallace Nussbaum."

"Good!" said Heinrich Nussbaum. "I hope you really thwart him this time."

"That is my intention," said the detective. "Now—one

thing more. When we meet again let there be no mention of werewolves, of our plans, or anything that has transpired this evening—we do not know who may be listening. We will simply meet for a pleasant evening's entertainment. I myself will discourse brilliantly on a number of subjects, and everyone will have a lovely time. After our meal we will all go in cars to a place I will suggest—and then, whatever happens will happen. Now, I bid you all good night."

DANIEL PINKWATER

When the meeting at the Deadly Nightshade Diner—We Never Close broke up Winston couldn't get the Peugeot started. Rate had a look under the hood and said that it needed a rare French engine part, a sort of terrycloth mitten that fitted on top of the carburetor. Winston looked depressed. Rat said she was pretty sure she had the part under her bed at home. She said she'd come back the next day and fix it for him. We got a ride with Rat and Heinz, also known as Heinrich Nussbaum.

During the ride, Heinrich told us something about the history of the Nussbaum family.

"There have been master criminals in our family from the beginning of history," Heinrich told us. "The Nussbaums were once a wandering band of barbarians, like the Vandals, and the Visigoths. Even earlier, it is believed, our ancestors were no-goods, chasing honest folks away from the carcasses of mastodons they had killed for food, and raiding peaceful Paleolithic settlements. Some people think Attila the Hun was a Nussbaum, and some of the nastier Roman emperors are supposed to have had Nussbaum blood.

"In modern times Moriarty Nussbaum was considered to have had the finest criminal mind in Europe, and Fu Man Nussbaum operated a vast network of spies, assassins, smugglers, thugs, and blackmailers the like of which the world had never seen. My father, Dennis Nussbaum, made the Old World too hot to hold him and emigrated to South America. He always liked my brother Wallace better than me.

"As far as I know, I am the first honest member of the Nussbaum clan. It was quite a blow to my mother when I became a member of the Peruvian police. I have been trying all my life to single-handedly offset the horrible record of my family."

"It must really bug you to have a brother like Wallace," I said.

"You have no idea," Heinrich Nussbaum said. "Oh, I hope he gets thwarted this time! I hope Mr. Sigerson really thwarts the dickens out of him!"

"You have a lot of confidence in Osgood Sigerson, don't you?" Rat asked.

"He is my benefactor," Heinrich Nussbaum said. "It was Osgood Sigerson who helped me to get into the police. They were reluctant to take me because of my family."

Then Heinrich Nussbaum broke out in evil-sounding laughter. "That fool Sigerson will never thwart my plans!" he hissed.

I felt a creeping horror, and confusion. It was as though Heinrich had suddenly gone mad—or as if he had been the evil Wallace Nussbaum all the time. Winston and Rat shuddered too. Then we realized that it had not been Heinrich who had spoken. It was the radio speaker. A voice identical to Heinrich's, but somehow evil and scary, was coming over the radio—which, to the best of my knowledge, had not even been turned on.

DANIEL PINKWATER

"Yes, my dear fat-headed Heinrich, this is your brother, Wallace. You may tell that pathetic detective that he couldn't thwart his old granny. I listened to his idiotic conversation over the little jukebox in the booth at the Deadly Nightshade Diner—We Never Close, and it is to laugh. The whole time you simple fools were sitting around theorizing and making your feeble plans, my werewolf was just outside. If I had wished, I could have had him run into the diner and give you all such halyatchkies as you never had in your lives. Ha ha ha ha!"

Then the car radio went silent. Rat, who was sitting in the front with Heinrich, fiddled with the knobs. It had been switched off when Wallace Nussbaum's voice had come over the speakers.

"How did he do that?" I asked.

"Halyatchkies?" Winston asked.

"Oh, I hope he doesn't give us halyatchkies," Heinrich said.

Rat had her Swiss Army knife out and was taking apart the panel which held the radio in the Matthews family limousine, a luxurious Edsel touring car. Having removed a few screws, she yanked out the radio, reached into the cavity in the dashboard, and felt around. "I've got something," she said. She pulled out a little box wrapped with black tape, with wires dangling from it. "Look," Rat said, "it's a little tape recorder. Wallace Nussbaum must have rigged it so that it would start playing when the ignition was turned on. The first part of the tape is probably blank. After a few minutes it spooled along to the place where his message was recorded. He must have thought it would scare us."

"It scared me," I said.

"That Wallace is so tricky!" Heinrich said.

"First thing tomorrow I'm going to check out the jukebox in the booth and see if there's a microphone in it," Rat said. "Then I'm going to go over the Peugeot very carefully and see if there's another tape recorder, or maybe a bomb. Chances are that Wallace is the one who fritzed your engine."

"Good idea," Winston said, "especially about checking for a bomb."

"Don't worry about a thing," Rat said.

DANIEL PINKWATER

                                    WHO'S THIS GUY
                    NUSSBAUM?

                                    I

                                    THOUGHT

                                    A

                                    WEREWOLF

                    WAS   BAD

                                    ENOUGH

BUT

        NOW

                I

                        HEAR

                            IT'S

                                    ALL

                                        ABOUT

                                                        THIS

                    NUSSBAUM

GUY   WOW

PEOPLE   WILL   GO   TO   ANY   LENGTHS

                                                    TO

                                                    MESS

            UP
                                                                        A

                        POET

                                    571

Rat didn't find a microphone in the jukebox. We did get into a certain amount of trouble with Gus Bowlingpin. We went to the same booth everybody had been sitting in the night before and ordered crullers and coffee, and then Rat whipped out her Swiss Army knife and had the jukebox in pieces in a matter of seconds. Gus hollered at us and was going to throw us out.

"Don't you want me to put it together again?" Rat asked.

This gave us the advantage. Gus grumbled, but let us stay and finish our crullers and coffee while Rat put the jukebox back together. "At least we know that Nussbaum was bluffing about listening in on our conversation last night," she said.

"Let's make sure there isn't a bomb in my car," Winston said.

"Even if he had listened, I don't know what he would have learned," I said. "I didn't understand half of what went on. It was mostly Sigerson spinning theories—and we have no idea what he's got planned for Thursday night."

"I have to go to the bathroom," Winston said. "You guys go ahead and start looking for the bomb in my car."

"Well, if any of Sigerson's theories were correct, and Nussbaum was listening, that would put him ahead of us," Rat said.

"If you find the bomb, just go ahead and neutralize it," Winston said. "Don't wait for me."

"What do you think Sigerson has planned for Thursday night?" I asked.

"It beats me," Rat said. "I don't know any more than you do. All he said was that we were going to meet for a meal of borgelnuskies—which, by the way, I can't stand—and then we would all go someplace. We're not supposed to talk about Nussbaum or the werewolf or any of that."

"Just knock on the men's room door after you disarm the bomb," Winston said.

From *The New York Times*, June 6th, 1983:

By William E. Geist

One night in 1933, Richard Hollingshead, Jr., took a projector outside, flashed a movie on the side of a building, and sat in his car to watch it. Friends and family were very worried about Mr. Hollingshead. He next patented a ramp system allowing the occupants of a car to see a screen over a car in front of them, and on June 6 of that year he opened the world's first drive-in movie theater, the R. H. Hollingshead, Jr., Theater on Admiral Wilson Boulevard in Camden, N.J.

From *The Times of Africa*, Nairobi, May 28th, 1966

Eleven non-paying customers turned up at the Riziki Rafiki Drive-in Movie Theater on Kimenge Road last night. The occasion was the first showing of the film *Born Free*, which deals with Elsa the lioness and her cubs. During the presentation of the film, eleven lions from the Nairobi Game Refuge came over the wall, no doubt attracted by the growling and roaring on the sound track, and watched the film. The lions took up positions on the roofs and bonnets of cars, and stayed until the end of the performance.

From the *Baconburg Free Press*

In response to the revival of interest in monsters arising from the Baconburg Horror incidents, the Garden of Earthly Bliss Drive-in and Pizzeria on Route 9R has scheduled a Season of Horror festival. Beginning this Thursday at nightfall, the Garden of Earthly Bliss Drive-in and Pizzeria will show five different horror features every night.

An alternate tradition contends that it was not Richard Hollingshead, Jr., who first opened a drive-in theater, but a Romanian named Tesev Nussbaumscu who opened such an establishment in the town of Blint in 1893. Some historians argue that this was not a true drive-in in the modern sense of the word, as neither automobiles nor movies were known then, and the theater remained open for only one performance which consisted of Nussbaumscu and his family falling upon the curious, who had come in carts and wagons, beating them with halyatchkie sticks, and taking their money and possessions.

A Bucharest firm which opened a chain of drive-in movies throughout Eastern Europe in the 1930s was unaware of this event, and were taken by surprise when their Blint location was burned to the ground by an angry and suspicious populace—some of whom still remembered the Nussbaumscu affair.

Coincidentally, Louis Grotshkie, the head of the firm which built the ill-fated second drive-in movie theater in Blint, emigrated to the United States and, in time, opened the very finest drive-in movie ever, the Garden of Earthly Bliss Drive-in and Pizzeria in Baconburg.

Even more coincidentally, half the population of Blint also emigrated to the United States and settled in and around Baconburg.

577

Some believe that there is a connection between the Blintish colony in Baconburg and the constant outbreak of fires at the Garden of Earthly Bliss Drive-in and Pizzeria. In any case, one of Mr. Grotshkie's constant concerns has been the repeated arson attempts at his theater. On two occasions the entire screen was immolated, and Grotshkie was forced to hire extra security guard and to install a state-of-the-art fire prevention system in the pizzeria/projection booth.

Following these innovations, would-be firebugs began bringing combustible materials into the drive-in and setting huge bonfires. This necessitated the installation of high-pressure fire hoses at strategic points in the parking area.

This was the state of affairs at the Garden of Earthly Bliss Drive-in and Pizzeria at the beginning of the Season of Horror film festival.

DANIEL PINKWATER

The moon is my friend. I sneak and hide. I love to howl. I love to pounce. I love to eat. I love to eat. I love to eat borgelnuskies. Borgelnuskies. Want borgelnuskies. Really hungry for borgelnuskies. Borgelnuskies. Is it Thursday? I smell them. The Deadly Nightshade Diner—We Never Close. Borgelnuskies. Yum. Get borgelnuskies. I drool.

Thursday night. It looked like everybody in Baconburg had turned up at the Deadly Nightshade Diner—We Never Close. There's always a mob scene when borgelnuskies are served. The parking lot was just about full. People were standing in line waiting to get in, and people were coming out with faces that expressed supreme contentment and pleasure mixed with nausea and gastritis. Rat, Winston, and I arrived in the Peugeot. Heinz, the butler who was, in reality, Heinrich Nussbaum, twin brother of Wallace Nussbaum the master criminal, was driving on his own in the Edsel limousine. We could smell the grilled onions two blocks away.

Osgood Sigerson was already in the diner. He had reserved a large booth which was rapidly filling up with people. Dr. Ormond Sacker was there, of course. Also Winston's uncle, the Mighty Gorilla, who did part-time bodyguard and strong-arm work for Sigerson. Phelps Feldman and his son Scott were there, eating corn flakes. K.E. Kelman, PH., the phantomologist, and his mother, Lydia LaZonga, were there. Jonathan Quicksilver, the poet, was there, and also his guru, the Honorable Lama Lumpo Smythe-Finkel and Howling Frog, the bookseller. Rat was surprised to see her English teacher, Mrs. Starkley, and a man who turned out to be Mr. Starkley sitting in the booth.

There was barely room for us to squeeze in—and Heinrich Nussbaum hadn't shown up yet.

"I've already ordered," Osgood Sigerson said, "you are all my guests. It's borgelnuskies for everybody—and don't be shy about asking for seconds. It's a party! Whoopee!" The world's greatest detective was in unusually high spirits. He was wearing his deerstalker cap, and was obviously excited and ready for action. He was bouncing up and down in his seat and annoying other patrons by blowing the paper sleeves off soda straws. If Winston or I had acted that way we'd have been thrown out.

"Look! Look! Here they come! Bring on the borgelnuskies, chef!" Gus Bowlingpin was carrying a tray crowded with platters of hot borgelnuskies. "Bon appétit!" Gus said.

"Hooray!" the great detective shouted, and "Dig in! Get them before they get you!"

The Mighty Gorilla made the least noise but ate the most borgelnuskies. It was a frightening spectacle, even though he didn't begin to have trouble breathing until the ninth helping. Even the Feldmans nibbled a borgelnuskie apiece, although they expressed fear that they might have indigestion later.

"Nonsense," Dr. Ormond Sacker said. "I am a medical man, and I can tell you for certain that there is no reason to worry. You *will* have indigestion later. It's the price you pay—but there's no cause for alarm. No one is apt to die from eating borgelnuskies—except perhaps the Mighty Gorilla."

"Ah!" Osgood Sigerson said. "Is it not my old friend, Flipping Hades Terwilliger?"

"Sigerson!" said Rat's uncle. "And everybody else! What a pleasure!"

"Join us," Sigerson said. "We're just having some borgelnuskies."

"Exactly what I came for," Flipping Hades Terwilliger said, "I'll just instruct the chef. Gus—a triple order of borgelnuskies, if you please, and topped with confectioner's sugar, pineapple slices, and instant-whip as usual!"

"Yick!" the Mighty Gorilla said. "Speaking as a confirmed gourmand and pig-out artist, that is the most awfulsounding combination I've ever heard of. Even I could never eat that—nobody could."

"It's the way I like them," Uncle Flipping said, "and, as I understand matters, one of the benefits of living in a democracy is that a man may eat his borgelnuskies any way he likes."

"But not in front of the children!" Lydia LaZonga said.

"It's all right," Rat said, "he's my uncle."

"You poor dear," Lydia LaZonga said.

"I say, Sigerson," Dr. Ormond Sacker said. "Do you notice anything odd about that kitchen helper?"

"Yes," Osgood Sigerson said, "I've been observing the poor devil for some time—but let's not discuss such matters at the moment."

I caught a glimpse of the kitchen helper they must have been talking about. He was a poor devil if I'd ever seen one—stoop-shouldered, flat-footed, and hairy as an ape. A really ugly guy.

"I say!" Sigerson shouted. "I've been neglecting my

promise to entertain you all with some brilliant conversation. Now, who here knows why tennis balls are fuzzy when they're new?"

Sigerson astounded us with obscure information for the next hour or so. "I wonder if anyone here knows how many varieties of salami there are throughout the world?" the world's greatest detective asked. "There are over a thousand! One thousand six hundred thirty-three, to be exact! Salami is one of the most ancient foodstuffs—probably originating when the first caveman, unable to finish his meal of pterodactyl cutlets, shoved the leftovers into a bag and then forgot about it for a month or two. I include in the general category of salami such delicacies as Chinese lop cheong and Bavarian jaegerwurst, as well as the more readily recognized varieties such as the kosher gut buster and the Hungarian black beauty."

Sigerson certainly knew a lot. From salamis, he went on to tell about the history of cuckoo clocks, favorite footwear of the pre-Socratic philosophers, and whether there is life on other planets. Cuckoo clocks were first made in Turkey, not Switzerland, most of the pre-Socratic philosophers liked open-toed sandals, and in Sigerson's opinion, beings from other planets not only exist, but visit Earth regularly. It isn't often that one gets to listen to a really brilliant person. I was impressed.

While Sigerson talked he munched borgelnuskies. The rest of us ate quite a few too. We all began to feel quite full— which, when you've been eating borgelnuskies, is what you feel just before the pain begins. Sigerson interrupted himself in the middle of an interesting account of the different varieties of African zebras and said, "I say! Who's for a movie?"

For myself, I was more in the mood to go home and writhe on my bed until the effects of eating borgelnuskies had worn off. I would have thought the others felt the same way, but Dr. Ormond Sacker said, "By Jove! What a capital idea! What precisely did you have in mind, Sigerson?"

"I believe we have the honor to have among us three—no, four of the greatest exponents of the art of snarking," Sigerson said. "I refer, of course, to young Rat, Walter, and Winston, and the distinguished scientist Flipping Hades Terwilliger. May I make so bold to suggest that they lead us all on a grand mechanized outdoor snark?"

"A grand mechanized outdoor snark?" Winston asked.

"Precisely," Sigerson said. "With such a large group of distinguished persons, it seems to me that the ordinary sort of snark might call upon us for less than our best effort. What I propose is that we all get in cars, and just go."

"Go?" the Honorable Lama Lumpo Smythe-Finkel asked. "Go where?"

"I thought it would be fun if you all didn't know exactly where quite yet," Osgood Sigerson said. "We will all get into cars and begin driving. Before that, I will give you sealed envelopes—one envelope to each car. Once we are all rolling, someone in each car will open the envelope. Inside the envelope will be instructions for our snark. It's something like a treasure hunt or a game. Doesn't it sound like fun? Now, who wants to go?"

Everybody wanted to go except Uncle Flipping. Uncle

Flipping said he had some work to finish at his laboratory—but if Sigerson would give him one of the sealed envelopes, he would try to catch up with us later.

"That will be no problem at all," Osgood Sigerson said. "Here is your envelope. Now, shall we all get started?"

It was Rat, Winston, and me in the Peugeot. Osgood Sigerson and Dr. Ormond Sacker went with the Mighty Gorilla in their famous Studebaker Lark touring car. Heinrich Nussbaum took Jonathan Quicksilver, the Honorable Lama Lumpo Smythe-Finkel, and Howling Frog in the Edsel limo. Mrs. Starkley, Rat's English teacher, and her husband, Mr. Starkley, had a big motorcycle—Mrs. Starkley drove. K.E. Kelman, PH., and his mother, Lydia LaZonga Kelman, had a black van with the word PHANTOMOLOGIST lettered on each side. Phelps and Scott Feldman drove in their Gremlin with automatic transmission, cruise control, deluxe wheel covers, and vinyl roof. Osgood Sigerson had given the driver of each vehicle a sealed envelope.

"Have fun, everybody!" Osgood Sigerson had said, and belching exhaust fumes and borgelnuskies, we roared off into the night.

"Let's see what's in the envelope," Rat said. She tore open the envelope and read:

> Greetings!
> Tonight we catch the werewolf! Proceed to the Garden of Earthly Bliss Drive-in and Pizzeria. Pay your admission and drive in as though you were going to enjoy the films. Park

anywhere. It is my belief that the werewolf will not be able to resist showing up, as the films tonight include *The Werewolf; The Werewolf of Poughkeepsie; I Was a Communist Werewolf; Werewolf Wars;* and *Werewolf Stewardesses.* Sit in your cars and enjoy the show—but be on the lookout for the signal, which will consist of the lighting of a flare or torch by Dr. Sacker. When you see the signal, instantly come to the refreshment area, where I will give each of you a bouquet of wolfbane with which to confuse the lycanthrope. We will then spread out and chase the werewolf. At all costs prevent him from leaving the drive-in theater. Mr. K.E. Kelman and his mother, Lydia LaZonga Kelman, will be on hand with werewolf-capturing equipment. If we can direct the creature toward their van, which will be located at the center of the parking area, they assure me they can do the rest. Be vigilant! Be courageous! Be swift! Good Hunting!

—O. Sigerson, Esq.

"Wow!" Winston said.
"Definitely. Wow!" Rat said.
"Yeah. Wow," I said.

A horrible voice crackled through the loudspeaker. It was another recorded message from Wallace Nussbaum, coming over the car radio.

"Fools! You will never capture my creation! My werewolf is strong and clever and mean—and he can move so fast, it's as though he were in two places at once. I shall let you continue with your pathetic little exercise—just so you can see how really formidable my werewolf is. Don't blame me if you get a halyatchkie. You've been warned! Ha ha ha ha ha!"

"He's bluffing," Rat said.

"Right. He's bluffing," I said.

"Right," Winston said.

"Right."

"Right."

The Garden of Earthly Bliss Drive-in and Pizzeria, built by Louis Grotshkie, is generally agreed to be the finest outdoor movie theater in the world.

The giant screen is the size of two football fields. The projection system, specially made by Zeiss of Germany, has such superior powers of resolution that only brand-new prints of movies can be shown, because scratches and small imperfections on a film would appear as large as watermelons on the screen. The speakers, which are hooked over the windows of the cars of patrons, are in stereo pairs, and of the highest quality. There is a special noiseless gravel in the parking area, so that latecomers will not disturb with the sound of crunching tires.

Invisible bug-lights protect the patrons from mosquitoes. There is a full-scale amusment park for the children, complete with ferris wheel, pony rides, and an Olympic size swimming pool. Three European chefs supervise the preparation of pizza, which is baked and delivered directly to your car by an automated Japanese pizza chef robot, which runs on wheels and presents your pizza, piping hot, directly into your car window.

Full medical services, including a psychiatrist, are available should any patron become indisposed—and any baby born in the drive-in during the showing of a film receives a free pass, good weeknights, for life.

In addition to these regular services, the Garden of Earthly Bliss Drive-in and Pizzeria offers occasional door prizes, including grand pianos, trips to Europe, mobile homes, and gold coins.

The visitor will note that the ticket kiosk and pizzeria/projection booth are built in the architectural style of the Mogoshoaia Palace, and the swimming pool is a replica of the Herculane Baths in the Cerna Valley in Romania. Before, after, or during the film, one is free to walk in a large formal garden built to resemble the Cishmigiu Garden in Bucharest.

The Garden of Earthly Bliss Drive-in and Pizzeria has received several awards from the Association of American Drive-in Movie Theaters and the International Brotherhood of Pizza Makers.

DANIEL PINKWATER

The fact is, I had never been to a drive-in movie. Neither had Rat. Neither had Winston. We drove out on Route 9R, looking for the Garden of Earthly Bliss Drive-in and Pizzeria. When we saw it, we flipped. It was great!

The place where you pay your admission looked like a castle or something. The screen was enormous. Band music was playing on all the loudspeakers, hundreds of them. The pizza smelled great. It was like a circus or a parade. Cars full of people were lined up for a mile, waiting to get into the drive-in. Once inside, the cars cruised around—the drivers trying to make up their minds about where to park. All this time, the band music was playing and colored lights were flashing on the great screen. There was this castle-type building in the middle of the place. Great big loudspeakers at the corners were blasting the band music, and this thing on wheels was running up and down in front of it.

The thing on wheels was a robot pizza chef. You could call your pizza order in by pressing a button and talking into one of the car speakers, and the robot would bring you your pizza, shove it through the car window, take your money, and give you your change. The card attached to the speaker said the Garden of Earthly Bliss Drive-in and Pizzeria could make *any* kind of pizza—just ask. What a great place!

The back part of the drive-in was like a carnival or an

amusement park. There were colored lights, rides—a ferris wheel, a roller coaster, ice cream stands, a swimming pool, and a big garden you could walk around in. And everywhere, band music.

I nearly forgot that we were there to catch a werewolf. The place itself was so spectacular, I would have been happy just to have come out there to watch five werewolf movies, maybe eat some pizza, and then go home.

We could see the Kelmans' van parked in the middle of everything, and we also could see Heinrich Nussbaum in the Edsel. None of the other cars were visible to us, but we assumed they were somewhere in the drive-in. Sigerson's instructions had been to sit in our car and enjoy the show. The show hadn't started yet, so we sat in our car and enjoyed the band music and the colored lights on the screen.

Ignatz the Igniter, a well-known Romanian pyromaniac, put fifteen or twenty books of matches in his pockets, checked his small bottle of gasoline, stuffed some automobile emergency flares into his shirt, wound several feet of slow-burning fuse around his ankle and covered it with his sock, filled his cigarette lighter, tucked several days' copies of the *Baconburg Free Press* under his arm, said a small prayer before a statue of Saint Barbara of Blint, kissed his mother, and went out for an evening's entertainment.

"Have a good time, son!" the mother of Ignatz the Igniter called.

ORDINARILY

I

DON'T   LIKE

DRIVE

IN

MOVIES

THEY'RE DECADENT, AND APPEAL TO THE LOWEST ELEMENTS IN

SOCIETY

BUT

THIS

ONE'S

DIFFERENT   I SORT OF LIKE IT

AND MY GURU PAID MY

ADMISSION

SO I GET IN

FREE

*

Hark! Somewhere in the city, I hear a werewolf giving voice. Can it be that I am not alone? Somewhere one like me is growling. Humans are shrieking. It sounds like a party. I go to find the sound.

I, *Wallace Nussbaum, have done this thing. I alone have loosed upon the city my masterpiece of evil, my arch-awful impossible imp, my werewolf. How I love you, my sweet little werewolf! Wolf! Wolfy! Wolfaleh! Now I will take my rightful place among the Nussbaumic evil geniuses of history.*

Go, wolf-baby! Terrify! Destroy!

Osgood Sigerson, eat your heart out!

A car of foreign make pulls up to the ticket kiosk of the Garden of Earthly Bliss Drive-in and Pizzeria. It is a Wartburg, seldom seen in the West, but popular, because it's all you can get, in certain Soviet-bloc countries.

When the driver rolls down his window to pay his admission, the ticket-taker is struck by a whiff of Romanian "suicide-squad" salami mixed with the aroma of gasoline, paraffin, and other combustibles.

All types, high and low, enjoy the Garden of Earthly Bliss Drive-in and Pizzeria, and the Wartburg enters the great theater unhindered.

Dr. Ormond Sacker peered through a set of werewolf-spotting glasses. "I don't see anything yet, Sigerson," he said. "That is, I don't see any sign of the werewolf. The behavior of some of the citizens of Baconburg, not to say the citizens themselves, I have been watching with immense disgust."

"Keep scanning for the werewolf, old chap," Osgood Sigerson, the world's greatest detective, said. "He's bound to turn up once the films start, if not sooner."

"How curious, Sigerson! Those people over there seem to be preparing a barbecue of some sort."

"Romanians from the village of Blint, no doubt," Osgood Sigerson said. "The security guards will be along in a moment to extinguish the fire and eject them."

"Amazing, Sigerson! You're absolutely right! The security guards are putting out the fire and making the people leave. Why do they do that, Sigerson?"

"Why do people from Blint set fires in drive-in movies?"

"Yes, Sigerson. Why do they do that?"

"All I can say is that I'm grateful that the strange proclivities of the former residents of Blint are none of my concern. I doubt whether they know themselves why they behave in that singular and annoying fashion. Since Blintians are law-abiding, apart from their penchant for arson in open-air theaters, I have had no occasion to deal with any of them. As you know, my ethnological interests are largely limited to people who specialize in crime. There is a village in Sikkim, for example, which produces nothing but high-grade felons. Nobody knows why."

"Lordey, this is boring," Dr. Ormond Sacker said. "I wish the werewolf would show up."

"Daddy, do you think we'll really catch the werewolf?"
  "Shut up, son—the movie's starting."

"O.K., Sonny, let's go over it once more. Rope made of wolf-bane."

"Check."

"Stainless steel handcuffs."

"Check."

"Stainless steel footcuffs."

"Check."

"Net."

"Check."

"Silver-headed clubs."

"Check."

"Garlic."

"Check."

"Mirrors."

"Check."

"Assorted religious artifacts, relics, and symbols."

"Check."

"Stereo recording of werewolves growling."

"Check."

"Bottle of synthetic werewolf fragrance."

"Check."

"Gas masks."

"Check."

"Bite-proof gloves."

"Check."

"Bite-proof boots."

"Check."

"Bite-proof trousers."

"Check."

"Extra-strong stainless steel cage, blessed by the Transylvanian monks."

"Check."

"Chain."

"Check."

"Muzzle."

"Check."

"Liver treats."

"Check."

"That's everything, Sonny. Now, let's just hope he shows up."

"Check."

Behind the wheel of his Wartburg, Ignatz the Igniter picks his teeth with a match. And waits. And watches.

"Sigerson! I think I see something! It's moving between the cars!"

"Just let me have those glasses, old fellow. Yes. Yes. I think our werewolf has arrived. Now, take this magnesium torch, and when I give you the word, run as fast as you can to the front of the theater, light the torch, and wave it about. That will be the signal for our friends to get out of their cars and dash like mad to the refreshment area, where I will be waiting with these bunches of wolfbane. Ah, this is the part I like. The game's afoot, Sacker, old thing. Now, be off with you!"

I run between the cars. I snarl and drool. Look! Up on the screen! Is it? It is! A wolfman like me! Oh, how beautiful! What a sad story! It seems so real! I feel! My senses reel! Never have I known such a thing. Can this be emotion, art-inspired? Does my wolfish heart feel sentiment, pity and terror? What shall I do? I am confused. Now, in this flickering movement of frame after frame, I stand transfixed, an unmoving picture. Oh, see! On the screen, my likeness is pursued. A posse impossibly persecutes my shadow. I must act. Never before have I hesitated, even for a moment.

What? A light! A flash! A torch! A flare! An idiot waving a torch! Something in my mind ignites! I have been thinking! Drat! That is something I never do! I scorn the images of light. I extinguish thought. I am myself again. I go to mangle the pizza kitchen.

The doctor waves his torch beneath and in front of the great screen.

Osgood Sigerson prepares to distribute bouquets of wolf-bane to his helpers.

The snarkers, deputies of Osgood Sigerson, leave their cars and head for the refreshment area.

The werewolf is shaken loose from his moment of inaction, and moves off toward the refreshment area.

Wallace Nussbaum, sitting disguised in a nondescript Datsun, guesses what's what and starts out for the projection booth above the pizza kitchen.

Ignatz the Igniter thinks another firebug is about to steal his fun and bolts from his car, intent on making things hot.

On the screen, a giant werewolf cavorts and capers.

When we saw Dr. Ormond Sacker waving the torch, we headed straight for the refreshment area in the middle of the drive-in. Everybody arrived more or less at once. Osgood Sigerson handed each of us a bunch of wolfbane and told us to head for the edges of the parking area and work our way in toward the center, waving our wolfbane and hollering.

I felt something rush past me. For some reason, I pictured a dark wind. "A sudden storm coming up," I thought—but things were happening too fast to think clearly. Then there was a lot of noise and banging in the pizza kitchen—it sounded as if they were having some trouble with the equipment.

"Hurry to the edges of the parking area," Osgood Sigerson said. "I shall stay here with K.E. Kelman, PH., and Lydia LaZonga Kelman, and prepare to snatch the werewolf when he arrives, terrified and confused by all the noise you'll be making."

"Listen," Jonathan Quicksilver said, "about getting a werewolf terrified and confused . . . it isn't as easy as . . ."

"There's no time to exchange opinions now, Mr. Quicksilver," Osgood Sigerson said. "I respect the arts as much as anyone, and I have no doubt that you are a fine poet, but I must choose to accept the advice of professional werewolf experts."

"Well, I come from Transylvania originally, and . . ."

"Mr. Quicksilver, please! I must ask you to get busy now. We can talk after the werewolf is captured."

Quicksilver mumbled something under his breath and hurried off to the edge of the parking area to start waving his wolfbane and hollering. Rat, Winston, and I took up positions maybe fifty feet apart, and started closing in. We waved our wolfbane and shouted at the top of our lungs. The movie patrons, who were involved with the movie—it was the one in which a werewolf menaces Poughkeepsie—all told us to shut up.

They didn't have time to complain for long—something more distracting took their attention.

"FIRE!" someone shouted, and another voice in another part of the drive-in shouted "FIRE!" At first, I thought it had to do with Dr. Ormond Sacker, who was still waving his torch and being abused by people still waving his torch and being abused by people in the cars nearest to him. Then I smelled smoke and became aware of a flicker of flames at the base of the great screen.

The screen—or that part of the screen which was supposed to represent some architectural marvel in Europe—was on fire. The movie was still being projected onto the screen part of the screen, but flames were creeping up the sides, making a sort of flame-frame around the picture.

The reaction of the crowd was mixed. Some were screaming—some were cheering—and a group of people were singing what I later found out was a Romanian anthem of joy.

From his position near the pizza kitchen, Osgood

Sigerson shouted, "Never mind the fire! There's no particular danger! Just keep waving the wolfbane and shouting and moving toward the center! Keep calm!"

Nobody was keeping calm. People were leaving the drive-in in droves. Others, apparently happy about the way things were turning out, stayed; still others seemed to be horrified and unable to tear themselves away from the events as they unfolded. Giant fire hoses were turned on. Mounted on tall poles throughout the drive-in, they were spinning like pinwheels, drenching everybody. The movie, now encircled by flames, was still showing. The Romanian choir was singing. We were shouting.

It's funny what you shout when you have to keep making a lot of noise. I found myself hollering *"Boo!"* over and over. Winston was sort of yodeling and shouting *"Yippee!"* like a cowboy. I heard Rat shouting *"James Dean, I love you,"* as she waved her bunch of wolfbane around.

We kept closing in on the center of the drive-in, where Sigerson and the Kelmans were waiting near the pizza kitchen and projection booth. There was a lot of smoke coming from the pizza kitchen, and a strong smell of burned pizza crust. That place was about to go up in flames too.

Something was careening crazily around the parking area. At first I thought it was the werewolf. Then I saw that it was the automated Japanese pizza chef robot. It had gone out of control. It was zooming up and down the aisles at high speed shooting hot pizzas out of its slot at car window height. Some of the Romanians got painful cheese burns.

As we converged on the center, we heard one another's

shouts plainly. *"Oh, goody! We're going to catch the werewolf,"* I heard Scott Feldman shout. "What a shnerd!" I thought.

The film was still being projected onto the screen, surrounded by fire, only now there was an immense black shadow dancing and capering. It was a werewolf—but not one on film. Something unmistakably horrible had gotten between the projector and the screen. It was the real thing! It must have been on the roof of a car, but with all the smoke and water from the fire hoses, and confusion, I couldn't see the werewolf, only its shadow. I was about to get scared by that, when something else scared me.

The voice of Wallace Nussbaum came over all the loudspeakers in the drive-in. I recognized it well enough—but even those who had never heard it stopped screaming, shouting, escaping, fire-fighting, and singing, and were terrified by the sound of it.

"Listen, fools! My werewolf cavorts.

I, Wallace Nussbaum, creator of the werewolf, and with whom the werewolf is in cahoots, cavort also.

The Mitsubishi Medium-Range Pizza Chef spits hot cheese at mine enemies.

Sigerson is a dumb-dumb.

Blintish Romanians sing their ancient song, unaware that they are witnesses to the beginning of the end of everything.

The firehoses spin and drench and are of no use.

The film unreels and becomes reality.

Sing, you inhabitants of Blint.

Shout, you friends of Sigerson.

See, citizens of Baconburg, the end of the film comes soon.

The end of all you know and hold dear.

The end of culture—if you call this culture.

This is the vengeance of Nussbaum.

The beginning of my power.

I am your master—and you will be my slaves.

Hee hee hee hee hee!"

There was a noise as of scrambling and thumping, also shouting and gurgling. Somehow it was clear to all of us that what was happening was Nussbaum being shouldered aside, or the microphone grabbed away from him. The sounds of struggle lasted only a few seconds, and then another voice could be heard over the loudspeakers.

There was no describing whose voice this was. Looking at the screen to see that the silhouette was no longer there was just a matter of checking that which I already knew. What I was listening to—and what everybody else in the Garden of Earthly Bliss Drive-in and Pizzeria was listening to—was the voice of the werewolf—the Baconburg Horror.

There is no describing the quality of that voice. All I can say is that a thousand horrible images ran through my mind at once. I pictured claws scraping on a blackboard, breaking glass, a barrel of herring overturned, a McDonald's milk shake left overnight in August, rusty razor blades, industrial pollutants, Ronald Reagan singing Neapolitan ballads, bus fumes.

More horrible than the voice itself was what it was saying. It was too unbearable to listen to, but I had the sense that the werewolf was reciting a poem—a poem so monstrous, so vile, so evil that to listen to it for long would drive me insane.

"*I think that I shall never see,*" the werewolf recited, "*a poem lovely as a tree.*"

At that moment, K.E. Kelman, PH., and Lydia LaZonga Kelman jumped the werewolf. It was lucky timing. I don't know how much more of the werewolf's reciting I could have endured.

There was a tremendous struggle. I didn't get to see any of it—it took place inside the projection booth. Later, I was told that the fancy equipment the Kelmans had brought was of no use. The special net, the handcuffs and footcuffs—none of it did any good. The werewolf snarled, knocked everybody sprawling, and bounded out of the projection booth, which was already on fire.

One good thing did happen. Sigerson managed to get handcuffs on Wallace Nussbaum, who was crawling around on the floor after having been shoved away from the microphone by the werewolf. Sigerson and Heinrich Nussbaum dragged Wallace out of the burning building.

"You're going to be thwarted this time," Heinrich said to his brother.

"That remains to be seen," Wallace Nussbaum said. "My werewolf is still free. By the way, how's Mommy?"

"She was fine the last time I saw her," Heinrich said.

"Look! There he goes! After him!" Osgood Sigerson shouted.

The werewolf was streaking away, darting among the remaining cars, the still smoldering pizzas, and the wreckage of what had once been the finest drive-in movie on earth.

THE MOST SPECTACULAR FIRE YET AT THE GARDEN OF EARTHLY
BLISS DRIVE-IN AND PIZZERIA . . . AND, . . . IS THE BACONBURG
HORROR AT AN END? DETAILS AT ELEVEN.

It was Scott Feldman who caught the werewolf. The creature was making its way through the wreckage at high speed when it ran into Scott, who was waving his bunch of wolfbane and shouting "Oh, goody! We're going to catch the werewolf!" The werewolf paused, possibly to laugh, and Scott stuck his hand out and said, "Hello, my name is Scott Feldman." At the same time, he gazed at the creature with his well-known hypnotic stare. "I liked your poem," Scott said.

Louis Grotshkie, now a very old man, had been following the werewolf as best he could. He was convinced that he had at last caught up with Ignatz the Igniter, who had many times torched Grotshkie's great creation. Ignatz, in fact, was at that very moment sprinkling paraffin on the last gondola of the great ferris wheel, having already prepared the others.

Grotshkie, coming up behind the werewolf, raised his silver-headed walking stick and prepared to strike.

Ignatz raised his last waterproof kitchen match and prepared to strike.

"I liked your poem," Scott Feldman said to the werewolf.

At that moment, Louis Grotshkie brought down his walking stick with the utmost force.

At the same moment, Ignatz the Igniter lit the ferris wheel and pulled the lever setting it in motion.

At the same moment, the automated Japanese pizza chef,

traveling at top speed and spewing fourteen-inch pizzas piping hot in every direction, struck the werewolf broadside, causing Grotshkie's blow to fall with a sickening thwack on a double-cheese-with-sausage-and-anchovies in midair.

Essentially unharmed, but slightly dazed by the impact of the robot, the werewolf was also distracted by the simultaneous splattering of the pizza and the sudden spectacle of the ferris wheel in flames.

At almost the same moment, but actually in the next one, K.E. Kelman, PH., and his mother, Lydia LaZonga Kelman, frustrated and inspired to superhuman vigor by their chagrin at the lycanthrope's earlier escape, fell upon him with stainless steel handcuffs, footcuffs, elbowcuffs, kneecuffs, and earmuffs, yards of wolfbane rope, extra-strong black electrical tape, and miracle glue.

In the next moment, or possibly the one after that, the werewolf was immobilized.

All of this was illuminated bright as day by the revolving flaming ferris wheel, visible all over the county.

By this time, the fire brigades had arrived. The streams of their hoses arched over everything. The Garden of Earthly Bliss Drive-in and Pizzeria was a battleground, soggy, smoldering, flickering, pizza-strewn.

"Next time, I build the whole thing out of asbestos," Louis Grotshkie said.

Rat was disgusted that it had been Scott Feldman who had, essentially, caught the werewolf. "We'll never hear the end of this," she said.

"What's more," Winston said, "he intends to take up snarking. We'll be seeing him here at the movies. He got permission from his father—can you beat that? Asking permission to sneak out of the house? Yick."

"When does Uncle Flipping get out of your soundproof room?" I asked Rat.

"I think Osgood Sigerson is going to let him out soon," Rat said. "It's a week past the last full moon, and this time he just got slightly hairy—no howling or anything."

"So the marifesa Nussbaum was feeding him has just about worn off."

"So it seems," Rat said. "He still doesn't remember anything about being a werewolf."

"I read where they're deporting that orangutan—the one Nussbaum had working as a kitchen helper and doctoring Uncle Flipping's borgelnuskies at the Deadly Nightshade Diner—We Never Close."

"Well, the way I see it, it wasn't really his fault. Nussbaum hypnotizes the apes, and makes them do whatever he wants."

"Heinz—that is, Heinrich Nussbaum—is going back to Peru," Rat said.

"Yeah? He's a nice guy," Winston said.

"Not like his brother," I said.

"Yeah. That Wallace is evil. At least they've got him where he can't escape—the Château d'If."

"Yeah."

"Sigerson's going to leave town."

"Yeah. I heard."

"Well, anyway, Uncle Flipping will never be a werewolf again."

"No. That's true."

"Did you know that Jonathan Quicksilver is a manager at Ms. Doughnut now?"

"Is that so?"

"Oh, he's very serious about his work—hardly has time for poetry anymore."

"Hum."

The house lights started to go down. It was time for the movie to start. We settled down in our seats.

Then something amazing happened. Instead of the opening credits for *Utamaro, Painter of Women* there was the face of Wallace Nussbaum, filling up the whole screen. Nussbaum was laughing.

"Fools!" Nussbaum was saying, "I have escaped from the Château d'If. It was easy. I have spliced this film onto the beginning of every movie in every movie house in the world, and also in the middle of most television commercials—the only thing on TV anybody pays attention to. My purpose is to tell the world that I will strike again! I have plans! Horrible plans! And that fool Osgood Sigerson and his friends can do

DANIEL PINKWATER

nothing to stop me! You have not heard the last of Wallace Nussbaum!"

Then the screen went dark. The movie house was silent, except for the sound of the three of us clapping and cheering.

F I N I S

Aladdin Paperbacks is the place to come for top-notch fantasy/science-fiction! How many of these have *you* read?

The Tripods, by John Christopher

- ❏ Boxed Set • 0-689-00852-X • $17.95 US / $27.96 Canadian

- ❏ The Tripods #1 *When the Tripods Came* • 0-02-042575-9 • $4.99 US / $6.99 Canadian

- ❏ The Tripods #2 *The White Mountains* • 0-02-042711-5 • $4.99 US / $6.99 Canadian

- ❏ The Tripods #3 *The City of Gold and Lead* • 0-02-042701-8 • $4.99 US / $6.99 Canadian

- ❏ The Tripods #4 *The Pool of Fire* • 0-02-042721-2 • $4.99 US / $6.99 Canadian

The Dark is Rising Sequence, by Susan Cooper

- ❏ Boxed Set • 0-02-042565-1 • $19.75 US / $29.50 Canadian

- ❏ *Over Sea, Under Stone* • 0-02-042785-9 • $4.99 US / $6.99 Canadian

- ❏ *The Dark Is Rising* • 0-689-71087-9 • $4.99 US / $6.99 Canadian

- ❏ *Greenwitch* • 0-689-71088-7 • $4.99 US / $6.99 Canadian

- ❏ *The Grey King* • 0-689-71089-5 • $4.99 US / $6.99 Canadian

- ❏ *Silver on the Tree* • 0-689-70467-4 • $4.99 US / $6.99 Canadian

The Dragon Chronicles, by Susan Fletcher

- ❏ *Dragon's Milk* • 0-689-71623-0 • $4.99 US / $6.99 Canadian

- ❏ *The Flight of the Dragon Kyn* • 0-689-81515-8 • $4.99 US / $6.99 Canadian

- ❏ *Sign of the Dove* • 0-689-82449-1 • $4.50 US / $6.50 Canadian

- ❏ *Virtual War*, by Gloria Skurzynski • 0-689-82425-4 • $4.50 US / $6.50 Canadian

- ❏ *Invitation to the Game*, by Monica Hughes • 0-671-86692-3 • $4.50 US / $6.50 Canadian

Aladdin Paperbacks
Simon & Schuster Children's Publishing
www.SimonSaysKids.com

Would you get out alive?

FACED WITH DISASTER, ORDINARY PEOPLE FIND
UNTAPPED DEPTHS OF COURAGE AND DETERMINATION
THEY NEVER DREAMED THEY POSSESSED.

Find Adventure in these books!

#1 TITANIC

On a clear April night
hundreds of passengers
on the *Titanic* find
themselves at the mercy
of a cold sea. Few will
live to remember the
disaster—will Gavin and
Karolina be among the
survivors?

#2 EARTHQUAKE

Can two strangers from
very different worlds
work together to survive
the terror of the quake—
crumbling buildings, fire,
looting, and chaos?

#3 BLIZZARD

Can a Rocky Mountain
rancher's daughter and
her rich, spoiled cousin
stop arguing long enough
to cooperate to survive a
sudden, vicious blizzard?

#4 FIRE

Fate and fire throw Nate
and Julie together on the
dark streets of Chicago.
Now they must find a
way out before the
flames spreading across
the city cut off their only
chance of escape!

ALSO:

#5 FLOOD   **#8 TRAIN WRECK**
#6 DEATH VALLEY   **#9 HURRICANE**
#7 CAVE-IN   **#10 FOREST FIRE**
#11 SWAMP

Simon & Schuster Children's Publishing Division
www.SimonSaysKids.com

Lizzie Logan

will make you laugh!

Read all three books:

Lizzie Logan Wears Purple Sunglasses 0-689-81848-3
$3.99 / $5.50 Canadian

Lizzie Logan Gets Married 0-689-82071-2
$3.99 / $5.50 Canadian

Lizzie Logan, Second Banana 0-689-83048-3
$3.99 / $5.50 Canadian

Simon & Schuster Children's Publishing
www.SimonSaysKids.com

Mysterious things are always going on at the Bessledorf Hotel. Don't miss any of **Phyllis Reynolds Naylor's** other zany adventures featuring Bernie Magruder and his friends:

The Face in the Bessledorf Funeral Parlor
Atheneum Books for Young Readers · 0-689-31802-2
$14.00 / $19.00 Canadian
Aladdin Paperbacks
0-689-80603-5
$4.50 / $6.50 Canadian

The Treasure of Bessledorf Hill
Atheneum Books for Young Readers
0-689-81337-6
$15.00 / $22.00 Canadian
Aladdin Paperbacks
0-689-81856-4
$4.50 / $6.50 Canadian

The Bomb in the Bessledorf Bus Depot
Atheneum Books for Young Readers · 0-689-80461-X
$15.00 / $20.00 Canadian
Aladdin Paperbacks
0-689-80599-3
$3.99 / $5.50 Canadian

ALADDIN PAPERBACKS
Simon & Schuster Children's Publishing
www.SimonSaysKids.com